About the Au

Rachael Stewart adores conju
heartwarmingly romantic to wildly erotic. She's been
writing since she could put pen to paper, as the stacks of
scrawled-on pages in her loft will attest to. A Welsh lass
at heart, she now lives in Yorkshire with her very own
hero and three awesome kids. If Rachael's not tapping out
a story, she's wrapped up in them or enjoying the great
outdoors. Reach her on Facebook, Twitter @rach_b52 or
rachaelstewartauthor.com

Dare Me

Dare Me
to Need You

RACHAEL STEWART

MILLS & BOON

First Published in Great Britain 2023
by Mills & Boon, an imprint of HarperCollins*Publishers* Ltd,
1 London Bridge Street, London, SE1 9GF

www.harpercollins.co.uk

HarperCollins*Publishers*
Macken House, 39/40 Mayor Street Upper,
Dublin 1, D01 C9W8, Ireland

NAUGHTY OR NICE

To my kids, who will be doing their utmost to get on Santa's nice list! I know you're too young to read this – in fact, you'll always be too young – but I can't have a Christmas book without dedicating it to you. I love you regardless of your naughty little antics.

To my family and friends for making every Christmas as special as it can be.

And to my gorgeous readers, too… Are you on the naughty or nice list this year? How about joining me and straddling them both? Ho ho ho ;-)

Happy Christmas to all, and to all a good read!

Rxx

PROLOGUE

I TWIST MY hands in front of me, the heel of one stiletto grinding into the plush carpet of my father's study.

I know Lucas is going to follow me here. I saw it in his eyes. That same look I've caught several times over in the past few months…the same look I know I sport: want, desire—*love*.

I've loved him for years—long before Mum and Dad became his guardians…long before I really knew what it was that had my heart trying to leap out of my chest, my body throbbing, my tongue tied.

I'm eighteen. It's my birthday party. It's as good a time as any to tell him—or so I keep telling myself. I can't go on keeping it locked up inside. But I'm scared. It doesn't matter that I sense he feels the same, that I see the way he looks at me when he thinks no one else is watching.

I pin his expression in my mind, focus on it as I grab my flute of champagne and throw back the remainder. The hit of alcohol makes me wince, but I need it—Dutch courage. I return it to the side as I watch the door.

You love him. You can tell him. You have to.

I hear footsteps in the hallway, louder than the music from my party, underway further down the hall, and I take a breath, pressing my hands into my thighs, forcing them to still and hoping their dampness doesn't mark the bright white of my dress.

The door opens and I can't breathe.

'Evangeline?'

His voice sends blood rushing through my body, my pulse rate skittering out of control.

'Yes…' It comes out like a whisper, my fear coming through, and it frustrates me. I want to be confident. I want him to see me as a woman, not the little sister of his best friend, Nate.

Get it together.

His head appears around the door, his gaze hesitant as he looks from me to the hallway and back again.

'Hey.'

He steps inside but pauses, the confident twenty-one-year-old I usually see oddly absent. He's boyish, uncertain, and my heart turns over.

'Hey,' I manage back, breathless.

We don't move closer. My knees feel like jelly and his fingers tremble a little as he rakes one hand through his hair, his other still hanging on to the door handle.

Take control. You need to do this. You need to show him.

'Close the door.'

I'm surprised at the confidence I've injected into my tone—am surprised all the more when he does what I ask. But his eyes don't return to me. They burn a hole in the floor at his feet.

I take a small breath. 'Why won't you look at me?'

His eyes waver and I can sense the fight in him.

I step forward, my progress slow as the tight mini-dress restricts my movement, riding ever higher up my thighs. The moment I'd chosen it I'd had this in mind. To confess my love, maybe even seduce him. I want my first time to be with him and tonight would be so perfect.

'Lucas?'

He shakes his head, but then his eyes lock with mine and I feel their burn. Need is etched in the tightness of his jaw, in his hands fisting at his sides.

'We shouldn't be in here…alone.'

'Then why did you come?' I press.

Please let him be torn. Please let him confirm what I suspect.

'I—'

He shakes his head again but his eyes are still fixed on mine. His internal fight is clear in their depths, and he runs his teeth over his lower lip. The move distracting me with the glimpse of his tongue, the mouth I so desperately want to taste.

'Being alone with you, like this…' He waves a hand up and down my length, his eyes travelling over me and setting my skin alight.

'Don't trust yourself?' I tease, forcing out the playful jest even though I know how much rides on his response.

I pause less than an arm's reach away and look up at him from beneath my lashes, not quite ready to reach for him. That fear of rejection is still there.

'You know we shouldn't.'

It's my turn to shake my head. 'Why?'

'Because—because of who you are. Of who your family are to me.'

'In a way, we're your family too.'

'Exactly, Eva—they're all I have.'

I risk another step and hold his tormented gaze. I want to kiss it away, take away the pain of his past, his loss, his loneliness. He never had a father. His mother, although best friend to my own, was hardly ever present, and now she's been dead almost a year. But I have been here. I've always been here for him. I can be enough. If only he will see it.

'And we will always be here for you. But I have to tell you how I feel. I have to tell you I…I…' My voice cracks and I curse the show of weakness.

'Don't, Evangeline—don't say it.'

His words are a warning that I can't abide, and it's the push that I need.

'Why?'

'Because it will change everything.'

'And why is that so bad?'

He takes a breath and it shudders out of him, but he says nothing.

Now. It has to be now.

'Lucas.' I slip my hands over his shoulders, feel him tense beneath them, but there's no going back. 'I love you.'

He squeezes his eyes shut, closing me out, and when he opens them again they're blazing. His hands are reaching out, tight on my hips as he forces me away.

'I love you too, but not—not like *this*. I can't.'

He turns to leave and I move, stepping between him and his escape, so swift that he ends up pressed against me, my back against the door as my lips part on a gasp.

It's not just surprise—it's the strange frisson that runs right down my front as my body absorbs his heat, the very hardness of him.

His eyes drop to my mouth and there's no need for words. His intent sears me seconds before his lips claim mine.

Christ, I'm in heaven.

He isn't soft, tentative, uncertain. He's hard, determined, his tongue forcing my mouth apart, demanding entry, coaxing me into doing the same.

I've been kissed before, and I've kissed boys before, but I've never been devoured—not like this.

My body thrums, my breasts prickle against his chest, and the dull ache in my gut swells and throbs with mindless need. My hands are in his hair, clinging him to me, his own rake over my body, feverish, trembling. I can't believe this is real. I feel drugged, dreaming.

And then he groans into my mouth, pressing me back harder, and I know it's real. I know this is happening… my dream is coming true.

His fingers drop to my naked thighs, encouraging my dress higher. I don't know whether I lift my leg to hook it around him or he does, but the hard swell of him inside his jeans presses at the throbbing heart of me and I moan my pleasure.

He curses, his teeth nipping at my lip as he shakes his head once more. 'I've wanted you, so long.'

His confession jerks me alert. I want more of it. More words. More to affirm how he feels.

'How long?'

'Too long.'

Happiness bursts within me. Everything's falling into place.

I find his lips again, desperate to seal his words with my kiss. 'And you can have me. I'm yours. I've always been yours.'

There's a strange knocking sound—one that doesn't compute with the whirlwind that is my mind—and suddenly I'm thrust away from him. I try to focus through the haze. I see his widened gaze, his alarm clear.

'Lucas? You in there?'

The handle shifts with my brother's voice, but the door doesn't budge. I realise Lucas has turned the latch. It fills me with hope, but hope dies just as swiftly. He looks as if he's seen a ghost as he stares at me in horror.

'Lucas! Come on, man. Someone said they saw you head in here… Eva too.'

Oh, God.

He was pale before. Now he looks deathly. His eyes leave me, his head shaking.

'I'm an idiot. A *fucking* idiot.'

He says it under his breath and I tiptoe towards him, my hand reaching out. But he moves away from me just as quickly, his eyes throwing daggers. 'Don't.'

There are footsteps down the corridor and then my father's voice. 'What's going on?'

'Nothing... I'm just getting Eva. Mum wants her to cut the cake.'

'The last place Eva will be is in my study, son.'

Nate gives an awkward laugh. 'Sure...of course. I'll check upstairs.'

They move off, their voices growing distant, and I know my brother is protecting us. But I don't want protection. I don't want to hide any more.

'Lucas, please don't push me away. I don't want to deny this any more. I know you feel the same. I know you—'

'You don't know anything.'

'You want me—'

'Yes, I want you.' He launches the words at me, so certain. 'But that's not love.'

'It is—because I love you.'

'You don't love me. You're infatuated, confused, doped up on hormones.'

My heart starts to split in two, ice running through the middle. 'You don't know what you're talking about...'

'I know you and your family are all that I have. That without you I have nothing.'

I don't know what to say to that. I know the truth of it. But it makes my reasoning all the more valid. It's so simple.

'Then accept that we love one another and that my family will be happy for us. Once they adjust.'

His head shakes violently. 'No, they won't. Don't you see? Nate was banging this door down to *stop* us. He *knows*.'

'But—'

'No, Eva, he's already made it clear you're off-limits and, hell, he's right. What happens to me a year or two down the line when this…whatever this is…fizzles out?'

'It won't.'

'You can guarantee that, can you?'

'I…I…'

He rakes both hands through his hair, his torment written in his haunted brown eyes. Eyes I've dreamed about for so long.

And then he's turning away and heading for the door.

'Please,' I hear myself say. 'Don't go.'

He doesn't even pause—doesn't even look back as he unlocks the door and slips away. Leaving me standing there, my heart in tatters, as I realise he means it.

That no matter how much I love him he can never be mine.

CHAPTER ONE

THIS IS MY MOMENT. For the first time in my life I know that I've made it. That I stand apart. My family name hasn't handed me this. Aside from a small investment from dear old Ma and Pa, this is all me.

My baby is finally ready, and companies are clambering over themselves to head up its manufacture, its distribution, wanting to join forces, to conquer the field.

But I have weeks to decide.

Tonight is about enjoying the buzz…feeding it.

The room is fit to bursting with prospective producers and vendors alike. And here's me, confident in a festive red silk dress that just sweeps the floor, my blonde hair knotted up high, sophisticated, yet softened by the loose locks that fall free. The delicate bubbles of the champagne in my hand are feeding my ego and my mood to perfection.

'Well, you did it, angel.'

I turn and lift my chin to meet my father's eye. I can see the admiration in his gaze—something I've hungered for since I found I could outrun my brother at fourteen.

It's not that I'm naturally competitive, but when you're always deemed the less capable, the *girl*, it can happen. Even more so when your brother can apparently do no wrong, when in truth he does plenty wrong, and *still* has admiration dished out in spades.

'I know.'

He tenses, and I fear he's read the bitterness in my tone. But, no, his eyes leave me and narrow. Something else has caught his attention.

'What the hell...?' he mutters.

I follow his line of sight, but already my nerves sizzle. My father doesn't ever show unease—he doesn't do emotion, particularly in a business setting like tonight's launch party. *My* launch party.

'Did you invite him?'

'Wh—?' The word dies and my entire body draws tight.

I see him. I see the exact cause of my father's unease and feel it seep into my very skin. My mood dies with it. The champagne flute trembles in my hand and I know I should look away, but I can't.

Ten years and still my eyes are hooked on him.

Lucas Waring.

My family's nemesis.

My heart's downfall.

'No,' I manage to say.

I shouldn't be surprised—not when the room is full of his peers.

Peers? Are you dreaming?

They're not his equal. No one is. Waring Holdings has it all and now here is Lucas, wanting...*what?*

'He can't possibly think you'll be interested in working with him.'

My father speaks my mind exactly. He can't. But what else?

'There's only one way to find out.'

I'm not the eighteen-year-old girl I once was, and I'm not the woman I became soon after that, determined to evade him. I am in control now. This is my night. This is work.

'Excuse me.'

'No.' My father steps into my path. 'I'll get rid of him.'

I hold his eye as my lips twitch. What I want to say is *Stop treating me like a child*, but in my mind that sounds petulant and childlike in itself. Instead I smile up at him. 'He's made the effort to come. I should at least see what he wants.'

'But—'

'But nothing, Dad. Giving someone as powerful as Lucas the cold shoulder tonight of all nights would send the wrong message to the room.'

My father grunts and swigs his champagne. He knows I'm right. He didn't get where he is today by letting personal differences get in his way. But then it's the first time I'm aware of that Lucas has dared venture near any of us in five long years.

Ever since my family shut him out and the blame

for the demise of the company he co-owned with Nate seemed to land firmly at his feet.

I questioned it at the time. I continued to question it each and every time Nate screwed up after that. It couldn't have been down to Lucas—not entirely. But it seems Lucas has suffered the same as me.

Nate's golden halo failed to shift.

I can't deny I'm curious as to what truly went down. And I also can't deny that his presence here tonight only serves to help my cause, my product. It'll feed the frenzy already taking hold as companies vie for my business.

Or it'll send them running, because they'll think there's no chance in hell you'll look anywhere else but him.

Not him—his business, Eva!

I give my head a small shake, the loose curls from my updo brushing against the prickled skin of my nape. It loosens up my thoughts, the tension.

'Why don't you make sure Mum doesn't flip at his presence?' I say, and with another sip of champagne I start to make my way towards him, praying he doesn't spy me before I'm prepared.

But already his head is turning, as if he senses my approach, and then his eyes are locked on mine and I can feel a startling rush through my system. It doesn't matter that I'm used to the sight of him on the TV, in the tabloids—that same old zing is in my belly, that heat that only his physical presence has ever instilled creeping into my cheeks.

I want to look away, but I won't give him that. I am stronger now, wiser, and the better for it. And so I enjoy him, my eyes sweeping over every inch of him. His black hair, long on top. His prominent brow arching over heavy-lashed eyes that narrow on me, dark and intense. I ignore the hiccup to my pulse and cut lower, to his wide, angular jaw with its intentional stubble.

I avoid his mouth entirely.

I don't need the memory of its brief contact all those years ago. *I really don't.*

I move my eyes lower, to the broad set of his shoulders—wider than I recall. Imposing. I don't dwell on the muscle behind that. Instead I focus on the designer cut of his deep grey suit, the white shirt and his defiantly skinny black tie.

My lips lift at the edges, I can't help it. *Always the rebel...*

I lift my eyes back to his and they flicker. There's something there. I just don't know what. Unease?

Maybe.

Like hell.

He owns the room. His presence commands attention even when he's not looking for it. Just like he's commanding my own, against my will.

A waiter passes between us and he reaches out for a glass, but not once does his gaze release me, and I can feel myself being drawn in like the besotted eighteen-year-old I once was.

Careful, Eva.

'Lucas…'

I draw his name out, feel it fall softly from my lips, and I see his eyes flit to them. I know they're red and glossy. The perfect match for my dress and the countrywide festivities, and I imagine him looking hungrily over them now.

If only…

'I wish I could say it's a pleasure to see you.'

I'm proud of the steadiness in my voice, its hard edge— it's what he deserves for what he did to me ten years ago and for the last five, too, if my family are right… In this second I'm not sure which I want to hurt him more for.

Yes, you do…liar.

He watches me with that intense stare that I can't even begin to read and raises his glass to his lips. Too late I'm looking, remembering, and my betraying tongue sweeps over my own lips…

'It's rude to stare.'

My eyes leap and I curse his very presence, his very effect over me. But there's a tightness to his voice, a flare to his eyes that he cannot hide, and I know he's not immune to me—not any more. It gives me power and I feed on it.

'It's rude to attend a party without an invitation.'

He smiles, the movement small and soft—and, *dammit*, my insides quiver.

'I'm used to being welcomed with open arms. Invited or not.'

I raise my brow, the idea of being close enough to embrace him not helping my focus.

It's a figure of speech, idiot.

I cock my head, masking my unease. 'Once upon a time that may have been true, but not here, not now, and not with me.'

'Not with you, or not with your family, Evangeline?'

If I could melt to the floor I would. No one calls me Evangeline—no one. Unless they're my parents. I am Eva—strong, dependable, Eva. A woman who has proved her worth a hundred times over.

But when *he* says it, the *way* he says it, it's not like Mum and Dad do it. It doesn't make me feel like a girl, weak and vulnerable. I feel empowered, worthy of so much, catapulted onto a pedestal and ready to be worshipped.

By him. At my feet.

Oh, yes.

I swallow, the bolt through my body jolting me straight.

It scares me. *He* scares me. And I know I need him gone—that no matter what I said to Dad I don't dare to entertain him for longer than is necessary.

'Cat got your tongue?'

'No,' I blurt.

'So?'

I can see a pulse working in his jaw, and his eyes are intense as they watch and wait for my response.

'Is it you or your family telling me I'm not welcome, Evangeline?'

'Both.' I say it and immediately regret it. It's too personal, too unprofessional, but I can't think clearly. Not with him so close.

'Is that your way of asking me to leave?'

I sense nearby heads turning, ears tuning in.

Careful, Eva...

I'm losing myself in the fierce glint of her blue gaze, almost daring her to throw me out. There's something about the fight in her that I want to provoke.

It's so much easier than dealing with all the shit buried ten years deep.

'No, Lucas, I'm not asking you to leave.'

She wets her lips. Again. And the red shines ever deeper, the carnal colour driving a string of sinful thoughts—none of which have a place in this room, with this audience.

Or fit with the reason you're here.

It's about business.

Not her.

Not...

A pulse flutters in her throat and she raises her hand, her red-tipped fingers circling over the delicate ripple. Christ, I want to do that—be the person with his fingers over that creamy skin.

I tighten my hold on the stem of the glass, slipping my other hand inside my pocket. Out of trouble.

'Good.' I tear my eyes away, looking towards the grand Christmas tree and the big screen that stands proud alongside it, streaming highlights of the product

I'm here to secure. 'Because I think we have a future together…in business.'

I suck the inside of my cheek.

In business? What the actual fuck? Do you want to make it any more obvious you want her in your bed too?

I hear her laugh, and the sound is as surprising as its effect, rippling through my body like an aftershock. I'd forgotten how she can do that—be it with a laugh, a smile or a song when she thinks no one's listening.

'Of course, Lucas. Of course in business. What else could you possibly be suggesting?'

She watches me over the rim of her glass, the depths of her eyes alive with suggestion, amusement, confidence. And it's the confidence that's my undoing. It's new. To me, at least. Where there was once a questioning innocence there's now the maturity of a woman who knows her own mind, her own desires.

And where do those desires lie now?

Ten years ago she made it obvious, but now…

Hell, most women desire me—it's par for the course. My money and power attract all sorts, even without the body I work hard to hone.

But you don't care about other women. You only care for her.

Cared—not *care*. Because that would be damn stupid.

Ten years ago she was forbidden. As the sister of my best friend, as the daughter of the closest thing I had to parents—*real* parents.

But, let's face it, here I am now, her family's worst nightmare, and all that loyalty no longer applies.

Just think what you can do with that.

I look her over, slowly, purposefully, and before I can hold back it's out. 'It wasn't my intention—I came here tonight to secure a deal, to offer you a very lucrative contract… But now I find myself wanting a whole lot more.'

Her eyes widen and the glass quivers beneath her chin, not quite lowering but not quite lifting either. She's shocked and I seize the advantage.

'What's it been, Evangeline—seven years?'

'Six.'

She says it so certainly it makes me wonder. Has she counted it down to the exact day, the exact moment? Because I sure as hell have, despite my intentional miscalculation. And even then it had been a brief passing—a moment at the Beaumonts' home before Nate and I flew out on business. But it's ingrained in my memory. The sight of her with another man—her *fiancé*. Happy.

'How is Peter?'

I don't know why I even ask it. I can see she isn't married—her bare finger gives that away. And there's no reason for me to think he's still on the scene, so why I need the added reassurance is beyond me.

'I have no idea. We broke up not long after that night.'

My question hasn't even jarred her, and that tells me enough. She remembers the occasion.

I don't want to feel the pleasure-filled rush that

comes from this, but it's there anyway—as is the burning need to taste those lips that keep goading me with their illicit colour, their inviting sheen.

'And Nate?' I manage to ask. 'I can't see him here.'

Her lashes flutter at my change in focus. Moving from one unsettling topic to another. But the need to talk business, to get back to safer ground, is lost on me.

'My brother had some work to tie up in Hong Kong. He'll be back for Christmas.'

I nod and ignore the weird ache her mention of Christmas kick-starts inside me. Christmas at the Beaumonts' was my tradition for so long. I never dwell on how much I miss it, but in that second I feel it. The cold, dull ache of what once existed but is no more.

And Nate still has it all, whereas I—

For fuck's sake, Lucas, get with it!

'Good for him.' I crush the ache, but the bitterness is there in the chill of my tone.

Her eyes narrow and I look away, forcing my shoulders to relax as I sip at my drink, wanting to quash the past just as much as I want it brought to the fore and dealt with.

But what would that accomplish? *Nothing.*

'I see your parents made it.' I gesture to where they're standing together at the bar, their eyes drawn to us as inconspicuously as they can manage. But I know they are watching. I can feel their penetrative stare as much as I can feel the heat of her proximity.

'They wouldn't miss it. It's in their interest to see me and my business do well.'

'I understand they have a twenty-five per cent share?'

'You've done your research.'

'I *always* do my research.'

I trust no one. Not any more. What little trust I ever gave was destroyed by her brother five years ago.

'I make it my business to know all there is about the companies I wish to work with *and* the people who run them.'

'And what does your research tell you about me?'

'You or your business?'

'Both.'

If it had been any other woman I might have thought she was fishing, but looking into her eyes I see she is not. That fierceness is still there, that sense that she has proved herself over and over again, and knows I won't have found her wanting. And it drives me to the brink.

Would that confidence extend to the bedroom too?

'Your product has an eager market, but its patent will only protect it for so long. Time is of the essence, and you need a ready production line and a route to market that is as speedy as we can make it.'

'We?' Her brows rise. 'That's quite presumptuous of you.'

'You know my company can give you both.'

She hums low in her throat and it resonates through me. My eyes fall to her lips, to their provocatively tight line. How I want to probe it with my tongue…make her yield…

'And what of me, Lucas? What does your research tell you about me?'

I want to tell her that I'd value her business, but more than that, I'd value *her*. I want to tell her that I'd trust her. That everything I knew of her all those years ago hasn't really changed…that all I've learned in the intervening years only reinforces that view. That there is nothing in her to spark my doubt.

Except my experience with her brother—an experience which has made me an outcast of her family…

You're getting personal. This is business. You only have to trust her as far as the contract you draw up dictates.

Yet already I can feel myself wanting more. Wanting to see how far I can push the perfect, composed businesswoman before me and make her crack. Make her desire me like her eighteen-year-old self did.

If only I could go back, take what she offered so willingly instead of—

'Are you ready, Eva? The floor awaits you.'

It's her father. He appears by her side from out of nowhere. Fuck her red lips. If not for those I would have sensed his approach. Been ready for it. Instead I'm forced to look straight from them to him, and I can see displeasure in every hard-cut line to his face.

It's as if he can see inside my soul to the ingrained need I have for his daughter and is telling me where to shove it.

'Mr Beaumont.' I say it smoothly and raise my glass, giving him the half-smile I reserve for business.

His eyes flash. I can see he wants to ignore me, and

Eva positively thrums with tension as her gaze flits between us.

'Yes, of course—thank you, Dad.'

She lifts a hand to her father's chest, clearly telling him to stand down, and it riles my blood. I'm not a man to tell tales, and I'm not about to start now, but the truth of what happened five years ago is burning to get out.

I wash it back with champagne and turn to Eva, my hand falling to the curve of her back as I move to speak and feel the words evaporate on the heat of her skin beneath the silk.

She turns to look at me, her mouth parting in what I think is surprise—until I see the flush to her cheeks, the flare to her eyes, and I know, in that moment, that she feels it too. The desire. And if I were a betting man I'd put money on it being stronger than ever before.

'Let's talk later.'

I don't wait for a response. I turn and walk away. Seeking out the shadows where I can regain my prized composure in peace.

I'm not used to losing my cool. I depend on it to face the many challenges that come my way. But something tells me that working with Evangeline would be a challenge like no other—because, regardless of my intentions when I set out tonight, I want her.

Her *and* her business.

Trouble is, I know which one I want more...

I watch as she takes to the podium, her entire body glinting under the fairy lights of the tree, and my body stiffens with a need so fierce I know it should have me running in the opposite direction and yet I'm rooted.

I owe the Beaumonts nothing.

But I owe *her* a ten-year-old debt. And suddenly I can't wait to pay up in full.

CHAPTER TWO

I DELIVER MY speech to the room and my words flow. I've rehearsed them a zillion times over and could do it in my sleep. Which is a good job, considering my attention is off the product and on the dark corner of the room where I know *he* waits. Listening…

I can feel his intense stare, his hunger. It was there in his touch, in his eyes that burned into my back all the way to the podium, and it's still there, fuelling my own.

The audience is enraptured. I've been reeling them in for the last twenty minutes. But still my mouth dries with anticipation. For *him*.

I pause to sip some champagne, my smile sweeping the entire audience before coming back to him. I need this to be sated. Before it consumes my every thought, drives my every action.

I raise my glass and offer a toast to the future. It's an excuse to loosen my vocal cords further, before I leave the stage and do what's expected of me—circulate the room.

Most people I've spoken to already. But now it's

about verbally agreeing to meetings and having my PA follow them up. Sealing their interest.

I know *he* will be on that list of interested parties. I owe it to my product.

It won't sit well with my family, but I'll deal with that as I do any business dealing—with professionalism. My parents can't fault me for that, and whatever deal I sign will buy them out. It's money back in their pocket and the business wholly my own. It's what I've dreamed of for so long. And if that money comes from a deal with Lucas, so be it.

Yeah, and what about Nate?

I bury the instinctive snort. I'm sick of him getting a free ride. I love him. I do. But I'm almost certain that whatever happened five years ago had more to do with him than the tale I've been given: that Lucas simply ran when the going got tough, leaving Nate and my father to clean up the mess.

But what about what he did to you? What about your heart?

Now my tummy turns over. My heart has no place in this. Not any more. I will consider his business offer, but as for the unvoiced part of his proposition…

I find him in the room. He leans against a pillar, one leg crossed over the other, his body relaxed. But his eyes as they lock with mine are anything but.

I moisten my lips. For that my body is already willing—my eighteen-year-old self still craving satisfaction, longing to experience what he cruelly refused all those years ago. Only this time it'll be on *my* terms.

I'll show him what he's been missing, get this carnal need sated, and then it can all be about business.

If I choose to sign with him.

'You were amazing, Eva.'

I drag my eyes away to smile at Clare. She's a fabulous assistant—her excitement bubbles over as if it were my own. 'Thank you.'

'If anyone had the slightest doubt they'll be utterly convinced now that they want it—even if it's to gain a piece of *you*.'

I know she means it professionally, but I can't help thinking of Lucas, and again I'm distracted, my eyes hunting him out. And then a crazy urge takes over.

'Clare, do me a favour and hold the room for five. I just need to take care of something.'

'Sure.'

I'm already heading for the exit, the restrooms, giving a polite 'I'll be back in just a moment…' to anyone who pauses to speak to me.

I know I don't need to beckon him, that he'll be hot on my tail. And he is. As soon as my hand presses into the restroom door he's at my back.

'Escaping?'

I turn and smile up at him. 'Wait here.'

His brow pinches together. He's unaccustomed to being commanded—that's obvious. But he does as he's told and I walk through the door, scanning the stalls. They're all empty and I don't hang around. I pull open the door and reach for the skinny black tie that reminds me so much of the defiant teen I loved.

'Come.'

I walk backwards and he moves with me, feeding the power swimming like liquid heat through my veins, my core.

'What is this, Eva?'

'What do you think?'

'I hope it's you calling in a ten-year debt.'

I keep moving, ignoring the brief spike of pain, of heartbreak. Knowing I'm about to replace it with something far more satisfying.

'Do you remember that night?'

His jaw clenches, his eyes ablaze, and I know he's reliving it.

'Yes,' he grinds out.

His tension is palpable and I take conceited pleasure in it.

'I remember.'

I push open a stall door, thankful for the opulent finish, and nudge him inside. A toilet wouldn't be my ideal place to feed this need, but it's certainly the most convenient. And, as far as toilets go, this is designed for a certain clientele—a sleek private vanity area, with space for a woman's multitude of possessions or her derriere, should the need arise. How very convenient.

I back him inside, blindly locking the door behind me. 'Do you remember how you left me?'

He falters and shakes his head.

'No?' I raise my brow at him, my fingers toying with the slit in the silk that rides high up my thigh.

'I do remember.'

His voice is tight. It reverberates through my spine as I circle the exposed skin and raise the slit higher. '*What* do you remember, Lucas?'

'I remember you wore a white number that barely covered your arse.'

I can feel the effort it takes him to form the words and my confidence edges ever higher. I hook my fingers into the fabric of my dress and spread it open across my thigh, loving how his eyes track the move, his breath hitching.

'What else?'

'I remember how your skin felt beneath my palms… the taste of champagne on your tongue.'

He gives a small shudder and his fists flex at his sides. I know he wants to reach for me, but something is stopping him. And I'm glad. I want to be in control. The one driving this…

I lift the fabric until it exposes the lace of my nude thong and watch him swallow heavily.

'Do you want to know what *I* remember, Lucas?'

His eyes lift to mine, burning deep, and I don't wait for his answer. I focus on the sex, the need, the desire that has lived on in spite of my shattered heart.

'I remember aching for you so badly… I remember being wet and ready for you…'

I ease my hand between my parted legs and he exhales sharply, his eyes falling away once more, his fists tight.

'I can remember wanting to do just this…'

I slip my fingers beneath the lace. Christ, I'm so wet. My thong is damp against the backs of my fingers. *He* does this to me. Without a touch he has me primed and ready.

I catch my lower lip in my teeth as I pull my fingers back over my clit, pleasure ripping through me, my hips gyrating into their touch. His eyes flare and I lock onto them, getting off on his reaction as much as the skilful touch of my own fingers.

I could come like this. I know it. Come and leave. Make him suffer. But it's not enough.

'Come here,' I tell him.

He doesn't hesitate. He steps forward, his hands reaching to cup my face, but I lean away from him. I don't want him to kiss me. Not on my lips at any rate. It's too personal—too close to my teenage dreams.

I press my free hand to his chest and look up into his questioning gaze. 'Make me come.'

He cocks a grin at me. 'My pleasure.' He lowers his hand.

'No.'

He frowns.

'With your mouth.'

His eyes widen. 'You like being in charge now?'

'Always.'

I slip my hand out of my thong and gather up the skirt of my dress. 'On your knees.'

As he follows my instructions, surprise floods me. I didn't expect this swift agreement. And then he's upon me, his mouth encasing my mound through the lace, the heat of his breath making me shudder, and my knees go weak.

He probes me with his tongue, his teasing through the fabric enough to make my legs buckle completely. He palms my behind. Holding me steady.

'Why don't you sit?' he murmurs against me, encouraging me to the countertop. I go willingly, my dress hitched up to my hips, and the cold surface a shock to the cheeks of my arse. I spasm and he laughs. The sound resonates over my clit.

'Easy…'

I fork my hand over his head and draw him against me. My other hand clutches the edge of the countertop. 'I don't want easy.'

This time his laugh is tight, and his eyes are now black with his own need. He catches the lace of my thong in his teeth and tugs. 'These need to go'

I am captivated by him. For all I want to be in charge, I would actually let him do anything to me in this moment. I nod my head, my hand releasing him to grip the countertop.

He takes hold of the waistband just as the sound of people approaching reaches us—the unmistakable click of stilettos, women talking. The door opens and I tense. My eyes widen on to his, but he merely smiles as he continues with his task.

A stall door opens, a tap runs. The women are still talking, but I'm not listening. I'm focused entirely on not giving us away, my knuckles white with the effort of holding everything in as well as keeping my perch upon the vanity.

He shimmies down my thong, the thin cord stinging

against my skin as he pulls it from underneath me. He brings it to my calves but doesn't take it off. Instead he bends forward and lifts my ankles, ducking to position himself between my legs. The sharp points of my heels dig into his tailored jacket and for a split second I worry about damaging it—but then his eyes lock with mine and my brain empties.

I am spread open and bare before his hungry gaze. Outside our stall the women talk and talk, but all I care about is him and the crazy tumultuous heat swirling through my limbs.

His eyes lower as his fingers part me and I whimper. It's a small choked sound that I cannot help and the women pause in their chatter. I have no idea if we're discovered, but in that moment all I want is his mouth on me, drinking up the need I feel slipping from me.

Yes, Lucas, now, I beg silently.

And slowly he leans in.

His breath reaches me first, warm and teasing, and then the probe of his tongue. Its very tip flicks against my clit. I buck wildly, the whimper becoming a strangled squeal, and he breaks away, his eyes flashing in warning.

I bite into my lip so hard I fear I may draw blood. But the women continue with their chatter, and whether they've heard or not I don't care.

He leans back in and this time I'm ready for it, my body set rigid as I anticipate the spasm, the pleasure, the—

Oh, my fucking God.

* * *

She ripples beneath me, her muscles straining to keep still, and I can't help the smile that lifts my lips. How I've wanted this. Dreamt of it, even. Working her is a pleasure like none other.

Working her? My body mocks me. I am *drowning* in her. Her taste, her essence, her every reaction. She's working me. And I don't care.

I surround her perfect pussy, my nose nudging, my tongue dipping into the place I so want to plunge, and my cock swells harder, thicker, in the confines of my trousers.

She pants above me, her hands clawing at the counter. Everything about her urges me for more, to go faster, but I'm in my element…exploring, tasting, probing.

She shivers as I run my tongue over her clit, her breath a hiss between her teeth. I repeat the move, slow and hard at first, lapping at her. Jesus, I could stay like this for as long as she would let me. And then she writhes and I sense her climax building. I change my tempo, make quick flicks of my tongue in tune with her movements, then faster as she tenses.

I can't wait to tip her over and start anew. To feel her lose it and then go again and again.

I break away just enough to watch as I slip two fingers inside her, plunging deep and bringing them out wet and slick. She is so ready, so hot and needy, all for me.

I hear her pant my name. The sound mingles with the noise of my fingers inside her and with the muttering taking place outside the cubicle door and my smile grows. I want her to scream my name. I want her to forget her place, the perfect persona that she presents to the world, and break...*for me.*

I grow hungry...two fingers become three...and then her frenzied hands freeze, her knuckles flashing white at the counter-edge. I look up into her face, feasting on the desperate heat of her gaze, the fierce pinch of her teeth as she draws back her lower lip. I drop to her clit, sucking over her hard, and she cries out. The room stills but I don't stop. I can't stop. Not until she shatters under my hand, my mouth...

'Lucas... Lucas...'

I keep going, and then her thighs close around my head and her entire body convulses with wave after wave. She's coming hard and my body is at bursting point, living it with her. For a split second I worry I might lose it too—and then a cough breaks the air from the other side of the door. A prim, *what-do-you-think-you're-doing?* type of cough.

I look up at her, my grin as reckless as I feel, but something in her eyes holds me still, robbing me of breath. It's not their satiated blaze. There's something almost vulnerable—something that takes me back ten years.

And then she blinks. It's gone. Did I imagine it?

She releases the counter to comb her fingers through my hair. Her touch is like fire upon my skin and I shoot the thought down.

The heels outside retreat, the restroom door opens

and shuts. We're alone, and I'm not wasting the opportunity. I throw my focus back to her, leaning into her warmth, her wetness, and I drink her down, cleaning up every last drop.

She quivers around me, gives a small whimper. 'I…sensitive.'

I know she means in her body, the orgasm having left her raw, but I think of that look. I need to replace it with the wild heat of seconds before, so I soften my touch upon her, I tease… I can feel her shifting away from me, as if the moment is over, but I'm not ready. I've not had my fill.

'We should be…getting back…before we're missed.'

Her words are hitched and I know I'm getting to her. Her hand in my hair has turned rough, and her body trembles with resurging tension.

'I can't…not again…not so soon.'

Wanna bet?

I hold her apart, my mouth and my tongue unrelenting. My body pleads for release. I know I should stand, take her now. But I can't. I am lost to her pleasure.

'Oh, God, Lucas!'

This time she cries it so loud the sound echoes through the empty room—hell, it probably reaches the outer corridor too. This is madness. But I'm all for it.

She grips me against her with both hands now, her hold fierce as her legs spread wide over the marble top. She's clinging to me as if her life depends on it, but I'm not going anywhere. I catch each wave of her orgasm with my mouth. It's perfect, heavenly, and as I get to my feet my cock spasms painfully.

Now.

I look down into her sparkling gaze. Her smile is soft, warm.

'I didn't think—' She breaks off, her cheeks flushing deeper, her lashes lowering.

Her sudden embarrassment makes me ache—and not with need, but with something I don't want to acknowledge. I use my hands to stroke her inner thighs gently, holding her open to me. I don't know why I'm waiting. I should bury myself in her and be done with it. With this.

'It's a well-known fact that women can enjoy multiples.'

'In general—just not me.'

So I'm the first. That feeling swells inside me and I drop my head. I need to kiss her. To taste those cherry-red lips. But she turns her head away. It's a rejection. A shot of ice water in my face.

'No kissing.'

'Fuck me, Evangeline, what we've just shared goes a whole load further than kissing.'

Her thighs tense beneath my fingers and her palms drop to my chest. 'I must get back.'

She has to be kidding.

Her hands forcing me away tell me otherwise.

I'm lost for words.

Carefully she closes her legs and slips from the countertop, bending to retrieve her thong from the floor. I get there first. Scoop it up into my hand. Our gazes lock in silent challenge. Hell, if she's leaving me like this I'm taking *something*. Even if it's to reassure me that I didn't dream it.

She wets her lips, their glossy redness killing me. 'Fine—keep them.'

She smooths down her dress as she rises. I follow suit but make no attempt to leave. There's something about her I just can't shake. Call it too many years of absence, a need to make up for lost time, an opportunity to take what I've always wanted at last.

I have a ridiculous urge to say something—but what?

She reaches for the door latch and my hand covers hers on instinct. There are voices approaching once more and her eyes flicker in their general direction, away from me. I want so much to read her thoughts.

'You need to go, Lucas.'

Her voice is cold. Unsettling. And then she looks at me and I can't work out whether it's with hatred or sadness, or both. But it's enough for my hand to fall back to my side.

She pulls open the door, forcing me to move out of the way. It doesn't matter what her eyes tell me now. She wanted me—and that doesn't just die out on a simple tongue-fuck or two.

She turns to me, her hand hot against my chest as she backs me out of the cubicle.

'This isn't over,' I say.

But she smiles—it's soulless—and her hand shifts from me to curl around the edge of the cubicle door.

'Yes, it is… *Now* we're even.'

I register her meaning, shaking my head. *Like hell we are…*

'We're not even.' My grin is one of sheer arrogance. 'Not by a long shot.'

Her brow lifts into an elegant arch—I can't tell if it's in disbelief or challenge—and she closes the door in my face, the lock twisting into place.

It's a first for me. I should feel humiliated, cheapened—*used*, even. But I'm feeling none of those things.

Fire burns in my veins—fire for the chase, the thrill of the conquest. She will be mine. My groin pulses and I adjust myself, lifting my hand to sweep it over my face as determination settles in.

When I'm buried deep inside her—then we'll be even.

I turn and head for the door. I should clean up, but the lingering taste of her keeps me hungry. If I get my way, I'll have what I crave before the night is out.

And I *always* get my way.

CHAPTER THREE

I FEEL LIKE JELLY. It's the only way to describe how my insides tremble and my legs are weak.

Two orgasms.

Two.

I would have been content with one.

Whatever. You want more already—more a thousand times over.

And even then I know I'd still be wanting.

Because it could never just be about sex with him.

He's dangerous. To my senses, my sanity—and, if I really dwell on it, my heart. All over again.

I was foolish to even go there.

I circle the room, talking with prospective partners, my business persona enough to hide my distraction.

Him.

I feel his presence with every word I say, every breath I take, every clip of my heel against the gleaming floor as I walk. I can feel his eyes following me and I purposefully evade him. My schedule for the next two weeks is filling up and I know he'll be wanting his share. Perhaps that's why I leave him until last. Because I'm goading him. *Not* because I still want him.

He's at the bar now. I know it without looking. I've been aware of his movements ever since he appeared.

'Your feet aren't going to touch the ground over the next fortnight,' Clare tells me as she scans her tablet. 'And we still have those few that weren't able to make it tonight…'

He's moving. I can feel it.

Don't turn.

'I can offer them Friday,' she says, 'or later the following week. Of course, we still need to schedule in Waring Holdings, but if—'

'Good to see I'm on the radar.'

Shit. He's right behind me already.

I don't want him to know how I feel, and I don't want Clare to read it. So I school my expression, turning to face him with a polite smile that I hope masks a multitude of sins. I took what I wanted earlier to get him out of my system. I need him to see that. To hell with what my body is still saying.

'Of course you are, Lucas.' I gesture to Clare. 'My PA will arrange a convenient time for us to meet the week after next.' I add the timing for my own benefit, I need those days to get myself straightened out. 'Now, if you'll excuse me…?'

I move to leave but he steps in front of me, his frown so genuine I'm momentarily struck still.

'Does your PA deal with your after-hours schedule too?'

Now it's my turn to frown. He's not ready to let me

go. That much is obvious. 'Can you excuse us a second, Clare?'

'Sure.' She doesn't even quirk a brow at his remark, such is her professionalism, and I'm grateful for it.

I watch her walk away and purse my lips as I turn back to him. Refusing to acknowledge the excited tremble that runs up my spine as his eyes sparkle at me, glinting in the fairy lights adorning the tree beside us.

'Do you mind keeping this professional?'

If I expect my cold demeanour to rub off on him, it doesn't. He actually looks as if he's about to laugh.

'I was merely suggesting you might be hungry.'

His eyes trace a slow path to my belly and back up, teasing me through the silk.

'The hors d'oeuvres were delightful, but hardly enough to keep one going *all night*.'

I swallow. It's the way he draws out the words *all night*...the sequence of carnal images it paints...

'So, are you free for a late dinner? The place is emptying out.' His hand, still holding a glass, sweeps the room, but his eyes are all for me. 'For old times' sake, Evangeline. We've so much to catch up on.'

There's my name again. There's that same excited shudder. My brain is screaming at me to turn him down, to keep this all about business from here on in. It's wrong on so many levels—not least of all my family's. I want to be stronger. I want to be able to stamp this out and move on.

'Slow to work out that you're not wanted here, Waring?'

Shit. Dad.

I'd been so focused on Lucas I hadn't sensed my parents' approach. Now they're both standing directly beside me and I can feel the war building. This can't be happening. Not tonight of all nights. My night.

Fuck that.

A pulse moves in Lucas's jaw. He's mad. Really mad.

'I don't believe anyone has said that.' He raises his drink to his lips, the movement casual, but I can feel the barely restrained anger thrumming off his rigid stance.

My mother touches a hand to my father's arm. 'Now, David—'

'*I* am,' my father says, talking over her. 'And *she* will—won't you, Eva?'

He's looking at me. They both are. And I see red. This is what I've been fighting to escape—my family's control, interference, whatever you want to call it. For all that they love me, I'm tired of being under their thumb, dancing to their tune. And this is *my* product, *my* life. I've earned the right to say who I get involved with.

The way my brain phrases that last bit—*involved with*—isn't lost on me, but I push past it and look to my father.

'Waring Holdings is a good fit for the business.'

My father's colour deepens, his eyes widening as my mother's hand tightens upon his arm. But anger has given me the strength I need. Not just to deal with Dad, but with Lucas too.

'They will be on my list for consideration.'

I feel Lucas's chest puff and my eyes snap to his.

'Please ensure that Clare has your details before you

leave, so that we can arrange a mutually agreeable time to meet.'

My words leave no room for misunderstanding but rather than looking rebuked, he appears amused. The spark in his eye an open challenge. 'Of course.'

'Now, shall we go?' I say to my parents. 'We don't want to leave François waiting.'

My mother looks warily between us all. 'I thought you…?'

She's right. I told them before the night began that I wouldn't be joining them for dinner at their favourite French restaurant afterwards. I had some grand plan of a fancy takeaway, a hot bath and more champagne. Wallowing in my triumph, so to speak, and soaking away the stress of the last few months—years, even.

Now I know that a bath would only encourage debauched fantasies of what I might be doing with Lucas…

'I've changed my mind,' I say over the heat that starts to swirl, and I face him off. 'Thank you for coming, Lucas.'

His lip twitches and I read the double meaning in his eyes. Christ. I almost expect him to say, *Not me, but you did…twice.*

My cheeks flame as his eyes dance. 'I look forward to our next meeting.'

Look forward to it? I'll be on heat for it—*and* at my wits' end if I don't get this under control.

Still, I have at least a week—maybe more.

Plenty of time.

* * *

It's late when the door to Je l'adore opens and she emerges, her parents in tow.

I don't know why I'm here. Or rather I know why, but I don't approve of my actions.

Seems seeing her again has broken something in me. Something I kept locked away when I had a friendship to protect, a surrogate family to honour. Without it, I can't shake free.

I want to blame it on unsated desire. Sex. Simple as.

I tell myself that if I have her, then I can move on. It's an ability that's served me well in the past. I don't form attachments. Not any more.

I look at her now from my vantage point in the back of my limo across the street. She's laughing, her arms around her mother as they bid each other good-night. There is so much love between them and my gut lurches at the sight of it. There'd been a time when I'd been part of that. Had loved and been loved, or so I'd thought.

Then she turns to her father and that lurch turns into a twist. I don't want to care any more. It's old ground. But I owe part of myself to that man, my only real father figure. He shaped me, and my success is in some way because of him.

Love, respect, anger—they all collide. I flex my fists, breathing through it. I always knew tonight would be hard, but there's so much I didn't bank on.

And right up there is this rush of feeling for her. An emotion I thought well and truly dead.

Seems she *is* my weakness after all.

She pecks her father on his cheek and I can almost sense his need to say something. I know him, and I know he's not going to let this go, but whatever he says she shakes her head at it and gestures for them to get in their waiting car.

I know she has an exclusive apartment around the corner—one of many homes owned by her family—and I'm banking on her heading back there tonight.

Just as I'm banking on getting what I came for...

I'm wired by the time I say goodbye to Mum and Dad. I could blame it on the amazing party—the culmination of my hard work. But it's not. It runs a whole lot deeper.

Loving Lucas had been as natural as breathing in my teens. And just as impossible to prevent. He'd always been a part of our lives, his mother constantly using mine as a sitter so she could go on date after date, never finding anyone permanent.

I don't know whether she was picky or desperate, but it had made me mad. Mad at how she could neglect Lucas, not care about him. The day he got his exam results I remember her delivering a swift 'well done, honey' before planting a kiss on his forehead and leaving for the night. There was no celebration—no nothing.

It had been my parents who had cheered him on, congratulating him, spoiling both him and Nate because they'd done well.

We'd even taken him away with us on family holidays. It had been inevitable, really.

He'd been gorgeous, athletic and toned, intelligent, a rebel, but never taking it too far—not like Nate, who never knew when to quit. It was always Lucas reining him in, looking out for him.

He'd looked out for me too, and my heart had revelled in it. Loving the way he didn't disregard my opinion, unlike Dad and Nate, who saw me as just a girl. Lucas made me feel special.

But when his mother had died suddenly things changed. We truly became his family, gave him a home, and as much as Nate was his best friend, and my father a man he respected and could call on for advice, my mother the one to feed, water and look after him, I was Lucas's ear. It was my turn to be there for him.

I was the one he talked to about how he felt, about his grief which was tainted with guilt at not having been the closest of sons to his mother. But his remorse only succeeded in making me more angry, more protective, as I tried to tell him it wasn't his fault. She should've been a better mother. She should've been there for him more.

Like I had been.

Until my eighteenth birthday, that is. Until I pushed him too far.

I was naïve to think he would consider me worth the risk. Naïve to think he could have loved me enough.

I take a shaky breath and duck my head against the bitter cold wind. I know better now. I won't go there again.

I teeter down the pavement towards home and I

shiver. The champagne topped up with wine had been doing a fine job of warding off the chill until now.

How could things have gone so wrong five years ago?

Ten years ago I messed up and he broke my heart.

But five years ago, he and Nate and their business… I just don't get it.

My parents loved Lucas—*Nate* loved him. I can't believe he just bailed on the company, as my father and Nate claim. They hate him for it, but the Lucas I know—I *knew*—wouldn't do that. And the anger, the resentment—it's there on both sides.

If we're to work together I need to get the full story. I need to know I can trust him. Which means I need Lucas to tell me his side of it. And that means dragging up the past.

I wanted to press Dad at dinner, to be honest and tell him that I suspect Nate of playing a greater role in what went down five years ago. But I didn't. Instead, Lucas just became the elephant in the room.

A rather sexy, irresistible, *fuck-me-now* elephant.

I remember how he looked on his knees, his head buried between my legs, and the chill evaporates with a lick of heat. I wonder whether his trunk would be just as impressive as the oversized animal's…

A surprised laugh erupts over my crazed thoughts.

'You know, talking to oneself is the first sign of madness.'

Lucas. Oh, God.

I misstep and quickly correct it. Straightening my

spine I turn to face him, praying that the low light hides the excitement rising beneath my shock. 'Technically, I was laughing, and *that* is a sign of good character… not that you'd know much about that.'

His brow lifts over eyes that flicker and I wonder if my words sting. Guilt fires inside me—*it's a low blow*—but I bury it.

'What are you doing here, Lucas?'

'I would have thought that was obvious.'

I take a shaky breath and remind myself of the trillion reasons why this needs to stop. 'I thought I made it clear earlier that we're even.'

He steps towards me and heat flares with his proximity. My lungs drag in air that is tainted with his cologne.

'And I told *you*,' he murmurs, 'we're not…not even close.'

I hear the desire ring in his voice, feel it echo in my blood, and I force myself to turn away, to walk. 'It's close enough, Lucas.'

'That's not what your eyes were telling me earlier, Evangeline.'

He follows close behind me and I ignore the shiver of delight, wrapping my arms around my middle, hugging my faux fur coat tight.

I can't tell him that I'm scared of falling for him again. But I can tell him that my family hating him makes this a very bad idea.

But part of me suspects he is doing this *because* of my family and their vendetta.

I know my product is good enough to warrant his attention, but *this*—this has nothing to do with my product and everything to do with me.

'Are you denying that you want me?'

I can hear the disbelief in his voice and it annoys me. Like my father—like my brother, even—he assumes he knows what I want. Is he going to start dictating what's best for me too?

'No, I think you know that well enough,' I admit. There's no point in lying about the obvious. 'You knew it ten years ago and you know it all over again now. But here's the thing, Lucas…'

I turn to face him. My apartment is a building away now. Sanctuary is close. I just need to hold it together a few more moments.

'I'm not the kid I was then. I won't jeopardise my work for some…' I struggle for the right phrase and settle for the easiest, most innocent. 'Some silly distraction.'

His laugh is low, seductive, and he takes advantage of my stationary state to close the distance between us, reaching out his hand to cup my jaw. I want to move away, to stop the frisson at his touch, but I can't make my body obey.

His thumb is soft, warm as he brushes it over my cheekbone, and my eyes are lost in the darkness of his, so close I can just make out the rim of brown, the flecks of gold that dance in the snow-white lights adorning the trees that line the street.

'There's nothing silly about the way I feel right now.'

Dammit, does he have to look so sincere?

A group of revellers round the corner and start moving down the street, their voices deep and loud as they roll out a rendition of 'Good King Wenceslas'.

'Seems we're destined to have spectators,' he says.

And as my lips part on no words I'm swamped by the memory of our previous encounter and the fear that I want him to kiss me. So much it hurts. But it'll be my undoing. A ten-year-old memory stoked, refreshed, and my feelings with it.

And a hope for something that just isn't possible.

My tongue sweeps across my lower lip.

It's nerves. I'm just nervous.

My clit pangs painfully, mocking me.

'Please, Lucas, this has to stop.'

I think of his mouth, his tongue, the dizzying pressure he administered so expertly over me. *Stop. Don't stop.* My thoughts are as chaotic as the blood racing through my veins.

'Tell me to leave…'

He steps forward, close enough to stop the chill wind breaching the gap between us, and now I'm just hot. Hot and confused.

'…and I will.'

'I…I…'

'*Tell* me.'

'Please…' I try again and fail. I don't want to breathe—don't want to inhale his scent, his warmth, his appeal. All my barriers are collapsing.

'Evangeline…'

My name rolls over his tongue and his head dips.

The air sits in my lungs as I neither rebuke him nor pull him in. And then he sweeps past my mouth, along my cheek to my ear, his lips gently brushing over my skin with his words.

'I want you.'

A strange whimper sounds, and as he lifts his head, his lips curving, I know it's come from me. I see the triumph in his gaze as he moves for my mouth and a slice of sanity erupts.

'Don't kiss me.'

I palm his chest and he frowns.

'Don't make this about more than sex.'

His head tilts to one side as he studies me, the meaning of my words sinking in. 'Last time I checked, kissing was quite an essential element—quite an irresistible element.'

He looks to my mouth, eyes hungry, and as though emphasising his point he runs his teeth over his lower lip. *God, yes.* My tummy contracts on a rush.

'Oi-oi! Get yourself a room!' one of the passing revellers declares, and there's a string of cheers and laughter from his crew.

Lucas doesn't flinch—doesn't even back away. 'A room sounds like a good idea to me.'

He reaches around me with his other hand and brings me closer. Close enough to feel his hardness pressing between us. Damn suits and their forgiving cloth. I didn't need any confirmation of his impressive trunk. Not when I'm hanging by a thread.

My hands soften against him. 'This isn't a good idea.'

'*Au contraire.* I see it as the only way to get our business off on the right foot.'

He leans back in, his mouth hovering by my ear once more.

'I need to know how it feels to be inside you…to cease the raging fantasy and know the real thing. I need to know so I don't spend every meeting thinking about what it would be like to bend you over and fuck you hard.'

Air flutters past my lips. I could come just listening to his dirty talk. No one has ever spoken to me like this. No one.

'Lucas…'

It's not his name that betrays my every want. It's the husky intonation, the plea-like quality of my voice. I don't care that the revellers are now wolf-whistling and cheering, entertained by our display.

My body surrenders and my lashes close… 'Your room or mine?'

CHAPTER FOUR

SHE OPENS HER eyes and for a second, I wonder if she will still refuse me.

Something vulnerable, something edgy persists in her gaze, but then she turns and walks away.

No refusal, then...

I follow.

She hasn't told me to go. She hasn't told me to stay.

But one thing I'm sure of, Evangeline does what she wants and I'll go along with it until she tells me otherwise.

Hell, I don't want this to be about more than sex either. It will only muddy the waters, exposing us both to a future headache neither of us needs.

But not kissing her?

That's like being gifted a three-course dinner without the main course.

And those lips...

She turns to look at me now as she pushes the door open and holds it for me. They curve a little and her lashes lower as I step forward. I want to taste them... to feel them part beneath my pressure...to swallow her moan with the one I know I'd give.

Because I've only tasted them once, and the memory is burned into my soul.

She says nothing as we cross the harsh white vestibule. It's all glass, high ceilings and bright lights, but she lifts its starkness just by being there and I can't look away.

A warning sparks in my gut—a warning I want to ignore.

So much time has passed since I loved her. The sweet, feisty, fun-loving girl that she was. So many women have come and gone since, none of whom have inspired a need for more or warranted a trust I feel incapable of giving. I date. I have fun. I move on. They're not relationships as such. Merely acquaintances who satisfy the basic urge for companionship, sex.

I want it to be the same with her. Safe.

But it's not.

I had so much to lose back then and it served me well, kept me protected.

But now there are no barriers against what's burning between us, and I should be running the other way.

But I'm not.

We reach the lift and she presses the button to call it. I half expect her to turn, tell me she's changed her mind, but she doesn't and the warning starts to trickle through my spine: *Are you sure you can keep a lid on this?*

She sneaks a look at me from beneath her lashes, her thoughts hidden as she nibbles over her lip—that deliciously full lip that I want to trace with my tongue—and a tide of longing drowns out the panic.

The lift opens and we walk in. It's vacant and small. I expected it to be vast, to give me room to stave off the heat her nearness is driving. I've wanted her for so long. Fantasised about it even when I knew I shouldn't. And now I'm going to have her I want it to last—not to erupt like my teenage self would have done.

But it's impossible to put down the semi-permanent erection I've been sporting since sitting between her legs. Hell, even before then. From the moment she gave me that look across the room, daring me to follow her. It was there with her intent, her desire.

I fist my hands inside my pockets, fix my gaze to the lift doors and count to ten...twenty... The ground shifts to a gentle stop. The top floor. The penthouse. Only the best for the Beaumonts.

As the doors slide open there's more white, more glass, more coldness. It's similar to my place, further into the city, but it reeks of her family—not her. Not the girl I knew. But as for the woman... What do I truly know?

We should have gone to mine.

'You don't like it?'

I realise she's caught me frowning, my hands still deep in my pockets and my shoulders tense. I force myself to relax and give her a smile. 'It's not what I expected.'

She shrugs off her coat and opens a concealed closet, hanging it up. 'It's my parents' place, and it's *exactly* how they like it.'

'Not you.'

It's a simple statement, and I guess I could be wrong but I want to know I'm right. I see a flash of colour run along her cheekbones, her lips twitching.

Not only am I right, I've pleased her—and, Christ, does it feel good.

'No, not really.' She closes the closet and starts to head off towards an open living space. 'I have a place I'm renovating in Notting Hill. This is a stopgap.'

My smile grows with my confidence as I follow her. I still *know* her. 'What colour?'

She eyes me over her shoulder as she enters the kitchen and reaches for a glass. 'Colour?'

'The house...'

She gives a soft laugh. 'What makes you think I've gone for a colour?' she asks, dispensing water from the sleek black fridge door. 'I could have gone for *au naturel* stone.'

She leans back against the countertop and takes a sip from the glass, her eyes holding mine.

'Again...not you.'

She smiles approvingly. 'Pink.'

'Pink?'

My brow rises—she *has* to be teasing. I search her gaze and it dances with humour. I would have had her saying blue—yellow, even—but *pink*...

'Now you look like my mother when I told her the same.'

I laugh as I imagine the scene and see humour reflected in her gaze. She looks beautiful, amused, so at ease suddenly, and it warms me through. It feels like old times. When the banter was so quick to spark between us.

I smile. 'I bet she was all for yellow—am I right?'

'Yellow, or even blue, anything but pink.'

She shakes her head softly and there's a silent exchange, an acceptance that we still *work*.

I can feel it.

And then it's gone.

She stiffens as the mood shifts and I grapple to get it back. 'Whatever floats your boat, I say.'

She takes a breath, visibly composing herself as she turns away to place her glass on the side.

'You do,' she says, her eyes coming back to me, her voice low, her eyes intent. 'Right now.'

The swift change from light-hearted to sexual unsettles me. My eyes narrow. Is she forcing us back to sex? Taking away our connection? The personal talk?

You should be happy.

She gives her head a small flick as her eyes stare into mine. 'Or have you changed your mind?'

Fuck that.

I'm moving before I know it.

Fuck personal. Fuck talk.

She's in my arms, her hands beneath my jacket shoving it down my shoulders. I throw it to one side, pulling her back against me and seeking out her mouth, instinct driving me, making me forget not to kiss her. She turns away, arching her neck and offering up the creamy expanse of skin instead.

The gesture cuts deep and I scrape my teeth against

her—a nip of punishment and acceptance in one—and the whimper it draws triggers a groan of my own. *Christ*. The series of things I want to do to her, *with* her, is rampaging through my brain, and my arousal strains painfully between us.

I run my hands over her dress, seeking out the fastening—a zipper, buttons, anything. It's frustrating as hell. 'If you don't get this off, I swear I'm going to rip it.'

She laughs at me. The husky lilt driving me crazy.

'So impatient…'

'I've had ten years to wait for this. I call that patience enough.'

Her eyes widen as she stares up at me and she's momentarily still.

Shit. Too much.

'Off,' I command, wanting her back in the moment, to forget what I said.

And she turns away to pull the escaped curls over her shoulder. 'The zipper is concealed in the back.'

I find the fastening and slowly—too slowly for my tortured cock, but too quickly for my struggling control—I lower it, exposing her exquisite skin, her spine that I want to trace with my fingers, my lips, my tongue. Goosebumps prickle where the fabric parts, calling to me, and I press a kiss to the nape of her neck, breathing her in.

'You are beautiful, Evangeline.'

She shudders on a breath, turning her head so that I'm on the periphery of her vision, her lashes low, her forbidden lips parted. The zipper stops over the curve of her bare arse and I remember her thong sitting pretty in my pocket. I smile. She went to dinner like this, bare and exposed, thanks to *me*.

And then all sane thought leaves me as she slips the dress from her shoulders and it pools at her feet. Her perfectly round cheeks are exposed to my hungry gaze and I can't breathe, can't move, can't believe.

Her eyes lift to mine above her shoulder. 'Are you just going to stare?'

'I'm savouring.'

Engraving this moment in my memory, worshipping it—you, Evangeline.

I reach out to smooth each mound and she curves into my touch, her teeth biting into her lip.

'Please, Lucas, I want you now. You can savour later.'

Later? How much later? In an hour? Two? A day? A week?

I don't pose the question; the answer is too depressing.

And if I only get to be inside her once, I'm going to make it the best she's ever known.

I bow my head into the curve of her neck, my lips gently brushing her skin as I say, 'Now who's impatient, hmm…?'

I grasp her hips and pull her back against my clothed erection, relishing the moan she gives in return, the feel of her cheeks cradling my arousal. And when I release her to trail my fingers up her sides she doesn't move away. She stays curved against me, her palms planted on the cold white countertop as she pushes into me.

I lift my lips to the edge of her ear. 'What would your parents say to you fucking in their kitchen?'

She whimpers—she likes my dirty talk. I know it and I love her for it.

Enough with the love!

I focus on my hands. I want to touch her everywhere, claim her everywhere, coax out every sound of ecstasy she's capable of making. I stroke along her back and unclasp her bra. The nude lace obediently falls open, the straps landing loose down her arms before I encourage them off. Her breasts fall free. I can't see them, but knowing they are there, waiting, has me aching, painful, *desperate*.

I trace the curve of her waist around to her belly, higher... I stroke beneath the curve of her breasts, feel their weight shift as she writhes.

'God, Lucas, *please*.'

I grit my teeth against her heated plea, feel my control fraying as I rotate my palms and surround each breast. I shudder on my own breath even as I feel her do the same, feel her hardened beads pressing into my palms. I roll her nipples between my thumbs and forefingers, making them harder, prouder, feeling the tautness in the ripples that surround them.

Just perfect.

Perfect and mine.

For now.

I pinch them tighter and she inhales sharply between her teeth.

'God, *yes*.'

'You like that?'

My voice is strained, my balls heavy. I'm so close, and I know she is too.

'Yes...'

It's practically a hiss as she leans back, her body arched. Her bra hits the floor as she flicks it away so she can raise her hands to my neck, and I do it again and again, making her writhe. Her naked body against my clothed one. It's one hell of a contrast and it's pushing me over.

I'm tempted to make her come like this. It's clear she would. But I need to feel her—feel her wetness, the evidence of her need.

I trail one hand down her belly and she sucks her tummy in.

'I can't get your pussy out of my head,' I tell her, kissing her shoulder. 'The way you taste...' I nip her skin. 'The way you move...' She claws my neck as I cup her and her legs shift apart, granting me all the access I need. 'The way you're wet just for me...'

I move, sliding my middle finger in deep, and pull back until her clit is beneath my fingertip. Slowly I rotate it over her and she whimpers, the noise sending my balls heavenward. The smooth undulation of her hips is pushing my release and I grit my teeth.

Not yet.

I'm losing it.

It's the only way to explain how we've got to this point. In my parents' perfect, clinical abode. All orderly and cold. Me naked. Him clothed. Me on the brink. Him…

Oh, yes…

I can feel he's close. Every taut muscle is pressing into my back, and his stance as he rocks with rigid precision against me is so fucking hot. I ride my arse against him, staving off my own release.

I want him to come. I want him to come inside his clothing. I want to feel that power—to know that a man like Lucas Waring can lose it, still caged inside his underwear, over *me*. It's that which keeps me just this side of sane.

I drop one hand to move it with his and feel his body jerk.

'Christ, Evangeline.' His breath rasps. 'What are you *doing* to me?'

I smile through the salacious heat whipping around us, pushing his fingers lower, encouraging him to sink inside me as I move with him.

He breathes into my neck, his stubble grazing my skin as he buries his face there. His other hand drops to my thigh and grabs it, lifting it, granting himself greater access, greater friction over my clit as his wrist rubs against me and his cock presses harder, more urgently.

'Yes, Lucas, yes…' I pant, and my control is slipping.

But his is too. He's trembling against me, his body ever more tense, and then I am gone. Wave after wave crashes over me, and my head is swimming with ecstasy. And then I feel him, hear his growl into my shoulder, feel his teeth biting as he bucks and shudders, his own release wild and sudden.

I hang off his neck, holding him to me, keeping us locked together, and my lips stretch in a triumphant smile. I look to the pristine white ceiling, catch our reflection in the rim of a chrome spotlight, and it's a reminder that this is *real*. So very real and so electrifying.

I should be scared—scared of what it means for the future, scared about whether I can give this up. Instead I'm content in his arms, naked and at home.

'Fuck, I haven't… I shouldn't have…'

He shakes his head and his disbelief, his sudden vulnerability, resonates through me. I turn and hook my hands behind his neck, eager to see off any hint of real emotion—because *that* I can't deal with.

'Oh, yes, you should…because *that* was erotic as fuck.'

He lifts his lashes; his eyes meet mine and I am winded. They are almost shy as they search, seeking out a lie that doesn't exist. It *was* fucking hot. It was everything I wanted.

'You have to be kidding me…?' His hands drop to my behind, soft, yielding.

He doesn't believe me.

'No.'

I almost kiss him—can feel the urge burning through my veins. But where would that leave us?

And then his crazy statement replays in my mind: *'I've had ten years to wait for this.'*

Shit.

I push it away. I can't think about what that means.
It's too hopeful. And I learned my lesson once. I won't
go there again. *Focus on the sex.* It's tangible. It's what
he came for and it's the one thing I agreed to and can
give. For tonight.

'Just thinking about it turns me on all over again,'
I say.

As if on cue my nipples prickle into his shirt and I
run my teeth over my lower lip. I'm not kidding. Three
orgasms and still I want more. I know it's a bad sign,
but as I curve into him, breathing him in, I couldn't
care less.

Slowly his smile lifts, his eyes with it, and he presses
his forehead to mine. 'Keep talking like that and I'll be
taking you to bed next.'

'I like the sound of that...' I smile, all sultry. 'But
how about a shower first?'

I take his hand and before I can question my senses
I head to the bathroom, loving how he comes with me.
No question. No hesitation. This feels like a dream.

One that I don't want to wake up from.

Again, it's a warning. Again, I ignore it, pushing
open the bedroom door and heading straight for the en
suite bathroom.

Lucas releases my hand and I look at him over my
shoulder.

'I'm stripping for this,' he says.

Then it hits me—we've done so much but I've not
seen him naked. *Not yet.*

I reach into the bathroom to set the shower going before sauntering towards him. He's placing his cufflinks on the dressing table that blends into the shelving system that runs along one wall. His dark, erotic presence is at total odds with the crisp white room. He doesn't belong here. Hell, neither do I. But it only makes my blood rush faster, my ache build.

He's tugging his tie undone when I reach him, and I go to work on his shirt, pulling it out of his trousers and moving on to the buttons. My eyes follow my progress, and my mouth dries further the more skin I unveil, the more muscle, the more toned ripples that are triggered with each scrape of my fingers.

I've seen him shirtless before. He only ever slept in lounge pants when he stayed with us. And he was captivating then—in a boyish, trim way. But now he's all hard, lean muscle and I can't believe I'm getting to strip him.

'I've waited ten years for this...'

His voice reverberates through my mind. Ten years ago he refused me, and didn't give me a backward glance. Or so I thought. Now he's hinting at something else...something more.

My insides twist. My heart aches. I want this to be about sex. I don't want to feel anything else—not on that level.

'Hey, are you okay?'

I realise I've stilled, my eyes unseeing on his chest, my fingers frozen.

You fool.

'Of course,' I say softly, pressing a kiss to his chest

and breathing in the thought-obliterating scent of him as I tell my brain to shut down. To go with the flow.

I release the last button and smooth my hands over his shoulders, coaxing off his shirt, exposing the beauty of him to my appreciative gaze. He really is exquisite. I've had men—of course I have. I almost married one in trying to forget Lucas.

That foolish move seems ever more idiotic as I drown in a sea of sensation over the man before me now.

I could never forget Lucas. Never carve him out of me.

I trace his pecs, watch them flicker, then I lick my lips as I trail my hands lower, over the taut expanse of muscle to the hint of hair that thickens above his belt buckle.

I move to unfasten his trousers and he catches my wrists, halting me. I look up, questioning, praying I can hide the swirl of emotion running away inside me.

'As much as you found it a turn-on,' he says with a lopsided smile, 'I'm taking myself in there and getting these off alone.'

He steps around me and I watch him go, mesmerised by the movement of his shoulder blades, by the sharp waist and the curve of his behind in those trousers.

Fuck, how I want to bite that.

I giggle at my own crazed desire. It's so unlike me. As if a dormant part has suddenly awakened inside of me and is taking over. Pushing out all else.

Thank God.

I give him a minute, until I hear the sound of the

water change, and then I know he is in there…ready and waiting.

I go in. My sanity well and truly gone. There'll be time for that tomorrow. I need him inside me now… filling me, making me whole.

I enter the cubicle and he's there, slicked up, his eyes dark and needy. I step forward and my smart-watch beeps. I don't know why I look at it. Maybe it's because he does. But I immediately wish I hadn't.

The incoming text message glares up at me, and with it everything changes.

I can't *un*-see it.

I wish I could. But I can't.

I should be grateful. But I'm not.

CHAPTER FIVE

FIVE DAYS SINCE I've seen her.

Five days since she told me to finish my shower and leave.

I'd blame it on the fact that I lost my load like an inexperienced fool if not for the fact she was so turned on by it. She told me so herself and I believed her. It was written on her face…in her actions.

And then her watch beeped and she morphed into someone else entirely.

A cold replica.

She had no time for me…for *us*.

Not that there would ever *be* an 'us'—but, hell, in that moment in her kitchen…before, during, after…I felt things shift between us. I thought it felt *right*, picking up where we'd left off ten years prior, saying to hell with everyone and everything else.

Clearly I was wrong.

She offered no explanation. Nothing. As if I didn't even warrant one. And I wasn't about to give her the satisfaction of grovelling for justification.

I cleaned up, dressed and left.

Two days later Monday morning hit, and my PA informed me that my meeting with her had been scheduled for a week Friday.

I laughed. Actually laughed. Did she really think she could keep me hanging on for two weeks like some insignificant prospect?

But you've only got yourself to blame.

I've hardly covered myself in glory, following her around like some fool, giving her the impression she can wrap me around her little finger.

But no more.

It's time she saw the real me. The one who stays in control.

So now I'm here, in her building, more than a week early and ready to face the music.

I know she's not going to like this, but I have a score to settle. Not just professionally, but personally too.

'Mr Waring, I'm afraid Miss Beaumont has an appointment with Houston Logistics right now,' her PA says to me, her smile polite but confused. 'I believe we have an appointment scheduled for next week on Friday?'

I give her a smile loaded with charm. 'That *was* the case, but Houston and I have decided to swap.'

'To…swap?'

Her brows lift past the rim of her thick black glasses and I want to laugh. It's a worrying sign. Laughter tells me that I'm nervous. And I'm never nervous.

Control, Lucas. Control.

I clear my throat and slot my hands into my pockets,

letting my eyes drift across the office and back to her. 'That's right. We—'

'Lucas?'

Eva.

My pulse skips a beat. Her sudden presence triggers an adrenaline shot and I'm slow to turn to face her, to neutralise it.

'Evangeline, it's good to see you.'

Good? Christ. 'Good' has nothing on the reality.

She's striking in pink today. A simple shirt that looks anything but simple clings to her curves and disappears into a tight black skirt. Her legs are exposed from the knee down and accentuated by heels that trigger a carnal hit, making me think about things that have no place in this room right now.

Control.

I drag my eyes back up to her hair—something innocent. It's twisted high on her head, smart and professional and sexy as fuck.

Dammit all.

I meet her eyes. They're bright. Their blue depths alive and popping. I could say it was down to effective make-up, but I know it's her reaction to me.

And then I find my control. I'm not alone in this. She feels it too.

It puts us on an even footing, at least.

My chest eases and I step forward, offering my hand. She eyes it suspiciously before taking it for the briefest handshake I've ever experienced. But I feel the current that sparks between us, and I see it reflected in her dilated gaze as she looks up at me.

'I'm afraid I'm too busy to see you today.' She crosses her arms, her lips giving a delightful little tremble as she breathes. 'If you'd called ahead we could have saved you the disappointment.'

She looks past me to her PA.

'Clare, when are Mr Waring and I scheduled to meet?'

'Well, you—'

'Now.' I cut over her. There's no point dragging this out. 'Shall we…?'

I gesture to the open door behind her. Her office. But she's busy looking at her PA, as though she needs saving, and I allow myself a momentary sense of satisfaction because I've unsettled her.

It doesn't beat my experience last Friday night. No, I had the rug well and truly pulled out from beneath me then. But it's a start.

'It seems Mr Waring and Houston Logistics have made an arrangement to swap appointment slots.'

I almost feel sorry for her PA as her voice pitches, and I know she can sense the undercurrent between us.

'Swap?' Eva looks at me incredulously. 'Clare, could you ring and confirm that's the case?'

'Sure.'

'No need—use my mobile.' I extract my phone. 'Houston's in my recently dialled—we played in a golf tournament Sunday. Great chap.'

'Of course you did.'

She doesn't take my phone—she doesn't spare me another glance. She simply turns on her heel and starts for her office.

'Clare, would you mind bringing me a coffee, please?'

Something tells me she wants something stronger than coffee, and I have to stop myself from grinning.

'No problem.' Her PA looks at me, hesitant. 'Can I get you one too, Mr Waring?'

I force my attention off Eva's elegant curves as she strides away—she's so damn sexy when she's pissed off. 'Black, no sugar. Thank you,' I say, and follow her in.

Her office is contemporary. A geometric pattern adorns the grey walls, but there are splashes of colour everywhere. Splashes of her. It has a bright couch with co-ordinating chairs, and a glass coffee table adorned with industry magazines. Her desk is large, a mixture of modern glass and old twisted oak. Interesting, fascinating…just as its owner.

I close the door behind me and wait for her to offer me a seat. Actually, I'm waiting for the eruption that I sense is coming.

She's standing at the room's only window, looking out. From here, I can't make out what she sees, but I'm guessing it's the park across the road. Her building is in a residential area of the city—it's pleasant. Especially on a day like today, when the sun is out, not a cloud in sight.

Her shoulders lift as she takes a long, drawn-out

breath. 'It's a shame you didn't have the decency to let me know about your little arrangement with Houston.'

Her voice is brittle. As if I've done something to offend her. As if it's me who kicked *her* out and not the other way around. My teeth grind.

Control, Lucas. Today is about business.

Except it's not.

If it was purely work I would have left it until next week to prove my company's worth. Instead I'm here now, trying to push past Friday night.

'An oversight—my apologies.'

My tone is careful, restrained, and she turns to me.

If looks could kill...

'I like to feel prepared for my meetings, don't you?' she asks.

She has a point. 'Of course.'

She walks to her desk and wakes up her computer. 'Then you'll understand my request to rearrange.'

I laugh before I can stop it and her eyes flash to me.

'Something funny?'

'Look, I'm here with the perfect deal, tailored to your product—there's nothing you need to prepare. Unless...'

I look at her—really look at her. The quick undulation of her chest is giving away her rapid breath, and there's a persistent flush to her skin. I had it tagged as annoyance, but now I'm not so sure.

I close the distance between us and she backs up, her eyes widening. 'What is it, Evangeline? Did you want more time in the hope that whatever this is between us would go away?'

She scoffs and looks back to her screen. 'So bloody full of yourself, aren't you?'

I raise my hands in defence. 'You're the one acting all angry. A simple switch in meetings shouldn't warrant this. Although, let's be honest, it's me who got the brutal rejection—a naked one at—'

'Stop it, Lucas.'

'What? Reminding you of the truth? Of what we were about to do before that—'

'Look, you want to talk business? Fine. Let's do that.'

She drops into a seat and gestures for me to do the same. She won't look at me, though, and I'm itching to push my luck, to walk around her desk and lift her chin, force her to accept it's still there, riding strong.

'But stick to business, Lucas, or you're out.'

I move to the seat she's offered me and stand before it. 'Just tell me one thing...' I shouldn't ask, and part of me doesn't want to know, but... 'What changed?'

She looks up at me, eyes hesitant, the bob of her throat giving her away. 'I don't know what you mean.'

'You do know what I mean. One minute we're having the best sex of our lives...' I see her entire body clench, her fingers fisting over her keyboard, and I know she's fighting it—fighting the heat the memory triggers. 'The next your watch tells you something and you turn into an ice queen... So what gives?'

She closes her eyes, her fingers relaxing over the keys, and I can't bear it. She's shutting me out and I want to know why.

'Or should the question be—*who*?'

Her lashes lift. Her eyes are unreadable—hatefully unreadable. There was a time I could have read her like a book, but this new skill she has is driving me crazy. All the more so because I'm letting it get to me.

'That has no place in this conversation.'

'Are you sure about that?'

'Positive.'

She looks at her phone and activates the screen, calm as the day outside. 'I have another meeting this afternoon, so I suggest we get on with this.'

I feel my mouth gape and quickly snap it shut.

'I'll find out what's keeping Clare first.'

She stands and leaves. Her absence is just as frustrating as her presence.

'That has no place in this conversation...'

That makes the reason personal. And if it's personal, does that mean she has another man? Was it guilt that had her kicking me out?

I can't believe it of her. The Eva I know wouldn't be unfaithful, no matter how strong our connection. But if it's not another man...

I look to her phone on the desk. Whatever that notification was, there'll be a record of it on there. The temptation to lift it and take a chance on it being unlocked, or possessing an easy-to-guess PIN is there, but I'm not going to sink that low. I'm not.

As if I've summoned it, the phone starts to flash with an incoming call: *Nate.*

Something twists deep inside me and I feel I have my answer.

She took me back to her place straight off the back of seeing her parents. Their hold over her wasn't enough to stop it. *But Nate*...

My lip curls; the bitter, acrid taste of betrayal stings my throat.

I let him get between us before, there's no way I'll let it happen again.

This contract was important enough when it was purely business—now it just got personal, *real* personal, and I'll do everything within my power to see it signed. Pull every trick in the book if I have to.

She *will* sign it.

And do a whole lot more if I have my way.

The business is revenge enough, but Eva... She's the icing on the cake.

As I walk back into my office, I notice two things that stop me in my tracks.

Firstly, Lucas has made himself at home, and I don't want to feel the excited rush that comes with the sight. His jacket is slung over the back of his chair and he has his laptop propped open as he taps away, his crisp white shirt rippling with the movement of his shoulders, his hair falling forward over his forehead.

Too appealing. Too comfy.

Secondly, my phone has moved. It now sits alongside his laptop and my eyes rest there as my heart lurches.

Has he...? Could he have...? It's my birthdate— would he remember?

He turns his head to look at me, but barely acknowledges my presence before he looks back to his screen and slides my phone across the desk, to where it was before.

'It kept ringing, so I silenced it.'

I come alive at his voice—so matter-of-fact, so deep and thrilling. 'Right. Sorry.'

Jesus. Why am I apologising? I remember the coffees I'm holding on to and kick the door closed behind me before striding over and slapping one down next to him.

'It's not quite barista standard but it does the job well enough.'

'Thank you.'

His lashes lift but I don't wait for our eyes to meet— not at this proximity. Not even excusing myself on the pretence of chasing up Clare has helped me get my head back in the game. I quickly scoot to my side of the desk, putting a whole chunk of glass and wood between us. Better.

'Don't you want to see who's been calling? They've been quite persistent.'

He doesn't look at me as he asks the question but there's an edge to his tone—something that has my skin prickling.

'It can wait.'

Now he looks at me and his eyes are cold, piercing. 'You sure about that?'

I swallow. 'Yes.'

'I think you should at least check.'

He's goading me, and I don't want to give him the satisfaction, but I can't stop curiosity getting the better of me. I reach out and activate the screen, glancing at it with my trusty poker face. Not that I think it will fool him.

Three missed calls. Nate.

Shit.

I shut the screen down and lean back in my chair, taking my coffee with me. 'I'll call him back later.'

'Three missed calls, though,' he pushes. 'Could be urgent?'

I give a dismissive shrug and his eyes lower briefly, burning into the fabric of my blouse. It's buttoned high, it's perfectly decent, and yet I feel as if he's stripped me. Heat swamps my belly, my breasts, my nipples prickle against the lace of my bra.

'It's fine. I'll call him back later.'

I'm repeating myself, but this time the words are harder, stronger, fed with the strength of will it's taking for me to fight this dogged attraction. Because that's all this can be—attraction. I don't know Lucas now, and I don't know the truth of what went down five years ago with Nate, or the true reason he is back. I want to think it's for my product, but is it really?

He gives me a slow smile and closes the lid of his laptop. 'Okay.'

I watch him take up his coffee, watch him sip at the hot, steaming liquid, and not once does he release me from his gaze. *I* could look away, but it feels like a challenge: first who does admits defeat.

Well, not me...

'Shall I start from the top?' he asks. 'Me? My company? The basics? Or is that a bit like covering old ground?'

How is he doing it? Remaining so calm when I know he's not? He wanted me to see that Nate had called. He wanted to test me…assess my reaction. Has he worked out it was Nate who ruined Friday too?

'I know enough about Waring Holdings,' I say, grateful for my projected confidence.

'Is that so?' He shoots me a grin as he settles back in his seat. 'Please enlighten me.'

I wonder if this is a test too, or if he's genuinely curious as to what I know.

I humour him, reeling off facts and figures, cities of presence, high-profile partners—the lot—and I know I've surprised him. I can see it in the swell of his chest, his pumped-up reaction as I feed his ego. I don't mind doing it—not when I'm stating facts.

He runs his forefinger along his lower lip and rubs at his chin. 'You've done your homework.'

'Of course.'

I don't want to say I knew all this anyway. That he might have been out of my life but I couldn't help keeping tabs on him. It's not like anyone can ignore him anyway, not when he's splashed all over the media to enjoy.

'I thought you said you needed time to prep for our meeting?' he says.

My cheeks colour. He's got me, and I look at my mug to avoid his eye, taking a sip. 'I like to know who I'm meeting. If I'm expecting Houston Logistics, I want to see Houston Logistics.'

'Are you saying you prefer dear old Leslie's company to mine?'

'I think from a distribution point of view you're on a par.'

'You know that's not what I meant.'

'Isn't it?' I challenge—and, God help me, my belly flutters excitedly. Sparring with him is too much fun.

He gives a soft laugh. 'Fair enough, but I disagree. We're not on a par. Open your email. I've sent you some comparisons to look at it.'

'Comparisons?' I place my coffee on the desk and look at my computer screen, doing as he asks.

'Sure. I figured I'd make it easy for you. In the attachments you'll find a whole host of competitors and the reason Waring Holdings outperforms them all.'

I open up his email and the first attachment, giving it a quick scan, and then the next, and the next.

What the hell?

'How can you—?'

'How can I know who I'm up against? Your launch party told me that, and my research team did the rest. I may be missing a few—in fact I'm sure I will be—but if they're not on my radar they're not worth worrying about.'

I can't believe it. A thorough analysis worthy of myself or my team is laid out before me. It wouldn't take me long to check what the reports say for accuracy, but I know in my gut that I won't find anything to fault.

And then Nate's words come back to haunt me—his

timely text from Friday night, the multitude of communications since: *You can't trust him.*

I look at Lucas now and Nate's warning clashes with what I know for myself, with what I feel.

Why did he want me to see that Nate had called? Was it his way of saying his conscience is clear? That he's not worried about him or what he has to say? And if his conscience is clear, then what does that say about my brother? My family?

A wave of uncertainty washes over me and I throw my focus into the spreadsheets and the words before me. But they simply blur.

Lucas left, though. The company collapsed, my brother and father dealt with the fallout, and Lucas was long gone. Why didn't he stick around and protest his innocence? At least help? Why did he go without saying goodbye?

And there it is—the crux of it.

Christ, it was hardly like you spent any time together by then. He owed you nothing.

But the pain is there, and I know it's a huge part of it all. He left without so much as a nod in my direction, without even attempting to clear his name with me, and he must have known the crap my family would lay at his feet.

'What really happened?' I say, looking at the screen.

'Excuse me?'

I look at him now, my eyes narrowed. 'Between you and Nate…the company?'

He stills, his posture straight as his eyes fall away from me. 'You should talk to *him* about it.'

'I'm talking to you.'

Not to mention that it's the last thing I want to raise with Nate. He went off the rails for two years after the company collapsed, drinking heavily, socialising day and night—he was a mess. No one talks about it. Least of all me.

'If we're potentially going to work together, I want to hear your version of events.'

'It's not my place.'

'The hell it's not! You left when the going got tough—is that how it was? Because that's exactly how my family see it. Things got a touch hard and you legged it, leaving them to pick up the pieces.'

Colour seeps into his cheekbones, his knuckles whiten around the mug he still holds, and his eyes harden as they land on me.

'You don't know what you're talking about.'

'Then tell me—give me your side and I'll consider you as equally as I am everyone else.'

'My company stands for itself. I'm not justifying the past to you.'

'You told me Friday night that you make it your business to know all there is about the companies you wish to work with and the people who run them. This is me doing the same due diligence.'

He leans forward in his chair and I think he is about to speak. I hold my breath, waiting. This is it: the truth, his side to balance out theirs.

'Thank Clare for the coffee.'

What?

He places his mug on the desk and gets to his feet.

I stand abruptly. 'You can't leave.'

'Changed your mind already?'

There's humour in his words but not in his eyes.

'We have things to discuss, to go over,' I say.

'It's all there in the email. The last attachment details the arrangement I propose. I think you'll find it fair.'

'But—'

'Speak to Nate, Eva, or drop the past.'

His tone brooks no argument, but how can I tell him I don't dare have it out with my brother for fear of a relapse?

'My business references speak for themselves. Speak to anyone about Waring Holdings and they will put your mind at ease…if it's truly the business you're worried about.'

He lifts his jacket from the back of the chair and shrugs it on, taking up his laptop and case.

'My number is in the email—call me when you're ready to talk business.'

And with that he leaves. I haven't even managed a goodbye. I'm still floundering under the mess that is the past and the present, my family and my business— and, if I'm truly honest, my heart.

To think I had believed it possible to be around him again and keep it tucked away was ridiculous.

Maybe in some way I hoped the past would protect me, keep me safe from falling again. And maybe it would have, if not for the fact that the past as I know it—as my family know it—could well be based on a lie. Or a clever manipulation of the truth. My brother was a pro at doing both when he wanted to.

And Lucas's words in my kitchen about his ten-year wait… They told me there was more to his rejection than I believed all those years ago.

But where does any of that leave me now?

If the company failure was down to Nate, why would Lucas want to go into business with another Beaumont? Why would he sleep with me?

I don't want to think of it as some sort of vendetta, but I can't help it. The rejected eighteen-year-old still inside me can't believe his sudden turnaround. *Get in business with the little sister…get in bed with her.*

It makes for the greatest revenge. But…

'I've had ten years to wait for this.'

Surely that shows he cares about me? Not my family, not my business, but *me*?

I want answers. To explain ten years ago, five years ago. I want the whole damn lot.

And that means going after him.

My phone starts to buzz, along with my watch, and I know it's Nate again without even looking. I ignore it.

I'm going to finish going through the email. I'm going to get my meetings done for the day. And then I'm going get my head around all of this.

If only it can be as simple as it sounds.

CHAPTER SIX

I POUND THE paving beneath my feet, trying to run her out of my system, to forget her family and the past. Tower Bridge and its array of lights against the night sky make the perfect scene to lose myself and regain peace. And normally it works. But not today.

I've had five years to bury the anger the Beaumonts spark in me, the resentment, the betrayal, but it's still as raw as if it was yesterday.

I've done this to myself. I should have stayed away.

There are other products, other investment opportunities—plenty to occupy me. The truth is, when you have money it's easy to make money—so long as you're careful. Nate should have remembered that five years ago, instead of taking it upon himself to sign a deal that I'd already warned him against.

No, not warned. *Forbidden.* Yet he'd broken my trust and done it anyway.

And, hey, presto: today's mess.

Although I can't really blame him for what's happening right now. For *her.* Life was fine. I wasn't fulfilled, but I was a damn sight happier than this.

Yes, it would have been easy enough for me to find opportunities elsewhere, but did I? No. I went knocking on her door, telling myself it was for the product.

The reality hits me—winds me, even—and I double over, my fingers gripping my thighs as I stare unseeingly at the ground.

I went for *her*.

It's obvious now. So obvious I can't believe I didn't see it in the first place. I told myself it was the instant hit of mutual attraction at the party that blurred the boundaries, but like hell it was.

Idiot. I smack my knees in frustration and take off at a sprint, uncaring that people are looking at me as if I'm crazy.

I *am* crazy.

Crazy to have reopened this old wound, brought back the past, her, Nate, the family I once belonged to, was loyal to.

I always cited that loyalty as the reason I stopped myself from giving in to the feelings I had for her. Now that loyalty is gone it's bloody obvious it was an excuse, a handy barrier to stop myself getting too close to someone else.

If my own mother wasn't able to love me, and my father was never in the picture, how could I expect someone else to? Someone who didn't *have* to? That kind of unconditional love doesn't exist. Eva's family proved that to me when they booted me out to protect Nate's arse. Now no one gets that close to me—no one has that kind of power over me.

No one but her, it seems. *Fuck.*

I round the corner to my building. I have an apartment above the company headquarters, which makes life easy when I'm working late. It's time to hit the shower and go out. Maybe a few drinks and a female companion will fit the bill.

Even my cock mocks me. No one will make me forget her—not now. Everything we've shared, every intense second has only ramped up the way I feel. It's like an obsession, an addiction, and neither is healthy or acceptable but I am powerless to stop it.

And as if to prove my point I see her—in the foyer of my building, chatting to security. She's leaning on their high-rise desk, legs crossed at the ankles. Judging by the sin-inspiring shoes, she hasn't changed since I saw her at work, only donned the black coat that's tied tight at the waist.

I stop short, staring through the glass as though at any moment she will vanish. And then I hear her laugh. It escapes through the door as someone opens it to leave and there's no mistaking it.

I realise belatedly that the person is holding the door open for me, and I give him a brief nod of thanks as I take hold of it.

But I don't enter—not yet.

I'm wrapped up in watching her, so relaxed, at ease, chatting, and the way others respond to her, get caught up in her happy web. Just like at the party, where everyone hung on her every word. Now she has Ron—a security guard, built like a wrestler, with a face that doesn't smile—beaming like a man-child.

And then he spies me, clears his throat as he gives a brief nod.

She steps back, turns to face me.

I move before her eyes reach me, striding into the foyer. 'I wasn't expecting to see you again so soon.'

I scan her face as I get nearer, looking for any hint as to what's brought her here.

Has she spoken to Nate? Does she know the truth? Is she here to discuss it? Or the deal?

All these questions blaze through my mind, racing with the crazy heat her nearness instils, but I can read nothing other than surprise in her face, in the flare to her eyes and her parted lips.

Which is odd since it's *my* building—who else does she expect to see?

And then heat flushes up her chest, her mouth snaps shut, her eyes drop and she fiddles with the handbag over her shoulder. 'I thought we could talk…'

She wets her lips nervously and looks up into my face. She's all demure and inviting at once, and I can only just about manage, 'Now?'

'If you're free…'

If I wasn't, I know I'd be making myself so. 'Have you eaten?' I ask.

I don't know why I'm proposing dinner, but I haven't eaten, and I suspect she hasn't found time to either. And dinner feels *safe*.

Safer than the other thing that springs to mind.

My body throbs with it. Sex with Eva. I want her so much it hurts. There's the ache of longing, of desire, but there's a greater ache—a riskier one, the one I know I should listen to. Dinner in a public place will help.

'Erm…no.'

'Let's talk over dinner. I just need a quick shower.'

The mention of a shower has her cheeks flushing deeper. 'Shall I wait here?' she asks.

My sanity says *yes*. Having her in my place would be too intimate. It would be too easy. And the look in her eyes is feeding that realisation.

'Don't be ridiculous. Come up and I'll fix you a drink.'

She looks to the security guard as I move off. 'Thanks, Ron.'

And then she falls into step beside me as I head to the lift, the doors already opening to greet us.

Every one of my senses, pumped up from my run, is doing overtime as we enter the space together and that warning ache builds. I use my pass to send the lift to my private floor and step back—a feeble attempt at creating distance.

'Nice run?'

I murmur an incoherent 'yes' and keep my eyes fixed ahead. It's hard enough that her perfume fills the space. To look at her in this private enclosure will tip me over. Make me think to hell with security cameras and giving Ron an eyeful.

'Something wrong?'

She's looking at me. I can make out her confused

frown in my periphery and it's killing me. The urge to pull her to me and be done with it.

I never realised this lift took so long.

Jesus.

I let go of a trapped breath and the lift doors finally open onto my private foyer.

I gesture for her to lead the way and hang back a second longer than necessary. Again, *space*. Much-needed space.

I want to point her in the direction of the drinks cabinet and tell her to fix her own drink, but I'm a sucker for etiquette.

You'd think restrictive running shorts would provide some resistance against the nagging erection I'm already sporting, but it seems not. I feel exposed, both physically and mentally, my brain constantly teasing me with memories of her naked and writhing over me.

I clear my throat and stride forward to the kitchen, assuming she will follow—which she does. I can sense her continued frown, but I need that shower. *Fast.*

'What would you like? Wine? Gin and tonic? Beer?'

She used to like a beer. When she wasn't supping champagne with her well-to-do chums. Like that night... Her birthday bash, her white dress, the taste of her lips, those lips that I've yet to enjoy again... It's all there, singeing my body, my mind.

She laughs as she shrugs off her coat and slings it over one of the bar stools that line the centre island. 'You know, no one ever offers me a beer.'

'You forget how well I know you.'

It's out before I can stop it—the reminder of the past and how well we used to know one another. But this time she doesn't shrink away from it. She only smiles at me, a reminiscent look in her eye that has me heating up further, and I snap my gaze away as I pull open the fridge and grab myself a beer.

'I guess you just don't look the type.'

'No—much to my parents' pleasure, I'm sure.'

The smile is still in her voice, the connection, and it's pulling me in.

'They hate seeing me with a bottle.'

'Well, they're not here now. Beer?' My tone is tighter than I'd like, but she doesn't seem to notice. Her eyes sparkle into mine with such mischief... Christ, I want her, need her... *So* bad.

'Why not.'

I'm practically climbing inside the fridge in my need to cool down and hide my raging hard-on from her gaze. I grab her a bottle too, and place both down on the counter, turning away as I swing the door closed and pull a bottle opener out of a drawer.

I'm so fixated on breathing steadily that I barely notice her move until she's right alongside me, staring at the wall. No, not at the wall. At the shelf and the photo framed atop it.

Fuck.

It's been there so long it's part of the furnishings. I curse my stupidity. I should've remembered—should've done something.

'You still have this?'

I can hear the incredulity in her tone. Hell, I'm incredulous with myself.

I look at the bottles as I open them and inject nonchalance into my tone. 'It was a good night.'

She's leaning across the counter; her eyes slide from the incriminating photograph to mine. 'No wonder you remember what I was wearing...'

I couldn't forget. Photo or not.

She looks back to the picture, her lower lip caught in her teeth as she smiles wistfully. 'You and Nate look so young...so happy.'

I take a slug of my beer and let my gaze drift to it too: Eva, Me, Nate, our arms over each other's shoulders, doing a rendition of...

'The cancan, wasn't it?' she says.

'Yes.' I have to force the simple syllable past the wedge in my throat.

'It was a bitch in that dress—but worth every second to see you and Nate falling over yourselves to see who could get their legs the highest.'

She gives a soft laugh and then she turns to face me, her eyes curious. *Too* curious.

'I'm going to take that shower. Help yourself to anything—living room is just through there.'

I'm already moving, escaping her magnetic pull, but she's not letting me. She's on my tail.

'Why keep it?'

'I told you—it was a good night.'

Really it's a memory of a lesson learned. Never to get that close to anyone again. Not just Eva, but Nate too.

It's also the night things changed. The night she made
her feelings so clear, her passion. Her switch from besotted spunky teen to—

Christ, don't go there.

'It was ten years ago, and you've had nothing to do
with us for five—why would you keep it?'

I turn to look at her and she's practically upon me.
Her eyes are wide, probing. She's looking for a deeper
meaning that I know I can't give her. I can't open myself up to her. I trust her, but I don't trust her with *that*.
There can be no future for us. To confess now would
be pointless and would only complicate things. I don't
want her pity and, knowing her like I do, that's what
I'll get.

Pity for all that I've lost.

Even without the knowledge of what really went
down between Nate and I, she will pity me. She knows
too much of my past, of my childhood and of what the
Beaumonts meant to me.

'Tell me.'

Her voice is soft, coaxing, and her fingers reach out
to stroke along my jaw, gentle and coaxing like her
voice, her eyes, and I'm falling. I can feel it just as well
as I can feel her touch upon me.

'Lucas, please…'

I'm looking up at him, cradling his face, and I'm past the
sexual magnetism of his sweat-slickened body that struck
me so dumb downstairs. I'm all over what I can read in
his eyes, in what his keeping that photograph means.

'I've had ten years to wait for this.'

It's as if some kind of screen has lifted—as if I can see him clearly now and see him clearly then. So much emotion in his face. Did he feel something deeper for me all those years ago…something akin to what I felt… is he feeling it now?

I can see the fight in him. He won't speak. And suddenly I don't need words. I need *him*. *All* of him.

'Lucas…' I whisper, my lashes already lowering and my body lifting onto my toes as my head tilts back to find his mouth.

His body turns rigid, but he doesn't push me away. I kiss the corner of his mouth, its hard line, his five o'clock shadow grazing me. His scent is musky and all man, and I'm high on it. Every sensation teases me, even the slightest press of my lips against him.

He stays rock solid, unmoving, but I press on. I'm ready. For this…for whatever is to come. It feels right— *he* feels right.

I keep my eyes hooked on his, my hand upon his cheek as I reach for his beer bottle, taking it from his unresisting fingers and placing it on the table at my hip. Nerves rear up inside me, mixing with the thrum of anticipation, but I *want* this. And I think—*I know*— he wants it too.

I lift myself towards him again and gently nudge his mouth with my own. So hard, unrelenting. But I persist, taking what I've always wanted. Repeating the move, slow and coaxing. He tastes of beer, of him…

'Evangeline… *Don't*…'

He sounds gruff, pained, and I look into his eyes, see need shining back at me shrouded in fear.

'Don't what, Lucas? Press you for answers…?' My lips brush against his as I speak. 'Or do this?'

I tease the joining of his mouth with my tongue and his lashes flutter closed, his body shuddering on a stilted breath. And then he comes alive. His eyes open and there's no hesitation, no fear, just the burning heat of desire as he forks his fingers in my hair and swings me back against the wall.

The first sweep of his tongue against mine turns my body molten, and the explosive heat swirling in the pit of my stomach is mounting the further he invades, the harder he moves over me. Hungry, fierce, possessive.

I match him move for move, telling him with my body what I want, what I need. No games, no taking control. This is about *us*. I feel as if I'm drowning in a multitude of emotions and sensations and I can't cling to a single one. I'm hungry for them all.

'If we let this go on I won't stop,' he says, intense.

I drag him back to me, press my body into his hardness. 'I don't want you to stop—not ever.'

Christ, that's a sweeping statement, but I'm done holding back. I'm living for this moment.

He breaks away from me completely and I look at him, pleading. *Please… Don't stop…not now…*

His eyes blaze at me and his jaw pulses with such tension. I know he wants me. I *know* it. I can feel it, for Christ's sake.

Before panic truly sets in, he grasps my hand and

starts to stride away. I don't know where we're going and I don't care. As long as we're together…as long as we complete this.

The foyer is vast, with several doors, and he pushes open the double doors that sit at the end.

The master suite. *His* master suite.

It's masculine, stark, moody—so *him*.

He releases my hand but is still walking as he drags his sports tee over his head. I am rooted, just watching him—every muscle that ripples, the trace of sweat, the strength of his arousal as he turns to me and kicks off his shoes, his socks, his shorts, his boxers—

Oh, God.

Heat assaults my gut. Sheer, intense heat.

'You owe me a shower,' he grinds out.

My mouth is so dry I don't think I can speak. Instead I lift my fingers to my blouse in answer and begin unbuttoning it. All the while I watch him. Watch how he follows my fingers and his cock lifts. A whimper sounds in my throat. I can't contain it. I feel as if I'll burst if I don't have him soon.

He draws in a breath, flexing his fists at his sides, and then he's across the room before I know it, his hands on my blouse, parting it, thrusting it down my body. The force of the move spikes my libido, making my tummy contract with the rush.

'Too slow,' he complains, yanking it free of my wrists and tugging me against him so hard I gasp.

The heat of his body sears my bare skin, my breasts surge within my bra and his impressive arousal presses between us, making the dull ache down low a pulsing knot.

He reclaims my mouth, his tongue plundering, taking my all.

'I can't believe you kept this from me.'

He says it between kisses, as if at any moment I might pull away, and I know he's referring to my *No Kissing* rule.

'You feel incredible. You *taste* incredible.'

He sounds like a man half-starved, and I cling to him as he reaches down my back, his fingers grazing over my tingling skin to unzip my skirt. He forces it down my hips, letting gravity do the rest as he drops his hands to cup my arse, drawing me harder against him.

He pulses between us, a growl erupting low in his throat, and I raise my leg to hook it around him, encouraging him closer, bringing his rigid length right up against my clit. Pleasure ripples through me, and his mouth swallows my moan as he keeps on kissing me.

And I'm kissing him back. Intense, possessive. As if we're branding one another with our claim.

He drops his hand to cup my thigh and goes still, his forehead pressing into mine as he twists his head to look at where his hand is on me over the lace band of my hold-ups.

'*Fuck*, Evangeline… You're too sexy.'

I laugh, almost delirious at hearing those words come from his lips. I'm dreaming, surely. But his hardness, his heat, his breath as it sweeps over my chest in ragged gusts is all real. Erotic, carnal and *happening*.

He grabs my other leg and hauls me up against him, wrapping them around his waist. Then he's moving, his mouth back on mine and his eyes on the direction in which we're travelling. He strides across the room into the adjacent bathroom and presses me up against the cold tiles. My body shivers at the chill even as I worship the sensation: the cold at my back, his heat at my front...

He reaches out to mess with a dial.

Water pounds the marble floor, the sound blending with the rush of blood in my ears and the moans of sheer abandon that I'm barely aware of making. I hold his face in my hands. Gripping him to me. My mouth, my tongue are unable to get enough of this. And then he sets me down and tears his lips away to trace a searing path along my jaw, down my throat.

I lean back against the wall, my body trembling with need as I arch into him, encouraging him lower, *needing* him lower, running my hands over his shoulders, down his back.

He undoes the clasp of my bra and my breasts bloom, heat rushing to their tips as he eases the cups aside and the straps down. It falls to our feet as his hands roughly cup me, his mouth claiming one pleading bud, moving tantalisingly over it, his tongue flicking before drawing it in deep.

Christ.

I claw at his shoulders, my desire mounting, out of control. 'I *need* you.'

He takes in the other nipple, his hands turning more

urgent, his mouth unrelenting. We move against one another, our bodies building into a crazed rhythm.

I reach for him, desperate to feel him, to ride him.
My fingers close around his cock, its heat feeding into
my palm as I draw my hand upwards. He hisses, throwing his head back, and I repeat the move, watching his
efforts to fend off his climax so clearly building.

And then he grabs at my wrist, pulling away. *'Not
again,'* he bites out, his fingers rough as he yanks my
thong down.

I step out of it and he turns to my high heels, stripping them off so swiftly I'm sent off balance. But his
palm is there, on my torso, pinning me against the wall
as he drops to his knees. The heat of his touch contends with the intense heat swelling out of control just
beneath, and then his mouth is there, at the heart of it
all, his tongue sweeping over my clit and making me
buck, making me cry.

His fingers smooth around my thighs, slipping beneath the tops of my hold-ups. He rolls them down, and
all the while his tongue is circling my clit, gently goading me, driving me crazy.

He lifts one foot to pull the nylon free, then the other,
but he doesn't stand. He's too busy feasting off me, his
hands coming up to part me, to give his mouth, his
tongue, deeper access, and I know I'm going to come.
I can feel it building in my limbs.

But I want him inside me. I want all of him when I do.

I pull at him, my nails running up his shoulders.
'No, not like this.'

His voice rumbles over me. He doesn't agree.

'Lucas.'

Something in my voice makes him pause and he leans back on his haunches, looking up at me. I'm wondering why the hell I stopped him, but...

'I need you inside me.'

The pulse works in his jaw and then he's on his feet, striding away.

What the fuck?

He's back in seconds, sheathing himself, and the sight of his fingers moving masterfully over his erection is so fucking erotic, even as I acknowledge that he's had the sense to get protection when I didn't.

I start backing into the shower, pulling the pins from my hair, undoing my hair tie, dropping them to the floor. All the while my eyes are fixed on his, taunting him to come and get me.

Water rushes over my body and I tilt my head back, lifting my fingers to comb through my hair. And then his own are upon mine, completing the move. His lips claim me, hard and demanding. Water runs between us, slips into our mouths, our eyes. His cock presses against my stomach, stoking the fierce ache within.

'Please, *now*,' I beg.

He runs his hands down my body in answer, cupping my thighs to lift me against him.

I encircle his waist and he takes himself in his hand between us, positioning himself, positioning me. His look of concentration damn near pushes me over. And then he's there, his tip nudging at my entrance, and I

clamp down on my lower lip as I take his sweet invasion. He's slow, measured, his restraint taking all his
effort, and I know he doesn't want to hurt me. He wants
it to be right.

I move over him, coaxing him further, deeper,
stretching to take him. More. *More.* Until he fills me
completely and I moan, contracting around him even
as he stills, his breath hissing between his teeth. He's
trembling, fighting for control. But I don't want his control. I want his total abandon.

I nip his lower lip with my teeth, drawing his mouth
back to me, pushing his concentration away, and I un-
dulate over him, slowly at first, using my every yoga-
toned muscle to guide him, tease him.

And then he's moving, taking the driving seat. He
forces me back against the wall, his rigid length riding my clit from within as he pumps harder, faster. Our
teeth clash, our tongues twist, our kiss as erotic as the
action below.

Yes. Yes. Yes.

Pleasure radiates from my toes up and the muscles
of my legs tighten as it builds. I can't move now. He
drives it all as ecstasy renders my body immobile and
then it erupts, shaking through my entire body as I cry
out. He thrusts deeper, his own cry drowning out my
own, and he loses it with me.

It's so perfect, so utterly right. But even as I come
down from the crest of the wave, my legs still hooked
around him, now limp with release, I know that's a
fanciful notion.

Because whatever his words mean, whatever his keeping the photo means, whatever the cause of his fall-out with Nate, it doesn't change the fact that my family won't accept him. They won't accept *this*. I doubt even Lucas will accept it when all is said and done.

And if that's the case, what the hell am I doing fantasising about the impossible? Teasing myself with *what if...?*

He brushes his lips against my neck, his caress soft and barely there, and my thoughts fragment, disperse as sensation takes over...

'I could get lost in you, Evangeline.'

CHAPTER SEVEN

I FEEL HER tense around me.

Fuck.

I curse my mammoth mouth.

What the hell is wrong with me? I don't *ever* speak without thinking first. Yet she's done this to me, with the turnaround in her no kissing rule and what it means to her, to me. There's no way in hell I would usually say anything as sentimental, as deep as that—not if I'd taken the time to think first.

It was impulsive, reckless.

There can be no getting lost for me in *anyone*. Especially her. A Beaumont. The one woman with the power to crucify me, to rip my heart out and leave me stranded. Lost. I've been that person. I won't be like that again.

'What did you say?'

She encourages my head up and I shut my expression down with a grin. 'Nothing.'

She's frowning at me and I spin her into the water flow. It's noisy in here—noisy enough for her to doubt she heard me right. I cling to that, setting her down on her feet.

'Let me get rid of this… Stay here.'

I stride out of the shower, avoiding my reflection in the mirrors that run along one wall as if my reflection will only incriminate me further. There's a bin in the bathroom but I don't use it. I keep going until I'm in my bedroom and I can take a steadying breath out of sight, take a few seconds to gather my wits before I face her again.

Lost…

It wasn't a lie.

My lungs contract, my chest aches. I strip off the condom and toss it in the wastebin beside the dressing table. My reflection in the mirror above it catches me, and I see the torrent of emotion in my face.

But it's just sex. It has to be.

Sex now. Work later. The end.

I'd laugh if it wasn't so brutal. So impossible to think of bringing an end to this thing between us.

She appears in the entrance to my bathroom, a towel wrapped around her, her brows drawn together, and I shut everything down under the wave of warmth the sight inspires.

'I said stay there.' I stride towards her, swinging her up into my arms.

She laughs in surprise, her hands hooking around my neck. 'I thought you'd run out on me.'

I look into her face, my grin purposefully easy. 'Would I do that?'

There's a moment's hesitation in her face and then I'm kissing her, pushing out everything else as I walk straight back into the shower, uncaring of the towel still wrapped around her.

'Lucas…' She pants as she presses me away, her eyes dancing. 'The towel…'

I look down at it. 'Ah, well, too late now.'

I set her down and strip it from her, tossing it aside as I flick my wet hair from my eyes and take her in my arms. Her flushed skin is wet, and marked where I've been, and a primal surge of possessiveness assaults me, winds me.

Her eyes flicker beneath the droplets of water, as if she's read it all, and she lifts her palm to my chest. 'Keep looking at me like that and I'll think it's *me* you're wanting for dinner.'

I comb her hair back from her face, the water with it. 'How about actual food for dinner and you for dessert?'

Her smile is soft, and she lowers her eyes—to avoid the run of the water or to hide, I'm not sure. And I do the one thing I know to bring her back to me and get the answer I want. I kiss her. Slow and teasingly. Until she's kissing me back and her hands are holding tight.

Then I break away. 'Deal?'

'Deal…' she breathes.

I draw her tight against me, feeling her approval upping the rush of my desire. I know I have to let the real world back in soon, but for now it can stay the hell away.

Reality comes sooner than I expect or want—in the shape of her blasted smartwatch again. I want to rip it from her. Insist she put it away, and her phone with it.

We're sitting on my living room floor, not too far from recreating a scene from our teens, with Chinese takeaway boxes strewn across my coffee table. She's in one of my T-shirts, her hair loosely piled atop her head, her face clean and glowing from our hot shower and the multitude of heated acts since. I'm on one side of the table and she is on the other, stretched out and perfect.

Save for that damn watch.

She looks at it and that frown is back.

'I assume it's your watch and not the food doing that?'

'Hmm…?' She looks at me, distracted, and I lean over to touch her brow, smoothing it.

'The frown?'

She gives me a look which I interpret as an apology and wraps her legs beneath her as she takes up a spring roll. She's forcing a calmness she doesn't feel—I know it. But I'm silent, pressing.

She takes a bite and the food breaks into her mouth, vegetable strands escaping as she licks them up. Her dainty tongue is efficient and far more sexual than it has any right to be. She's doing it on purpose—trying to distract me, I'm sure.

But there's also unease building, and I want it gone.

She makes a delectable little hum in her throat. 'No, the food is fantastic.'

I barely hear the words I'm so focused on the satisfying sound and on her lips as they turn the food over.

Distracted?

I force my focus. 'So, what is it?'

Silently she chews, her eyes on me as if she's gauging my potential reaction.

'I'm not about to kick you out in just my T-shirt if that's what you're worried about—you can tell me.'

Her lips quirk. 'No, I don't think you'd do that.'

'Then tell me.'

She looks me over and that unease mounts.

'It's nothing, I'm just…' She shrugs. 'I'm just enjoying this. It's nice…like old times.'

'I've been thinking the same.'

I like that she feels it too. *Really* like it. And it's a problem—I know it is—but the warmth it brings is there regardless.

Suddenly she gives a little giggle and that cosy feeling inside me blooms, edging out the unease. 'What?' I ask.

'You remember that time when Mum went all vegetarian on our arses and wouldn't let a scrap of meat into the house?'

My smile is instant, the memory as vivid as yesterday. 'You mean the ribs fiasco?'

She giggles again and I hook on to the sound. It's so carefree, so easy. 'I don't think that Chinese takeaway had any left by the time you, Nate and I finished raiding it.'

'True—but Nate was the worst offender. He could put away a truckload.'

'Yeah, but it was *your* idea.' She looks at me and licks her lips. 'You were mortified when Mum found the remains in the bin the next day.'

'Can you blame me? If you'd only taken the bin out, like you were supposed to, that never would have happened.'

'Well, you and Nate got your own back—tossing me into the pool fully clothed.'

A wicked rush surges south and I tense against it. I remember that moment too. And I remember when she stepped out of the pool, soaked and ranting, not realising that her white tee clung to her every curve. It was a month before her eighteenth birthday, and the day I acknowledged that my feelings towards her had changed.

Unfortunately Nate had sensed it too.

I clear my throat and shake my head at her. 'You deserved it.'

'Hmph...' she says over her spring roll, her eyes alive and holding my own.

I don't want this to end.

'Stay the night?' It's out before I can stop it, but I manage to avoid adding *please*, begging.

Her lashes lower; her eyes flicker away.

The mood is shattered—once again thanks to my big mouth.

She drops the last bite of spring roll onto her plate and wipes her fingers on some kitchen towel. 'I can't.'

'Why?'

It's more abrupt than I want to be, but I know that after she leaves we won't get this back—this moment, this connection.

Her watch goes off again, her phone echoing the buzz, and she glances at it.

Anger fires in my veins. I know the answer even before I ask, 'Who is it, Eva?'

Her eyes flick to mine, her cheeks now pale. 'I think you know.'

'Your father…mother…Nate…?'

'Try all of the above.'

She suddenly sounds tired, weary, and my body pulls with the need to comfort her. Which is madness, since I'm likely at the heart of it all. But I'm pissed off. I'm sick of being seen as the bad guy. I loved every last one of them and they…they…

Fuck, what does it matter?

'What's so urgent that they have to bombard you at this time of night?' I can't keep the bitterness out of my voice.

She gives an incredulous laugh, surprising me. 'You can't guess?'

I take up my beer, having a slug before answering. 'Are they worried the evil Lucas Waring is leading you astray?'

'Don't say that.'

'Why? It's the truth, isn't it?'

'They're just worried about me.'

'Good for them.'

'Lucas, please—if you just tell me what happened then maybe I can help…maybe we can see a way to put the past to bed.'

My laugh is derisive. 'You really don't know your brother if that's what you think.'

Hell, I thought I knew him and look where it got me.

'You'd be surprised.'

There's something in the way she says it that has my ears pricking, my attention shifting. 'What's that supposed to mean?'

'Things changed after you left—*he* changed, and not for the better... He's...suffering.'

The admission is weighted, and she looks away from me as if she's said too much. I don't know whether to push or let it go. I should let it go. Digging further implies I care too much. About her, about Nate, her family. But I can't.

I lean back into the sofa behind me and take another swig of beer. 'Why don't you be straight with me and I'll be straight with you?'

He looks so relaxed in his stonewashed jeans and white tee, leaning back against his deep grey sofa, beer in hand. But it's his eyes that tell me otherwise. There's a dangerous glint to them that tells me to shut up. Even though I know we need to do this, get it all out in the open.

'Why don't you be straight with me and I'll be straight with you?'

It's what I came for.

And maybe if he understands the way things are with Nate now, he'll understand why I have no desire to interrogate my brother. Why I need to hear it from him.

I look at my near-empty bottle of beer. 'Can I get another?'

'You stalling?'

'Call it Dutch courage.'

I remember the last time I used that kind of courage to do what I needed to with him and my cheeks colour as I roll my shoulders, shaking it off. The move draws his eye and I tug at his T-shirt, feeling suddenly naked against his fully clothed state.

'You're sure you're ready to hear the lurid details of what happened five years ago? Sure you want your golden-boy brother tainted?'

Golden-boy? I almost snort and he sharpens his gaze. He doesn't miss a trick.

'About that beer…?' I say.

'About Nate…?'

I take a breath and raise my chin. 'I'll tell you exactly what the last five years have been like if you promise to tell me what happened.'

His eyes flicker; his jaw pulses. 'I've already agreed, and I don't go back on my word—no matter what *your* family think.'

The way he stresses 'your' isn't lost on me, and he slaps his beer bottle on the coffee table as he rises.

'But also know I still want dessert.'

My insides clench and my lips part. I'm so glad he isn't looking at me to see the effect his words have had. It doesn't matter how deep our conversation goes, how much pain it dredges up, his effect on me is impossible to prevent, and I need to muster my strength if I am to get through this unscathed.

Perhaps walking out, ringing Nate, dealing with his ineffectual tantrum, would be preferable to opening myself up even more to Lucas. I was vulnerable enough before, but now…

I don't finish the thought. Instead I scoop up the empty trays and roll the leftovers onto one plate. My mind shifts helplessly to 'dessert'.

What the fuck, Eva?

I know I shouldn't be contemplating it. Loyalty is a huge thing in my family—we stand by one another through thick and thin. The Beaumonts stand united, as Dad would say. But everything I've done with Lucas, everything I *am* doing, goes against that.

Or does it?

I'm only trying to get to the truth, to get the other side to this tale.

I join him in the kitchen. 'Where's your bin?'

I scan his super-smooth cupboards, the walls—avoid looking at the solitary framed photo.

'Here.' He presses a rectangle and out it pops. I drop the rubbish in as he turns to me with a beer bottle.

'Ta.'

My hand rests over his as I take it. Our eyes lock and the crazy narration taking place in my brain ceases and then starts again tenfold.

Why does he have this power? No one else has ever come close. No one…

'Evangeline.'

His voice rasps and suddenly it annoys me. I'm sick of being out of control with him. Sick of being hounded by my family to do *the right thing*.

'Let's talk.'

I stride back to the living area and sink onto the sofa, my legs curled up alongside me.

He's slower than me to return. 'Is it safe to sit next to you?'

'If you like.'

I don't look at him as he lowers himself onto the sofa. I focus on chucking back a mouthful of beer rather than on the way my body reacts to his proximity, the fuzzy warmth that radiates all down the side that's closest to him. I taste nothing.

'So?' he probes, looking at me.

But I don't turn. Reliving the past isn't something I find easy. It changed me for the better, made me stronger, more determined to go after what I want and gain my independence. Nate's the opposite.

'Nate's not the man you remember.'

'So you say.'

I give him a quick look, more to shut him up than anything. His cold dismissal isn't what I need right now.

'It wasn't like it happened overnight,' I say. 'At first it just seemed like he was putting in enough hours for two, filling in for his AWOL partner—'

'I wasn't—'

I cut him off with another look. 'You want me to tell you how things went down over here when you swanned off to the States or not?'

'Apologies—go on…' He retreats, his shoulders relaxing as he sinks back into the sofa and gestures with the tail end of his bottle as he drinks.

I tear my gaze from the movement in his throat as he

swallows and look at my bottle, toying with the corner of its label as I work out where to start.

'He started to become hard to reach,' I say eventually. 'We'd have people messaging us to say they'd seen him in this bar, this club, this restaurant, asking if he was okay. Which was bizarre in itself. I mean, Christ, he was a grown adult, but even I, his younger sister, was getting concerned messages.'

Hair falls over my eyes as the memory makes me animated. I scrape it behind my ear and throw back some beer, letting it settle before I carry on.

'We put it down to him networking at first—trying to pull in investors to save the company. But of course that was a load of rubbish. The company was past saving. The highlight came when he got himself into a fight. I mean, I knew he was quick to temper—how could I not, being his annoying little sister? But losing it with a sibling is very different to a public fist fight with a billionaire you're trying to impress.'

Lucas clears his throat and I sense he knows this already—the incident made it into the papers so it's no surprise.

'Dad insisted he come home for a bit. He helped him get straightened out, gave him a role in the family business and what-have-you, but he was never the same… not without you.'

I expect Lucas to say something, but he doesn't, so I press on.

'He doesn't trust himself. Dad thinks he's okay now but he's not. He calls me too often, asking my opinion, needing advice on things that he really shouldn't need me for. And then when things go south it's me that gets the call.'

'Christ, Eva, you have your own work—you shouldn't be wiping his arse.'

I see red. Hot tears burn my throat as my eyes snap to his. 'Maybe if you'd stuck around longer it never would have come to this. He missed you—needed you.'

He pales, and I wonder who I'm really talking about. Me or Nate.

Does it really matter when the same applies?

I look at the bottle in my hand, stare through it. 'Maybe if you'd actually bothered to pick up your phone and help, you could have changed things.'

Bad enough that he'd upped and left, but then he'd ignored my phone calls, my pleas for help…

It didn't matter that we had nothing much to do with one another any more. That avoidance was my way of coping after the lesson of my eighteenth birthday. But I still thought I deserved something—he owed us, owed *me*.

'I called you almost daily at first, and I texted, emailed. Then one day your phone stopped working and my emails bounced. You were really gone.'

'I'm sorry.'

I glance at him. His hand is so tight around the beer bottle's neck I fear he's going to break it.

'What for?' I demand. 'Ignoring me? Or what you did to Nate?'

'I had to cut myself off.'

'*Had* to or wanted to?'

He shakes his head. 'It was a choice that was made for me.'

I scoff. 'No one tells you what to do, Lucas. You've always done what you want, when you want.'

'If that was the case I wouldn't have stopped myself at your eighteenth.'

His voice is harsh, formidable, the truth in his words undeniable. I don't know what I expected but it wasn't that. I can't find any words—can't seem to make a sound.

'That really surprises you so much?'

'Lucas, I…'

This isn't getting the right answers—this is getting into *us*, and 'us' isn't going to help me get my family straightened out, end their feud and bring me the decision I need to make for my business.

'I wanted you, Evangeline. I wanted to drag you off to a quiet corner, ride that dress up your hips and take all that you were offering me.'

My heart rises in my throat. I can't breathe past the desire and the bigger emotion that's holding my lungs tight. 'Then why…?'

It's a whisper so quiet I can barely hear it above the racing pulse in my ears.

'I told you that night—because of *Nate*.'

He says it so fiercely, his body rigid as he considers me.

'He told me to keep away… What? You didn't believe me?'

'No. Yes.' I shake my head. I can't believe Lucas would give up on us because my brother had ordered it so. 'I don't know.'

'He left me in no doubt as to what would happen if I went there with you.'

I flip. The pain I suffered, my heart ripped in two. 'He was your best friend—not your keeper! *Christ*, you even went out with his exes and vice versa. Why was *I* so different?'

'You were out of bounds. You were his little sister.'

My scoff is more of a snort this time. But this is madness. I *won't* believe it.

'You can't blame him for wanting to protect you. My reputation with the opposite sex didn't exactly work in my favour.'

No, I remember his reputation well enough. It made it all the more painful when he rejected me—as if I didn't come up to scratch.

'Look, Eva, he was my best friend—the closest thing to family. You all were. Why is it so hard for you to believe I didn't want to jeopardise that?'

I can read the truth in the softening of his eyes. I want to scream that I should have been more important, that I wanted him, loved him, but it all seems so selfish now.

And ultimately it didn't matter. He lost it all anyway. Nate, their friendship, my family…

'Fat lot of good it did you.'

I neck my beer, washing down the bitter bite of my words.

'Believe me, I'm more than aware of what I gave up then.'

I ignore the flare to my heart his passion instils. His old feelings towards me don't help now. If I was out of bounds before, when my family loved him, I'm on another playing field now.

He reaches for me, his fingers brushing the hair behind my ear. 'Evangeline, I *am* sorry.'

I risk a look and butterflies flutter in my throat at what I see—his sincerity, his intensity. He's so close. I'd only have to lean a little to meet him, to kiss him. And I want to so much. To drown out the pain with the crazy passion that simmers just beneath the surface.

I know he's thinking the same—I can feel it in the touch of his fingers still stroking at my skin, see it in the parting of his lips, the darkening of his eyes.

'I really am sorry…'

He's closer—too close. I have a second to stop this, before it goes too far, and I almost don't. It would be too easy to forget it all in his kiss.

I suspect he knows it—that he's doing it on purpose—and it's that which has me pushing at his chest, straightening my body and forcing his hand to fall away.

I need answers. I need to know.

'It's your turn,' I say. 'What happened five years ago?'

CHAPTER EIGHT

HER EYES ARE fixed on mine. She's not going to let it go.

It wasn't as if I'd tried to kiss her to make her forget. *Honest.* Although it would have been preferable to this.

I place my beer on the table and rake my hands through my hair. I don't owe Nate anything. And yet talking about it doesn't come easy. Last time I spoke up I lost the entire family. Her father pushed me out and told me I'd failed them, failed Nate. He was angry, but his words stung. More than he can possibly know.

And how would she take it—*the same way?*

I meet her determined gaze and realise it doesn't matter how she reacts. She isn't going to let it rest until she knows. And I have nothing to be ashamed of.

Nothing.

Not that her father saw it that way.

'Well?' She tucks her legs tight beneath her, the challenge in her eyes bright. It beats tears. They knotted up my insides, crushed me with guilt.

I speak over the painful reminder. 'You know what your brother was like growing up: outgoing, a people-pleaser, a constant beam of optimism?'

She frowns at me, but nods. I know she's comparing how he was to the man he is now, as she's just described him to me.

'He was also hot-headed, excitable—he would always act first, think later, if it meant he could lead the way with whatever had caught his eye.'

I take up my beer for a swig and let the memories in.

'He definitely did that when it came to women.' I can almost laugh at that. 'We had some seriously fun times…and some fallouts. But it was the same in business too, and together we *worked*. So long as I was there, watching his back, and so long as he listened to me we were okay, the business was okay. He was the go-getter and I was the level-headed one, doing the research and giving final approval.'

'Yeah, I know. Dad made some sweeping comment not long after it all came crashing down, referring to you both as yin and yang, the perfect system…until you went AWOL.'

'I *didn't* go AWOL.' It comes through gritted teeth, and I see my anger surprises her. 'I left after your brother went too far with one of his schemes. He'd been pulled in by a woman he was dating. She'd convinced him this product they were working on was the next big thing—that they just needed enough investment and it would make us all billions.'

I laugh bitterly now, as I remember the conversation, the stupidity of it all.

'I told him it was a bad investment, that we couldn't risk it. We still had your father's money to pay back and we were on track for that. A few months and we could have been clear—well on our way to making a small fortune. Of course, your brother wasn't one for waiting, but I never thought for a second he would go ahead and do it without me. He lost it all. Bankrupted the company… lost your father's money…left us with nothing.'

'But…' She's staring at me as if she doesn't believe a word. 'I don't understand. Why did you leave if it was all him?'

'I was angry. I tried to speak to your father but Nate got there first—claimed I'd been on board, that he might have sourced the deal but I was with him on it.'

'No, he wouldn't lie like that.'

She's shaking her head at me, but her voice is soft, lacking in conviction. Not that I care whether she believes me or not. Her father didn't—why would she be any different?

'Wouldn't he? Nate was always trying to prove himself, to outperform all around him, to prove his worth to your father. Can you imagine what this did to him…? No, you don't need to imagine—you *know*.'

'But to lie…to blame you.'

'I don't think he realised at the time just how badly his accusation would land. He was just covering his back, protecting his position with your father.'

'Fuck that, Lucas! You were kicked out because of this.'

I don't need her sympathy or her anger. This is old news to me.

'Your father chose to believe him. I tried to tell him

but he wouldn't listen. Ultimately I don't think he cared. He just wanted to place the blame squarely on me.' I take another swig of beer, douse the choking heat in my throat. 'I wasn't *blood*.'

'But, Lucas...' Her voice is whisper-soft. 'You could've come to *me*—at least told me, explained...'

'What good would that have done?'

'I could've spoken to Dad, defended you, made Nate come clean—anything.'

I shake my head at her. It doesn't change anything. The past is done and dusted. There can be no going back.

'I was better off out of it. I wasn't about to plough any more time and money into that company. I couldn't trust Nate any more—not in business and not personally either. He betrayed me, Eva. He was like my brother, and then he did something as huge as that behind my back and lied about it.'

'But what about *me*?'

'What about you?'

She chews her lip, eyes wide. 'Didn't I deserve to know?'

'You expected me to turn up and say, *Hey, Eva, not seen you since you were at your folks with your fiancé, all happy and whatnot, but get this: your brother just screwed me over and bankrupted the company, so I'm off. Sayonara*?'

The words come out rapidly and then it hits me. It wasn't just Nate and her father I ran from. It was her too. Her and her soon-to-be marriage.

Christ. I rake a shaky hand through my hair and evade her eyes.

'Don't be so ridiculous!'

I barely hear her. I'm reeling from the realisation that I am screwed. That coming back to her has opened me up, made me defenceless again. Vulnerable.

Her phone starts to ring, her watch vibrates. She flicks her wrist and cuts the call.

'Who was it?'

'Nate.'

The pain of the past, the potential future, has me snapping, 'Tell you what—why don't you leave so you can call him back?'

Her eyes widen. I can see I've hurt her but I can't hold back. I need to bury this crazed emotion boiling inside me.

'Don't push me away.'

'Your family did that a long time ago.'

'And I want to fix this.'

'You want the impossible.'

'No, I don't. Nate's not been the same since you left. It makes so much sense now why he doesn't trust himself—why he comes to me before Dad, why he's always looking for a sounding board. He needs you in his life again.'

Screw Nate. All I care about right now is *her*, and the dawning realisation that I ran from her all those years ago and I don't want to run any more.

'And you, Evangeline? Do *you* need me?'

'I—'

She breaks off as her phone rings again, and this

time she pushes to her feet and strides away, grabbing up her coat from the bar stool and taking her phone out of its pocket.

She lifts it to her ear. 'Just give me half an hour.'

Her eyes flick to mine as she listens to the person on the other end.

'I'm busy right now… Just busy… Out… Dinner… No, no one you know…'

'No one you know…'

I flex my hand around the beer bottle, keeping my face expressionless.

Her silence extends and she wets her lips. 'I get that… No, I know… Yes, I'll call you… Bye.'

She hangs up and pockets the phone, her eyes coming back to me, shadowed. 'Thank you for telling me the truth.'

'So I'm *no one you know*?' Anger at her lie heats my words, my body, my blood.

'What did you expect me to say?'

'I don't know.' I get to my feet. 'I'm not sure where I fall. Am I the guy you're fucking, or the guy you're going into business with?'

She swallows hard. 'Neither.'

My laugh is harsh. 'Well, your state of undress places me in the former camp, for sure.'

She tugs at the hem of my tee and her cheeks heat. 'We *were* fucking—now I have no idea what we're doing.'

'No? Want me to help with that?'

I walk towards her and she backs into the counter.

Perhaps a revenge fuck will kill off this insane sea of emotion. Something has to.

'No. I can't do this.' She raises her palm to me even as her nipples bead against the tee. Air rasps from her lungs. 'I need time to think about what you've said. It changes so much and yet changes nothing.'

I stop walking and my smile is tight. 'Okay, and while you're thinking it through can I take it that my business proposition meets with your approval?'

She starts moving towards my bedroom, her coat hooked over her arm. 'We need to talk about that.'

'Talk?'

I follow her. She's looking for her clothes, dipping and bending as she collects each item from its place on the floor. If not for the edge to her voice I'd be all over the sight of her bare arse each time my tee lifts.

'You say we need to talk like it's a way off?'

She dumps her clothing on the bed and with her back to me pulls my T-shirt over her head. My pulse leaps, heat streaks to my groin and I pocket my fists. She's not making this easy.

'I have concerns.'

She steps into her thong and shimmies it up her legs, her hips, over her perfect round arse. *Christ.*

'What kind of concerns?'

'Like how you can do it so cheap.' She dons her bra, the cups facing me momentarily before she tugs it around to the front and slips her arms in.

Effortless, easy....so sexy even in reverse.

'I care about my workforce, whether they work for

me or my suppliers. I need to know you're not crossing any human rights lines.'

She bends forward to step into her skirt but all I hear are the last three words. '*Human rights lines?* Who do you think I am?'

She looks at me over her shoulder as she fastens her skirt. 'Don't act so defensive. You wouldn't be the first company to present me with a proposal that takes advantage of child labour and suchlike.'

'*Child labour...*' I choke the words out—*is she kidding me?*

She's not looking at me now. She's thrusting her arms into her blouse and fastening it up, acting as if she has no awareness of how deep her words cut.

'Anyway, I don't want to discuss it now.'

She tucks her blouse into her skirt and strides into the bathroom, emerging with her shoes and stockings. She pushes her foot into one shoe and then the other, her eyes anywhere but on me.

'We can pick it up at work.'

She grabs up her coat and stuffs the delicate nylon strips into its pocket as she heads towards me, past me, back into the foyer, her eyes scanning the lift for a call button. I press it for her and she clears her throat.

'Thank you. My PA will be in touch to arrange a meeting.'

'Your PA?' I raise my brow at her, daring her to meet my eye. 'Why not you?'

'My PA and your PA can sort it out. It's the way of things, is it not?'

'Normally.'

She still won't look at me and it's driving me crazy.
I want to reach for her and pull her in. I don't want her
to go with this uncertainty hanging over us. I want to
know where I stand.

And deep down I know it's not the business proposition I care about. It's her and her opinion of me. Is it
so low that she could truly question my business ethics? I don't want to think it possible, and yet she's im-
plying just that.

But then I never thought her father would think me
a liar either...

And she's a Beaumont, after all.

The lift doors open and she sweeps inside, turning
just quickly enough to offer me a parting look before
they close.

And that look swallows me whole.

'What is it, Nate?'

My temper is frayed. I feel oddly naked with my
stockings stuffed inside my coat pocket. As if every
Londoner can tell I've just run out on my lover and
didn't have the inclination to dress properly.

Your lover? Really, Eva.

'What do you mean: *what is it*?'

I tune in to my brother's scornful tone and take a
breath before replying. It never pays to react in kind—
especially with him.

'If this is about Lucas again, I'm not interested,' I say.

'If?'

I weave through the heavy stream of pedestrians, their loaded bags making it more awkward than usual. I really need to start my own Christmas shopping, but it's been at the back of mind, buried beneath work… *and now him*.

'What else would it be about?' asks Nate.

'I don't know—your issue with the wife of Mr Chan and her roaming fingers and the price hike they're insisting on? Or how about your laundry going astray?'

Okay, so I'm not doing a great job of keeping a lid on my frustration. I blame it on the ice-cold air whipping up my skirt and the thought of the heated body I'd much rather be curled up against and had to bail on to make this call.

No, not to make this call—to avoid getting in too deep.

Honesty was supposed to help. Instead it's opened me up…made me fall.

No. No. No. Not again.

'You're not funny, Eva.'

'Funny?' This really isn't what I call 'funny'. 'I wasn't trying to be.'

I look at the entrance to the Underground and decide against it. I can't face being hemmed in—not like this.

'Then quit the avoidance and tell me what you're playing at, still talking to him.'

I pause and a laden pedestrian curses, right on my tail.

'Sorry.' I grimace, ducking out of her way.

'Sorry?'

'Not you.' I scan the traffic, looking for a yellow taxi

light. 'I'm talking to him because he could be good for my business. He has everything I need.'

'Need?' Nate scoffs down the phone. 'There are plenty of other suitable firms. What about Rosalie and Janus Industries? She's flying in next week. I thought you were speaking to her?'

'I am.' I spy an available cab and hail it, moving to the edge of the kerb, careful to avoid being run down by either a person or a car. 'We're scheduled to meet on Tuesday.'

'So wait for her.'

I shake my head incredulously. 'Don't be ridiculous, Nate. I'm doing my research—both Rosalie's and Lucas's are among the many companies I'm considering. I'm getting this right.'

The cab pulls up alongside me and I open the door, hopping in. 'Jermyn Street, please.'

'Sure thing.'

The driver scans me over his shoulder a second longer than feels necessary. *Bare legs, middle of winter, that's not normal.*

I tug my skirt lower.

'Still staying at Mum and Dad's, then?' asks Nate.

'Until my place is ready—yeah.'

I look out of the window as the taxi pulls away, but I'm not really aware of the passing world or what I'm saying. My head is full of Lucas, of how he felt towards me, of what Nate did. And I don't want this conversation with my brother over the phone. I know I need to have it, but not now. I'm tired, and he's thousands of miles away getting a deal signed. It's not the right time.

'Don't do it, Eva'

'Do what?' I ask, even though I know.

'Go into business with him…bring him back into our lives.'

My anger erupts, spurred on by guilt at how we mistreated Lucas. The royal 'we'—the Beaumonts. And my brother is still sticking the knife in.

Remember, now isn't the time…

'*I'll* decide what's best for my product and for my business, Nate.'

'And what if he's doing this just to stir things? Have you thought about that?'

Christ, when haven't I? Isn't that why I'm terrified, in part…?

'He could screw you over just as easily as—'

'*Nate.*'

I hear his breath, heavy down the phone.

'Fine. But keep me posted, okay? And keep Dad in the loop? No nasty surprises.'

'No, no nasty surprises.'

Not like the one I just got, learning how you screwed Lucas over. Not that I was truly surprised.

'So, how is Hong Kong and the lovely Mrs Chan?'

He laughs down the phone at me and my body eases into the seat. 'Eva, I'm not kidding. The woman terrifies me…'

For the remainder of the cab journey he fills me in, and then quizzes me on what to buy Mum and Dad for

Christmas. The conversation turns easy, and it's the perfect distraction—until I let myself into the apartment, into the kitchen, and in my head I'm naked, with Lucas pressed into my back...

My body tightens on a shiver of heat, of longing, and I reach a hand to the cool surface of the worktop, dragging in a breath.

I'll never have enough of Lucas. He's the only man I've ever loved, the only man who's truly got under my skin. And now I've learned the truth. He's not the enemy my family painted him as for so long. *He's* the one who's been wronged.

Where does that leave us? Leave me?

Scared.

If I listen to my fear then I'll take his business off the table and run—because being around him and keeping my heart under wraps is impossible. And if I don't— if this love has chance to take hold again—what am I risking?

Everything.

There can be no future. Not with the past as it is.

But what if it could be changed? What if the air could be cleared? What if he could be welcomed back?

Was it even possible?

I feel a lightness creep its way in, see the future opening up with possibility...

There *has* to be a way. Mum and Dad are good people; they're controlling, overprotective, but *good* people. And Nate isn't himself—he hasn't been since the day he and Lucas went their separate ways. It has to be rooted in guilt, shame for what he's done, a desire to avoid Lucas and the memory of it all.

But surely if Lucas is willing to forgive, Nate can stop this whole *don't trust him* shit. He can take responsibility for what he's done and stop insisting that Lucas is on a revenge mission. Because I don't believe it. Not after all Lucas has said.

And he can't be lying. That photo isn't a lie. His desire for me can't be fake. So the rest has to be the truth too...

But what if it's not?

CHAPTER NINE

DESPITE TELLING LUCAS that our PAs would handle it, I'm still surprised when it comes to Friday and I've not heard from him.

I was so convinced he'd call. But then I didn't exactly leave him on fabulous terms. I gave him my warning that his deal was questionable and then ran off to deal with my family and the mess that is me, my feelings.

I've been trying to come to terms with both since—to come up with a plan, even.

It's less than three weeks to Christmas. Three weeks until the Beaumonts do what they do best and celebrate the season all cosied up at the family home. The family home Lucas was once a part of. And I want that again. More than anything.

I pull open my office door and Clare looks up with a smile.

'Do we have a new meeting scheduled with Waring Holdings yet?'

My cheeks flush a little and I damn my inability to stay cool.

If Clare notices, she's ever the professional and

doesn't comment on it. A few clicks of the mouse, a scan of the screen and then she's frowning.

'I don't see anything—should there be?'

'No... I mean, yes.'

She looks at me oddly and I shake off the madness. It's five p.m. on Friday. If his PA was going to get in touch she would have done so by now. Is he getting cold feet? Has talk of Nate given him cause to rethink?

Well, would you want to get back in bed with the Beaumonts after...?

Less of the bed, Eva.

'Eva?'

My eyes focus on Clare, my brain playing catch-up with what we were saying. 'Sorry, I expected his PA to get in touch to arrange one, but maybe he's expecting me to initiate it.'

It's possible. Unlikely, but possible.

She squints at me. 'Would you like me to do it?'

'Hmm...?'

Even Clare's professional mask is slipping now, at my dizzy behaviour.

'Would you like me to get in touch and arrange something?' she asks.

Would I?

My mobile starts to ring and I check my watch—Dad.

Great. No guessing what he wants to talk about.

I look back at Clare, but I'm not confused now. I'm fed up with being told what do, being controlled and manipulated into whatever action suits the Beaumonts.

This venture was meant to be my chance to break away and it still is.

'Yes, give Waring a call—see what you can work out.' I look back to my watch, still flashing at me. 'Sooner rather than later, Clare.'

'On it.'

'Thanks.' I turn back into my office and swing my door closed, bracing myself for Dad.

I take up my phone from the desk as the missed call alert appears and activate callback as I head towards the window and look out at the twinkling Christmas lights lifting the street below. They're beautiful, innocent, a real contrast to the chaos going on in my head.

The phone doesn't even complete a full ring in my ear.

'Evangeline.'

Now I'm five years old. The contrast between Lucas saying my name and my father is marked. 'Yes, Dad.'

'You've remembered who I am, then?'

My head nods of its own accord and a surprising smile lifts my lips. This is just how it is with my family—how it's always been—but I feel in control now, and it's different.

'I saw you a week ago, and it's not like we haven't spoken.'

'Yes, well… I just expected a call, you know… A status update on how things are…progressing…'

He sounds shifty. With good reason. 'You mean things in general or things with a certain someone?'

'Your brother called—he said you were seeing him.'

'In so much as it suits my business, yes.' Okay, so that's a lie. But it's not like I let Dad in on my sex life anyway.

'Evangeline, why would you *do* that? You know it's only going to cause ructions, and God knows what his true intentions are.'

'You sound like Nate.'

'You should listen to him—he knows better than most.'

'Really, Dad?' I can't stop the angry pitch of my voice. 'And how's that?'

'You *know* how.'

'Oh, that's right—Lucas did a runner when their company collapsed and now he's back to mess things up for me. Have I summed it up?'

My father is quiet on the other end of the phone and I see no need to rescue him. If he has a sound argument—the truth, even—I'll listen to it.

'Or shall we talk about how Nate did that dodgy deal all by himself?'

'You don't know what you're talking about—'

'Don't I?'

But I can hear the hesitation in his voice—can sense he's not as convinced as he's trying to make out.

'So Lucas *didn't* come to you after it all kicked off and tell you what Nate had done?'

'Yes, he did… But—'

'But you chose not to believe him. Lucas—a man who was always solid, trustworthy, dependable. Who doted on you as a father figure and balanced out Nate's crazy antics.'

'It's not that simple—'

'Isn't it? You said it yourself, Dad. They were yin and yang, Lucas kept Nate in check. And yet you were so quick to listen to your son, never mind that you destroyed Lucas.'

'I hardly think I destroyed him. He's hugely successful—a pillar of the business commun—'

'And what does that matter when he has no one to share that success with?'

My voice cracks and I purse my lips together, fighting back the well of emotion.

Dad is quiet. I want him to say he's sorry. I want him to tell Lucas he's sorry. But there's nothing.

'Speak to Nate,' I say, pushing him. 'Or I will. It's time he came clean.'

'It's in the past, Eva. Why do you want to go dragging it up now?'

'Because it affects the future—you know it does. And why should Lucas be tainted by it? We should *all* know the truth. Mum included.'

'But you know how your brother is… If we do this—'

'If we do this, *what*? He relapses?' I snap. 'Christ, Dad, he needs to take responsibility for it—he needs to grow up.'

'Maybe if Lucas hadn't abandoned the company—'

'*Don't*, Dad. You're still defending Nate over Lucas.'

'I just want you to be careful, honey. I don't want you hurt in some twisted attempt at revenge.'

My laugh is scathing. 'That's the *last* thing I need to worry about.'

'I'm not so sure…'

'I am,' I say, sounding more confident than I feel. 'This is *my* product, *my* company. I will make the best decision for both and see your investment paid back in full.'

'I don't care about getting the money back. All—'

'I *do*, Dad.' I want to be free. 'And I want you to speak to Nate.'

He's quiet again and I let the silence hang between us, pressing.

'Okay,' he says eventually. 'I'll try.'

'Don't just try—make him come clean. You're his father, for Christ's sake, he never should have lied to you in the first place.'

'No… I know.'

And there's something in the way he says 'I know'—*guilt*—that has me wanting more. I almost tell him that he should look at himself, too, to see why Nate was driven to do what he did, but I don't dare. I hope that in talking to each other it will come out anyway, and he'll shoulder his part in all of this.

It's a start, and it's as good a time as any to cut the call before he can backtrack. 'I have to go.'

'Evangeline, wait.'

'What is it?'

'Your brother gets back next week. We thought a family dinner would be nice.'

'Will you speak to Nate before that?' I ask, too eager to stop myself.

'Perhaps not before, but after—when the time is right.'

I want to ask exactly when he thinks that might be, but my dad is not a man to be pressed and I've already done plenty of that.

'When are you thinking of for dinner?'

'Friday—a kind of welcome home and pre-Christmas planning session. You know how your mother loves to plan for the festivities.'

I smile. It's instinctive. I love Christmas. I love my mother's obsession with it. And I love my family, no matter how they rile me. And now I have my father's assurance that he will talk to Nate I feel lighter, almost happy.

'Sure. I'll see you then.'

I hang up and head to the door just as someone raps on it. 'Yes?'

Clare walks in, eyes wide.

'What is it?' I ask.

'Erm…you're free this weekend, right?'

'Aside from some Christmas shopping I have planned, yes. Why?'

'Great, that's all I need to know.'

Lucas strides in as he speaks. *Lucas.*

'Thanks, Clare.'

He's dismissing my PA and I'm on another plane, I swear to God. My eyes rake over him, my brain disengaging over the mere sight of him. He's wearing a dark blue suit, his white shirt tie-free and distractingly open at the collar.

The door clicks shut. We're alone and there's so much I want to do with that—none of it conducive to work.

And didn't I just tell Dad I'm doing this for work? For work and to fix the past.

Liar.

'It's good to see you.'

He speaks again—not that he has much choice. I'm still struggling past the heart-shaped wedge in my throat.

'Evangeline?'

Better. So much better coming from him.

I smile and walk back to my desk, setting down my phone and leaning my hip against its edge as I look back to him. 'So, what's this talk of the weekend?'

I'm so damn curious my blood is pumping with it, excitement quick to follow.

'You questioned my ethics…'

My eyes narrow. 'Ethics?'

'You made some sweeping remark about crossing human rights lines.'

He's right. I did. But it was a fair—if unlikely— assumption based on the figures he presented.

'I have concerns, that's all.'

'And that's why I'm here.'

He clears his throat and shoves one hand into the pocket of his trousers, the other through his hair—*is he nervous?*

'I'm going to put your mind at rest.'

He's actually rather cute when he's nervous…

You're supposed to be talking work, Eva.

'How so?'

'My jet's on standby. I'm taking you to Singapore.'

Singapore? I straighten. *He can't be serious.*

'I can't just up and leave.'

'Seems you can.' He holds my eye, any trace of nervousness gone. 'You have no plans, you can shop in Singapore if need be and Clare has cleared your Monday too.'

'But—'

I break off. There's no reason for me to say no. In fact my body is screaming *yes*. With such force it's scaring me. I am so hooked on him, so keen…

Oh, yes, definitely scared. And excited. *Say yes.*

'Seems to me the best way to convince you of my upstanding ethics is to show you in practice—wouldn't you agree?'

'I…'

'And besides…it'll be fun.'

Fun. So much implied in that one word…

'Okay…' I say slowly, processing, considering…

'Great, the car's outside. We'll swing by your place en route to the airport.'

'Now?'

His grin is unhurried, and electrifying as fuck.

'Yes, now, Evangeline.'

I'm on my best behaviour. This is about convincing her to work with me.

But the way she keeps looking at me…the way her face lit up when she stepped onto the jet and asked if it was mine…

Impressing her is like a drug, I want to do it again and again and again. And, luckily for me, this trip is all about that.

The Beaumonts have money—serious money—but they don't have wealth like this.

'Can I get you something to drink, Mr Waring?'

I pull my attention from Eva, who's been exploring the cabin area since we hit cruising altitude, and look to Frederick, my on-call flight attendant. Ever efficient, polite and discreet.

'Please—champagne.'

Eva's eyes flick to me, widening.

'What?' I ask innocently.

'A bit extravagant, don't you think?'

We're on my private jet and champagne is what she deems 'extravagant'?

'No.'

Her smile is provocative as much as it is coy. 'Celebrating a bit early, aren't you?' she asks.

'No.'

She settles herself into a sofa, her hands reaching out to smooth along the upholstery—*yes, she's definitely impressed.*

'This has nothing to do with work and everything to do with a drink worthy of the company.'

She laughs and it ripples through me, heat tightening me up like a coiled spring. 'Some water, too, please, Frederick.'

'Of course, sir.'

He disappears, and Eva watches him go before looking back to me, her brow wrinkling. She's serious and happy all at once—speculative, if I had to put a word on it. But she's not wary...not like she was before.

'Are you hungry?' I ask.

It's almost nine in the evening and I know she's not eaten. We've been together since we left her office. And I've loved every second.

Something's changed since that night at my apartment—whether it's what I told her, or something else, she's different. She seems relaxed—*hell, I'm relaxed*. It's rubbing off on me, blurring the boundaries of this trip. Personal or business...?

Something flares inside. Something akin to hope.

'Ravenous,' she says.

My breath catches. *Jesus*.

It's an honest answer, perfectly platonic, but to my hyped-up body she might as well have begged me to screw her with that very sweet word. Frederick present or not.

And, speak of the devil, he appears, champagne in hand.

'Miss Beaumont.'

He offers her a glass and she takes it with a smile.

'Thank you.'

Frederick beams back at her. Frederick my professional and extremely impassive flight attendant. Yet another person who breaks character for her and they've barely shared two words.

I can't blame him either. Eva has this look in her eyes when she's relaxed that seems to encompass the world.

They're so bright, so caring, so captivating. And I'm hooked on them as I take my own glass.

'What has Andreges prepared for dinner?'

I barely hear as Frederick runs through the menu. I'm watching as Eva's lips part with growing surprise and, if the colour in her cheeks is any indication, with pleasure too.

'Wow,' she says when he finishes, 'that sounds fabulous.'

'I trust it's acceptable?'

Frederick is asking me, of course, but I'm still looking at her.

'Is it?' I ask.

Her smile fills the cabin, contagious as it sweeps us both. 'Acceptable? It sounds delicious!'

'Wonderful.'

Frederick clasps his hands together, still beaming. This is the most animated I've ever seen him.

'I will bring it through shortly.'

He glides away and silence descends. Her eyes are off me as she frowns into her champagne, and her switch from exuberant enjoyment to quiet introspection is so rapid I struggle to keep up.

Despite the cushioned leather I'm suddenly uncomfortable, and I shift in my seat, running a finger through my open collar. I can take a guess at what she's thinking about, but I don't want to go back to that. We've done the past. Now I want to look to the future.

'I spoke to my father,' she says, before I can think of a conversation-starter to stop her.

I drink my champagne but barely feel its chilling progression down my throat or even taste it. The Beaumonts make me numb. It's a defence mechanism—effective with all bar her. But I've come to accept that. I don't want to be numb with her. I like how alive she makes me feel.

'And…?'

'I told him he needs to get the truth out of Nate and acknowledge they did wrong by you.'

She sits straighter and brushes her free-flowing hair over one shoulder, all calm and controlled and breathtaking with it.

'I also told him to back off as far as my business goes. This is my decision—they have no say in it.'

I don't react, keeping my face deadpan even though inside my pride in her swells. The Evangeline of our youth would never have stood up to them.

'You said it just like that?' My lip quirks as I imagine it.

'Pretty much,' she says, and the glint in her eye hits me with the blue of her sweater. I love her in blue. Hell, I love her in every colour.

I realise she's staring at me, waiting for a response, and I ask carefully, 'How did they take it?'

She drinks her champagne and shrugs. 'Dad's still coming to terms with Nate's lies—he needs to hear it from him.'

I nod. 'And our potential working relationship?'

She doesn't look away. 'I think they're both of the opinion that you've got some devious plan to screw me over,' she says. She narrows her sights on me and leans forward slowly, provocatively, 'So, Mr Waring, *do* you have some wicked plan to take revenge?'

I have a thousand wicked wants in that second, with her lips slick with champagne and pouting at me. But I sense that, for all she jokes, this is important. I can't deny that I've thought about it, that there would be something just in that kind of revenge, my anger towards Nate bringing out the worst in me. But it's not what drove me to her.

'I'm a busy man, Eva. I don't have time to exact some ill-considered revenge.'

She cocks her head to one side, her teeth scraping over her lip as she quietly considers my words. 'Which brings me to my other question: Why come to me at all?'

I go to answer, but she continues.

'I know you want my product, that you want to join forces with me, and that's all perfectly acceptable. But *you*—why are you doing all the leg work? You must have a multitude of very capable employees to entrust with the task of gaining my business, of coming to the party, attending meetings, even taking me on this tour... But it's all you.'

'Why shouldn't I? The potential is huge, the competition for the work fierce. I wanted you to know I'm serious.'

'Wanted *me* to know, or my family?'

She leans back in her seat, crossing her legs over one another, and even though she's now wearing jeans, following a quick change at her home, the skinny fit of the fabric is doing nothing to help ease the appeal of those long, lithe legs I've traced with my mouth, my fingers...

'Why does it matter?'

I don't know why I ask it. A delaying tactic, I suppose. Because, as I've come to realise, there is one reason above all others that I came, and I'm not sure she's ready to hear it yet.

'You *know* it matters.'

'I didn't think it fair to send in one of my people when I wasn't sure how well my company would be received.'

She raises an eyebrow at me. Amused. 'And you thought your own physical presence would be preferable?'

I laugh. 'I wouldn't go that far.'

'No?' She toys with the stem of her glass, her eyes following the rotation of it in her fingers.

'I figured that if there was a personal block to our companies working together it was best I confronted it head-on and in person. I didn't expect...'

I trail off and her eyes lift to me.

'Expect what?' she asks.

'This.'

I'm not going to lie to her. I'm done with secrets, cover-ups.

'Ten years...' She smiles softly. 'Who would think something could flare up again so readily?'

I wonder if she means it. Is she genuinely surprised at this force determined to pull us together? Whatever the case, my body is already gearing up to pursue the suggestion in her gaze, regardless of my good intentions when we boarded.

'Indeed.'

My agreement is tight, loaded, and the silence that ensues is heavy.

She looks to the door through which Frederick disappeared. 'When do you think the food will arrive?'

I follow her line of sight, my body rigid as I read her intent. 'Soon.'

'Shame…'

I smile as I try to set my body to chill. 'I thought you were hungry.'

'Absolutely famished.'

'Evangeline…'

It's a warning. To her. To me.

'I'm guessing you're already a member,' she says, looking at me from under her lashes.

'A member?'

My heart is thrumming in my ears now, the warmth coiling through my body reaching breaking point. She takes a long, slow sip of the straw-gold liquid, her throat moving hypnotically, her little appreciative hum teasing me.

'Come on, Lucas, you're not *that* innocent.'

I swallow, hard. Of course I know to what she's referring. And there's a bed next door…ready to be used. But I don't want this to be about sex. Me and her. I want it to be about business. About convincing her I'm the right company for her. Not cloud it with this.

But then, after the way we parted, this is the last thing I expected to be heading off.

'Tell me…is it as amazing as they say at high altitude?'

She's still sitting out of reaching distance, but I feel her words like a caress over my cock, and a stream of erotic scenarios streak through my mind.

'They say it's to do with the dip in atmospheric pressure…' she practically purrs. 'The reduction in oxygen levels messing with your brain, making you feel more stimulated, intensifying the pleasure…'

She curves a hand over her upper thigh and I fight the urge to move, to cover her hand with my own.

'I wouldn't actually know.'

'With your reputation, you expect me to believe that?'

I laugh, projecting mock-offence. 'Why is it so hard to believe?'

'Come on, Lucas, you *own* this jet—don't tell me you haven't brought a date on it?'

'No, I haven't.'

I date women, sure. And I have connections around the globe. But they're connections, not relationships. They serve a purpose when I need it. The jet is simply my transport for work—it's not a social vehicle.

Not that I really *do* social.

'Give over. Once a player, always a player,' she murmurs into her drink.

I sense she's teasing me, but I don't like it.

Let it go.

I can't. It's the same reason I couldn't let her remark about human rights slide. I want her to see the good in me. And if not the good, then at least the truth.

'Is that how you see me?'

She lowers her glass to the side table and her eyes soften. 'Sorry. I didn't mean to insult you. It's just… you know. *All* those girls when we were younger…you and Nate were horrendous.'

She's not wrong. I remember it well. But I also remember the reason, and I want to tell her. But it will open me up, expose me.

My neck prickles. I'm not used to talking so much. Even though I want to tell her, there's a part of me that fears the power it will hand her.

And isn't that as bad as confessing the real reason I came to her personally instead of sending an employee?

But is it so bad if it's the truth?

'Look, it's okay, Lucas. You're not the only one playing the field.' Her cheeks colour and she waves a carefree hand. 'And, hey, you're a desirable bachelor. I'm not judging you. I'm just…you know…saying that if you had…'

She's babbling and flustered and I fucking love her for it.

I stop thinking. I sweep across the cabin and pull her with me onto the sofa, crushing her mouth with my own, swallowing her startled moan.

She moulds to me instantly, her kiss just as fierce, as hungry.

God, this feels right. Being here like this with her.

Totally wrapped in one another. I try to tell her, I need to tell her, and then I hear movement—

A trolley. Frederick. Christ.

I pull away from her and give her an apologetic smile. 'Time to satisfy that hunger of yours.'

She blinks at me, dazed. All hot and bothered and embarrassed at once, And then she turns to Frederick and musters a sheepish grin.

To his credit, he barely bats an eyelid. 'Dinner is served.'

He lays it out on the dining table before us. The smell wafts over to me, mixed in with the lingering scent of her still tingling my senses.

'Thank you,' I say, and he dips his head before turning and leaving once more.

I move to the table, retrieving our drinks as I do so, and wait for her to sit before I follow suit, placing her drink before her.

She raises it to her lips, her eyes locking with mine. I do the same. And this time I taste it. I feel the fine stream of bubbles dance over my tongue, taste the caramel, the hint of lemon...

It's exquisite.

As is she.

The perfect match, just as I told her.

And she deserves the truth. I need her to know.

'All those girls you saw me with...'

She takes up her cutlery and shakes her head softly. 'Don't worry about—'

'It was because of you.'

Her fingers still, her eyes return to mine. 'Me?'

Her frown is delectable. I want to lean over, kiss it away, trail kisses right down to her open lips.

'Yes, you.' I reach out, brushing my thumb across her cheek as I lose myself in her eyes.

'I was trying to prove to myself that I could look past you.'

'Past…me?'

'You were off-limits. I had to go elsewhere.'

It's so simple, so honest, but she doesn't seem to accept what I'm saying.

'It was a foolish notion,' I add.

She licks her lips and her cheeks heat beneath my palm. 'How so?'

'Because there's only one you.'

There—I've said it. It's out there.

Her lashes flicker, her eyes water. *Jesus, she's going to cry.*

'I…I don't know what to say.'

'Nothing. You need to eat. And then you need to sleep.'

She's staring at me as if I'll give her more, but I'm done with opening up. My body is tight with it.

Fear. That's what it is. Fear of where it puts us now. Because the one thing I'm sure of is that I love her. Still love her. And she loves her family. Her family who hate me.

I watch as she cuts up her food, but I sense that her mind is racing with what I've told her. Hell, mine is. What did I hope to gain? A sweeping confession of something similar from herself? And even if she had, then what?

The problem is I'm selfish. I have no one else. I only have to look out for me.

Which means I should be going after not just her business but her heart too, and saying to hell with the Beaumonts.

I should make her choose. Them or me.

I should.

But I can't.

She forks the food and places it in her mouth. Her shoulders relax, her lashes lower and then she smiles, pleasure ringing through her and pulling me in.

Screw the Beaumonts—make her choose.

CHAPTER TEN

DINNER IS INCREDIBLE. Fine dining at its best, all at forty-odd thousand feet in the air. It's almost too good to believe, but my taste buds are still zinging over the lemon tart I ate for dessert and I'm still crushing over the jet itself.

It's real.

I blame it on the designer in me. I've only seen a glimpse of the galley kitchen beyond the door behind me—all black and glossy, with crystalware on display in a high cabinet and accented lighting that you'd expect in a slick city apartment.

The cabin we're in features a plush sofa, seats that swivel and recline, a high-tech TV and sound system, and the dining table at which we sit is laid out like a high-end restaurant. All in colours designed to soothe and relax.

And I am *so* relaxed.

The flight is smooth; only the gentle hum of the engine, the dry air and the strange headiness that comes with flying remind me that we are truly on a plane.

This kind of luxury is beyond belief. I knew people

did this sort of thing—of course I did. I just never expected to be one of them.

And it truly does beg the question... *What would it be like?*

I look at him sitting across from me. He's checking his phone, his face serious and so goddamn sexy. It should be a crime to be this attractive, this distracting.

And the way he watched me through dinner... My body warms at the memory. He wants me as much as I want him. I know it. And who *wouldn't* want to experience an orgasm at altitude just to know if it's truly that good?

And just maybe the fizz is going to your head quicker than normal and your inhibitions have gone the way of your brain. Hmm...entirely possible... But do I care?

His eyes lift to mine and my breath catches, my pulse making a little trip of its own. *No.*

'All okay?' I say, amazed that I sound relatively normal.

'Yes.'

'Care to share?' I ask.

What the actual fuck?

His brow cocks and I want to slap myself. As if I have *any* right to know what he's up to on his phone. But it was supposed to be a flirtatious prompt—like *Hey, I'm interested.*

Oh, God.

The fizz and altitude have definitely gone to my head.

'Just catching up on messages and firing one off to the team in Singapore to confirm our arrival.'

I nod and automatically lift my wine glass. I do a mental recap: three glasses of champagne and a bit of red—*no more for you*—and put it down again.

'Isn't it early there?' I check my watch. It's half-ten at night, UK time. 'What is it? Eight hours ahead?'

'Yes.'

'So that makes it six-thirty…?'

My voice trails away. That look is back in his eye—that look that has salacious heat swirling in me so readily that I forget what point I'm even getting to.

'You should get some sleep.'

'Sleep?' Sleep is not what I'm thinking of. Far from it.

'Yes—you know…that thing babies hate, teens crave and us adults scarcely get enough of.'

I give a laugh, but it's tight with need. I know it is, and he does too, judging from the way his eyes drop to my mouth.

'Why break form, then? Sleep can come later…' I say.

The lights have been dimmed, the plates cleared away. Frederick is gone—dismissed until his next summons, I assume—and I'm curious to see what other thrills this plane has to offer.

I stand and step around the table. 'Tell me, Lucas, where do you sleep?' I walk around the cabin, my fingers brushing over the back of a chair. 'Here?'

To be fair it looks as comfy as any hotel bed, but he shakes his head, his jaw tense. It's as if he's fighting his instincts and I wonder why…

I look to the back of the cabin, to the closed door, and I know the answer before I ask. 'What about through there?'

I walk towards it and look at him over my shoulder. He's still seated, rooted, but his eyes follow me.

'May I?' I say, my fingers over the handle.

I move before he answers, sliding it open, and I can't stop the gasp that parts my lips. I shouldn't be surprised—not having already enjoyed the living space, glimpsed the kitchen. But I am.

It's incredible: sexy, dark, alluring. Much like its owner.

I sense him move and suddenly he's behind me.

'That bed just calls to me…' I murmur, taking in the mink throw, the cloud-like pillows and inviting duvet.

He laughs softly. 'Good, because you're sleeping there.'

I turn to him, my palm lifting to his chest, feeding off his warmth. I can't meet his eyes, though. I feel suddenly unsure, nervous of his answer despite all he's said. 'You've really never brought anyone else here?'

'No.'

'So I'm the first?'

'Yes.'

My tongue sweeps over my bottom lip and I feel his chest tighten beneath my palm, his breath brushing over my forehead.

'What are you thinking about?' I ask.

'I'm thinking you should get into bed,' he says, backing away a little. 'I'll sleep out here. We've a busy weekend planned, and this is all about our two companies working together. I want to keep us focused on that.'

I smile. My eyes are still lowered. He's trying to do what's right. Trying to maintain some form of professionalism and I love him for it. But I love the sexual undercurrent even more—the tightness in every word he speaks, the tension thrumming off his body.

'Is that why you kissed me earlier? To keep me focused on work?'

He clears his throat. 'I shouldn't have.'

I look up. 'Oh, yes, you should.'

I lift myself on tiptoes, my lashes closing, and he moves swiftly, his hands reaching out to grip my arms. 'Come on, Eva—bed.'

My eyes flick to his. 'You're coming with me.'

'No, this is *your* bed for tonight.'

I pout. Actually pout. Like some naughty child. He can't be serious. He's given me signs all evening that this is heading somewhere, that this isn't just about work.

And now he steps back out of the room while my cheeks burn.

'There's a bathroom through there—help yourself to anything you need, Frederick has already brought your suitcase in.'

'Lucas?'

I don't want to sound affronted. But I am.

Or am I tipsy? Is that what this is? Some drunken plea and he's saving me from myself?

My cheeks flame deeper and his smile is small, warm. 'Sweet dreams, Evangeline.'

He slides the door closed, leaving me alone, and I have to stop myself from striding after him and demanding he *do* something. Anything to see off this need he's evoked.

It's his fault.

Entirely his fault.

So why am I still loving his decency?

I flop onto the bed and am instantly cocooned in softness. The kind that makes every muscle in your body go weak, your brain quiet. *Bliss.*

He can have his way for now—his bed is an inviting compromise—but there are hours ahead. Many hours in which he can change his mind...

All he needs is the right kind of nudge.

I smile as I strip down to my underwear and climb beneath the quilt. I'll just give him a few hours of thinking he's won first...

I flick my phone over, face down on the table, and lean back into my seat.

Ignore it. Ignore him.

But Nate's text burns into me:

Leave her the fuck alone.

And she really thinks that talking to her family, her father talking to Nate, is going to fix this?

Like hell it is.

I grit my teeth and close my eyes, riding my shoulders into the soft upholstery, seeking comfort, seeking the blissful ignorance of sleep. But my conscience laughs at me. There's no way sleep will be forthcoming when I know she's lying in the room next to me. Wanting me.

I know she's pissed off with me. My rejection has goaded her. And I can't blame her—not when it comes so soon off the back of that kiss, when all my good intentions disintegrated, incinerated in the heat of a need that won't shift.

I'm torn between doing what I want and encouraging her down a path that she might regret.

If I'd told her one of my messages was from Nate— the first message I've received from him since I changed my number all those years ago—would she still have tried to jump me?

It's a question I can't stop tossing around—have been for the last two hours, since closing the door on her.

I swing from wanting to send an equally angry retort to her brother and then taking what's on offer in my bed, to protecting her from herself…from me. I'm not blind to the anger that still bubbles beneath the surface. The resentment. It fizzes in my blood at every mention of her family. But my need for her, my love, swamps it.

Or maybe it feeds it?

Maybe there is an unconscious need to have what I shouldn't—to have what pisses them off the most.

I force my hands to relax and shimmy my shoulders further back—*sleep, just sleep.*

Logic tells me to get the deal signed, get her in my life and *then* go after more. Not to jeopardise the business by encouraging a relationship I'm not sure she can accept. Not when her family are so against it.

But the alternative—the platonic route—is impossible. No matter how short-term. I need her as much as I need my next breath.

And then I hear it: the soft glide of the door.

My fingers twitch; my chest tingles.

'Lucas?'

Her voice is soft, whisper-like. Has she just woken up?

I try to appear asleep. I can't begin to imagine how she looks right now, dishevelled by sleep. Or, if she hasn't slept, from tossing and turning. Either way my body heats at the very idea.

'Are you awake?'

Her feet pad towards me and I try to even out my breath, relax. The room goes quiet and I know without looking that she's studying me.

One breath in. One breath out. In—

Her fingers brush gently over my forehead, taking back my fringe, and then her lips are there, soft, caressing.

'Lucas…'

Oh, God.

Her fingers slide down over my front and I realise how stupid playing asleep is. Awake, I can stop her. Awake, I can stop the progress of her fingers…

'Lucas, I know you're awake.'

My lips curve in a lazy smile. 'Not one to be easily fooled, are you?'

'No.'

'What gave me away?'

I open my eyes to meet hers. She's so close I can inhale her scent, feel the warmth of her body, and that's when I realise she's naked, with the low light of the cabin hinting at every glorious curve. *Fuck.*

'This.' She rakes a nail over my hardness, and my eyes and body feast on the simple stroke.

Sure enough, even in this light there is no denying how awake I am—awake and very much under her spell.

'You're supposed to be asleep—'

She grips me, and my words become a groan as I shift within her grasp.

'Eva.'

'The way I see it...' She runs her hand over me, and heat rushes to greet her touch. 'It will be near enough evening when we get to the hotel. There'll be time for sleep then.'

There is no hotel, but I'm damned if I can correct her. I'm trying to focus through a heavy haze of lust. Trying to hang on to what's right.

My fingers bite into the upholstery of my seat and my thighs tremble as I press into it, away from her, but she has me. I should extract her hands, make her move away, but I can't even do that.

'You don't like being told what to do?'

She shakes her head, and her teasing lips curve into a smile as she lowers her head to my ear. 'Especially when I want something as much as I want you.'

She trails her hot mouth across my jaw as she hooks her leg over me, spreading her heat over my erection.

'And I can feel you want me too.'

She rides against me and I'm back in that kitchen, with my cock getting the better of me.

Now I can move. I grip her hips, steadying her, halting her.

She pouts down at me. 'Don't be a spoilsport.'

Christ, if only...

I force an arrogant smile. 'You wouldn't want Frederick to hear, would you?'

Her eyes flick briefly in the direction of the kitchen. 'Worried I'm going to make a noise?' she asks.

She tries to move in my grasp and my hold tightens. She's a minx. An electrifying, dizzying minx. And suddenly I have the desire to do something extreme. Something that will stick the finger up at Nate. Something that will put me firmly in control and to hell with my good intentions.

'Come.' I lift her away from me and take hold of her wrist, striding to the bedroom before the lustful haze can lift and common sense can prevail. We make it to the bedroom. 'On the bed.'

She bites into her lip and lowers herself down onto it, every bend of her body, each slip of her hands over the duvet intentionally seductive.

'I like you like this,' she purrs.

Holy fuck.

I pull my gaze away, stripping off my clothes as she watches me. Not until I'm naked and have the cupboard that contains what I need open do I turn to her, the scarlet strip of silk in hand. A tie. One of my finest.

She looks from it to me, her brows raising. 'And what do you intend to do with *that*?'

She's provoking me and my cock fucking loves it. *Too much*.

I turn back and take out another tie. I need the second one to keep her under control—to keep *myself* under control. She's too efficient at tipping me over. Her hands, her body, her mouth—all dangerous.

I stalk towards her and she glides back on the bedcovers, her eyes pulling me in, her lips parted, anticipation in her breath.

'Have you ever been gagged?'

Her eyes flare as she shakes her head.

'Another first, then.'

'Yes.'

She leans up towards me, offering herself, accepting, and heat sears my gut. So much for keeping it under control.

I wrap the tie around her mouth, my eyes on hers as I gently tighten it. Her trust, her desire, her… *Her what? Love?* Hell, it looks like love. It looks like how I feel.

A very different heat swells, close to my heart, and with it comes that same edge—*fear*.

I can't deal with that right now.

I tug the strip of cloth tight, the sound of silk on silk a sharp whisper before softening as I tie it into a bow and lean back to take her in.

Her eyes are wider and her nose flares as she

breathes. Her cheeks flush pink and her lips form an erotic O as she tests the binding with her teeth.

'Okay?' I ask, even though I can see her answer. Her eyes blaze, her nipples are tight, her breasts flush the colour of her cheeks and I know if I dipped my fingers between her legs I'd feel it too.

She nods, a small sound quivering in her throat.

'Good. Hands?' My voice is tight with the command and dutifully she straightens up to offer them out.

I wrap the silk over her wrists, tying them together. She watches every move I make, her breath rasping over the gag, goosebumps prickling over her skin. She is so fucking sexy I'm starting to worry that just the sight of her is going to tip me over.

'Lie back.'

I help her down and raise her hands over her head, the tip of my erection nudging at her stomach as I move over her. She purposely arches into me, caressing me further. *Jesus.*

I fasten the tie-ends to the bar that decorates the bookshelf above the headboard and then back away to kneel over her, drinking in her naked beauty, willing her to be powerless and all mine.

She wriggles and whimpers, begging me for something, and I smile as she opens her legs to encase me, to draw me in. She's so wet... Her need glistens in the low light and I take pity. Just a little.

I reach forward and run my thumb up her slickened seam.

She cries into the tie, working her body against my

touch, and heat assaults my cock, pre-cum beading at its tip. It's goddamn erotic, having her like this, at my mercy, and I want to draw it out.

I climb off the bed and she moans after me, eyes pleading.

I take a fresh glass from the nightstand and head to the kitchen. Opening the freezer, I fill the glass with ice then return to her, my eyes lazy as they trail over her flushed skin.

She writhes towards me, her body outstretched, her whimpers begging, and then she spies the glass and stills, her eyes widening.

I lower myself to the bed, glass in hand, and she watches as I scoop out one ice cube and pop it into my mouth, rolling it around my tongue. She crosses her legs, her thighs clamped together, and I know she's feeding *that* ache. The same one that's throbbing through me for release as I move on all fours above her.

I drop my head to her neck slowly, teasingly, and I work my icy tongue over her skin, both cube and flesh caressing. Her breath hisses around the gag, her moans teasingly trapped.

I trail around to her front, to the hollow of her throat, where I dip and release the cube. It melts over her skin, where her pulse is beating a crazy tempo.

I take up another cube, running it down her front and beneath one breast. Her breath hitches and her body arches, her every reaction feeding my own. I work it in circles, getting steadily closer to where her nipple tightens.

I lock onto her eyes as I trace around the rose-pink bud. She shudders with a moan, turning her head into the pillow. I move to her other breast, teasing her with the ice, and then my lips drop to the well-worked nipple, my warm mouth a heated contrast.

Her body becomes tense, her legs wrap tightly over each another.

I know she's close, but not yet...

I rise up onto my knees and trail a fresh cube down her front, letting it rest in her belly button, where the ice water pools as she wriggles. Her eyes are glazed with lust, heavy and captivating, as she watches me part her legs.

I kneel between them, taking hold of the cube, and trace soft, light circles from her navel to the strip of hair. She is rigid now—ready, waiting—and as I tease her apart with the frozen edge she cries in her throat, her head thrown back.

I stroke the cube over her so lightly my touch is hardly there, but it's enough. I can see it in her heightened colour, in the way her breath is ragged over the silk.

I circle her clit, gently caressing, watching her writhe for more. Her fingers claw in their binding, and her muscles are tight. I know that with one suck of my mouth she'll be gone.

She lifts her head and looks to me, desperate, the crazy undulation of her hips begging. I toss the ice and grab her legs, lifting her to my mouth. I'm not soft, gentle, delicate. I'm rough, desperate, eager.

I claim her as my heart wants to. I drink from her. I dip inside her warm haven and then retreat, grazing her with the flat of my tongue as I slide all the way up.

The moment I strike her clit, her body spasms out of control. She's coming, her screams muffled and carnal and snapping my restraint. I flip her over, twisting her binding with the move, and lift her hips to meet me as I thrust, burying myself deep.

Her tight, wet heat closes around me—so mind-obliterating, so new. She pushes back on her knees, her wrists pulling at the silk tie, demanding more.

But then I still as the unfamiliar sensation strikes a second's clarity—*condom*.

'Shit.'

I grip her hips to stop her—to stop me.

She throws me a look over her shoulder, her pleading whimper threatening my resolve.

'Protection,' I grind out.

She shakes her head, rocking her body in my hold, clamping her pussy around me. She's telling me no. And, hell, I know I shouldn't—but, Christ, I know I'm safe, and I trust her.

And, oh, my God, she's pumping me. Back and forward again, her gorgeous body riding me, milking me. Heat rips through my thighs, my gut, my cock, and I'm thrusting hard and fast. There's nothing delicate about it. I'm fucking her. My hands bite into her skin, her moans are wild, and I want more from her, louder...

My thighs slap against hers. I take hold of her arse and grip it tight. I rub at the plump flesh and test the surface with the flat of my palm. She looks at me, daring me to do it, her eyes glinting, and I spank her, the slap mixing with the heady sound of her cry.

I do it again. My blood pulsing with the crazed heat of it. Of letting go. No control. No nothing. Just me and her.

I feel like I'm punishing her. Some crazy kind of punishment for the sins of her family. But I can't help it. And she's taking it all, giving as good as she gets. It's messed up, but I can't stop.

And then I'm coming, pleasure streaking though my limbs, frenzied and out of control, and she's there with me, her body spasming around me. My cry is so loud the whole jet will hear, but in that second I can't care.

I only care for her. And it feels right. *So* right.

Fuck Nate. Screw the Beaumonts. She's mine and I'm keeping her.

CHAPTER ELEVEN

I THOUGHT THE plane was impressive. I truly did. But now I'm standing in the penthouse of a skyscraper—our home for the next two nights—and I'm starting to forget what reality looks like.

I have a suspicion that Lucas owns this place. The private elevator to which he has access, the respectful greeting of the staff, the similar decor to that in his London apartment... There's just something about it that's all him.

And now I have it to myself. He's gone out on some work errand, leaving me with strict instructions to call Room Service for food and get some sleep.

But, seriously, how do you sleep when you're surrounded by this?

I twirl on the spot, my eyes tracing a spiral staircase that looks as if it's been carved out of a solid marble block, the mezzanine gallery that leads off to the bedrooms, and the outside area that I've only just glimpsed. I know there's a pool out there, just waiting to be used.

My stomach growls, reminding me of his orders.

But Room Service? Really? When Singapore by twi-
light awaits? No way.

As Lucas is already learning, I might have followed
instruction well as a child, even as a teen, but no more.

I also have this bubble of nervous energy inside me,
and being surrounded by something that is so entirely
him is too distracting.

I rub my wrists. The flesh still tingles where he tied
me, and the bubble balloons. Nervous energy. *Need*,
more like. Need and so much more…

Time to go out.

I lift my clutch from a sofa that could seat at least ten
and head out to the lift area, where I stop in my tracks.
There's a glass wall alongside the elevator that I didn't
see before. I was too wrapped up in Lucas and in following him inside. Now my jaw drops as I take in the sight
beyond the glass. A bright red Ferrari and a vibrant blue
Porsche stare back at me. I can't even hazard a guess at
how high this rooftop penthouse sits, but surely too high
for this, an *en suite* garage.

And the cars… I *love* cars. I have a Porsche too—
it's my one real indulgence. But it's clear to see, even
from this distance, that his is custom-made everything.
Unique to him.

Unique *as* him.

I roll my eyes at my heart, which is getting so carried away, and continue to the lift, using a touchscreen
to beckon it. Of course it opens immediately, as if it
anticipated my request.

I scan my clothing in the lift mirror: skinny pants and a deep blue silk cami. It'll do. And I step in.

It takes me a few tries to navigate the touchscreen inside, and it occurs to me that I don't have a clue how to get back in. There will be some code—some pass that I need. But I tell myself it's fine, I'll speak to the lovely staff we saw on the way in. Nothing is insurmountable.

It's exactly what I'm planning on doing when the doors open and I step out into the vast lobby. Instead I'm frozen, my feet stuck to the glossy white floor.

The thing about Lucas is that he stands out. Even more so in Singapore. And there he is, in the middle of the bustling lobby, with a lady. A tall, statuesque Asian woman who is all poise and elegance, exotic and captivating.

My teeth grit and my heart clenches in my chest.

Business—*she's* business?

The past rips through me: Lucas the player, all those girls, the women since… *This woman.*

And he told me it was *me*! That *I* was the reason there'd been so many. And I believed him.

My body overheats. I'm not only hurt, and embarrassed over my foolishness, I'm *livid*.

He moves, and for the first time I see he has a red box under his arm. He hands it to her and she beams, leaning in to peck him on the cheek. I see the intimacy of the gesture, see her stroke the box affectionately, and I've had enough.

I stride forward. I don't know what I'm going to say but I'm not letting him think he can get away with this.

But you're not together. You're not in a relationship. This trip is about business for him. You're the one who turned it into more.

No, *he* turned it into more when he tied me to his bed, when he screwed me—

Oh, God, don't think about that now.

He cups her elbow and I see they're about to move off. I'm almost upon them and it's as if he senses my approach. His head turns and his eyes are on me. They narrow before they lift and he smiles. *Actually smiles.*

'Evangeline, you're supposed to be getting some rest.'

I pull myself up in front of him, hating how hot my cheeks feel and how the beautiful exotic creature with him balances *his* beauty so spectacularly. Even now, as she studies me with open curiosity, I acknowledge that she is perfect for him.

'I wanted to go out to eat,' I say. I turn to her, holding out a hand. 'Hi. I'm Evangeline Beaumont.'

'I know exactly who you are.'

Even her voice is exotic, captivating. She smiles at me, her eyes alive with appreciation, and I feel my heart stutter, confusion hot on its tail. She takes my hand and shakes it softly, her delicate perfume wafting up to me, and suddenly I feel dizzy.

'I have been so eager to meet you.'

'You have?' I retract my hand, my frown impossible to prevent.

'Yes, of course—to work with you would be such a pleasure.'

'Go easy, Maylene, she hasn't agreed yet.'

My eyes dart between them both, my brain too slow to play catch-up.

'Sorry…' Lucas says, gesturing between the goddess and I. 'Eva, this is Maylene—she heads up operations for me out here. And, as Maylene says, she knows exactly who you are.'

He smiles at me, so proud, and I feel it all the way to my toes. As well as feeling the wash of shame at how quick I'd been to misjudge the situation.

His brows draw together and I know he's reading me. Reading my *faux pas*. I need to cover it. *Quick*.

'It's lovely to meet you,' I say. And now I need to leave, before I humiliate myself further.

My eyes drop to the box in her hands and up close I can spot the famous Fortnum & Mason label, see a glimpse of mince pies through the clear square on its top.

'Mince pies?' I'm so surprised it just comes out.

'Ah, yes,' she coos. 'You *can* get them here, but it's never the same. It's my naughty indulgence—we can't be good all the time, hey?'

She winks at me and my cheeks flare. My 'naughty indulgence' is currently looking at me as if I'm the most intriguing specimen he's ever seen.

'I'll let you get on.'

'No, wait.' She looks to Lucas. 'It seems a little unfair that we go and enjoy the best curry Singapore has to offer and leave Evangeline to do her own thing.'

'I don't want to bore her with work, and she's supposed to be resting,' says Lucas.

Maylene rolls her eyes at me. 'And who are you? Her mother?'

I laugh. I like her. 'I'm *so* glad you said that.'

Lucas looks to us both. 'If you're going to gang up on me, I'm not going anywhere.'

'I have a feeling we'd get along fine without you,' I tease him. 'And, as it happens, I *love* curry.'

We look at him pointedly and then it occurs to me that maybe he doesn't want to discuss work in front of an outsider.

I forget my teasing for a moment. 'Unless you need to talk in confidence?'

Maylene waits for Lucas to reply and he gives a shrug. 'I guess you're here to see how we operate, so it can't hurt for you to sit in.'

'Great!' we say in unison, and her friendliness and Lucas's easy inclusion of me buries the dregs of my embarrassment and we head out into the evening.

A car is waiting for us. Of course it is. Like everything with Lucas, it's slick and high-end.

And I am totally swept up in it. In him.

If I really concentrated I'd hear my phone vibrating, my watch attacking my wrist with an incoming call. I'd also hear my eighteen-year-old self trying to issue warning after warning.

Don't get in too deep. Not yet.

But I'm having too much fun.

The food was good. The company exceptional.

Maylene and Eva hit it off. It's no surprise. They're

both intelligent women with personalities to match. And, of course, when they're together they can unite and rib me better. *Better for them.*

It's late when we get back. As the lift doors open into my suite Eva's already sweeping forward, confident in the new space—not like when we first arrived and she followed in my shadow.

She turns to face me now, her smile wide, her eyes alive, and she waves a hand at the exposed garage that's lit with LED spots from the floor. It's flash, but I love it.

And I know she does too.

Eva has always loved her cars. One type in particular. And I know it's drawing her eye now...

'*That* is impressive.'

'Are we talking about the feat of engineering required to get them up here or the cars themselves?'

'Both.' She beams. 'How do you get in?'

A few taps to my phone and the glass door slides up. *'No way.'*

And here I go again. Impressing her. Getting high on it.

She glides forward, her touch delicate as she strokes the red bonnet of my Ferrari. Normally I'd cringe—and if she was any normal woman I would—but I know Eva and I know she loves this particular car. I knew it when I bought it, and think of her every time I get in it. Maybe I've always secretly dreamed of this moment.

'Trust you to own one.'

She looks at me over the hood and tests the door handle. It opens, and she gives a giddy squeal before she drops inside. I'm grinning like a fool as I watch her, but there's no stopping it.

She settles herself in, her hands flexing around the wheel, and I join her, climbing into the passenger seat.

'It's no ordinary Ferrari, is it?' she asks.

'Ordinary?' I raise my brow at her. 'No Ferrari can be classed as *ordinary*.'

'True—but come on, tell me. What have you changed?'

I laugh at her eagerness. I miss this. Having her to share everything with. Just like we used to. It's nice. Really nice. I sit back in the seat and give her the low-down, watching the way her hands caress the interior, feeling her excitement build my own.

'She's a beauty.'

'That she is,' I say, and I'm looking at her—all her—and she knows it.

She meets my eyes, her smile softening as she places the back of her hand over her mouth and stifles a yawn. I feel it too—jet lag creeping in.

'Come on. Let's get you to bed.'

'Us,' she says. 'Let's get *us* to bed.'

Us. I love how that sounds. My body warms over it as I climb out of the car and walk around to help her up. She takes my hand and folds into my side as we walk out of the garage. I set the glass sliding back into place and make for the staircase.

She pulls on my arm to stop me as she kicks off her shoes, and then we're moving again and I'm thinking about sleeping. Sleeping and logistics.

'I had the spare room made up for you.' It feels ridiculous even as I say it and her laugh confirms it.

'You *know* I'm not going to use it, don't you?'

My smile is easy. 'I didn't think so.'

'Sweet of you, though.'

She hangs off my arm and rubs her cheek against my shoulder, almost catlike and loaded with affection. My heart squeezes in my chest.

Where is this heading? Am I a fool?

We reach my bedroom and she pulls away from me, heading for the bed that takes centre stage. She starts to strip as she walks and my throat tightens. But it's not all lust. There's a sense of her belonging here, a sense of comfort. And the fact that she clearly feels it too isn't lost on me.

I follow suit, taking off my jacket and unbuttoning my shirt. I don't remember ever doing this. Bringing a woman home and just undressing as if it's a nightly thing. In fact, I can probably count the number of women I've had in here on one hand.

I sit on the edge of the bed, stripping off my shoes, my socks. I feel her weight as she slips onto the bed too, the quilt shifting as she lifts it and slides under. The warmth that's been setting up camp in my chest since I came back into her life swells inside me.

I stand to unbutton my trousers and strip both those and my underwear away in one swoop, tossing them to the side.

'Do you always sleep naked?' she murmurs, her words drawn out and low.

I look at her as she blinks at me, her eyes heavy. The quilt is pulled to her chin and a pillow cocoons her head. She looks comfortable and inviting all at once.

'Yes.'

I smile and climb in beside her, careful not to let the air-conditioned draught in too much. Immediately she scoots over, resting her head on my chest, and my smile grows as I wrap my arm around her and hold her there.

'Lucas…?'

'Hmm…?'

'Don't you get lonely?'

I flinch and mask it with a shrug; her simple question has cut deep. 'I'm too busy to get lonely.'

She shakes her head. 'I don't believe you.'

She sounds strange, remorseful, so different from how she's been up until now, and I find I'm struggling for words. Too busy fending off the truth.

'You don't really have anyone—thanks to my family.'

Oh, God. Too close.

My gut writhes as I squeeze her shoulder. I'm aiming to reassure, but I can't speak past the chill.

She presses a kiss to my chest and turns her head to rest her cheek over my pec.

'I'm so sorry,' she whispers, and I feel a damp trickle over my skin—she's *crying*.

'Evangeline…?'

Oh, God, don't cry, baby.

'I'm so sorry.' She shakes her head again, her breath rasping. 'You don't deserve it—you don't deserve how my family has treated you. You don't deserve any of it.'

I turn her onto her back and gaze down into her face. Her eyes are clamped shut, tears escaping to trail down her face.

I press a kiss to her brow. 'Evangeline, look at me.'

She doesn't.

I lightly kiss the bridge of her nose. 'Please?'

Her lashes flutter open.

'You have nothing to be sorry for.'

I seal my words with another kiss, ending any denial with the gentle pressure of my mouth. I only want to comfort her, to make her happy again, but as her body curves into mine her nakedness draws me in, and my body stirs, my heart warms.

'Make love to me,' she whispers against my lips, hooking her legs around my hips, opening herself to me.

Something inside me eases, like a balm being smoothed over old wounds. I trust her—heart, mind and soul.

Make love to me...

Always.

I press home and in one swift move she surrounds me. Comfort, love, light. Everything I could ever want, ever need, is here...right now.

And I won't let anyone take it away.

Not Nate. Not her father. No one.

CHAPTER TWELVE

I AM BLISSFULLY COSY. Wrapped in the most luxurious quilt, my limbs entwined as I cuddle it to me.

But I'm alone.

My senses come alert. I'm not worried, though. He's here somewhere. The heady scent of fresh coffee is in the air and I can hear movement somewhere in the distance.

I open my eyes, blinking against the sunrise that fills the room with a golden glow. It's breathtaking, lighting up the sea and the sky beyond the glass, and I'm basking in it. I roll over and stretch, loving how my body still tingles after everything we have shared since we left London.

I smile and a little kick of glee erupts inside me. This is too good to be true.

But it is true.

And once I get my family in line it could be perfect.

My eighteen-year-old self is becoming an increasingly distant memory, her warning just as weak.

I leap out of bed and the sound of water breaking reaches me—*the pool*. I imagine him almost naked, his muscles rippling as he moves through the water, and my body sighs over the image.

I dip to collect his shirt from the floor and slip it on, heading in his direction. My pulse is already dancing, but as I step outside it skitters with my intake of breath.

The pool is outstretched before me, filling half of the long roof terrace. Two draped cabanas, a string of sun-beds and many decorative plants flank it on one side; on the other is the view. And there he is, gliding through the water, his back to me. A strip of black fabric sits tight over his behind and the rest is bare for me to enjoy.

I'm quiet as I pad out. I don't want to disturb his front crawl, and his perfect form delivering stroke after stroke is mesmerising. But of course he's nearing the end. At any moment he will turn and see me.

I lower myself to the edge and sit down, my toes test-ing the water. It's warm and I sink my legs in, swirl-ing them around as he disappears under the water and executes a perfect turn. Like a professional. Of course, that's Lucas all over…perfecting everything.

His head breaks the water and he flicks his fringe over—and that's when his eyes light on me, his smile wide and squeezing my heart tight. He picks up pace and reaches me before I can finish a breath, flicking his hair again, his smile sending butterflies loose.

'Morning, sleepyhead.'

He presses his palms into the pool edge either side of me and lifts himself effortlessly to plant a kiss on my lips. Water drips from him onto the shirt, down its opening, over my thighs, my skin alive to every patter.

'Sleep well?'

He drops back and I lean over to stroke his jaw, his stubble teasing at my fingertips. 'Very...'

'Thought you might.'

His grin tells me he's reliving the night and my body heats.

'I could get used to seeing you in my clothing.'

His eyes trail hot and heavy down my body, exposed save for the single fastened button at my waist.

'What time do we need to leave?' I ask. I'm already thinking about delaying and joining him in the pool. The water looks so inviting, and as for its single occupant... *mmm...*

'After breakfast. The coffee should be ready.'

I stroke my feet up his sides and he rests his hands over my thighs, making no attempt to move.

'Are you wanting a swim?'

'I didn't bring my costume.'

His smile turns wicked. 'It would be a waste anyway.'

And then he's pulling me in, shirt and all, his lips gentle as they find mine, his fingers in my hair combing, caressing.

I sigh into his mouth. 'Your shirt will be ruined.'

'I'll buy another.'

His lips turn urgent as he pulls it apart, the button disappearing somewhere on the pool-bed, his hands rough on my body as he caresses every curve, my breasts, my nipples. He presses me back against the wall, his groan of need echoed in my own.

I slip my hand inside his shorts and he bucks into my fingers—obedient, eager. I pull him out and, weightless in the water, lift my legs around him, positioning him so he thrusts, hard, deep, my slickness making it so easy, so welcoming.

He leans back, his face taut with desire, and he cups my arse with one hand, his free hand coming to rest over my pelvis, his thumb dipping to caress my throbbing clit.

God, yes.

He's circling over me, moving in me, and I stretch my arms out over the poolside, holding myself steady for his every move. It's electrifying, with the warmth of the rising sun and the water lapping over my exposed breasts an added thrill, and I'm coming in seconds, wave after wave racking my body.

I cry out, his name bursting from me, loaded with everything I feel. *'Lucas...'*

Tears prick the backs of my eyes, happiness welling so fierce, and I hear him join me.

His *'Evangeline!'* tips the tears over and I reach out to hook my hands around his neck, pulling myself tight against him as he pulses within me.

I want to tell him I love him. I want to so much, but something stops me. The rejected eighteen-year-old girl still hanging on? Or the fear of going through the same all over again?

And then there's my family and the rift I've yet to fix. Their suspicion that his motives aren't as innocent as he's made out. But I can't believe that. I won't.

'I could get used to good mornings like this,' he murmurs against my hair, his fingers stroking my nape.

I nod. It's all I can manage.

'Ready for some breakfast now?'

I rub my face against his chest, hiding my tears before I look at him. I don't want him to question them. Because I *am* happy. In that moment I really am.

I can deal with the rest later.

'Absolutely.'

Breakfast is perfect. A selection of pastries, fresh fruit, juice and coffee. But it's the company that truly makes it: *him*.

And as we tour his business that day he's in his element. Hell, so am I.

What he's achieved isn't to be sniffed at. It's incredible. He's maximising the skilled workforce Singapore is renowned for, and not only that—he's keeping them. His staff turnover is lower than any competitor, and when I quiz him on his costs and how he manages it he has an answer for it all.

His *is* the right company for me to go into business with. He can give me everything I need to break out on my own. I wouldn't be beholden to him *or* my family. As far as business goes it would be all me. That part has nothing to do with sex, or love. It's about doing the right thing for the product, showing I can really *do* this.

We talk not only to his managers, but to his workers too. They show me the clean, comfortable housing the company provides, and they tell me about the subsidised bills and all the amenities, which include a park area for children, a sports centre, a nursery. They tell me how Waring Holdings puts other big corporations that function in the vicinity to shame, and how people come flocking to work here. They tell me how his company has effectively saved them—*saved* them.

It's crazy to believe it, but I've seen reports from other companies around the globe—the undercover news articles, the suicides. It's exactly what I was worried about when I flagged the human rights issues at him.

But now he's more than assured me of his ethics— he's made me fall in love with him all the more. He's not only given these people jobs, he's given them homes, good lives to live and enjoy. In return for their fantastically skilled work he's given them the respect of a fantastic working environment.

It's so perfect. So Lucas.

I think of his easy relationship with Maylene, of the mutual respect so evident between them, and the report he's given me on what his company can achieve. He's the right choice. I trust his company. I trust *him*.

By the time we arrive back at his home that night I am sold. And he knows it. I can see it in his grin as he pulls open the cupboard for wine glasses.

'Red? White? Or am I permitted champagne now?'

I shake my head with a laugh. 'I haven't agreed to anything.'

'Your face tells me all I need to know… Come on— admit it. You were impressed!'

My smile is fit to burst. 'Perhaps.'

'Champagne it is.' He takes out two glasses and hunts out a bottle. 'Let's take it to the roof—the view is amazing this time of night.'

The view is amazing right now...

He's so handsome in his charcoal-grey suit, with his white shirt now open at the collar, his tie undone. I could hook my fingers through the ends and pull him in...forget the champagne...

'Come on,' he says.

Spoilsport.

I let him lead the way up to the roof and then I get it. The view by night *is* spectacular and he wants me to see it—he's still trying to impress me.

He places the bottle and glasses on a low table beside one of the draped cabanas and strips off his jacket and tie, tossing them on the foot of the double bed beneath before sitting down at its edge.

'You going to stay there all night or are you going to join me?'

'In a bit...' I say it teasingly, but if I get on that bed there's no way I'm looking at the view.

Instead I walk around to the other side of the cabana and hook my arm around the pole at the end, my eyes on the glittering lights of Marina Bay, the Gardens and their futuristic bubbles. It really is a sight to behold.

And then music starts flooding the bay and lights dance.

'What is *that*?'

He gives me a grin as he lifts the bottle and starts to unwrap the foil. 'You'll see.'

I look back out to the bay and see laser strobes hit the sky, coming from the ship-like rooftop of the structure across the water. They dance with the music, and the spectacular pods of what I know to be a shopping plaza below light up in tune, bouncing off the water. It's incredible, and I'm so transfixed I don't realise he's moved until he's alongside me, holding out a glass.

I take it blindly, not wanting to miss a second. 'Thank you.'

'A free light show…' He bends to my ear as he says it and a heated shiver travels up my spine. 'What more can you possibly want?'

'*Free?*' I laugh softly. 'You really are spoiling me.'

His return laugh is husky, low, and I bite into my lip.

'There'll be another one later,' he says. 'They're on every night. The tourists go crazy for it. I've had a place here for a year and I still try to catch it at least once when I visit.'

I sip at my drink, my eyes devouring the whole spectacle, my body alive with his proximity. I'd love to spend more time here—taking in the sights, being a tourist… There's a vibe that I just love. I want to 'do' Chinatown, explore the famous Botanic Gardens, enjoy a Singapore Sling at Raffles Hotel, relax…*with him*.

'I'd love to do the tourist thing.'

I feel his eyes on me. 'Next time we come we'll do just that.'

Next time we come…

I turn to him. Those words are there again but they catch in my throat. I wet my lips. 'Is that a promise, Lucas?'

He curves his hand around the back of my neck, stirring every excited nerve-ending.

'Yes.'

And then he kisses me and the world falls away.

Next time... There's going to be a next time... Oh, yes.

I've always loved this pad. The view, the location, the buzz. But lying here with Eva curled into my side, with the view outstretched before us, it truly is heaven on earth. As good as any paradise island or secluded hideaway.

'I wish we didn't have to leave in the morning.'

She toys with the buttons on my shirt as she says it, her contented sigh warming me through.

I trace circles over her bare shoulder and press a kiss to her head. 'Me too.'

'Thank you for all this.'

She looks up at me, her eyes dark in the soft white glow that comes from the decorative lighting cubes that line the terrace.

'What? For putting so much work into convincing you to go into business with me?' I grin. 'It seems a pretty selfish move, if you ask me.'

She digs me in the ribs and rolls on top of me. 'You know full well you didn't need to do all this.'

'Do I?'

'Yes, you could have documented all of it—in fact, if I dug a bit, I bet I'd find article after article about the fabulous Waring Holdings and its equally fabulous owner.'

'*Fabulous*, am I?'

Her smile turns shy and my heart blooms in my chest at her silent answer. She drops a kiss to my lips and folds her arms over my chest, her chin coming to rest upon them as she looks at me.

'Does that mean I have the job?' I ask.

I'm half joking, half serious. But she's all serious now, quiet, her eyes wavering over my face.

'I have people I've yet to see… It doesn't feel right, cancelling on them.'

'But why waste their time if you've decided?'

'Because they still deserve to be listened to and considered.'

'Are you saying that because you mean it or because you're worried about how your family will react?'

She presses herself off me and rolls onto her back, her eyes looking skyward. 'I'm not scared of them.'

She says the words, but there's an edge that I don't like.

I turn on my side and look down into her face. 'No?'

'I just don't want to hurt them or provoke them further.' Her eyes flick to me. 'I want to get this right—make them see what they did was wrong. But I can't push them out entirely. It's not fair on Mum, for starters, and for all they did wrong they're…they're still…'

'They're still your family.'

'Yes.' It's a whisper.

'So what will you tell them when the time comes? Because it will, Eva. You know as well as I do that our companies working together is the right move.'

I don't say the other thing I'm thinking: *We work, her and I...us.*

'The truth.'

'Which bit?' I test the water. 'The work or the per-sonal—*this*?'

'All of it.'

She nods her head emphatically, surprising me with her confidence.

'This deal gets me what I need. It buys them out of my business, and it buys me my total freedom. It's what I've wanted for so long—to be in control of my own destiny, my future, my company.' She pins me with her brilliant gaze. 'As for me and you...they have to see they've wronged you...' Her voice trails away, a frown marring her brow as her eyes narrow. 'Unless...'

Unease spreads like ice in my veins. 'Unless...?'

'Is there more to it?'

She's looking at me earnestly, searchingly.

'I just don't get it. They're good people, Mum and Dad. And Dad knows that Nate has his moments—well enough to suspect that what you told him was the truth—so why side with him?'

Why? I think about it. I think about what I told her. It's the truth—all of it.

Nate hated me for not stepping in, not saving his arse after he'd screwed up—again. I could've done, but

I didn't. Her father just protected his son…and to hell
with what was right, fair.

I rest my hand over her stomach, feel her warmth
seep into my palm. I lower my eyes to the touch and
use it to ward off the mounting chill.

'There's nothing to tell you that changes anything.
It happened just as I told you.'

She's quiet as she considers me, and then she shakes
her head and looks back to the view. 'I just don't get it…
Nate isn't a bad person deep down—he isn't. I wouldn't
look out for him if he wasn't.'

'You would. He's your brother.'

*Just as your father protected his son—his real son,
his blood.*

'No, I wouldn't—not if he didn't deserve it. He's un-
reliable, sure, and he messes up sometimes. He clearly
messed up with you. But he loved you, you were inseparable, and now… Now he—'

She breaks off, as if she can't even voice it.

'He hates me?'

She looks at me, her eyes stabbing me with their
pain, eyes that look so similar to Nate's in that moment, filled with the same blaze of hurt he wore the
last time I saw him.

'Yes.'

I don't really hear her. I'm transported back five
years. To that last argument…to his begging.

*'You owe us! You wouldn't be anything without our
money! You can save us. How can you refuse?'*

Their love shouldn't have been conditional. Mine

certainly wasn't. I thought I was loved. By Nate, by his parents. Eva. And look where it got me.

Shit. Don't tar her with the same brush.

I shut it all down and look at the view.

'Sorry,' she says. 'I know it's hard for you…the past. It's hard for me too—but we have to face it head-on if we're to get through this.'

My eyes fall to hers. 'And will we? Face this together when the time comes?'

She hooks her fingers through my hair, drawing me in. 'Yes. *Together.*'

She kisses me and all my doubts dissolve in the heat of her.

I trust her.

I love her.

And when the time is right I will tell her.

But not before she does what she says she will: confronts her family, Nate, and puts me first. Proves to me that *her* love has no conditions. Then I'll know for sure.

So, do you really trust her?

I groan with frustration, with need, as I kiss her hard, punishingly. I want to trust her—that's the point.

I tear my lips from her mouth and let my mouth travel to her throat. I nip her skin. 'I want you.'

It's as much as I can confess—as much as my heart and body will let me confess.

'I want you too.'

She forks her fingers through my hair, tugging me down, arching her body, her nipples already like marbles beneath her top.

I take one into my mouth, tease her through the fabric, drop my fingers to the apex of her thighs…

For now we have this, and I'm going to take it all. Tomorrow we'll return home and face it together. As one.

CHAPTER THIRTEEN

TUESDAY MORNING REALITY HITS—as it has to—only it's softened by the bed I wake up in: *his*.

The smell of fresh coffee greets me as I stroll into the kitchen and I know he's already gone. He warned me he had to be in Edinburgh early, for a meeting, that he would be away for a couple of days, but the fact he's set the coffee machine going in time for my wake-up call brings the goofiest of smiles to my face.

I could get used to this.

I know I have a huge ordeal ahead, breaking the news of us to my family, but it's the right thing. *We* are right. And the past has to be dealt with. Sooner rather than later. I want this Christmas to be special, I want Lucas in it.

I turn on the radio as I potter around the kitchen. Slade's 'Merry Xmas Everybody' fills the air and I'm dancing. Happy. Truly festive.

I am so convinced everything will be okay that I spend the next few days in a bubble.

By day I work, ticking off my back-to-back meetings as promised, sticking to my plan and being fair to all concerned.

By night I enjoy the countdown to Christmas. I hit the shops, I wrap presents, I decorate my mini-tree, bringing a much-needed pop of colour to the otherwise bland apartment, and I look forward to Friday. To seeing Lucas. My future. Our future.

I don't forget about Friday night's meal. I don't forget that Dad has promised to talk with Nate. I just have faith in my family to get things right this time.

It's Friday. Three days and three nights since I left her warm body in my bed. It feels like an eternity.

I've wanted to ring her—of course I have—but I also wanted to respect her decision to stick to her review process and the meetings she'd lined up.

I didn't want to mess with that.

I didn't want to appear desperate either.

I rake my fingers through my hair and take the stairs to her office, needing to burn off this incessant thrum of energy. I could put it down to excitement at seeing her again, but I know it's also nerves.

I hoped she'd call me, or at least email. But nothing.

And if I'm honest I'm scared she's changed her mind. About us, the business…all of it.

But it's time for our allotted meeting and she hasn't cancelled to avoid it, to avoid me. That has to count for something.

I get to her floor and her PA spies me before I'm across the room, her smile welcoming.

'Ah, Mr Waring, it's lovely to see you again.' She

steps out from behind her desk and offers her hand. 'Can I get you a coffee?'

I don't care what she gets me so long as I see Eva soon. I shake her hand with a nod. 'Thank you.'

She turns and leads the way to Eva's office; a gentle rap and she pokes her head through.

'Mr Waring is here.'

I can't make out Eva's response and I strain for it. Eager to hear her voice.

'You can go on through.'

She opens the door wider and I lose all sight of her as I seek out Eva.

'Lucas.'

She smiles and pushes up out of her seat to walk towards me, I meet her halfway and hear the door click shut as her PA leaves us.

She's a vision in pink again. This time a sleeveless dress that hugs her frame to the knee. Her hair is in a loose knot at her nape and silver snowflakes dangle from her ears. I itch to reach for one, to reach for *her*, to embrace her, to kiss her. A thousand wants and I can't even speak as I try to keep them contained.

She pinches the corner of her bottom lip with her teeth, hesitant, but her eyes are alive. 'Are you okay?'

'I'm just absorbing my first sight of you in three days.'

She laughs softly. 'Well, in that case, absorb away.'

She gives a little twirl and I'm undone. My hand reaches to cup her waist and pull her into me, my lips find hers.

She feels so good, sounds so good as her startled little whimper ripples through her throat and her hands grip me hard, needy. Her mouth, her tongue—every bit the same. It's intense and wild, and I realise with startling clarity that I could make love to her now, so easily, and her PA is returning with coffee.

Dammit.

I set her away from me, dragging air into my lungs. 'Your PA is bringing me coffee.'

Her fingers tremble as she touches her lips, her confused frown *so* fucking adorable.

'Coffee?'

'I may have agreed to have some.'

Her lips curve upwards, her eyes dance. 'So you're saving her from a scene?'

'Something like that.'

Heat streaks my cheeks and I'm not sure whether it's an alien sheepishness that does it or the lust still raging inside me, but the rap at the door is well-timed.

She smooths her dress out—it already looks perfect—and calls, 'Come in.'

'Here we go—two coffees and some festive treats.' Her PA places a tray on the desk and turns to leave. 'You know where I am if you need anything else.'

Her smile encompasses us both before she leaves, and I get the sneaking suspicion she knows exactly what was going down seconds before.

'She's a smart one.'

'If you mean she's got us pegged, then I'd say you're right.'

She returns to her desk and lifts a mug, places it on a mat before the visitor's chair, a mince pie following suit.

'Why don't we get business out of the way before we…er…?'

'Get carried away again?'

I'm grinning at her, high on her response to me, on what it means for us and the future. Everything is within reach. Everything that matters at least. Her suggestive smile across the desk tells me so.

I feel like I'm rushing to the end of our talk just to get back to where we were when Lucas first arrived.

I've told him I want to work with him. I've told him I've rejected the other offers. I've also made sure he understands it wasn't a simple choice to make—that he did have tough competition despite his claims and his report. Rosalie at Janus Industries, in the main. I liked her, and her offer was almost comparable—*almost*.

And there had been a moment's hesitation when I'd acknowledged to myself that going into business with her would be simpler…that the complication of loving and working with Lucas did go against him. But ultimately I fell in love with the way his business operates too.

'So we're agreed?' he says.

'I think so.'

I rise out of my seat and he follows suit, his eyes fixed on me. My pulse starts to race and I press my palms into the skirt of my dress, moisten my lips.

'So we're done with work?'

I nod. I want to race to him, but I force my pace to slow, my fingers trailing along the desk-edge as I approach him.

He turns to face me, his gaze flitting between my mouth and my eyes, dark, hungry. I reach out and wrap my fingers through the tail end of his tie, wrap and wrap until I'm almost to the knot, and then I pull him down to me.

Yes. No interruptions...no nothing now. This is all about us.

Our lips meet, soft, savouring, sampling. It's blissfully sweet. A moment's reacquaintance before all hell breaks loose with the sweet invasion of his tongue. My insides soar and his hands turn rough, pulling me against him as my grip over his tie tightens.

'I've missed you,' he says against my lips, his hands raking up and down over me.

'I've missed you too.'

He groans at my words, his fingers hooking under the hem of my dress, his palms on my skin, hot and urgent as he forces my dress up. It's at my hips when he lifts me, swinging me onto the desk, his mouth not once releasing me, his tongue delving deeper, driving me to fever pitch.

I wrap my legs around him, breaking our kiss long enough to take hold of his zipper, to ease it down. He's so hard as I draw him out, and my body contracts on a ripple of lustful heat.

'What the actual fuck?'

We freeze. Our heads turn to the door—

Nate!

His seething form fills the doorway.

Fuck.

I shove Lucas back, leaving him to yank his zipper up as I launch to my feet.

My brother looks as if he's about to commit murder.

'I fucking *knew* it.' He strides forward, slamming the door shut behind him, his fist raised. 'You son of a bitch.'

I watch in horror as he swings for Lucas, and then I throw myself forward.

I see a brief second of panic in my brother's face before his fist collides with my face. And then all I feel is pain—acute, throbbing pain—and my ears ring.

I'm on my knees, shaking my head, trying to focus, to get a handle on what's happening.

I can hear scuffling above me.

'See what you made me do!'

My brother is shouting, shoving Lucas back. I try to tell them to stop but I can't make my mouth work.

'I didn't make you do anything,' Lucas says. 'Now back off so I can check she's okay.'

'You've touched her enough, you sick fuck—taking your revenge out on someone too stupid to see it.'

I know what's going to happen even before Lucas's fist makes perfect contact with my brother's jaw, and inside I die.

This is wrong.

All wrong.

I don't want to believe it's happening.

Nate drops to the floor as Lucas rushes to my side and tries to lift me. *No.* I shake him off. Tears that I hadn't known I was shedding sting my cheeks.

'Don't touch me.'

I can't even look at him. Either of them.

It's a mess. A complete and utter mess.

'Get out,' I say, struggling to my knees. My lip smarts…it feels too big for my face. 'Both of you.'

The command is muffled and my cheeks flame in shame, pain, anger.

'But, Eva…' Lucas says softly, his hands hovering over me, not touching, but still there.

I shake my head again, putting the force that I can't give to my voice into action. I turn away from him. 'Get out.'

'Sis, come on.'

'Out! Out! *Out!*'

I stare at them both, my body rigid, and I almost lose it all over again when neither moves. I can't cope with the concern on Lucas's face, the anger and the swelling already building on Nate's, the throbbing pain radiating through my own. It's a real-life nightmare.

Lucas lets go of a ragged breath. 'Okay.' He looks at Nate, his disgust, his hatred, clear as day, and then he shakes his head and makes for the door.

'And don't fucking come back!' my brother throws at him.

I want to shout, to tell him to shut up, but I'm frozen in their hate.

Lucas looks to me for something—anything—but I'm trance-like.

And then he's gone.

'Good riddance,' Nate mutters, rubbing at his jaw.

Slowly, I turn, taking him in. Replaying it all. *'Stupid'* was what he called me. *Stupid.* After everything I've done for him these last few years. Everything he did to bring this raining down on us.

'Stupid…?'

My voice trembles over the simple word. White-hot anger laces every syllable.

He looks to me now, his eyes landing on my lip. 'Shit, Eva—I'm so sorry.'

He moves towards me and I raise my hand to stop him. 'Sorry for hitting me or for referring to me as stupid?'

I know that's what made Lucas snap—he was coming to my defence. It should make me happy. Instead I'm terrified. Terrified of the hatred that filled the room, the hatred between the two people I love. My worst fear coming to fruition.

He shakes his head and looks to the floor, appearing more like a teenager than the thirty-one-year-old he's supposed to be.

'I flipped out. I'm sorry. Seeing you, my little sister…' He raises his eyes to me, his shoulders bunching. 'And him…like that. I mean, for fuck's sake, Eva, you were about to let him screw you over your desk. *Him.*'

I'm still and controlled as I say, 'Who I sleep with is none of your business.'

'It is when it's him, and you know it.'

'Bollocks, Nate. *You* were the one who went behind his back and totally stuffed the company—him included.'

He stares at me, wide-eyed.

'Yes, he told me. He didn't want to. He said I should come to you, make you explain.' My smile is bitter, tight. 'Would you have admitted it if I had, though?'

'Eva—'

He breaks off and I wonder if he's going to lie some more. I can't bear it if he does.

'Look… I made a bad decision, okay? I know that, and I've regretted it ever since, but has he told you the whole story?'

My eyes narrow, a sudden chill making my skin prickle. I wrap my arms around my middle and remind myself that I trust Lucas. *I do.*

'What else is there?'

'He could have saved us, Eva—the whole business. He'd been investing for years on the side. How do you think he got so huge so quickly? He'd been stockpiling money…building up his own funds.'

I swallow. 'Stealing from the company?'

Nate snorts. 'As if! Lucas would never sink that low.'

Relief swamps me and my knees weaken. I plant my hands on the desk. The swell of nausea sudden and disorientating. 'Then what?'

'Don't you see? He was already loaded when the company lost it all.'

'When *you* lost it all.'

'Whatever…' he blurts, brushing off my point. 'I pleaded with him to reinvest. To take his private money and pump it in so we could get back on our feet, keep going, keep working together. We were supposed to be a *team*.'

I laugh—I can't help it. 'Don't you see the irony in that?'

His eyes flicker, pained, vulnerable, and I know he does.

'But he was like my *brother*, Eva, and I begged him—fucking *begged* him.' His voice shakes over the confession. 'And do you know what he said?'

His eyes stare at me accusingly. As if he's seeing Lucas, not me.

'No. Fucking *no*. Can you believe it? After all our family had done for him...all the money Dad had ploughed into the business from the start... He'd be nothing without us—*nothing*.'

'But you betrayed him, and then you lied about it to us all. How could he trust you after that?'

He shakes his head at me. 'You don't *get* it! I even offered to hand over enough shares to give him the majority, put him fully in the driving seat—that should have negated his trust issues. But did he care? Did he *fuck*.'

He forks his hands through his hair and starts to pace.

'I didn't know what to do. The look in Dad's eye when I told him...the disappointment... I couldn't stomach it.'

'So you threw Lucas under the bus instead?'

My tone is low, my eyes unforgiving as I watch him flounder. I can see the anger giving way to guilt, remorse, and it's what I'm hoping for.

'It was *our* company, *our* baby, and he gave up on it—we lost it all.'

'*You* lost it all.'

He looks at me, almost desperate. 'Will you drop the whole "you", "we" shit? What does it matter when it was one and the same company?'

'It makes a world of difference, Nate, and you know it.'

My jaw is throbbing like mad, and it hurts to speak, but I can't let this slide. If Lucas and I are to see a way through this I have to make my family acknowledge that they wronged him. And it needs to start with Nate.

'Just admit it.'

'Why? Because you want to get your end away—?'

The door swings open—no knock, no nothing—and in strides my father.

Jesus, could this day get any better?

'Eva, what the hell is—?'

He breaks off, his eyes landing on me—or more specifically on my flaming lip—and his skin pales as the door closes behind him.

'What happened?'

He softens his stride as he walks towards me, his eyes narrowing over the damage.

'Did Lucas—?'

My entire body flares as I back away from him. 'Don't you *dare* accuse Lucas of this.'

'Then who?'

'Why don't you look to your son—the guy who's to blame for this whole goddamn mess?'

He looks from me to Nate for the first time and his cheeks flood red. 'You struck your sister?'

'He was aiming for Lucas,' I rush out. 'I just got in the way.'

'And that?' He points to the swelling on Nate's jaw.

'Lucas—coming to my defence.'

He shakes his head, disbelieving. 'Is this really what we've come to? Fist fights in the office?'

'Don't you dare get high and mighty, Dad,' I say to him. 'You're not innocent in all of this either.'

He frowns with surprise. 'What does *that* mean?'

'All this hatred towards a man who did nothing wrong, Dad—*nothing*. You should've known—you should've seen through Nate's lies and sorted this mess out long ago, before Lucas lost everything.'

'The man is *loaded*, Eva,' Nate scoffs. 'He hardly lost everything.'

'He lost *us*, Nate—*us*. The only real family he's ever known. How the hell can't you *see* that?'

He stares, dumbstruck, then looks from me to Dad, as if our father will say something to ease the sting of my words. But instead he takes a shaky breath and suddenly seems to age before me. I can see my words sinking in, can feel the weight of them in the air.

Nate gives an awkward laugh. 'Oh, come on— the guy is doing fine. He always lands on his feet. Turns out he never needed us—not really. The man's invincible...'

He says the words but there's no power behind them.

'That's not true, son.'

My father's soft-spoken remark stuns me.

'Eva's right.'

'But…come on…look at him. He's loaded—a billionaire. What do we have that he could possibly think he's missing out on?'

I flip. 'Are you for *real*? You should be running after him, begging his forgiveness.'

'Like hell!' he erupts, staring at us both in disbelief. 'He bailed on *me*.'

'You know what?' I say. 'I used to think it was the shock of Lucas going that left you so broken, always coming to me for help, advice, support. Now I realise he'd probably been covering for you for years—and I ended up doing the same.'

'Hey, easy, honey…'

Dad steps forward, wanting to calm me, but I'm on a roll now. Five years of watching over Nate, coming to a head.

'Don't "easy" me. We were the closest thing to family he had and we turned our backs on him.'

'He turned his back on us first.'

It's Nate who speaks, and I want to swing for him, but my legs are like lead, keeping me rooted, and instead I twist on the spot to glare at him.

'It's true, isn't it? It wasn't the first time you'd messed up?'

Nate hunches forward, back in teenage mode, but his downcast eyes are admission enough.

My hands soar to the air as I fling them towards him and look to Dad. 'You *see*?'

'Yes, honey, I see. But this isn't helping. Why don't you just take up Janus Industries' offer and then we'll see what we can do about addressing the past—it's a separate issue.'

'*What?*'

'Rosalie's offer,' he says, focusing on the work, the business, and making my head spin at the change in focus. 'Your brother called me—told me she'd been in touch to say you'd rejected her offer, that you'd decided on Waring—'

'Yes, *I* decided, Dad! No one else. *Christ*, is that why you're both here? To tell me what to do?'

'Not tell you, just—'

'Get out.'

'Evangeline, take a breath…calm down.'

'Don't speak to me like I'm a child, Dad.'

'I'm—'

'Go.'

'Look, sis…' Nate tries.

'Don't you "sis" me.' I round on him. 'Until you can bring yourself to apologise to Lucas I don't want to speak to you.'

'Come off it—we've a family dinner tonight.'

I laugh over him. 'Tell Mum I can't make it.'

'Eva—?'

Now it's Dad who speaks.

'What? You'd rather I came and explained the fat lip to her?'

They both flinch.

'No, I didn't think so… I could always lie, I suppose.

It seems we're awfully good at that. Did you *really* believe the tale Nate spun, Dad?'

They look at one another, their open shame enough of an answer.

'How could you take away the only real family he ever knew?'

I shake my head. I still can't understand it. I just know I need them gone.

'I'll tell Mum I'm sick.'

'Eva—'

My dad reaches for me but I back away. The last thing I need is a hug right now—not from him. I need Lucas.

My rejection seems to do the trick and together they walk out. My brother is pulling the door closed when he stops.

'What?' I blurt.

'For what it's worth,' he says, looking at his hand on the handle and then back to me, 'I *am* sorry. I know I've done wrong, but I never wanted you caught in the middle like this.'

And then he's gone.

A heavy silence descends and I'm immobilised. Then I start to shiver. Delayed shock, I suppose. I touch my lip and realise I need ice on it before it truly does balloon and I have to avoid both Mum and all meetings well into next year.

I lift my phone and call Clare. She doesn't hesitate at my random request. My guess is that, having seen Nate, she has a fair idea what I want it for. She probably thinks I lamped him.

If only.

I drop into my chair and hug my middle, trying to ease the shakes.

I need to call Lucas, but I need to have this under control first.

I go straight to my apartment. I don't call into the office on the way. I'm in no mood to see anything but the bottom of a whisky bottle.

She kicked me out. *Me.*

Yeah, I totally get that she's upset—but, Christ, she needed to be taken care of, not left alone with that bastard.

I pour a double and take both the bottle and the glass into the living room, dropping onto the sofa and yanking my tie loose. The memory comes of her taking hold of it earlier, the look of passion and joy in her face…

My hand tightens around the glass and I throw back a mouthful, needing its burn.

Seeing her brother like that, hearing him speak about her like he did, the venom in his voice when he spoke to me.

Fuck.

I hunch forward, my elbows on my knees as I stare down into the amber liquid. It's never going to work. So long as they're around her, *we* will never work.

The way she looked between us both, her confusion, her torment… Who does she care about more? It all played out on her face as plain as day. I'm losing her. I can feel it. And my stomach twists, an ice-cold sweat prickling over my skin.

But we have a business arrangement. She told me that much. It's my one hope to keep her.

Hardly.

She can easily work directly with Maylene and the team in Singapore—she'll expect to. No CEO is going to get involved in the day-to-day. She won't need to interact with me. There'll be no contact.

Christ.

I need to think. Fast.

I know she wants the money to buy her family out of her business. She won't be able to do it immediately— she'll need income first.

But if she *had* the money it would be *Bye-bye, Beaumonts...*

Bye-bye, Beaumonts, and Hello, Waring?

I neck the remainder of my glass and toss the idea around.

I'll make it a condition of the contract. She uses my upfront investment to buy them out and bring me in.

She doesn't have to choose anything on a personal level. It's perfect.

Better than any fist to the face, Nate.

CHAPTER FOURTEEN

AT LEAST TWO hours have gone by since Nate and my father left and I'm hiding out in my office, waiting for the last employee to leave before I venture out. It was bad enough seeing Clare's face when she saw the state of me—I couldn't stand the entire floor gossiping. I've never been so thankful for the small en suite bathroom I have adjacent to my office.

And the mini-fridge.

I take out a cold beer and pop it open, wincing as I press it to my lips.

What a day.

Mum has already texted me back, telling me she hopes I feel better soon. Nate has texted me, too, to say he's sorry again—but it's not me he should be telling—and Dad has asked that I go easy on my brother… It's Christmas after all.

Go easy? Like hell. And I'm angry at him too. Angry because he should have seen the truth. He should have sided with Lucas and made Nate take responsibility for his actions.

What? Like you did when the fight broke out?

I squeeze my eyes tight against the memory. I hardly sided with Lucas. In fact I tried to kick them both out. The heat of the moment and divided loyalties made it impossible to think straight. Maybe it was similar for Dad.

But Lucas did no wrong. In either case.

I drop into my chair and take up my mobile. It's time I called him—screw my nerves… I need him, and I need to apologise.

I dial his number and he picks up in two rings.

'Evangeline.'

His voice is gruff, as if he's been drinking, and my heart squeezes in my chest. 'Hi…' I swallow past the wedge forming in my throat. 'I'm sorry I kicked you out.'

His breath shudders down the phone. 'I guess I can't blame you after that showdown.'

'No… Dad arrived after you left.'

'He did?'

'Yeah…' I trail off, working out how to phrase what I want to ask and realise I just need to come out with it. 'Why didn't you tell me Nate asked you to plough your own money into the business?'

'He brought that up, did he?'

'You could have told me.'

'It doesn't really change anything.'

'It does to Nate.'

'You sound like you agree with him.'

'No!' I rush out, hating his defensive tone.

'Look, I couldn't do it. I couldn't trust him not to lose it again. Every time something happened he'd always throw your family's investment at me—tell me

I'd be nowhere without them. He was so quick to lay that on me, so quick to remind me that I'm an outsider, not one of you. Let's face it, I was never going to be free of that guilt trip. I knew I'd always be beholden no matter what happened.'

'You don't need to defend yourself to me, Lucas. I get it.'

And I do—my heart swells for him and all he's been through. All he went through today too—for which I'm partly to blame.

'How's your hand?'

He gives a hoarse laugh. 'I can land a punch just fine. More importantly, how's your face?'

I can hear his concern and it makes me want to cry. Tears burn the back of my throat. I wish he was here with me. I should've driven to his place rather than hidden like this.

'Eva?'

'It's fine—or it will be soon enough.'

'You shouldn't have got involved. When you went down like that—'

He breaks off, his breath shuddering once more.

'Well, next time I promise to stay well clear—you're on your own.'

I'm trying to make light of it, lift the mood, but he's quiet. His silence is unsettling, and I can feel his hatred towards Nate all the way down the line.

'Look, he wasn't seeing straight,' I say. 'Catching us like that had him completely knocked for six.'

'You're making excuses for him again?'

'In this case it's justified. But as far as business goes, and the past, he's on his own—no more cleaning up after him.'

'Good.'

The line goes quiet again. The question burning to get out: *Does he still want there to be an 'us'?* But I'm scared. It doesn't matter that he has hinted strongly at a future—that was before the showdown with my brother, before I fell apart in front of them both.

'Lucas?' I say.

'Eva?' he says at the same time.

Hope sparks within me. 'You go first.'

'I want to amend our agreement.'

His words are clear as day, businesslike, and I struggle to shift gear, from personal to professional.

'What do you mean?'

'You want your family out of your company, yes?'

'You know I do.'

'Well, that works for me too, clearly.'

'My intention is to buy them out as soon as my sales revenue is big enough. It shouldn't take—'

'I want to give you the money now. So you can do it upfront.'

I shake my head. 'Look if you're worried about them interfering, they wouldn't dare.'

'What? Like your brother just didn't dare?'

Before I can speak he carries on.

'I'm not taking any chances.'

I hesitate. 'Okay...'

'But I want something in return.'

So many things stream through my mind, and hope is rising with every one.

I want us. I want you. I want you to tell your family we're together, that there's no getting between us.

'What is it that you want?'

'I want in.'

I frown, a cold tremor running down my spine as I straighten. 'You want *in*?'

'The twenty-five per cent share they currently have—I want it. We can come up with a gradual repayment of the shares over time—say a couple of years, which I imagine isn't too dissimilar to your current plan—but...'

'Back up, Lucas.' I struggle to draw breath, disappointment making my lungs contract. I can't believe what he's saying. What he's focusing on. 'Are you telling me you want me to replace my family with *you*?'

'If you want to look at it that way, then, yes. I don't want them anywhere near our arrangement going forward.'

It's all about revenge.

That's what they said and I didn't believe it. But then why was he so determined to push them out? Why insist on their share? Unless there's some truth to it?

And what about all I had told him about making it my own? Being beholden to no one. Did he not care about any of that? Him of all people...

'You told me this wasn't about revenge...you told me this was about wanting my product.'

'And it *is*, Eva.'

'Then why ask for a share? Why make me choose between my family and you?'

'Don't you see? I'm trying to avoid exactly that. There's no need for personal attachment on the surface. Your family can't resent you for making a sound business decision, and what goes on behind closed doors is our business.'

This just gets worse. Does he really want to dismiss us as some kind of fling? A dirty little secret?

'Oh, my God, Lucas—you *really* think that's the solution?'

'I don't know, Eva. I just know I can't face seeing you hurt like you were today.'

'There are other ways.'

'Name one?'

Being honest and open about our relationship, our love.

But what if it isn't love for him? What if after all he has said he doesn't feel the same way?

I can't bring myself to ask. I can't be that eighteen-year-old, wearing her heart on her sleeve again only to have it thrown back in her face.

Instead I ask a question just as revealing. 'So tell me, Lucas, if I say no are you taking your offer off the table?'

Silence.

'Lucas?'

'Yes, Eva.' He sounds resigned. 'If you don't let me buy in, the offer is off the table.'

My ears ring, disbelief coursing wildly through my

blood. I feel trapped, backed into a corner by the man I love with all my heart.

Scrap not wanting to be my eighteen-year-old self. I *am* her. Humiliated and rejected in one fell swoop. Even worse, I feel manipulated, controlled—*by him*.

I look at the family photo that sits on my desk, the similarities between him and them as unbelievable as they are unbearable. And I laugh, the sound high-pitched and alien.

Well, no more. I won't be controlled or manipulated by either of them. Yes, Rosalie might have been referred by Nate and my father, but she can give me what I need.

Without this.

Without the heartache.

My chest pangs painfully and I grip the phone tighter. 'In that case you can shove your offer, Lucas.'

'Eva, don't be ridiculous.'

I can hear his shock and it gives me the strength I need to hold my ground. There'll be time for tears later.

'There's no need to fly off the handle,' he says.

'If you really believe that then you haven't listened to a word I've said over the past couple of weeks.'

'Seriously, Eva, don't do this. Take the offer...at least think about it.'

'I don't need to think about anything, Lucas. It's over. All of it. *Over.*'

I cut the line dead, my entire being thrumming.

I'm alone. Truly alone.

And now I let the tears fall.

Ten years and I'm still no wiser.

I only have myself to blame.

Give over, Eva, you are wiser!

The old me would have rolled over and taken what Lucas offered. I can at least be proud that I took control—of both him and my family. I held my ground and my product will have a home with Rosalie.

So why do I feel as if I've lost everything?

I stare at the phone as if it's magically going to start ringing again, and when it doesn't I don't know what to do.

I want to ring her back. Hell, I want to drive straight over and make her see sense.

Working together gives us a way through this. A way that doesn't make it personal.

But it is personal. You love her. You let Nate come between you ten years ago and now you've let him do the same again. You fool.

I toss the phone aside and reach for the bottle.

One more.

One more to numb this.

One more to make me think clearly.

I watch the liquid slosh into the glass and know I don't need to think any more clearly.

Because I love her, I can't take her from her family. For all I said I'd make her choose, when it came to it in that room I realised I couldn't.

My gut turns over. I lost her before, but back then I'd never really had her.

Now I have...

CHAPTER FIFTEEN

I'M OUT IN the garden, avoiding them, and they know it. But, hell, it's Christmas Day, my favourite day of the year. I'm supposed to be happy and instead sadness hangs around me like an aura.

I only have to walk into a room and everyone else catches it. Even my mother's usual festive beam is dialled down.

Granted, the fact that Nate and I still aren't speaking doesn't help. But Mum knows the true extent of my sadness. She guessed it for the most part—my age-old feelings for Lucas were obvious to her astute gaze, and the second she probed it all came rushing out, a week of keeping it to myself proving too much.

And I think she's told Dad. I can see it in the way he looks at me. But he hasn't said a word to acknowledge it. It's driving me crazy, but I don't feel strong enough to have it out with him. I feel broken. Torn in two. And to what end?

It's not as if Lucas loved me back.

There's a whimper at my feet and I look down to see

my parents' Golden Lab, Frodo, staring up at me, his ears back.

'I know, kiddo. Sucks, doesn't it?'

I tickle his head and look out across the lawn. It's pretty out here. It's nearly lunchtime and the frost hasn't lifted so everywhere is crisp and white. Almost as festive as snow itself.

I breathe in fresh air and let it seep out in a puff of white. I'll have to go back in soon. I can't avoid them for ever.

'Eva?'

I turn. Mum's hanging out of the kitchen doorway.

'Could you give me a hand with the potatoes, love?'

I give a soft sigh and whisper, 'Time's up, Frodo.' Then I call back, 'Sure!' and start towards her, Frodo trotting in step beside me.

The festive favourite 'White Christmas' leaks through the gap she leaves in the door and my heart squeezes.

You've only yourself to blame, giving your heart away a second time.

'I thought Nate was on potato duty?' I say as I enter the kitchen and strip off my coat.

She's pulling the turkey out of the oven. Its scent fills the room, warm and inviting. But still my insides fail to smile.

'I've sent him to talk with your father.'

'Talk?' I pull open the larder door and root around for the potatoes. 'Sounds ominous.'

'They need their heads knocking together. I've sim-ply led the way.'

'*Mum*, what have you said?'

'Only what needed saying.'

'Which is…?'

'Never mind that—you just focus on those potatoes and leave their foolishness to me.'

She's basting the turkey, her manner brooking no argument. Not that I have the energy for one.

'And smile, please, Eva. It's Christmas and I have faith that all will be well again soon.'

I lug the heavy sack of spuds on to the side and swing the larder door shut, wishing I had her confidence. But then she isn't the one with the broken heart.

'Right, how many do you need?'

Mum goes about giving instructions and I do as she asks, my smile forced and firmly planted. I even start to sing with her. Nothing like a good Christmas tune to get you in the mood.

Not that I am—not at all.

But I'm trying. I really am.

'I think you've peeled more than enough, love.'

'Huh?' I look at her and see her frown, full of con-cern. I look back to the peeled potatoes, far in excess of the twenty she requested. *Oh, dear.*

'You always tell me it's better to have too many than too few,' I force out jovially. 'And there's always bubble and squeak tomorrow, right?'

'True.' She gives me a smile that I know says *It'll be okay* and goes back to her turkey.

I go back to peeling the spuds. And then stop. *No more potatoes.*

If only I could stop loving Lucas as easy.

But if ten years without him didn't work, why will the future be any different?

Dusk is settling as I pull up outside the house I once called home. It's set back from the road, its private drive bordered by trees and old-fashioned lamps, their soft glow lighting up the well-maintained garden. Well-maintained and just the same as it was the last time I was here...

Five years ago.

The night I realised I was no longer welcome.

And yet you're here now.

I drop my eyes to the steering wheel, to my knuckles that are white as I grip it tight. Maybe this isn't a good idea. It's Christmas. A day for families. A day for the Beaumonts. Not me, the outsider.

My eyes drift to the house, to the bedroom window top right—Eva's room. As if by magic her light comes on. I can vaguely make out someone moving around and then the curtains are drawn and a silhouette remains— *Eva?*

I'm no longer thinking. I'm getting out of the car and walking up the drive, my eyes fixed on that shadow, my body following my heart.

It's time I gave her the choice.

Time I wore my heart on my sleeve and took a chance.

I can feel no worse than I do already. Because I am nothing without her. Life has no meaning without her in it.

I need her to know that. I need her to know it's not her product, it's not her family, it's *her* that I want, that I love.

What the Beaumonts do with that is up to them.

I only care what Eva does.

I sit next to Nate, and Mum and Dad sit across from us. The table is fit to burst, with elaborate candelabra stuffed with holly, baubles, berries and pinecones— I spent several distracted hours making them—and a feast that could feed the entire village.

But no one is eating. No one is speaking.

If not for Frodo's intermittent whine for food and the gentle hum of Christmas carols playing it would be as quiet as a morgue.

I look to Mum, to the concern bright in her eyes, and guilt swamps me. I try for a smile. 'This looks lovely. Thanks, Mum.'

She doesn't seem to hear me. Instead she looks to Nate, and then to my father.

'Right, you two—out with it. I'm not having Eva force herself to get through dinner without hearing from you first.'

Dad looks at Nate, and I sense my brother shift in his seat.

'I've said I'm sorry…to her…to Dad…'

'And…?' Mum presses.

'And I *will* apologise to Lucas too. I *am* sorry for what I did. I just assumed he'd be okay. I mean…he's Lucas. He was always okay.'

He shrugs awkwardly, his smile filled with remorse as he looks to me for forgiveness.

'I need you to understand that, sis. I was hurt when he wouldn't help me, and I lashed out. I lied, and I'm sorry… I guess I was always a little envious of how good he was at everything, and too selfish to care about the consequences.'

I hear what he's saying, and I can read that he means it too, and my heart lifts a little. But it doesn't change how things have worked out. It doesn't change how Lucas feels for me.

'And you, David?' My mother turns to my father. 'What do *you* have to say?'

He clears his throat. 'I'll go with Nate. I'll make sure Lucas realises that we were in the wrong, and that you shouldn't be tainted by this, Eva. If you want to work with him—'

Mum elbows him none too subtly in the ribs and he clears his throat again.

'If you want to *be* with him, then you have our blessing.'

I want to cry and laugh at once. So much, too late. 'Thanks, Dad, I appreciate it.'

'Good.'

'But you don't need to worry. I've decided to sign with Rosalie.'

My father's frown is immediate, as is my brother's.

'Why?'

My throat clogs as my vision blurs, and I try to swallow, to force it back. I can't bring myself to say that it's over between Lucas and I. All of it—over.

'Sis…?'

Nate's voice is soft, his hand on my shoulder aimed to soothe, and I shake my head. My fingers tremble as I press them to my lips.

'He's gone… He's gone and he's not coming back.'

'But—'

My father's voice is drowned out by the ancient doorbell chiming through the house and Frodo's bark. Everyone looks in the direction of the hall, momentarily frozen, and it's my mother who comes alive first, standing and brushing off her skirt.

'How's that for timing?'

She bustles out, Frodo on her tail, but she's hardly gone a second before her voice reaches us.

'Eva, darling, you have a visitor.'

A visitor? On Christmas Day?

There's only one person I'd dare hope would turn up.

'Don't keep him waiting,' my father urges.

I rise up and head out into the hallway on autopilot. Mum is at the front door. Frodo is on his hind legs, fussing over my visitor.

Over—*Lucas*.

My heart leaps inside my chest, and my footing falters just as his eyes meet mine.

'Ah, there she is,' says Mum, turning to face me, her smile one of beaming encouragement as she leaves

Lucas and walks towards me. 'Come on, Frodo, let's get you some turkey.'

She gives my arm a gentle squeeze as she passes, but I'm barely aware of the contact as I drown in his gaze, forcing my legs to close the distance between us.

'What are you doing here?' I manage to say.

'Isn't it obvious, Evangeline?'

The sound of my name from his lips runs through me, comforting as honey. Is he really here? Is this some sick joke? Some weird dream that I'm going to wake up from any second?

'The last time we spoke you wanted my product with a bit of fun on the side.'

He cringes, his fists flexing at his sides. 'I couldn't care less about the product.'

I scoff—I can't help it—but it dies at the sincere look in his eyes. They're swimming. Or is it only mine that are? Making it impossible to focus clearly?

'Sorry—of course I *care* about your product, and Janus Industries will do an amazing job, I'm sure, but what I mean is… What I'm here for is… Hell, I love you, Evangeline.'

He reaches for me, his hands cupping my arms, his touch as real and as warming as his words.

He loves me…he truly loves me.

My head spins as I blink through the tears and see the passion, the love, in his warm brown gaze.

'I've loved you for far too many years to count,' he says softly. 'I wish I'd just come out and told you, but I was scared. Scared to take that leap…scared of putting you in the middle, making you choose and having you regret it.'

I shake my head. 'I'd never regret *you*.'

He groans and pulls me against him, his hug so tight I'm winded, and then his hands are in my hair, he's tilting my head up to meet him, and his lips are on mine, crushingly sweet.

I kiss him back, but it's not enough. I am finally free to say the words that have been burning through me for so long. No more fear. No more doubt.

I pull away, my hands framing his face as I look up into his eyes. 'I love you too.'

His grin is long and slow, and his eyes are moving over my face as though he's reading my sincerity, and then he breaks away, his voice soft as he says, 'I'm so glad you said that because…' He rummages in his pocket. 'I have something for you.'

'You bought me a present? But I haven't—'

I look down as he raises his hand. On his palm rests a small red box.

A small red ring box.

My lips part on a rush and my eyes lift to his, wide and questioning. 'Lucas…?'

'You're all the family I could ever want—you, me… kids if we so desire. I don't know how we navigate this with your family, but I know this is the right place to start. By giving you the choice.'

I watch as he drops to one knee on the weathered coir mat, his eyes not once leaving mine. I press my fingers to my lips, keeping back the sob that threatens. I don't want to break this moment.

He opens the box and inside is the most beautiful pink diamond ring—*pink*.

'Is it—?' I break off. It can't be. And yet I know that it is. This is Lucas.

'It's an Argyle Pink Diamond. It seemed very…you.'

My laugh is soft and shaky. 'It's exquisite.'

'So are you.' He blinks up at me once, twice. 'Will you marry me, Evangeline Beaumont?'

I am trembling. My head is shaking. My eighteen-year-old self is dancing like crazy inside.

'No?' He frowns, panic creasing his forehead, his hand dropping just a little. 'I'll work hard to make amends with your father…your brother. I'll do everything I can—'

'Shh…' I drop my hand to his lips, silencing him, laughter bubbling through the tears. 'Yes, I'll marry you—*yes!* Now, hurry and put that ring where it belongs and maybe I'll believe this is real.'

'Oh, it's real, all right.'

His grin is so wide, so happy, as he does as he's told, sliding the ring in place.

'If it doesn't fit I can—'

'It's perfect!'

I give my finger a little wiggle, watching the diamond catch the light in the porch, and then I start to sob and laugh all at once. I drop to my knees, flinging my hands around his neck, and kiss him hard, every ounce of excitement, happiness and love poured into it.

He breaks away first. His skin is delightfully flushed, his eyes bright.

'Merry Christmas, wife-to-be.'

Evangeline. Wife-to-be. The words work the same magic and my heart flutters and swells with sheer joy.

'Merry Christmas, Lucas.'

EPILOGUE

Christmas Day, one year later

'Mum, will you stop flapping? Dinner is going to be great.'

'But she's a chef—a celebrity chef—what if it's awful?'

I laugh. I can't help it. Ever since Nate brought home his new girlfriend, Florence, six months ago, Mum has gone into panic mode, not wanting to scare the woman off.

Not that I blame her. Florence has been great for Nate. He'd come a long way since he and Lucas cleared the air, and then he met Florence and the transformation was complete.

Mum looks at me as if she's going to tape my mouth shut. 'Really? You think laughter is going to help right now?'

I take pity and give her a quick squeeze. 'Mum, how many Christmas dinners have you cooked?'

'Too many to count.'

'And how many have gone wrong?'

She frowns. 'Too many to count.'

Okay, bad choice.

'Sorry to disturb the private party.'

Lucas appears in the kitchen doorway—my incredibly handsome saviour.

'But your dad's breaking out the champagne and itching to do a toast.'

He looks at me pointedly and a small smile lifts my lips as we share a silent exchange.

'Come on, Mum. Champagne will make everything better.'

We coax her into the living room just as Dad pops the cork and begins to pour.

I take in the entire scene. Everyone is happy, content— even Frodo is asleep in front of the fire—and I know it's about to get better. Inside my heart swells and Lucas wraps his arm around me as Dad starts to fill the last flute.

'Just a small one for me, Dad.'

He stops pouring and they all look at me, concern flaring. My smile grows. I look up at Lucas, search his deep brown gaze and share my elation with him.

'We have some news.'

The room falls silent. Everyone is waiting and I let Lucas finish it for me.

'We're pregnant.'

Mum gives a dizzying squeal. The men chortle. Congratulations stream through the air as Dad hands out the glasses and gives me my mini-one with a kiss to the cheek.

Nate comes up to us, patting Lucas on the back before giving me a hug. 'I'm so happy for you both.'

'Thank you.'

I look up at Lucas. He knows what I'm going to say next and part of me wants that final nudge from him first. I get it in the form of a kiss to the forehead and a squeeze around the waist.

'That's not all,' I say, my eyes returning to Nate. 'I'm going to need someone to look after things while I'm out of action, and I can't think of anyone I'd rather have than you—if Dad can spare you, that is?'

Nate colours. His eyes blaze. 'For real, sis?'

He knows how much this means. It's the biggest statement I—*we*—could make to show that the past is long since buried.

'For real.'

'You've got it.'

He pulls Florence into his side and offers his glass to the room. 'To the Beaumonts, the Warings and the mini-Beaumont-Warings!'

Laughter fills the room and my tummy gives the smallest flutter, calling my hand to it. Lucas traces the move, his hand coming to rest over mine.

'To family,' I say, raising my glass.

And we all drink to that.

* * * * *

LOSING CONTROL

For my husband, I never had any control over my feelings for you, they just were.

Dublin will always have a special place in our hearts, as does the location of the ending, which marries with our own HEA.

Love always, Rachael xxx

PROLOGUE

THINGS YOU SHOULD know about me.

I don't do trust.

I don't do love.

I don't do family.

I am me and I stand alone.

I run a billion-dollar empire and nothing can shake it.

Nothing can shake me.

Only I'm standing here at a double funeral, my brother and father both dead, and my collar is too restrictive, my chest too tight.

I shouldn't care. Not when they pushed me out years ago. Took all that mattered to me in one fell swoop. The family business, and her. Alexa Harrington. My ex-fiancée. The only woman I have ever loved. Now my brother's widow.

I run my finger along the inside of my collar, wishing the entire thing over. Wishing away the anger that still fizzes in my blood, the regret that shouldn't exist, the feelings that should have died a death seven years ago.

I'm standing at the back of the church while the priest commands the room. Far enough away from my family—my mother and *her*. Far enough away not to cause a scene. Far enough away to remain anonymous, should I choose to. The room is full to the brim, row upon row of pews crammed with people. No one need know I am here—not if I'm quick enough.

Why I came is anyone's guess.

A choked sob echoes through the rafters and I hone in on its source. My mother. She's hunched forward, head bowed, body shaking in tune to her cries. In response my own body shudders and I tighten against it. I can't breathe. I can't swallow. My eyes burn—

Fuck this!

I am not going to cry.

I am not going to care.

Only, Mum is the reason I came. Her plea. Her message full of regret, begging that I at least pay my respects, say a last goodbye. And for what? My father didn't deserve it—not when he made it so clear in life what a disappointment I'd been.

Well, screw you, Dad. I did it all and more.

She places a soothing hand upon my mother's shoulder. I can see her perfect French-tipped fingers gently rub, can imagine her whispered words designed to calm. My gut twists and I plunge my fists inside my pockets, tearing my eyes away.

She plays the part well enough, dear sweet Alexa. Behaves as if she cares. But how can she really, when she simply followed the money after I left. Swapped me for my greater counterpart. It doesn't matter what I've achieved since then. I will always feel inferior when presented with the past.

And that's why I shouldn't have come. Being weak is as alien to me now as the sentiment of love. I have no place for either in my life.

I have no place here.

I bow my head and start to move along the pew. I'm only four people away from the end, only a few strides from the exit, but it feels like a mile. It's hard to breathe, to see straight. In my mind's eye, the two coffins side by side at the front taunt me, my father and my brother's bond surviving even in death, pushing me out, leaving the two women to suffer— one I've missed more than I care to admit, and one I loathe myself for ever having loved.

I feel suffocated, unstable, and something catches my leg. There's a thud and I focus through the blur to see a hassock at my feet, a steadying hand upon my elbow that I can barely feel. I follow the arm, lift my gaze to meet an old man's eyes.

He's vaguely familiar. We lived in a small village growing up, the village in which my parents still live—no, my *mother* still lives. He's likely part of the community, and he'll know everything there is to know about us. There were never any secrets. So it's a surprise when I see sympathy shining back at me. Sympathy and compassion.

I feel as if I'm choking. I don't need his sympathy— not when the cause of all my pain is so far removed from what he suspects. I give a brief nod and withdraw, my focus once more on the door. On sanctuary.

I push it open and break out into the pouring rain, the Irish weather the perfect accompaniment to my mood. All I need now is thunder to meet my anger and I'd almost believe God was on my side. Not that I believe.

What kind of God would take away not only a woman's husband, but her son too? The better son? The worthy one?

I laugh at my cynicism, my twisted logic. My parents and my ex both deemed him better. I was almost ready to return, almost ready to prove my worth and face their disappointment, make them admit they were wrong.

I drag air into my lungs and look to the heavens. *Why?*

The rain beats my eyes closed and I blink against it, seeking out the sun in the looming grey above. *Why now?*

Is it the ultimate punishment for walking away? Is this what I deserve? No amends, no peace, no nothing?

I stagger forward. I can't bear it any longer. I never should have come.

'Damn you, Dad, for not believing in me.' I rake my fingers through my sodden hair, feel the weight of my rain-laden jacket and the fabric of my shirt clinging to me like a second skin. I throw my head back and curse the heavens. 'Damn you, Liam, for taking my all!'

'And damn *you* for coming back at all.'

I stagger back. I don't need to turn to know who it is. I'd know that voice anywhere. It haunts my dreams. My nightmares too.

I feel her presence as though it were the sun's rays beating down my back, feel the hairs upon my neck prickling to greet it.

The door swings shut. I hear her footfall on the path amidst the pounding beat of the rain and I urge my body to move. My car is at the end of the path, my driver ready and waiting.

Damn you for coming back at all...

Her words echo through my hangover-ridden skull, each syllable chiming with the emerging headache.

'Don't you walk away from me, Cain. Not this time.'

I spin on my heel to confront the angel who ruined me. *Angel?* Demon, more like. My lungs contract on a rush of air. She is beautiful—blindingly so. Her skin is pale against the dark grey stone of the centuries-old church standing tall behind her, her auburn hair like a comforting shroud of warmth as it falls around a face that is far too hollow and drawn, her eyes too big within it.

She's lost so much weight—too much. Just the slightest gust of wind and I fear she'll be gone. She's so far removed from the carefree, curvaceous woman I left behind, and right now she looks shocked into stillness, when seconds before she was the one commanding me to pause.

'You should go back inside.'

I say it, but I'm barely aware of the words. My voice sounds distant with the effort to ignore the racing of my heart, the twist to my gut, the pain.

Rain beads on her lashes, framing eyes that are so blue and look as haunted as I feel. She holds my own eyes trapped, her lips parted as rain rushes freely over them.

'You're getting soaked.'

Her eyes flicker, as though I've woken her up, and I can almost feel the shaky breath she takes, her chest shuddering in her simple black dress.

'Where are you going?'

The strength has gone from her whisper-soft voice and she presses her hands to her abdomen in a strange gesture that leaves her looking every bit as fragile as her slight frame suggests. The urge to offer her comfort, to sweep the rain from her lashes, her face, burns through me—instinctive, possessive, and wholly unacceptable.

She's not mine to warrant such care. She hasn't been for so long.

'I'm leaving.' I clear my throat and reinstate the wall around my heart. 'I never should have come back. Isn't that what you were trying to say just now?'

'I...'

She runs her teeth over her lower lip and I'm a prisoner to the move. Sent back in time. She used to do that when I teased her, when I turned her on. To remember it now is wrong—plain wrong—and yet my body reacts all the same. It seems my wall is not as solid as I'd like, and I don't need that realisation to tell me it's time I got the hell out of there.

'You should at least speak to your mother before you leave.'

'And say what?'

She shakes her head. 'She's just lost her son and her husband; don't you think she needs you now more than ever?'

What can I say? It's been seven years with barely a word spoken. My mother's plea to return has come from her grief. Her forgiveness has come from the same place. My eyes sting. I'm on shaky ground. Any moment now the tumult of emotion will out and I'll crumble.

But I can't.

I won't be weak—least of all in front of her.

'I'll call on her tomorrow…when we can talk in private.'

She gives a shaky nod and I drag my eyes away, force my feet to move once more.

My unspoken warning is clear: *Make sure you're not there.*

I watch him walk away, my shoulders easing with every step he takes. The rain is pounding down, streaming off my face. It's a welcome distraction from the pain that swells inside. It mingles with the grief, the hurt of losing Liam, of losing his father too. I wish I could be numb to it; heaven knows I've had enough thrown at me over the years.

My hands throb and I tear my gaze from his retreating form to stare at where my palms press tight against my abdomen, nursing the invisible wound beneath.

I've always known this day would come—part of me hoping for it, the other dreading it like the plague. But it *is* good he's returned—for his mother's sake. Marie has lost everything; he's all the blood family she has left.

And then there's me. An orphan, an outsider. Welcomed into the loving arms of the O'Connors when Cain brought me home to meet them all those years ago. I was fifteen and alone. And they took me under their wing, gave me a place to run to, a place where I felt loved, and that love never waned.

His did, though. Cain's. The boy who became the man I believed myself in love with, was destined to marry, have a family with.

My hands clutch tighter. He's the man who gave me the family I always wanted and then crushed me by walking away.

I look back up and see him stumble as he reaches the kerb, the downpour making the ancient path from the church unstable. I feel my hand reach out on instinct and snatch it back. He doesn't deserve my worry, my aid, and he certainly doesn't deserve the flicker of awareness that rippled through me the moment his glittering grey gaze collided with mine.

I felt his presence the second he walked into the church. It was the same as always—the strange flutter, the sudden awakening in my body. Almost as though I've been programmed from birth to detect him, to seek him out, with the rows upon rows of people between us doing nothing to douse it.

And Marie felt it too, in her own way. I saw her turn, saw the hope spark in her eye, a flash of something other than the grief she'd worn for the last few weeks. Waiting for the bodies to be fished from the sea, the plane crash to be investigated, the confirmation that the freak weather was to blame.

I couldn't stop myself chasing after him. It didn't matter that the service was still underway, that Marie needed my comfort. The fear that he would walk away and leave her with nothing, not even a word, drove me to follow him.

She deserved something, anything—no matter the cost to me of coming face to face with him again.

Seven years ago, he broke my heart, ripped it from my chest and left me with nothing…

No, that's not true.

He left me with a child—*our* child.

My hands are claw-like on my belly now, the nausea swelling thick and fast as the reminder rips through me. More death, more grief, more pain.

Thunder rumbles overhead, the sound vibrating through my skull, waking me up. At least I made my feelings clear, my curse falling easily from my lips on the tail-end of his. But then he turned and I was incapacitated with the rush of…of love, anger, betrayal, pain—more than anything, the pain.

A pain that he reflected back at me, blazing from him so strong I couldn't breathe through it. His masculine beauty, only intensified by his torment.

I think of the last time I saw him. Seven years ago. The lines etched in his face, nothing to do with age back then and everything to do with his anger. At life, his family…me.

I look at him now and a movement further down the pavement draws my eye. There's a driver waiting, the rear door of a sleek black car open. I know it's for Cain. I know of his wealth—hell, everyone knows of his success. Not many know the price he paid for it, though. The price we all paid.

But I do.

And that's why he doesn't deserve my attention. I've done what I came to do. I have his assurance that he will visit his mother tomorrow.

So go back inside and say goodbye to those who've always stuck by you…

I take a breath and smooth my shaky fingers over my face to sweep away the rain that I know is mixed with tears, then turn back.

Maybe he has a heart after all.

Shame it's taken him seven years to find it.

Not that I care.

I will never care for him again.

CHAPTER ONE

Three months later

'Isn't it time you went home, Alexa?'

I squint up at Janice, who's currently frowning at me as if she's my concerned counsellor and not my super-practical PA.

'I'm fine. I need to reply to Matthews before I call it quits today.'

She shakes her head at me, her frown deepening. 'Whatever you need to say, it can wait until tomorrow. It isn't going to change things right this second.'

No, it's not. She's right. But our investors are on edge. They have been since the plane crash that took out the company founder and his equally impressive son. And it's getting to me more and more. Making me feel helpless, ineffective, practically a failure. I can't bear it much longer.

Don't get me wrong—I *know* I'm worthy of this role, of being CEO. I was always Liam's equal. We graduated from Oxford together, top of the class, and companies were vying to take us on. But our hearts were in this firm. The one his father built up from nothing and dreamed his sons would take on. Together.

No one could have foreseen what had happened. Least of all the investors.

But no amount of reassurance from my lips will convince them, and I feel every bit the disadvantaged female when I sit with the board. All male, bar me. Their greying hair and condescension make it clear they don't believe in me. Not that I take it personally. I get the impression they don't think *any* woman should be at the helm of a *Fortune 500* company.

But I'll prove them wrong if it kills me.

Not for the first time I wonder… Would this be happening if Cain had inherited the shares? If he'd been forced to come back, to get involved? What if I'd taken him up on his departing offer of calling on him if we needed anything?

Not that he'd made that offer to *me*. No, it was what he told Marie on his one and only visit, the day after the funeral. At least I think there's only been one—the one she's spoken to me about. But then, would she have told me if there had been more? Would she have wanted to risk any more upset, any more pain…?

And there you go, thinking about him when you should be focusing on what matters…

'Maybe you should call him, you know. Just…'

I know Janice means Cain. It's not just me thinking about him; the majority of the company are.

His success knows no bounds, even when compared to ours.

'I don't need anyone's help, least of all his.' I smile to soften the acidity of my words.

She nods as she clutches her tablet to her chest. 'Forget I said anything.'

'I will.' I go back to my screen.

'Night, then.'

I don't look at her, only nod. There's too much emotion in my face, in my voice. I can't bring myself to speak any further. I'm tired and far too bitter not to say something about Cain that I'll later regret.

She leaves, closing the door softly behind her, and I feel a stab of guilt at my brusque treatment of her. It's not her fault I'm tetchy. It's all Cain's.

We're supposed to be ancient history, our relationship a whole other lifetime ago. So why, three months after the funeral, does his reappearance still have me reeling? And not just with shock, but with a multitude of feelings that I'd thought long since dead?

I rub at my face, my eyes, try to focus through the burning haze to read my computer screen. But it's no use. I've been staring at it for almost twelve hours and my eyes are protesting now. It really is time for home.

Matthews, my head of technology, can wait—just as Janice tried to tell me.

And as though I've conjured her back, there's a tap at my door.

'Yes?' I push out of my seat, start to rise, then

freeze, my hands clutching the chair-arms for support. *'Cain?'*

He fills the doorway to my right, the precise cut of his dark suit speaking of its price tag, the flint shade of his shirt an exact match for his eyes, which seem to glint at me from across the room. There's not a black hair out of place in its brushed-back style. His face is clean-shaven, his collar open—even his hands are relaxed inside his pockets. He's so at ease, in control... Nothing like the broken man I saw three months ago.

'We need to talk.'

I swallow, a shiver of fear running down my spine. It's not rational. This is *my* domain—my office, my company.

What can I possibly be afraid of when it comes to him?

Nothing can hurt me more than he already has. *Nothing.*

'I was about to leave for the night.'

'For the *night*? Hell, Alexa...'

And there it is—a slight crack to his calm exterior. He rakes his fingers through his perfect hair, a heavy sigh leaving his lips—lips I don't want to remember as though I devoured them only yesterday when over seven years have passed. But my body remembers. The rush of warmth low in my abdomen tells me so.

'You might as well stay a little longer and you'll be on a new day.'

'What's that supposed to mean?'

His hands are back in his pockets as he pins me

with a glare, half-censorial, half-something else that I don't understand and don't dare analyse. I got him so wrong before that I don't trust my instincts where he's concerned now. I won't even risk trying to read him.

'It means you should have left hours ago.'

I settle back into my seat, refusing to rise to the anger that flares at his surprising concern.

Yeah, it's anger that has you so worried...

'You gave up any right to have a say in my working hours long ago, Cain—or do I need to remind you that you walked out on me seven years ago?'

Too personal, Alexa.

But at least he can't see my insides wince at the revealing nature of my anger.

'You walked out on us all.'

There, that sounded better.

'I did what I felt I had to…at the time.'

'And now?'

For the briefest of seconds his lashes flutter, as though I've inflicted a physical blow, but then it's gone and I realise I imagined it. I also realise that whatever glimpse I thought I had three months ago of a man in pain, or just now of a man who cares about the working hours I keep, he doesn't really exist.

This is Cain.

And he only cares for himself.

'Going over old ground isn't the reason I'm here.'

I'm disappointed with his evasive answer. The rejected part of me—the part left to survive after he fled, the part that gave birth to our stillborn child without him—wants to have that argument. Wants him to acknowledge what he did and to see him beg forgiveness.

But only a fool would expect such humanity from Cain, and I'm no longer that fool.

'So, what *is* the reason you're here?'

I cross my legs and turn my chair slightly, angling it to face him. I don't miss how his eyes sweep my length. I'm wearing a teal satin blouse, buttoned almost to the collar, and a black skirt to the knee. All perfectly respectable, but I swear I see the flicker of what I know is dangerous, what I should ignore... Only the ache kickstarting down low has other ideas.

I watch his throat bob. His eyes strike mine, a second's fire, and then nothing. The mask slips back into place.

Cold Cain. Composed Cain. Downright callous Cain.

This is the man I can deal with.

'I haven't got all night and, as you so rightly pointed out, I should have left hours ago,' I remind him, sickly-sweet. And then I have to wonder... 'How did you know I was here, anyway?'

'My mother. I paid her a visit first.'

My mouth quirks up. 'You *paid* her a visit—how awfully dashing of you.'

His eyes flash, and his annoyance is like catnip to me. We never argued, Cain and I—not really. Unless you count that one occasion. The occasion that ended it all. And it's oddly thrilling to do it now, when I owe him nothing—no love, no respect, no loyalty.

'She told me you're often here until the early hours of the morning.'

He looks to my desk, the spread-out papers, the mess, and I fight the urge to scoop it all up into something orderly. He has no right to judge me. And I'm a scientist through and through—ordered chaos is how I live my life.

'Although I have to admit…' his eyes come back to me with some hidden question burning deep '…I'm surprised to see you here. I half expected it to be some cover for your extra-curricular activities.'

His words spike both ice and fire into my blood. 'Are you insinuating I've lied to Marie to cover up an affair?'

He shrugs. 'Can you blame me? The second I left you jumped into bed with my brother. Why shouldn't I think the worst?'

My stomach lurches. 'What would *you* know of it? You were long gone—completely off-grid, no contact number, nothing.'

'Oh, I came back. To see a ring on your finger and my brother at your side.'

'You…?' I can't even swallow. I feel dizzy, sick. 'When?'

'Three months later. Can you imagine my surprise at returning home only to find you were all out at the registry office, of all places? Of course I had to go there myself to truly believe it. And there you were, the blushing bride, all innocent and happy.'

A laugh chokes out of him and the blood leaves

my face, my pulse slowing down as I piece the night-mare together.

'It didn't take you long at all, did it?' he says.

I don't want to believe he truly witnessed that scene, but his anger is so visceral, so real... 'Why didn't you say anything?'

'Like what?'

His mouth is a grim line, his eyes hard, unread-able. And, Christ, do I want to read them now.

'Congratulations on your *fucking* marriage. I'm so happy for you both!'

I jump at his profanity, the force of it, and shake my head. The movement is negligible, but it's all I can manage as I'm transported back seven years to the life his brother offered me. Me and my unborn child. He was my best friend, my rock, offering me everything I could wish for to give my child a stable, loving home. Everything I didn't have growing up.

'And what do you know, Alexa?' His tone is hard, scathing. 'It's been three months since Liam died, which means you likely have someone else lined up to take his place by now.'

I can't speak. I can't breathe. His insult sends fire through my bloodstream. My ears are ringing with its pounding beat. I force in a breath, two, feel my eyes sting as I stare him down.

Don't let him win. Don't sink to his level.

I rise out of my seat and turn my focus to the computer screen, shutting it down. The silence in the room stretches...heavy, loaded...but I don't trust my voice. Not yet.

And then he moves and he's standing beside me, his proximity like a drug I can't resist, can't get enough of even now.

'Now I think about it, Lexi…' His voice is low, and the use of the name he gave me all those years ago is purposely teasing, crushing, cruel. 'Maybe I've come back at just the right time to take on that role.'

I twist on my heel, my hand gliding through the air to make for his cheek—*of all the goddamn nerve*—but he's quicker than me. He grabs my wrist a split-second before it collides with his arrogant, self-assured face and I'm panting, the ragged sound the only thing I can hear.

He's so close, I can feel his breath brush against my forehead, feel the heat of his body through his shirt, the old familiar scent of his cologne invading my senses.

I breathe him in—just a second's weakness—as my lashes lower and I'm transported back to a time *before*. A time when I didn't have to resist this persistent pull, this inherent need, this impulsive ache.

'Lexi…'

His voice is husky and it grazes over me like sandpaper, calling to the very heart of me. I wet my lips and look up, scared of what I'll see, hungry for it all the same.

His eyes burn into mine, his desire etched in every hard line of his face. And then his gaze falls to my fingers in his grasp, to the ring still on my finger, and I remember who he is—what this is. I clamp my eyes shut and shake my head, as though that will rid me of him.

'Don't touch me.' I pull my hand from his grasp and back away. 'Don't ever touch me again.'

I force my focus onto my desk, shoving papers into my bag and praying he doesn't spy how my fingers tremble, how my entire body quakes.

'Why don't you do us all a favour and disappear off again, Cain?' I don't look at him as I say it. I don't dare. 'It's what you do best.'

'I'm not going anywhere.'

I still, my hands deep inside my bag as I process what he means. I can feel my pulse beating in my neck, my lips drying up and my throat clamping tight.

I chance a look. 'What do you mean?'

'It means I'm here to stay.'

He walks away, over to the window that stretches along one wall of my office, but it does nothing to ease my panic.

'Stay?' I fight to keep the tremor out of my voice. 'Stay where?'

He doesn't say anything, simply stares out at Dublin's Liffey River and the bustling Beckett Bridge. It's as though I've lost him to the view as its myriad of lights dance in his darkened gaze and form shadows across his face.

I part my lips to speak, to draw him back and get answers, but then he turns to me and the intensity of his eyes alone dries up my words. My knees weaken and I lock them tight, forcing my mouth closed again as I wait for what he has to say.

'I'm back, Alexa, and this time nothing can stop me taking all that I'm owed.'

I wait for her to erupt, to demand my explanation and tell me to go to hell.

Instead she frowns, her brows drawing together as her hand—the one that still bears my brother's ring—rises to her neck. It taunts me. Fires my blood with the need to possess, to take back what was once mine. But she's no object. I have no hold over her.

Only, my body can't be told so easily.

She wets her lips, and when she speaks it's with a calmness I'm sure she can't feel. 'What, *exactly*, do you think you're owed, Cain?'

Her question chimes with my mental rampage. Calls my mind back to my choice of words seconds before. The double meaning is glaringly obvious to me and I wonder if she has any idea of it.

If I'd thought about it first maybe I would have been more careful, masked the personal entirely with business—just business.

But I was angry, bitter, my mind lost to how different things might have been—no, *should* have been.

Her by my side, wearing my ring.

My younger brother still alive and working alongside me.

My father proud, my mother prouder.

But, no. I'm back as the black sheep, half my family gone, and now... Now what?

Now I'm staking my claim to the business and...

I look to the single gold band around her finger. 'You don't wear an engagement ring.'

Her frown deepens. 'What does that have to do with anything?'

Hell, I have no idea. I came to discuss business. Instead I'm caught up in *her*, in the personal. In what we once had and what I lost.

'I'm just curious.'

She lowers her hand and rotates the gleaming metal between her thumb and forefinger, brandishing her love for another man with every twist. 'I didn't need one.'

I laugh; it's a bark. Harsh. Brutal. 'No one *needs* an engagement ring, Alexa. It's just expected...a loving gesture—' My voice catches and I mask it in a barren smile. 'It's tradition.'

'It was enough that he proposed.'

'Enough?' I stare at her, incredulous, my anger getting the better of me. 'How very romantic. You science folk really are clinical, through and through.'

Her eyes snap to mine, bright and fierce. 'If you've come here to lay into me and rip apart Liam's memory, you can leave right now. You don't get to speak ill of us—especially not him.'

'Why? Because he was so talented at everything? So good? The proper little Catholic boy my parents always wanted but had to wait two extra years for?'

She releases the ring and flexes her fingers. I

know she's itching to swing for me again. Funny, I've never thought her capable of violence.

Shows how much I knew her then.

And how little I probably know her now.

Or is her love for my brother so strong even in death that she just can't bear it...?

Ice pierces my heart, rebuilds my defences, reminds me of why I hate her.

'He was a better man than you'll ever know or understand.'

Her soft-spoken words cut deep, her meaning clear.

'Of course.' The words thrum out of me. 'I couldn't possibly know because I wouldn't know what it takes to be a truly good man.'

I raise a brow at her in challenge. I want her to refute it, tell me I'm wrong...

'Yes.'

The simple syllable vibrates with budding fury, making her affirmation all the more powerful, and I cling to it. To her honesty. To the fact that there is nothing between us any more. Only a mutual hatred that I can use. I need all the hatred I can get to keep my guard up. To resist this crazy pull that won't quit.

But what right does she have to be angry with me, when all is said and done? She's the one who betrayed me. Yes, I walked away—but I came back for her. *She* was the one who moved on. With my brother, of all people.

'And you think I should've just rolled over and accepted your relationship with him, the better man?'

She looks at me and I see her anger waver.

'Don't hesitate now, Alexa. You've stuck the boot in—you might as well keep on going.'

'I didn't… I don't…'

'You don't what?'

She says nothing, and my patience for this conversation is over. I never should've let it start in the first place.

'I'm sorry if you find me critical of your marriage to my brother but, given the circumstances, I would have thought it understandable. Even for someone like you.'

'Someone *like me*?'

'Did the affair start before I left? Or did you wait until a few days after I left?'

Her hands clench and her cheeks flare. 'We never had an affair.'

I pocket my fists and ignore the way my gut writhes at the idea, at the conjured-up images of the two of them together that I don't want to see and am powerless to prevent.

Maybe this *is* what I need.

Answers to the past before I can move on.

We're going to be working together—that's a given. My mother has already handed over my father's shares, and Alexa can't change the fact that we'll be equals as far as this business is concerned. I'll need my head clear to do what's needed, what's right for the company. Not enshrouded in anger, jealousy…intolerable desire.

'We *didn't* have an affair, Cain.'

'So you say.'

She shakes her head. Her cheeks are streaked with colour. She looks guilty as sin to me. It should make me despise her, but instead I'm thinking of how much she looks like she used to in my bed— the same colour in her cheeks, her eyes bright, her hair wild about her bare shoulders as she called out my name in sheer ecstasy.

Fuck.

I ram the thought out of my mind. It has no place in the present. It was so long ago. But I have no control over my dreams and they've teased me with it far too often.

'You only have yourself to blame for all this.'

She declares it as fact and I let out a harsh laugh— more to fend off the unwelcome heat plaguing my veins than at her words.

'You were the one who left, Cain.'

'Tell yourself whatever you like, if it makes you feel better, but it doesn't change the truth of it.'

'That *is* the truth.'

I suck in a breath, my lungs fighting my body's stillness to take in air. I shouldn't feel like this. She shouldn't have this power over me. And yet the tell-tale pressure building behind my fly knows otherwise.

Remember the pain.

Remember how she hurt you.

How *they* hurt you.

'Did you ever wonder why I left?' I ask, clinging to the memory as a lifeline.

'Are you serious?' Her eyes widen. 'You walk out without a word, go completely off-grid, where no one can reach you. Christ—of *course* I wondered. We all bloody did! It was only the fact you spoke to Marie that stopped us calling the police and sending out a search party!'

She's trembling from head to toe, her voice shaking, her eyes watering. I could almost believe she'd cared. Really cared.

'I had my reasons to leave.'

'Oh, yes, of course you did—and they all revolved around looking after *numero uno*. Yourself. And to hell with the rest of us.'

'I cared, Alexa, believe me. I cared more than you can possibly know.'

She laughs, and the manic sound drives me crazy. Pain collides with something more fierce, something more treacherous, and I move without thinking.

I'm across the room and pulling her against me. Her startled moan is drowned out by a growl I cannot contain and I realise my folly the second my lips claim hers.

Folly because she's not fighting me. She's on fire with me, her lips meeting me halfway and leaving me in no doubt as to how much she wants this too.

Fireworks erupt inside me—an explosion of sensation wrapped up in a warning so powerful it makes me dizzy. Drunk on her. On what's right. What's wrong.

I try to see sense even as my lips move with hers. Remembering. Reacquainting. But there's nothing soft or loving about this. It's harsh, demanding. Each of us taking what we want, what we need.

Her hands are pressed against my chest. I feel their heat burn a path to my heart beneath. And then she's lifting them to my hair, holding me, her body melding to mine. She's giving herself over to me. It should be enough. I should stop now. I should be the one to stop it. The one in control.

Instead I'm kissing her back like a drowning man on a quest for air. My hands are in her hair, and its softness is so familiar, her impassioned surrender so pure. It's pulling me under. It's not air I want—it's this sea of sensation, of incandescent need that she's always instilled in me.

I want to use it to obliterate my brother's touch with my own.

I want to use it to obliterate the past, the pain, the ache of loss.

But at what cost?

Do I really want to succumb? To lay down my defences? To be weak?

CHAPTER TWO

DON'T DO THIS, ALEXA.

The mantra is on repeat, playing at the back of my mind, but I can't listen. I don't want to listen. It's been so long since I've felt this way. Alive. The heat pulsating between my legs, robbing me of any coherent sense and making me feel again.

I'd started to think I was immune, that nothing would bring this feeling back.

But I'm not numb. I'm not dead inside. I'm thriving, flourishing, abuzz with it.

He's the reason you feel like that. And he's the reason you shouldn't be giving in to it now.

I kiss him harder, forcing out the dawning sense, the voice of reason. I only want to feed this budding ache, to go with it until it consumes me, and it's all I'm capable of thinking of.

I know he feels it too. I can feel his need pressing between us, his breath hitching in tune to mine, his hands fierce as they fork through my hair.

Our teeth clash as our pace outruns us and I laugh. I'm delirious at letting go, at not being in control.

I don't feel like myself. Or rather I feel like my younger self, with no cares, no worries. He pulls back and I look up at him. He's grinning, his eyes alive with mischief, and I *am* that young again. So is he.

But you're not.

The realisation ripples through my system, the chill contending with the heat as the past seven years rapidly replay and I'm in freefall. Lost to it.

The sudden burn of tears is my wake-up call.

Oh, God, no.

I try to draw a breath, my fingers freezing in his hair as I close my eyes to block him out until I can see straight again. I cling to the chill within my belly, the echo of my pain, of my loss.

'Lexi...'

It's part-groan, part-plea, and then his mouth is back, travelling along my jaw, his shadowed stubble teasing a rough path to my earlobe. The ice is melting. My fingers are softening in his hair...my disobedient deprived body is curving into him and letting his heat burn out the cold. This is better. This feeling. I don't want the chill. The grief that will overcome me if I let it.

'Lexi...'

The way he says my name is a tortured sound that meets my inner torment head-on. He knows we shouldn't do this. He knows it's wrong. He has his reasons and I have mine. Yet we are both losing it. Letting it win. And the battle makes it all the more powerful. All the more desperate.

I cling to his head as his teeth graze the delicate

flesh of my earlobe, shiver as his hot breath invades my ear and moan my approval. Not that he needs it. He knows my every erogenous zone and is using that knowledge to push me.

But I know his too.

And I'm eager to remind him of it.

I tug his shirt from his waistband, slip my hands beneath and feel the heat of his skin under my palms. He's harder than I remember. Hot, lean, chiselled.

My mouth waters anew and I trail my fingers up his back, feel his skin prickle, his body shudder against me, and I smile. Still the same Cain. The one who can't determine if he's ticklish, turned on, or both.

Confident, I rake my nails down his shoulder blades and he grinds his hips against me with a hiss against my throat. I want more than a hiss, though; I want him out of his mind. I want the controlled man of minutes before surrendering to the wild man of old.

I drop my hands to his waistband, go to pop the button, and his hands drop to my wrists, stilling me.

'Not yet.'

When? I want to ask, but I can't speak.

His mouth is moving down over my blouse, the light fabric allowing just enough sensation to draw my nipples through both it and the lace of my bra, betraying exactly what I want, what I need. He pulls my arms behind my back, clasps my wrists in one hand as he walks me backwards against my desk.

I'm restrained, captive, and all his. It shouldn't turn me on like it does.

He shouldn't.

But, hell, I'm turned on and willing to lay myself bare just to feel the completion of this. The promise of the climax to come. That height of bliss, of ecstasy, of what I've not had in over seven years. Ever since… Ever since…

He thrusts my skirt up my thighs and my breath hitches, my mind quits. His palms are hot and hurried against my skin, frantic—and, *fuck*, I am too. It's like a long overdue homecoming. Being here, like this, with him.

The breadth of his palm covers the front of my thigh, his thumb is so close to the heart of me, and then he skims over my underwear, a gentle brush that has me bucking and crying, arching my back to plead for more.

He makes a sound—half-laugh, half-groan—and then his mouth is covering one nipple, his teeth biting through the fabric. I curse the very existence of my clothing. Of any barrier. I want it all gone. Hell, I want the last seven years gone. A rewrite of every painful second. If only…

I'm too close to sanity again. Too close to ending this before I've had my fill—

No. No. No.

I don't need slow and steady. I don't need him savouring me. I don't need time to reconsider.

I want it hard and fast—no thought permitted.

I pull at my wrists, still encased in his grip, drop

my head forward. But my lips are silenced by what I see. Cain. He is heaven and hell all rolled into one. All strength and sinew, carnal and lascivious. His chiselled jawline emphasised as his mouth works over me, his eyes darkly intense as he focuses on drawing out my nipples, making them beg, making *me* beg.

I whimper and his eyes shoot to my face, their fierce intensity making my belly contract. The heated swell down low, so rampant I bite down on my bottom lip and watch his eyes flare in response.

I feel like he's testing me, pushing me, silently asking: *can we do this?*

I have no answer. Hell, he hasn't even put a voice to the question. But I feel it all the same. The question pulses through me, urging me to decide.

Can we?

Yes.

Should we?

No.

My fingers clutch the back of his head, his thumb rolls over me, and I want to cry and moan and say to hell with it. He keeps his eyes locked on mine, that question still blazing as he scrapes one protruding nipple with the edges of his teeth. Heat surges to meet his bite, pleasure on its tail. Pleasure and pain, desire and need. Then he launches back up to my mouth, his tongue delving inside, twisting with my own, making me whimper, making me fight back. Fencing, entwining…

Oh, God, yes.

He's back at my throat, my breast, my mouth again. I follow his every caress, and now I'm the one savouring every single touch as if it will suddenly expire—because it will. I know it will. There is no future here. Just like seven years ago, it will be whisked away. There'll be no warning. No nothing.

I claw his skull as pain spears me.

Stop thinking. Just feel.

He's crazy over me. His movements are frantic, as though he can't get enough of every part of me and he wants me all at once. I know that feeling. My lower body is grinding against his hardness, pleading for release, and he's meeting me. The hard length of his cock joins me at every rise and fall...our climaxes build as one. Like teenagers dry-humping for the very first time. Christ, just like our first time.

He was my one and only. In heart and in body. Not that he will know that—not unless I tell him the truth of my marriage to his brother.

I clamp my eyes shut as reality invades—another glimpse of pain threatening to destroy this moment, to take it all away. I can't have that. I won't. I have suffered for so long. Not even my own fingers are able to give me this heady, mind-obliterating pleasure.

There are so many reasons I shouldn't cave. So many reasons we shouldn't do this. But I can deal with those later. When I'm alone.

'Cain.'

It's the first time his name has left my lips like

this, and so much is loaded into that pleasure-filled tone I want to take it back. It gives up so much of me and I fear the exposure. But it only ramps up his tension, his need.

'I want you.'

He claims my mouth and releases my wrists in one movement. His hands grip my hips as he thrusts me back over the desk and lifts my legs around him. He's tight against my slick heat, his fingers vibrating as he holds me, his breathing ragged.

'Say you want me too.'

Oh, God.

His request is strained, gruff. But I can't do it. I can't. I do want him—but I don't.

He stares down into my eyes, our noses almost touching. I can see how much he needs the words. I close my eyes and kiss him instead. He caves for seconds, but he's no fool.

'Tell me you want me, Lexi.'

It's a command now, his entire body still as he waits on me.

'Say it.'

I risk a look into his face and the air catches in my lungs. So much pain tangled up with desire.

My fingers curl around his neck as I hold him to me. I part my lips, but nothing will come.

'You can't say it, can you?'

'I…'

He's Cain. He broke your heart. He'll break it again if you let him.

'No. No, I can't.'

It comes out as a whisper. I take a breath, then another, and watch his eyes flicker and his jaw clamp shut. I wonder if he'll come back to me anyway. I start to rise to meet his lips, but he's already gone, averting his gaze and stepping back, releasing me so quickly I almost fall.

I plant my palms onto the desk to steady myself and push myself to stand before he can turn and see the state I'm in.

His words come back to me: *'Nothing can stop me taking all that I'm owed.'*

'Is this why you're here?' I ask quietly. 'Is this what you mean by taking all that you're owed?'

He's tucking his shirt into his trousers as he sends me a look I can't decipher and my anger flares twice as strong, powered by my fevered pulse, by his demand, by his rejection.

'You just had to hear me tell you I want you? Just to win one over on Liam?'

I can't believe it, but at the same time I'm convinced it's true.

'It may surprise you, Alexa, but I don't make a habit of sleeping with women who don't want me.'

I laugh, the sound shuddering out of me. 'I think you know how much my body wanted you.'

He studies me intently, his eyes raking over me, exposing me. I fold my arms high on my chest, wanting to conceal the damp path created by his mouth, to block out the slickness between my legs that tells me how close I've come to making a mistake.

His eyes lift to my mouth, dark, intense, and he

takes a step forward, closing the distance between us. 'You and me both.'

He reaches out and I lift my chin, eyeing him warily. His palm comes to rest against my cheek, his thumb smoothing over my cheekbone, and I'm captivated by his sudden softness.

'I cared, Lexi—about you, about us.'

His eyes are fixed on my lips as he says it, his sincerity as bewitching as his touch.

'I loved you once.'

His eyes lift to mine.

'Don't ever question that.'

A lump rises in my throat, and my eyes burn as tears well.

'I loved you once.'

If he loved me, how could he have left? How could he have abandoned me and the unborn child I didn't know I carried?

I stare into his eyes, desperate for answers, and swallow down the lump to speak. 'But—'

'But nothing. It's in the past.'

Not when it still has the power to hurt. I need answers, I need to understand.

'How can it be?'

'Because it was a mistake I'll never make again. Ever.' His jaw pulses, his eyes harden and his thumb stills its caress. 'I won't love you. I won't mourn you. I won't be that fool again.'

He walks away, back to the window, and I stare after him. Cold. Confused.

'Then why kiss me?'

His eyes come back to me, his face set hard. 'It seems no amount of hatred can stop this fire between us.'

I feel sick. Sick to know he speaks the truth. Sick to know I almost caved.

'Well, I beg to differ.' I smooth down my skirt, ignore the damp cling of my blouse where his mouth has been, and face him down. I won't let him win this.

'It's a bit late to deny its existence now. That little display was enough to convince us both. We just established that.'

There is no answer I can give to that, so I go with my gut. 'Go to hell, Cain.'

I turn to start stuffing the rest of my belongings into my bag. The sooner I leave, the sooner I can get away from him and—

'I'd have a pretty hard time running the company from there.'

I freeze. My heart thuds in my chest. I can't have heard him right.

I glare at him. 'What's that supposed to mean?'

'When I said I was coming back to take what I'm owed…'

He faces me head-on now and I can see his power visibly seeping into every pore, his ease returning, his control.

'I wasn't referring to you—appealing as that idea is. I was referring to the company…to Dad's shares.'

I swallow. 'You're not serious?'

'Deadly.'

'But Marie wouldn't… She would have discussed it with me first. She would have at least mentioned it.'

'Be that as it may, they are mine.'

I shake my head at him. This can't be happening. It just *can't*.

He pockets his fists as he holds my eye. 'You need to practise looking happy about it. My personal assistant, Sheila, will be arranging a function in a fortnight, for the investors and some acquaintances of mine—a kind of welcome back into the fold, so to speak. It'll be good to make the right impression. Don't you think?'

'You can't do this…*we* can't do this.'

'Correction. We *need* to do this if the business is to survive and our investors are to be happy once more.'

'How do you know about the investors?'

'Everyone in the industry knows, Alexa. You can't keep that kind of thing a secret.'

My hand presses into my abdomen, the empty ache beneath increasing tenfold as I ask, 'How long will you be here?'

'Who's to say I won't make it a permanent thing?'

Is he goading me on purpose? Rubbing salt into the wound? There's no way he would come back permanently.

He can't.

'Because you have your business, your commitments… Ireland is hardly a convenient location for you. You have no presence here.'

He shrugs. 'Maybe it's time I changed that. A new

headquarters, a new operation—it'll be great for the local economy and it's time I had a base, a home.'

'A *home*?' I'm going to be sick.

'Are you not feeling well?'

My eyes narrow on him. Have I gone green? Then he gestures to where my hand clutches at my stomach and I snatch it away. It's too incriminating, too revealing of the painful secret I hold from him.

'How can you ask me that when you've just dumped this news on me?'

He has the audacity to almost smile as he nods. 'Fair enough—but the sooner we move past this and get started on presenting a united front, the sooner the investors will get off your back—*our* backs.' He straightens and clears his throat. 'We can talk properly on Monday morning. Eight work for you?'

'Monday?'

Try never.

But what choice do I have? If Marie has passed on those shares, she has done it because she has faith in her son. Faith she didn't have in me to pull the investors back onside.

Or maybe it's her way of getting her son back?

'Yes, I have to fly back to London for a few days. It'll give you plenty of time to get used to the idea.'

Whether it's for her son or for the company, I can't fight Marie's decision, and so I nod as I pull my bag up off the desk. 'Eight o' clock, Monday.'

I expect him to leave. Instead he hovers.

'You can go now.'

'How are you getting home?'

He looks and sounds as if he cares. But I know better—hell, he's told me he doesn't—and I resent having to give an answer. I do it in the hope he will then leave, giving me the space I so desperately need.

'I have a car in the basement.'

'Good.'

Thankfully, he heads for the door, and my resentment gives rise to strength. I call out. 'Cain?'

He pauses and looks at me over his shoulder.

'If we do this,' I say, square on, 'we're equals. You are *not* my boss, and you don't *tell* me what to do. We agree together. Is that understood?'

His lips quirk. 'Agreed.'

I swear I can see admiration in his gaze before he turns away again. Well, he can keep his fucking admiration.

'And Cain?'

Another look.

'I was a fool to love you once too. I won't make that mistake again either.'

His brow lifts. 'Tit for tat? Really, Alexa? I would have thought that beneath even you.'

Argh! I want to scream at him, pound at his chest until he acknowledges that *he* was the one in the wrong. Not me. And not Liam. *Never* Liam.

But I can't make him see that without telling him the whole truth, and I fear that more.

'If you want to see it that way, then fine.'

He's still, his eyes searing into mine, as if he can see all the way inside me to the truth. But I don't back down. I don't even flinch.

And then he's gone as quickly as he appeared and I succumb to the scream, fisting my hands and then flinging them out as I let it go. It feels so good that I do it again and again, and then I slump into my chair, my head in my hands, and breathe.

Just. Breathe.

It'll be okay. You just need to keep your guard up and all will be well. A piece of cake.

'Some cake…' I mutter into my palms.

CHAPTER THREE

ISN'T IT STRANGE how you can be someone to the out-side world, even believe you *are* that someone, but the second you walk into the home you grew up in, with the same smells, the same furnishings, practi-cally the same décor, you're transported back to the person you used to be? Exposed.

I don't feel like a successful billionaire who knows his own mind, who makes critical decisions on a daily basis.

I feel like a child.

Vulnerable. Angry. On edge.

I roll my head on my shoulders and shift back in the armchair my mother has set before the roaring fire especially. Dad's chair.

'Tough week?'

I smile at her, wanting to put her at ease. 'You could say that.'

She frowns at me from her own seat, angled like mine to face into the fire, but her soft green gaze is all for me and it's concerned. I really could be that schoolboy again, just come home after a run-in with his best mate. Or the teen who's just fallen out with his girlfriend and doesn't know how to feel.

She's much the same as she always was. Her long hair is woven into the same plait she's always favoured, only now it's greying at the temples. Her voice still possesses that melodic ring that Dad was so fond of and Liam and I were comforted by as children.

My stomach lurches. It happens every time I think of Dad, of Liam. And I know the added lines on my mother's face, the extra grey in her hair, have come in the last few months since the funeral. That the weight of facing life without them is taking its toll. But there's still a strength to her, a spark to her eyes when she smiles at me, that tells me I've done the right thing. That having me here has helped to ease that burden.

Yes, coming back was the right decision—even if it's brought me face to face again with Alexa and the unfinished business between us.

My mind replays the scene in her office. The crazy heat. The even crazier words that came out of my mouth. Out of hers. They burn through me even now, four days later, far more effective than the fire roaring before us.

I drag my eyes to the flames and watch them crackle and flicker.

'Do you want to talk about it?' Mum asks. 'A problem shared and all that…'

My fist pulses around the arm of Dad's chair and

I take a deep breath—only to have the scent of my family home attack my defences further. I don't even know where I'd start. Seven years ago? Three months ago? A week? And even so I'm not willing to voice the chaos underway in my head. To put words to it will only make it more real.

'It's nothing I can't handle.'

My own conscience mocks me, laughing at my projected confidence.

I want to be confident, though. I want to be in control.

But in Alexa's office I lost both, succumbing to the weakness of emotion, hormones, endorphins… I played myself for a fool.

'It can't be easy for you…coming back and working with Alexa—'

She breaks off, struggling for the right words, and I can't find any to stop her, to put an end to this conversation before it starts.

'I have a good feeling about this, though.' She nods, sounding far more certain. 'She needs you. She needs your help, your business acumen and your reputation.'

She reaches across to place her hand on my arm, her expression softening.

'She can be stubborn, but she'll see that eventually. She can't continue like she has been, and neither can the company. To see it pulled apart, failing… It's your father's legacy.'

Her voice is transformed with her grief, her concern. Just as it was a month ago, when she asked me to consider doing this. I balked then, but the more I heard about the company, the more I couldn't ignore what was happening.

And I trust myself to keep it all contained. The last seven years have taught me to think before speaking, to always be in control of myself, that it doesn't pay to act on emotion. It's how I've achieved all I have. I'm not the same man who left seven years ago.

Now, with hindsight, do I regret leaving? *Yes.*

But regret doesn't help me.

I have to look to the future.

So why did I lose sight of that in Alexa's office? Why did I allow my emotions to take the driving seat when I should have been focusing on the business? On what matters?

Why? my conscience mocks me again. *Because you're not over her. Because you love—no, loved her. And now you want her.*

Fuck—I do.

I don't love her. Not any more. How can I possibly love her when I hate her for what she did? I still can't believe the audacity of her parting words.

'I loved you too.'

How could she possibly have loved me, only to marry my brother within months of my departure? It was sick. Twisted.

And still I want her.

Maybe I'm the twisted one, for wanting what was taken from me.

Just like the business was taken from me when

my father decided to give a portion of it to Liam instead of me.

He said it was my wake-up call—that if I truly wanted to be a part of the business then I needed to demonstrate I was worth it.

'Knuckle down,' he said. 'Give up the sport, the mates, the fun. Grow up.'

I've definitely done all that.

And look at me now. Everything my father would have wanted. Only he's not here to witness it.

'I'm so glad you've come home, that you've agreed to help Alexa and the company,' Mum suddenly gushes, patting my arm. 'Your father would be glad too.'

And there it is: the confirmation I definitely want but don't feel prepared to hear. No matter that my thoughts had been going down that path seconds before.

'I hope so.'

'No hope about it, love.'

Her voice cracks with emotion and my stomach twists.

'He spoke about you often, you know. Liam did too. They always hoped... Well, you know...'

Oh, God. I don't want this conversation. I don't feel prepared for it. Emotionally or physically. I came for Sunday dinner—not to be emotionally battered by the past and my mistakes.

'We can't change the past, Mum.'

'No, no, you're right. And it doesn't help to dwell, does it?'

She reaches over to squeeze my hand, her smile bright even as her eyes glisten with unshed tears.

'I've made your favourite—shepherd's pie.'

I swallow. 'Brown sauce?'

'Always.'

And just like that the mood lifts, as it has every time I've returned over these last few months.

Every visit is an emotional rollercoaster that will get smoother as time goes by and will continue to get easier, I tell myself.

It will.

I open the wrought-iron gate and smile as it gives its familiar little squeak. I already feel calmer. The welcoming charm of the O'Connors' nineteenth-century cottage and its pretty little rose garden out front never fails to work its magic over me.

It's funny, really. You'd have thought with all the wealth they accumulated over the years Marie and Robert would have moved out—bought somewhere bigger, more impressive. But, no, Marie loved it, and therefore Robert loved it too.

My smile turns bittersweet as I let myself in, dropping my handbag in the hallway and toeing off my shoes. At least Marie still has me, and vice versa.

And now she has Cain too.

And that's just fine.

Absolutely.

Fine.

I push him out of my mind, though I know he'll make his way back in again soon—like he has done practically every minute of every waking hour these last four days.

I dip to pull from my handbag the bottle of wine I've brought and tell myself that this is mine and Marie's time and no one else can encroach on that. The wine is Marie's favourite red, and I bring it every Sunday. It's our weekly routine. We don our comfies—which for me means leggings, a big fluffy jumper and equally fluffy socks—and put the world to rights over good food and good vino.

'Only me, Marie!' I call down the hallway—as if it would be anyone else—and follow the sounds of crockery to the kitchen.

The house smells delicious, of comfort in all its glory. Marie's a terrific cook—something she's always been keen to pass onto me—and the homemade sticky toffee pudding I have hooked under one arm is all thanks to her teaching.

I kick open the kitchen door and walk on in, my smile wide. 'Hey, I hope you're up for something naughty—'

My eyes land on the tall, dark figure standing before the window and my smile dies. *No, it can't be.*

But of course it is. Cain's her son. This is her home. How naïve I've been to think things wouldn't change, that our easy routine wouldn't be upended with his arrival.

'Something naughty sounds thrilling.'

He pushes away from the window as he says it and stalks towards me. For one half-crazed second I think he's going to embrace me…kiss me, even…

Something naughty.

My mind races. Why did *those* have to be the words I used?

'Sounds perfect, love.' Marie is talking to her prized cast iron range as she finishes serving up some steaming veg. At least I think it's veg, but my eyes are hooked on Cain, my lips parted, my heart pulsing in my chest.

He pauses in front of me, his smile so warm I wonder if I've imagined the way we left things. And then I meet his eye and, no, it's there. The war blazing between us.

I can see it in the tightness around his eyes, the way his neck cords with tension. Tension and strength. I felt that strength first-hand four days ago, when I'd explored him in my office—and, damn it all to hell, that ache swells at the juncture of my thighs, my body reliving that scene in one vivid sweep.

Oh, fuck. Swallow.

He lifts his brow.

Shit—did I curse out loud?

Oh, please, God, no.

But Marie is still pottering, and my mouth is still gaping; it's so dry I don't think words could have formed even if I'd tried.

Then his finger is under my chin, and to my horror he pushes my jaw to close my mouth for me. I look away, but not before I spy the open amusement dancing in his gaze, and I want to slap myself. He's read me like an open book. But, hell, I didn't expect this. I'm unprepared, ill-equipped.

Excuses, excuses... I can practically hear him saying it.

I quit the mental rambling and say what I'm thinking—or close enough. 'I wasn't expecting you.'

I try to keep my voice neutral, but it's hard. So hard. I think of Marie, within earshot, and use it to claw back control.

'That makes two of us. Allow me.' He reaches out for the bottle and the glass-lidded dish, eyeing the dessert with open speculation. 'You cooked this?'

I thrust them into his hands, glad Marie can't see the aggressive manoeuvre, and make my voice sweet—sickly, even. 'I've been taught by the best.'

Marie's easy laugh breaks through the tension as she turns and sweeps me into a hug. 'I wouldn't say I'm the best—more that you're a good student.'

I embrace her, give her a kiss to the cheek. 'How are you?'

She releases me and steps back, her gaze sweeping us both. I don't miss the sheepish glint in her eye, the flush to her cheeks. The minx.

'Better now I have you both under this roof again.'

Marie. Don't push this.

I glare at her in warning and she purposely ignores it.

'Now, come on, I don't want dinner getting cold.'

One look at Cain and I know he hasn't missed his mother's guilt either. But we do as she instructs, carrying the food and the wine through to the dining room.

Marie sits at the head of the table and we sit either side of her, facing one another—far too close for comfort. I stare at the bottle I brought, not at him, but he's lifting it and my eyes follow.

He's wearing a simple sweater and jeans. At least it should be simple, but on him it's practically indecent. The jumper is thin, and it clings to his chest to the point that I can just make out the pearls of his nipples beneath, the pecs that surround them, the muscles of his arms flexing as he uncorks the bottle.

And then I remember what I'm wearing and my cheeks flush crimson. I look like Bridget Jones on a crying-into-a-tub-of-ice-cream night. Not the capable CEO I need to prove to him I am.

'Wine?'

Oh, God, he's looking right into my eyes—probably clocking my heightened colour and thinking it's all down to him and his damned appeal, rather than the fluffy bunnies adorning my equally fluffy socks. I plaster a smile on my face and nod, immediately questioning the decision. I'm going to need my wits about me to keep this chaos in hand and get through this meal unscathed.

'Ah, I've forgotten the brown sauce...' Marie pushes out of her seat.

'I'll go,' I say. Any excuse to leave and get my head straight.

The way his lips pull at the corners in a suppressed grin, I know he knows why I want to flee. And he thinks it highly entertaining.

I'm instantly irritated—to the point that I have the

most ridiculous urge to stick my tongue out at him. Very un-CEO-like. Very unlike me.

'Don't be silly.'

She's already heading for the door, and any moment now we'll be alone. No one to keep the peace— no one to stop me losing it.

'Stop looking at me like that.' I say it under my breath, but my cheeks are blazing crimson under his dancing gaze. His continued amusement is provoking me to the point that I can't zip it.

'I should tell you the same. You could have stripped me bare with your X-ray vision just now.'

Fuck!

My cheeks, my entire body, are flushing like a lobster. 'Don't mistake civility for anything more, Cain.'

'Oh, I know civility, all right, Lexi. But your thoughts were less civil and more of the X-rated variety—'

'Cain!'

My eyes flick to the door, the very idea of Marie overhearing him sending my blood pressure up another few notches. Not to mention his use of that pet name again. No one else uses it—ever. It was his endearment. His name for me. When he loved me… before…before…

God, woman, get it together.

'Your ego can tell you what it likes,' I say, grateful that my tone is hard, steady. 'But I'm being *civil*, Cain, for Marie's sake. And I will continue to be so for the company's sake too.'

His eyes flicker over my face, pause at my lips, and hell if I don't feel that heat from the inside now, burning low down. I cross my legs, fending off the dull throb that beats there.

'On that we can also agree.'

His voice is thick, his eyes dark. The table for eight feels small all of a sudden, as if the whole room is closing in around us and drawing us together. I can feel myself leaning, floating, drawn into his magnetic pull... And then I hear movement at the door and Marie is back.

I snap upright—*fucking smooth, Alexa*—and grab the chilled water jug, pouring myself a generous helping. It'll balance the alcohol and chill my insides. I hope.

I fill Marie's and Cain's glasses too, without asking. I think my voice would squeak if I spoke, and in truth I need something to do with my hands, which seem determined to wring themselves raw in my lap.

Four days. Four days I've had to come to terms with his return, to prepare for our meeting tomorrow, and I am no more ready now than I was when he first walked in.

'I'd like to raise a toast.'

My eyes flick to Marie as she raises her wine glass and I try to keep my expression neutral. A toast? Really?

'To new beginnings.'

I swallow and I swear it's audible. 'New beginnings,' I mutter, taking up my own glass.

I don't dare look at Cain as I drink. I don't want to see what he's thinking.

'New beginnings.'

There's that speculation again, ringing in his voice, and I'm pulled back to him, unwilling. He's studying me intently over his wine glass and I can't look away. I want to, I do…

'I'm sorry I didn't tell you both that the two of you were coming, but…' Marie shrugs merrily '…I figured it was best to face the music head-on, so to speak. It's so much better that way.'

I smother a startled cough, the remnants of wine catching. *Head on, indeed.*

'Cain, I am so glad to have you back here.' She reaches over to pat his hand, doing a good job of pretending not to notice anything amiss in the room. 'And Alexa…' She places her other hand on mine now. 'You have been running yourself ragged these past few months. Now you have someone to share that burden. Someone who will care for the company like you do.'

She smiles at us both, her hands resting on ours.

'So, please, indulge me with this.'

'There's nothing to indulge, Mum.'

He is so perfectly calm, and I envy him for that.

'You're right—it makes perfect sense for me to come back and help.' He places his hand over his mother's and smiles at her. 'I'm happy to be home too.'

My breath catches at what I see, what I hear. For the first time since he's been back he's completely unguarded, open, his face full of love—relief, even. I feel a stab of guilt. This is why I need to get myself in hand. To put on a front and make everything just so. Because he belongs here far more than I ever did or will again.

I wet my lips and squeeze Marie's fingers gently, my smile aimed to reassure. 'What Cain said…'

She studies me for a second longer and then she nods, her beam so full of relief, happiness. 'Good. Good.' And then she picks up her cutlery. 'In that case, let's eat.'

She looks as if a weight has been lifted. For the first time since the crash I see a glimpse of the old her and my smile is genuine, filled with the love I feel for this woman who has treated me as her own for fifteen years.

My eyes drift back to Cain and my smile dies a swift death. He's watching me, eyes intense, brooding, and so many emotions cross his face I can't latch on to a single one. I just know they centre on me. All me.

Where has the composed Cain from seconds before gone?

I pull my eyes away and lift my fork, preparing to eat, hoping he'll do the same.

He doesn't.

What have I done? Did I say something, do something, to put him on edge?

'This looks lovely, Marie.'

I stare pointedly at his plate and his lashes flicker.

He gives a slight shake of his head and then finally he follows suit.

'Smells as good as ever,' he says.

'Well, it always was your favourite. A mother never forgets.'

Shepherd's pie. I should have remembered. Should have realised. I want to kick myself over my stupidity.

Marie hasn't made this dish in over seven years. Not since that last family meal when his father announced the redistribution of his shares, cutting Cain out of the business. Not since Cain and I fell out in the O'Connors' front garden, of all places, straight afterwards, both flinging accusations that neither of us could come back from.

But we might have stood a chance if Cain had only stuck around. Instead he'd fled. Leaving not just me but the O'Connors too. A hate-filled goodbye, all he'd deemed us worthy of...

Jesus, Marie, you really are facing the past head-on.

I glance at her, seeing the hope in her bright green gaze, and I wonder if maybe, just maybe, she's right to do this. Maybe it's exactly what I should be doing too?

My hand goes to my stomach, stroking back and forth. There's so much he doesn't know. So much I need to confess in order to truly face the past. So much pain to dredge up.

Can I really go there and come out whole again?

Do I have a choice?

Now he's back, doesn't he deserve to know?

My skin prickles beneath my jumper as a cold sweat breaks across my back, down my front. I wish I'd worn a vest, so I could take off my suffocating fur-ball of a jumper, but even then I'd feel like this.

It has nothing to do with the warmth of the room and everything to do with the pain of past, of the memories I try to bury but not to forget, all at the same time. Because Rose shouldn't be forgotten. I gave birth to her. Held her. Her small body fragile and still.

My eyes sting and I avert my gaze, blink, reaching for my water glass and hoping they don't notice how my fingers quake.

Yes, telling him is the right thing to do.

In my heart I know that.

But confessing will also rip my heart in two, and I'm not sure I'll be able to piece it back together again.

Not this time.

CHAPTER FOUR

I EAT EVERY last mouthful of shepherd's pie and go in for seconds. I do it for Mum. To see the pleasure on her face as she dishes out another helping.

I give her a smile of thanks, then force my eyes back to my plate and away from Alexa.

I know why Mum made this meal. Yes, it's my favourite. But, more than that, she's doing just what she said she would: she's getting us to face up to the past head-on, in the hope that we can all move on.

Move on?

I manage to prevent the shake of my head as I take a forkful of food and chew it. My eyes drift back to Alexa, as they seem determined to do at every opportunity, and the past comes back to haunt me... The night we last had this meal. The night I let my anger get the better of me and made the decision to leave both my family *and* my fiancée.

It was the night Dad made his announcement regarding the company, confirming my ingrained suspicion that I would never stack up, that Liam would always outshine me. There'd been no discussion, no warning, no three strikes and you're out. He'd just gone and done it—written me out of the company as he wrote my brother in.

The food sticks in my throat and I force it down. I'm not angry about my dad's decision any more. I'm not bitter about it.

The past seven years have taught me about graft— the real hard graft of putting in the hours and proving your worth. Something my brother had done in spades back then and I had not. I've also had the last three months with Mum, talking to her, seeing it through my father's eyes, and although I may not agree with how my father went about it, I can forgive his reasoning now.

What I can't forgive is Liam. Liam and Alexa.

Their betrayal. *Hers.*

I glare at her now, and resent that my anger eases at the sight of her looking so pale. She's gone from flushed pink to deathly white, the smattering of freckles along her nose and cheeks striking out against the pallor of her skin. And I shouldn't care, I shouldn't be concerned with her discomfort. I hate that she makes me feel anything, but she does.

It will never be forgiveness, though, never love.

She wears no make-up today, and it riles me to admit that she looks all the more appealing for it. The reddish tone of her feather-like lashes setting off the blue of her eyes. Eyes which look even bigger with her auburn waves pulled back, her ponytail softened by the strands that fall free, all casual and sweet.

And her freckles—God, those freckles. They tease me, making my fingers itch with the need to trace their pattern like I've done a thousand times before. It was a lifetime ago, but I remember that path like it was only yesterday.

Does she have more now? More to discover, more to trace, more to kiss and tease?

My cock pulses, but so too does my heart. I bite back a curse and look for safety in my dish instead, only I have no stomach for food now.

She chose Liam. She married Liam. You weren't good enough for her. Remember that.

'How was your park run this morning, Alexa?'

Mum's been trying to get us to talk, and now that Alexa's plate is cleared and she can't stuff her mouth full she has to answer. I know this has been her tactic, because it's been mine too.

She smiles at Mum, but this time it doesn't quite reach her eyes. Not like earlier, when her smile shone with such love and affection for my mother that it lit me up from head to toe, strangling any warning my brain tried to give.

'I managed to get a PB…although I think that had more to do with Ed dictating the pace than me.'

Ed? Now my ears prick up.

'Quite eager, was he?'

Eager?

Alexa laughs softly, and the easy sound has my heart dancing in my chest.

'Very. I haven't the heart to rein him in either; he's too irresistible by far.'

Are they seriously talking about a guy? In front of me? Do they have no shame? No feelings? *Fuck*. Maybe three months really is all it takes for Alexa…

'Ed?'

They both look to me, and I see a faint flush of colour in Alexa's cheeks.

'Why, yes, love. Alexa takes Ed out for a run every Saturday and Sunday,' she announces proudly. 'Her neighbour works weekends, so it helps them out.'

'Ed's a Labrador.'

Alexa fills in the last blank, and although I don't want to feel it, relief washes over me all the same—even though it's none of my business…none at all.

'So you've taken up running?' I say with polite interest. 'Since when?'

I know straight away I've put my foot in it. The hint of colour in Alexa's face vanishes and my mother looks at her with a definite wince.

I know the answer already.

But it's too late to take it back.

Alexa clears her throat. Her fingers play with her cutlery and then she looks back at me, her face admirably still. 'A few years ago.'

Try seven, my brain supplies for her.

I stuff a fork full of shepherd's pie into my mouth and chew it with a nod, wishing for a rapid change in subject. My mother thankfully comes to my aid.

'So, how was your trip to London, Cain?' she rushes out, her smile forced as she looks at me. 'Was the event a success?'

I take a sip of wine to help the food go down. I can't remember ever having endured a meal as tense as this one. The second my father made his announcement seven years ago I ran. But there would be no running now. I'm not the same man I was then, and I don't run. Not any more.

I put down my glass and give another nod. Christ, if I keep on like this I'm going to come across like one of those ridiculous nodding dogs you get in the back of vehicles.

I force my head to still. 'I believe so.'

'Event?' Alexa asks, jumping on the change in topic too.

'I sponsor a youth centre back in London—'

'Don't be so modest, love.' My mother shakes her head at me before looking to Alexa. 'He *launched* that youth centre; without him it wouldn't exist.'

It's my turn to pink up. And I don't blush. *Ever*.

'It would have eventually,' I say. 'The proposal was already in place.'

'Yes—and you took that proposal, built on it, and made it a reality.'

I couldn't exactly deny it, but boasting about it…

I rub the back of my neck, which sure as hell feels hot. My cheeks burn.

I do these things to help people. Kids. Teens. People who need an outlet—somewhere to go to feel safe, less alone, to vent and let off steam.

'What does this youth centre do?' Alexa looks at me, and her interest seems so genuine I struggle to quash the spark of pride it triggers.

'It's a place for kids to hang out, play sport, study… or just get help.'

'Help?'

'We have counsellors on hand.' I shrug. 'Sometimes they just need to talk to someone who won't judge, won't hit back… It's a safe environment for them to work off steam and make something of themselves.'

'He funded it, and he helps to run it too. Tell Alexa what you were doing this weekend.' Mum smiles at me indulgently and then says to Alexa, 'You will *love* this!'

My cheeks burn deeper and I pick up my glass for another swig. At least I'm not nodding now. I can see what Mum's doing. She's trying to big me up in front of Alexa. No doubt looking for us to make amends, to get Alexa to accept that I may have walked out but, hey, I'm a good man really.

Well, screw that. I have no amends to make.

She moved on. I didn't.

'Cain?'

Alexa's soft prompt pulls me up sharp and I know I need to escape soon, that it's getting too much, but I can answer this question easily enough. I can talk about the youth centre in my sleep. It's my passion to help those that need it. To make sure they have a place to go to, to belong, when they don't have a home of their own or home is part of the problem. I know it chimes a chord with me—Alexa even more so, when I really think about it.

'We have a youth entrepreneur scheme. Once a year they get to pitch to investors and I always sit in.'

I look at my plate, which is almost empty, and I can't stomach any more. I roll my shoulders and try to think up an excuse to leave that won't disappoint Mum.

There isn't one.

'And do they get investment?'

I look at Alexa, note her continued interest and feel a sudden pull to tell her more, to share the importance of this venture and why I care about it so much.

But sharing with Alexa…it opens me up, makes me vulnerable. This past week—these last three months, even—have proved just how much I'm not over her. That no amount of hate will protect me from her.

'The ones that are ready, yes,' I say. 'The others get invaluable advice from the best in the business. It gives them drive and confidence in their abilities to succeed.'

'As well as giving them a place to call home when they don't have a real one to go to,' Mum chips in.

I don't know whether she realises it, but she's just described me. The man I was when I set up the centre. I wasn't a kid, or a teen with good reason to feel how I did. I was a man who should have known better—who had thrown it all away because I was jealous, obsessed with being pushed out and not feeling good enough.

Something that had only been reinforced when

I returned after those first three months, hoping to make amends, to win Alexa back, only to find they'd all moved on quite happily without me.

My body burns with the memory—the sight of them on the steps of the registry office, taking photos, laughing, smiling. I never should have gone. The second I learned of their location—from my father's PA, of all people—I should have bolted, put myself on a plane to America and not looked back.

Instead I stood there in the shadows, a frozen statue, incapable of moving until they disappeared out of sight.

And now I've come back again, when it's all too late and that family is irrevocably broken...lost.

No, not completely lost. You still have Mum. And she needs you as much as you need her.

But what of Alexa?

It seems she's part of the package, thanks to her closeness to Mum—a bond that only seems to have grown over the years. Hell, she's even taught her to cook, something I never thought Lexi would take to or show an interest in. And they have such an easy awareness of one another's routines, an obvious fondness in their eyes when they look at one another.

Yes, she's definitely part of the package.

I meet Alexa's eye and I don't want to see the admiration she's directing at me now. I don't want to react to it with the warmth that's spreading inside, soothing the hurt with scary ease.

'It sounds great.'

I know she means it. I know that in spite of our past she's praising me.

It's the kind of youth centre she could have done with when I first stumbled across her, lost in the corridor of our crowded school, wide-eyed and alone. She was the epitome of a troubled teen, tossed from foster home to foster home, school to school, as they struggled to tame her. And I, the sports hero, fell for her hook, line and sinker.

I took her under my wing, brought her home, gave her everything I could. And my family took to her too, her intellect making her the perfect study buddy for my brother. They were the same age, after all.

It didn't matter then. They studied together, but I got to date her, and our relationship grew over the years. But then so did theirs. They finished school together, graduated from university together, worked in the family company together...

My gut twists with that old familiar pang, but as I look at her now, in that oversized sweater, with those ridiculous socks covered in bunnies beneath the table, the last seven years evaporate. I'm transported back to cosy nights on the sofa when she'd lie with her legs across my lap, book in hand, while I'd catch up on the football. Occasionally she'd shake her head at me as I shouted at the screen, but her eyes would be filled with love, all for me.

The reimagined scene flickers to life inside me, and as I continue to watch her I feel that old protective need come alive once more, the desire to have back what we lost growing out of my control.

And if I can't depend on my control to keep those feelings at bay then I know I'm in trouble.

Heart, mind and soul.

'That was incredible, love.'

Marie smiles at me, having just finished the last of her dessert, and wipes her lips with her napkin.

'I told you—I've been taught by the best.'

I feel Cain's eyes on me and wish I hadn't finished that second glass of wine, let alone the dessert wine Marie insisted on pouring. I can feel its heady warmth soothing away my tension, blurring the boundaries I've worked so hard to draw up.

The problem is that I can stay angry at the Cain who left seven years ago. I can even detest *him*.

But the man opposite me… He's the same, and yet…

I sense so much is different.

He's more measured, less likely to jump in before thinking, less fun-loving too. He used to be quick to laugh—quick to act the fool, even—but I can't see that in him now.

If he hadn't broken my heart I might even feel sad that he's hardened over the years. But that youth centre initiative… If there was ever a way to soften my defences, that would be it. Wine or no wine.

Not that I *am* softening. He left once—there's nothing to say he won't do it again. In fact, he's even more likely to do it now he has a life to go back to. Regardless of his threats to stick around, to set up home. I'm convinced he only said those things to goad me.

And what of his life elsewhere? Does he actually have people to go back to? A woman? A family, even?

I realise I know so little about him and my stomach writhes over those missing years. There must have been women. Plenty of women. No one can look like Cain and keep an empty bed.

And, oh, God, why am I thinking like this?

The blasted wine.

Marie eyes us both. Our silence is heavy even to her, I'm sure. 'How about a spot of brandy?'

'No!'

It blurts out of us both and for a second our eyes meet. A smile—hell, almost a laugh—erupts, but I shake free of the weird connection.

'No, thank you,' I say, softer now as I look back to her. 'I could murder a coffee, though.'

An injection of caffeine. Sobriety—that's what I need to see the rest of this meal through. And then I can go home, take a bath and read a good book.

Anything to distract myself from this. From *him*.

Despite Marie's best efforts, I'm not ready to address the past head-on, and I hate that his return has put me in this position. If only he hadn't upped and left in the first place there wouldn't be this colossal secret between us. A secret with the power to cause so much more pain.

And, if I'm honest, I don't want to dredge up that last argument, the words that were said, the things that can't be taken back, no matter how wrong or twisted they were.

'Coffee it is. You head into the living room and I'll bring it through.'

We rise and she looks at Cain as he moves to follow her. 'Shoo, shoo—I can manage coffee on my own.'

If ever there was an order, that *is* one, and without thinking I raise my brows at Cain, who's pulling the same expression at me. And there it is again—that connection, our eyes dancing into each other's as Marie's shameless orchestration of 'alone time' unites us.

He clears his throat and gestures to the doorway. 'Shall we?'

'We best had.'

I try not to look at him as I pass him by. I even hold my breath so I can't get a hit of his cologne. But my body warms over the memory of it anyway. It's musky, welcoming, all male. And it took over my senses four days ago, when he kissed me—when *we* kissed. The intensity of it, the old familiar versus the new...

No, there's no way Cain has lived a life of celibacy these last seven years and I shouldn't care.

I want to blame his power over me on my abstinence. On the fact that while he was burning me out of his system with many a willing woman, I spent seven years with nothing more than a peck on the cheek, an awkward kiss to the lips...mine and Liam's one attempt at consummating our marriage, icky at best, and halting before we got anywhere close.

But is it really to blame?

The fire's crackling in the grate as we enter, its

glow the only light in the cosy room and making it feel even smaller. I immediately head to the lamps dotted around, knowing that Marie favours their soft lighting to the brightness of the overhead one, and start switching them on, keeping myself busy.

My ears are attuned to Cain, though. I can hear him tending to the fire, adding logs, stoking it, but I avoid looking at him. If I'm lucky Marie will return before I have to.

I walk to the glass doors that open up onto Marie's courtyard garden and watch as the various solar lights flutter in the wind. Their glow lends a magical, fairy-like feel to the pretty pots, the garden wall and the climbers she's planted. I try to empty my mind, focus on the soothing scene—until a sudden stillness in the room draws me back.

The spit and roar of the fire is the only sound I can make out, and as I turn I see Cain is standing rigid before it. He has something in his hand. Something…

Oh, God…

I feel my skin pale, the cold sweat returning. I've forgotten about the photo. Or at least I haven't had the foresight to recall it. It's just a feature of the room, blending in with the many other ornaments, pictures and paintings.

Why hasn't Marie put it away?

And why should she? my conscience berates. It was our wedding, for Christ's sake—of course she would keep it on display. It's also one of the nicest photos of the four of us—Liam and me, Marie and Robert—taken on the steps of the registry office by a passer-by. We're smiling, happy—though I know the truth is more skewed than that. Each one of us is missing the man who now holds the picture as if it's an instrument of torture.

I look away before he can see me watching, waiting for him to speak and dreading what he'll say all the same.

I hear the gentle knock of the wooden frame as he places it back on the mantelpiece, hear him take a ragged breath against the crackle of the fire at his feet.

'Taking the let's-be-civil act a bit far, don't you think?'

My eyes flick to his. He's facing me now, his hands deep in his pockets, his expression hard. I don't know what I expected him to say, but it isn't that.

'How do you mean?' I'm hesitant—confused, even—and I wrap my arms around my middle.

'"It sounds great."'

It's practically a sneer, and I know he's referring to my comment regarding his Youth Centre.

'It does. I'm impressed.'

He looks away and shakes his head on a short laugh.

'What?' I ask.

His eyes come back to me, but he says nothing. There's no hint of that easy connection now. We're back to how we were when we parted four days ago.

The silence stretches and I'm so aware of everything about him. I can feel his anger, his hurt… And, hell, guilt is what *I* feel. Guilt for the photo. Guilt at what I did. *Guilt!*

It's unbelievable. Why should I feel guilty when everything that happened was down to *him*? It was *his* blasted fault.

But even as I think it I know the truth is more complicated, that there were things I could have done differently seven years ago—things I shouldn't have said, things I could have said and didn't.

But he was the one who left, not me.

'Why don't you say what's really on your mind?' I ask.

He says nothing and I lose it, striding across the room towards him. He's no innocent in this and I'm going to make him answer.

'This is what you're thinking about!' I snatch the photo from the mantelpiece and thrust it out, making him look at it. 'This is what you're angry about. Not the fact that I dared compliment you on your youth initiative.'

His jaw pulses. He's so close now. Not even a foot between us. And as I drag in a breath his scent invades my senses…my head swims with it. The heat spreading through my body, nothing to do with the fire beside us and everything to do with my anger and the persistent need, the lust I just can't shake.

'It's *your* fault, Cain—can't you see that?' I force the words out, refusing to listen to the guilt, to the simmering heat, as I glare up at him.

'What's my fault, Lexi?' He leans closer, his eyes raking over my face, the flames from the fire flickering in their depths. 'How you feel this second?'

He reaches out, his fingers surprisingly soft beneath my chin, his eyes falling to my lips that I now wet and wish I hadn't. 'Don't, Cain.'

'Don't what?'

He traces my lower lip with the pad of his thumb and I shiver—too much heat, too much need. I feel the frame start to slip in my hand.

No.

I back away, out of his reach and tighten my grip on the photo.

'*Everything's* your bloody fault!' I throw at him, my body thrumming with it all. Frustration at myself for being attracted to him. Anger at him for not accepting the part he played. Desire. The carnal ache calling for satisfaction—*No.* I try and burry it with more words, more accusations. 'The whole damn lot is your fault! If you hadn't left…if you hadn't abandoned us all then…then…'

I shake my head, squeeze my eyes shut, haunted by the old, tortured by the new—the plane crash, losing my best friend, my father figure… Would they have even been on that plane together if Cain had never left?

Christ!

I open my eyes. Would Cain have been on it as well? Or instead of them?

My whisper is almost ghost-like. 'The plane crash…'

His eyes flicker dangerously. 'You may see me as some kind of God, Alexa, but even *I* can't conjure up a storm worthy of taking out an aircraft.'

'That's not what I meant, and you know it.'

He closes the gap that I've created. 'No, what you mean is if I hadn't left seven years ago then maybe there's a chance it would have been *me* on that plane instead of *Liam*.'

His lips curve into a smile that is all the more chilling, all the more immobilising for the pain I know it masks. And the hatred it doesn't.

'How tragic for you that I'm the one you're left with…'

'Right, I've brought both! Brandy and coff—'

Marie is halfway in the room when she freezes, a laden tray outstretched before her. Her eyes fall to the picture still in my hand and I see her skin pale beneath her make-up.

Damn you, Cain.

'Everything okay?' she says, her voice unnaturally high.

I move quickly, placing the photo back where it belongs and going to help her with the tray. I take it from her hands with a smile. 'Coffee smells lovely.'

She doesn't respond. Her eyes are on her son and I curse him again.

Say something, I urge him with a look alone.

'It does,' he says finally. 'But I'm going to have to give it a miss. I've an early meeting tomorrow and I need to get back.'

'But…' Marie wavers, her eyes wide with disappointment. 'Don't you want to call a taxi first? You can at least wait here for it.'

'No need. I can walk.'

'But you live miles away.'

He strides across the room and kisses his mother on the cheek. 'I could do with the air. Goodnight, Mum, and thank you for the meal.' He looks to me now. 'The pudding too.'

'Our meeting's not until eight—surely you can stay a little longer.'

For your mother's sake, I add silently.

'You're not my first meeting.'

And then he's gone, leaving an aching silence in the room that neither of us seems able to fill. I put the tray down on the table that sits between the two armchairs before the fire and drop down into one of them.

'You're going to have to tell him, you know.'

I hear Marie's words and I know exactly what she means. But, Christ…

'How can I? After all this time?'

'You just need to be honest with him.'

She moves to sit in the other chair, pressing down the plunger in the cafetière before picking up the bottle of brandy and pouring two glasses. She passes me one.

'I was just having coff—'

'Humour me.' Her smile is small. 'You look like you need it. The coffee can wait.'

I shake my head. 'You're incorrigible.'

But I sip it anyway. It's not as if I need my wits about me any more. He's gone. And instead of feeling relieved, I feel… I don't know how I feel.

I shake my head, not ready to examine it any closer.

'I know it's not going to be easy, love.'

Marie sips at her own brandy, her eyes not once leaving me, their sympathetic quality making tears prick.

'But he deserves the—'

'Don't say he deserves the truth, Marie. I know he's your son, but *he* was the one who left…he was the one who ran…he was the one who…who…'

'Broke your heart.' Her lips pull back into a tight line, but dimples appear in her cheeks as she nods. 'Yes, I know, love. I know. But he has to know the truth or it'll eat away at you, destroy any chance you have of being able to move past this together.'

'Who says I want to move past it together?'

Silently she studies me, her assertive gaze reading me far too well.

'You think you can carry on like this? With this secret between you?'

'I don't know.' My empty hand goes to my stomach; the other pulses around the brandy glass as I struggle to even think on it, let alone speak. 'I just know I'm scared—scared of telling him and not knowing how he will react. Of leaving myself open…bare…having him crush me like he did before.'

Her eyes glisten in the firelight. 'I know, and I understand. But you need to do this and trust that he'll do right by you. He's not the same man who ran away.'

'You say that like you know him now.'

'I know him well enough.'

'How can you? He's hardly been here.'

She doesn't answer me, and I get the sudden impression there's something she's not telling me.

'Marie?'

'He's been in touch a lot over the past few months…visited too, ever since the funeral. I didn't say anything because… Well, I guess it's been a habit for so long—none of us mentioning his name for fear of upsetting one another, and I guess more so with you.'

'With me?'

'Yes, love…' She looks at me, guilty now. 'Because every time he came up that look would come over you and…'

Her eyes fall briefly to where my hand still presses against my abdomen and I know what look she means. I know then that she's been protecting me. That while I've been trying to look out for her, she's been doing the same right back. And so the guilt returns.

'I didn't want to hurt you,' she finishes.

'I'm sorry.'

'Don't apologise.'

'You shouldn't feel like you can't talk about your son to me.'

She shakes her head. 'You've had enough pain, that's all.'

'And you haven't?' I raise my brows.

Her smile is soft, wistful. 'I love you like a

daughter—you know that—and I just want you to be happy. I want both of you to be happy.'

My heart squeezes tight in my chest. *Happy*. I just can't imagine it. Not with Cain back in my life as a constant reminder of what I've lost, of what *we've* lost—only he doesn't know it.

Our daughter, our little Rose, is a burden I carry alone. Yes, I had his family, all of whom suffered her loss with me. But they hadn't felt the pain of a mother, of a parent.

Liam would have loved her. He would have brought her up as his own. And, no matter how twisted, how messed-up that would have been, it had been our plan. To give her everything I'd lacked growing up: a stable, loving home, a mother and a father...grandparents.

I swallow as the brandy rises in my throat, the rolling of my belly meeting the pain in my heart. Would Cain feel it like this? This sickness? This empty hole inside? The skin-prickling grief that you don't want to believe it has happened to you, to your precious little bundle?

'Have you said anything to him?'

My voice is distant as I ask the question, my head still filled with images of being in that hospital bed, her frail body unmoving in my arms, my body in a weird state of post-labour numbness.

'No—good heavens, no.' Marie's eyes are wide with her insistence. 'It's not my place. Don't get me wrong, I hate keeping it from him—especially knowing how much the past haunts him. But—'

I scoff. I can't help it.

'It *does*, Alexa, and you know that deep down.'

I'm quiet. I can hardly deny it.

I wrap an arm across my stomach and lean forward, staring into my brandy as if the amber liquid will have all the answers. 'What if he can't forgive me?'

'Forgive you?' She frowns. 'For what?'

'For not telling him sooner.'

'He left you no choice. None of us could reach him. And by the time we could it was in the past and you had moved on with Liam. He didn't want to be reached. Not until he was ready.'

'Would he ever have been ready?' I wonder aloud, needing to speak my mind. 'If not for the plane crash, I can't help thinking he may never have come back at all.'

'He would.'

She says it like she knows for sure, but I'm not convinced. It's been seven years, for Christ's sake— plenty of time for him to get over it and return if he was going to.

But he did come back, my conscience reminds me. *He came back, saw you and Liam together, married, and he ran.*

His declaration in my office comes back to me.

'I loved you once.'

Were we the reason he stayed away? Liam and I? Did we leave him so broken he couldn't face returning?

'I loved you once...'

I hear those tortured words as though he's speaking them in the room now, and I shake my head to empty it.

He *left* me. He *left* us.

Whatever he felt, it wasn't love—not the kind I felt for him. Because if it had been then he would have stayed. He would have fought it out. And telling him the truth of our baby will be easier if he's the villain of the piece, the person who abandoned us and broke my heart.

But what if it's all skewed? What if I'm more to blame than I know? What if the words I threw at him that fateful night cut deeper than I could ever have imagined? What if my marriage—a marriage I have to accept was driven by my anger and pain at losing him as much as it was my lonely childhood and wanting more for my child—kept him away?

Do I run the risk of casting myself in the role of villain?

Am I the villain deep down?

The one to be hated, despised, cast out?

Alone again?

CHAPTER FIVE

I DIDN'T REALLY have a meeting before my eight o'clock with Alexa. I was making excuses, covering my need to get the hell out of there before I lost what scrap of control I had left.

Seeing that photo last night…having the memory of that day in full colour before me…

I don't know how I missed it when I was in there previously. I sure as hell wish I'd gone on missing it.

I rake my hands through my hair and grip my skull, hoping the pressure will somehow stop the incessant noise inside. The noise, the emotion, the inability to think straight…

It's useless. Nothing will rid me of her, of our messed-up past and our even more messed-up future.

Because it *will* be messed up if we can't get a handle on this. We need to be able to work together. To separate the personal from the business.

But I can't even look at her now without that photo taunting me. They looked happy. All four of them smiling in front of the registry office, her in a simple white dress, hooked on the arm of my brother, my parents beaming as they toss confetti over their heads.

Seeing it was like being an observer again, watching the scene of happiness unfold from across the street, feeling the pain that ripped through me and having it return twice as hard, twice as fierce, along with the grief I've yet to deal with.

I shove myself back from my desk—no, *Dad's* desk. This was his office, his space, up until three months ago.

I launch myself to my feet and stride to the window as I feel the familiar churning in my gut, the cold sweat pricking against the collar of my shirt.

I'm surprised to see the windows have latches and I push one open, breathe in the crisp morning air and let it calm my skin. A definite perk to being in a low-rise city, I guess. Something I rarely ever get to be.

I have bases all over the world. But they're just that—bases. Penthouse apartments in skyscrapers that dominate the streets beneath, hovering above ground level and keeping me apart…distant.

Nothing like this.

Everything feels smaller here, more intimate, and rather than feeling a part of it I feel ever more out of place…on edge. Yet I was born here—lived here for twenty-five years. The building in which I stand is owned by my family's company—the company I dreamed of being a part of and of which I now own a controlling share.

And still I don't belong.

Why?

Because Dad didn't give it to you... Fate handed it over...

And now, more than ever, I need to prove myself, to make myself fit.

I look at the harp-shaped bridge, rising proud over the river, at the early-morning rush starting in earnest now, and take another breath.

It doesn't matter how I feel—insider or outsider, fate or not—now I'm here at Dad's company, and that means leaving the past behind enough to be able to work alongside Alexa and convince the outside world, the investors—Mum, even—that all is well.

And all *is* well.

I close my eyes, feel the sun trying to break through the clouds and warm my face...

All will be well.

Movement inside the outer office has me turning sharply on my heel. It's six-thirty a.m.—hardly a time I would expect anyone to be in—and I'm already opening my office door before I think better of it. Before I acknowledge that there's only one person who'd be here at this time...

'Lexi?'

I want to wince as her name comes out in its pet form. It's as if I'm exposing the old me—the one who loved her—each time I do it. But she hasn't even heard me, and I'm too surprised at what I'm seeing to try again.

She's dressed for a run: skin-tight Lycra from head to toe, showing off every curve, hot pink earphones dangling from her ears and her hair swinging in a ponytail. She's obviously just finished, judging by the flushed sheen to her skin, and she's singing under her breath, practically skipping as she moves on, unaware of my presence.

I lean into the doorframe and watch as she goes to the water cooler. She bends forward to fill the bottle in her hand. Her perfect behind, round and full, hugged in black Lycra, is offered out to me, and I feel an unwelcome surge of heat rush south.

Her voice inches higher as she hits the chorus of a song I can only just about recognise from her high-pitched rendition and I feel my lips quirk upwards. I've not seen her like this—relaxed, happy even—in so long. Her hips start to rock back and forth to the music as she carries on filling the bottle—*Christ, how much does that bottle take?*—and I feel my cock pulsing, getting harder, hotter, with each sway.

Jesus.

I adjust myself, and to my horror she spins and falters and freezes as her eyes hit mine. Water erupts out of the bottle as she clenches it too tightly, her other hand still holding the lid.

'Cain!'

She's the picture of embarrassment, and *damn* if that doesn't make her sexier still, with her lips parted in a provocative O, her colour high. My gaze travels lower, to where the water from the bottle meets the sweat that runs down the unzipped V of her running top, which she's clearly yanked down, thinking no one will be in yet. And then there are her breasts, the teasing curve of each as she pants for breath—

Holy Mother of...

I drag my eyes up to her mouth, which is still parted, to her cheeks flushing darker still, to her eyes, which are bright... And then she blinks and the shutter falls into place, her easy spirit evaporating as if it never existed.

She yanks the earbuds out. 'You could have warned me you were here.'

'I tried.'

'Well, I...'

She opens and closes her mouth. When she does it again I'm hit with the oddest desire to laugh and I can't stop it. It erupts out of me. And I haven't laughed in so long my head spins with it. She glares at me, and that only makes me laugh harder. Maybe I'm starting to lose my mind a little. Is this what grief does when you don't let it out?

'What's so funny?'

I push off the doorframe and close the distance between us, my eyes on the earphones now dangling from her clenched fist.

'Still your favourite band, huh?'

She closes her eyes and shakes her head. 'You heard all that?'

'Yup.'

I take the bottle from her weakening grip and bend to fill it up once more. It keeps me busy and it's a nice gesture. I'm hoping that with enough nice gestures we can start the day on neutral ground. Do what needs to be done for the company's sake.

'Lucky for you, you have a well-paid day-job.'

She takes the bottle from me and screws the lid on. 'Thanks.'

'No, thank *you*—that little scene brightened up an otherwise shitty morning.'

'It's only six-thirty—what could possibly have gone wrong already?'

I run my teeth over my bottom lip, look down into her face, so near, and wish to God things were different—another life kind of different.

'Do you need to talk it through?' She takes a swig from her bottle and I can tell she's putting on a front, following my lead. 'I'm just going to take a shower and I'll be right out.'

She starts to move off.

'Wait! You have a shower in your office?'

Not even Dad's office has one.

Her eyes flick away, and I wonder what I've hit upon now.

'Liam had it installed so we wouldn't need to go home after our morning run.'

Of course he did.

I nod, try to appear uninterested, and know I'm failing miserably. 'No need to rush. It's not something you can help with.'

No, that mess is all me… Unless she suddenly wants to go another round in her office. This time I won't be fool enough to demand her verbal confirmation. I'll happily take the confirmation from her body. Because *that* had definitely wanted me.

Like mine wants her now.

'Okay.' She's walking away again, and I swear

she's purposely teasing me with the sway of her arse. 'I'll be in my office if you change your mind.'

Her office...

I'm treated to a mental replay: her leaning back over her desk, her blouse damp from my mouth, her legs tight around me, my ears filled with the heady moans she gave.

A truce. That's what you need. That's what the company needs.

A fuck I could go elsewhere for—because she would never be just a fuck.

It's seven-thirty, and I'm itching to cross over the outer office and get this started. Whatever *this* is. I have no idea what Cain intends to take on—what role he's going to play—but if he has some grand idea of pushing me out he has a fight on his hands.

I drum my fingernails against the desk and look at my computer screen. My calendar is open, today's schedule stares back at me, and my heart sinks further in my chest.

Back-to-back meetings. Another day of getting no real work done.

I want to go and brainstorm with our techies—I want to feel the buzz of innovation, of fixing problems people don't even know they have yet. And instead here I am, suited and booted, ready to talk the talk...but I can forget the walk...the doing.

Although come to think of it, now Cain is here maybe it doesn't have to be that way. The idea sparks a hopeful flutter inside me. Can I relinquish enough control to go back to what I really want to be doing?

And have him slowly push you out?

No way.

I immediately quash the idea. I don't know what his intentions are, and on top of that do I really trust him? Do I really believe he won't run again? What if this is some fleeting interruption for him, during which he shakes things up and then bails? What then?

There's movement in the outer office and I see the early birds are starting to arrive. I give a small smile through the glass in acknowledgment and push up out of my seat. He said eight, but he's here, I'm here, and I can't stand this stomach-churning wait any longer.

I leave my office, taking my coffee with me, and my pulse starts to thrum in my veins. Nerves. Dogged lust. I'm not sure which, but my mouth is dry. I sip my coffee and try to tell myself this is just like any other meeting.

His door is ajar, but as I go to rap on it my hand stills in mid-air. The last time I crossed this threshold it was shortly after the crash. Marie wanted Robert's personal effects to be taken home, and I didn't want to put anyone else through the pain of doing it.

His PA had served him for thirty years; she'd suffered his loss like a family member. And as for me… Well, it was something I could do to be useful—anything to distract myself from my own grief.

But it wraps around me now…a chilling blanket

that I have to straighten my body against as I force my knuckles to strike against the door.

'Yes, it's good to be back,' I hear him say.

I peer through the gap. He's on the phone, standing behind his desk. His eyes shift to me as I enter and I mouth an apology, turn to leave, but he raises his hand, stopping me.

'Yes, a week Friday, Ethan... Glad you can make it...'

His eyes are hooked on mine and I feel his attention on the call slip. Mine doesn't, though. I know exactly who he's talking to and my blood fires.

'Dinner? Let me check the diary and get back to you...' A frown mars his brow and I wonder if he's read the eruption that's coming. 'Look, I have to go... Will do...bye.'

I turn and close the door, telling myself to count to ten and remember that these walls are thick, but not entirely soundproof. Especially in an office building that isn't at full steam yet and lacks the usual background hum.

'Hey,' he says to me now.

'Ethan Tennant, I take it?' I drop the pleasantry of a greeting as I face him.

But his eyes are busy sweeping over me, his attention off my words and totally on my appearance.

What the...? And then I remember what I'm wearing. *Damn silly move.*

'You choose that outfit on purpose?'

He drags his eyes back to mine and they are dark, intense, openly feasting on what he can see, what he can remember from the last time I wore it. In my office, just last week. My stomach contracts, and the heat he injects is as visceral as if he's stroked the pad of his thumb over my clit.

I bite the inside of my cheek, stave off the betraying whimper that climbs my throat. 'I asked you a question first.'

His mouth quirks up to one side. 'Yes, it was Ethan.'

'You seem very...*chummy.*'

He pockets his hands and steps out from behind the desk as he considers me. 'He was Dad's best friend.'

'Yes... And you've not been around for seven years, but now you're best buds?'

He shrugs, the movement slow as he steps closer and leans his head to one side, narrowing his eyes.

'Tell me...' I wet my lips, my mouth once again parched. 'How long have you and Ethan been planning this?'

His eyes widen and he shakes his head. 'I don't know what you're talking about.'

'No?'

I step towards him, ignoring the buzz our growing proximity gives to my eager body. I'm not turned on. I'm angry. One hundred percent livid. And if the ache between my legs would just quit, I'd believe it wholeheartedly too.

'So, the company's most influential board member—the man I consider responsible for sowing the seeds of doubt about me, the *doubts* that brought *you* back here—' I stab him in the chest with one finger '—just happens to be on great terms with you?'

He holds my eye, doesn't blink.

'I'm here to help regain the board's confidence.' His voice is smooth as silk, brushing over my skin. 'And, as you so correctly state, he *is* the most influential board member—which means I'm starting with him.'

He catches my finger in his hand and the contact zings along my arm.

'It's good business sense...nothing more.'

I laugh, but it's high-pitched—either from his touch or my continued disbelief. I hope he sees it as the latter.

'Are you sure you didn't start with him three months ago? Start sowing those seeds of doubt yourself?'

I stare resolutely up into his face, refusing to let him catch a glimpse of what he's doing to me.

'I don't like what you're insinuating, Lexi.'

My stance softens at the pet name and I feel my temper soar, angry at my body's betrayal. 'Quit with calling me Lexi. It's Alexa.'

'No... To me, you're Lexi.'

I inhale, to fend off the dizzying dance his insistence creates, but instead his familiar scent invades me, cocoons me.

When will I learn my lesson? Don't get too close. Don't breathe him in. And, above all, don't fucking touch him!

I try to pull out of his grasp, but he has me held fast. 'That was a long time ago,' I say.

'Was it?' he murmurs.

Too close. Far too close. His free hand snakes around me, curving my frustratingly pliant body into his.

'Because right now I want you every bit as much as I wanted you then.'

'Cain...' It's a whisper, and my body trembles with it. The pent-up desire, the continued fight. My good sense battling my neglected libido.

He's the only man to have made me feel this way, and I have this irrational fear that he's the only man who ever will. It doesn't matter what we've been through, what he put me through.

I shake my head, try to kill the thought dead, and I feel the splash of something on my ankle. It forces me to focus on the coffee cup still in my unsteady hand, and I stare at it rather than him.

'How about some honesty?'

His voice is gruff and my eyes snap to his, surprise making me forget that there's a reason I don't want to look up at him this close.

'Shall I start?'

My tongue is tied, caged by an overwhelming urge to pull him down and form a tryst with his.

'What do you say?'

I nod. It's all I can manage when my lower body is pressed against his. And I know it's not his hand that's holding me there. I know it's my own treacherous need to feel his desire straining between us.

To have that heady reassurance that this is no lie. He wants me. Regardless of everything else, he wants me as I want him.

His gaze darkens as it falls to my lips and I realise I've wet them on impulse. I can feel their sheen in the cool air-conditioned room, feel how they're slightly parted and demanding what I won't dare to.

'This morning is the first time I've spoken to Ethan,' he says.

I go to respond but he stops me.

'Let me finish.'

I oblige and his hold around my fingers relaxes, no longer gripping as he starts to caress them, the gentle touch as hypnotic as his gaze.

'I haven't spoken to Ethan in over seven years.' His voice is soft, earnest. 'Yes, when I returned last week he soon learned of it, and he reached out to me. What you just overheard was me returning his call.'

I want to say I don't believe him. I want to throw his words back in his face. And he must know it, because his fingers over mine still and his jaw flexes.

'*Lexi...*'

He sounds pained now, and his eyes, staring down into mine, are just as tortured.

'I am not the enemy. I'm here to help you. Regardless of the past.'

'But...'

I give another shake of my head. Because if Cain isn't the enemy, then how can I protect myself? How can I protect myself from him and a future with him in it?

'It would be so much easier if you didn't fight me…if you just trusted me.'

I feel tears prick and curse my own weakness. 'How can I trust you? I loved you, Cain, and you left. You didn't stay and fight—you ran.'

'It was all I was capable of doing back then. I couldn't cope with my father's decision… I couldn't cope with…'

His eyes glisten and—*oh, my God*. He can't be. Cain doesn't cry. I've never seen him suffer the weakness of mere mortals and I feel a fundamental shift inside me—a shift I can't prevent and that's far too close to my heart.

Is he reliving that last argument? Is that why he can't bring himself to finish his sentence? And do I really want him to? Do I really want him to dredge it all up?

'I'm not the same man I was then,' he says eventually. The glisten is all but blinked away, but his voice is still thick. 'And I'm not going anywhere now. Just let me help you…*please*.'

I can't speak. I can't move. It's taking all I have just to stop my own tears from falling, to stop my toes from lifting, from my lips meeting his.

'Let me help the company my father created…the company my brother loved.'

Oh, Jesus.

It's a low blow. He knows I can't say no to that. I just can't. It doesn't matter what risk it poses to me, to my heart that has never healed, to my baby…our baby…the truth…

I can feel myself nodding—even though deep down I'm still tormented by the past, by what's still left unsaid.

'Good.' He breathes out. 'Now it's your turn.'

'My turn?' I frown, confused.

'For honesty?' He reminds me of our pact.

Oh, God. Oh, no.

He releases his grip on my hand, my lower body, but he doesn't release me. Instead his hands rise to my face, gently cupping my cheeks as his eyes burn into mine.

'Can you deny you still feel this?'

'Don't, Cain. Don't do this,' I whisper. 'You want a place in this company. You want to see faith in it restored. That's fine. But don't bring our connection into it.'

His lashes flutter. 'You're denying it, then?'

'No. I won't lie to you. I want you. I want you more than I've ever wanted another soul. But that doesn't make it okay. It doesn't mean I'm willing to go there again.'

I take his hands in mine and gently press them down and away.

My body pines even as I step back, but I lift my chin, ignoring it. 'Where do we start?'

'Alexa?'

At least he has my name right this time, and that helps rebuild my strength. I've given him my honesty and now it's time to focus on what we should be.

'Please, Cain, the business is what matters now. Let's just concentrate on that.'

* * *

I want to curse. I want to grab her, pull her to me and kiss the rejection out of her.

She wants me. She admitted it.

'I want you more than I've ever wanted another soul.'

Which puts me above Liam…

I'm instantly chilled, goosebumps rife across my skin. To think it is bad enough: getting one up on my younger brother…my younger and very dead brother. My gut clenches tight and I can't breathe. The grief I haven't yet surrendered to is building with force.

'Cain?'

Her voice sounds distant, miles away, as I swim in a misery of my own making. I feel my fingers shake as I rake them through my hair and turn away from her.

'*Please*,' I force out, 'can you go?'

'Cain…?'

I spin on my heel. 'Lexi, just go. I'll find you shortly.'

'But…'

I stare at her, my pain, my past, my present all in one. *'Please.'*

And she does exactly as I ask, quietly, with no more sound—nothing but the click of the door as she closes it behind her.

I turn a full three-sixty and I'm surrounded by Dad. But both Dad and Liam are gone. Dead. There's nothing bringing them back. Nothing.

I sink to the floor in a crouch, a winded, wounded

mess. I heave in a breath. Another. I slow it down until I can get my breathing under control.

I stay like that until my skin cools, my head quits and the sickness passes.

All better. Almost.

I head to my desk, straightening my tie, my hair. Another deep breath and I'm calmer now.

One day I'll mourn. One day I'll feel strong enough to let it out. But not now.

I have a job to do and I'll get it done.

I will.

CHAPTER SIX

THREE MONTHS OF working alone—or rather, working without an O'Connor alongside me—has been hard. Lonely, even. And the pressure—I don't mean the pressure of the workload, I mean the pressure from my peers and from the board—has been unbearable.

It doesn't matter what I say or do, nothing can convince them I have this. I don't need help. They just need faith. And I'm convinced that doubt stems from my gender—my gender and my age: a combination it seems no amount of hard work on my part can fix.

But, of course, the second I caught that whiff of a conspiracy between Cain and the board via Ethan I pounced on it, desperate to blame someone other than myself. It came from my frustration, my anger, my dwindling motivation as I struggled to hang on under the constant weight of having to prove myself while keeping my grief private.

Days given to work, nights to tears. That was my routine for so long I'm finding it difficult to adjust to this new state of affairs.

Two weeks Cain has been back. Two weeks since he officially re-joined the fold and the transformation within the firm is marked. I wasn't enough, but Cain, it seems, is plenty.

News of his return rippled out swiftly, with calls coming in from investors and clients alike, the office abuzz with it. He already has Sheila, his PA, in position outside his office. John, his second-in-command, is in the office next to him; and a whole host of others are infiltrating my teams, gleaning what they can, helping rather than taking over.

No one is pissed off.

No one except me.

Although 'pissed off' isn't the right term to use. Don't get me wrong—I'm pissed off that all he has to do is walk back in and suddenly everyone feels safe again, confident, with the kind of faith in him that's something I've failed to earn, no matter how hard I've tried. But I have to acknowledge that my work life has eased. I'm starting to enjoy my job again, focusing on the things I'm good at rather than paying lip service to nervous board members, investors, peers, all of whom should've had faith in me from the off.

As for Cain and I, we seem to have found a way to function that doesn't involve sniping at each other one minute and ripping each other's clothes off the next... Although the desire to do the latter is there, simmering under the surface. It's a constant recognition that all it will take is one moment of weakness and we'll be re-enacting his first visit to my office and this time there'll be no stopping.

It's a dangerous tease that I try not to think about, but I have no power over my dreams, and it seems my mind is happy playing out a multitude of teasing scenarios that often leave me breathless and panting before I wake with a start.

And, as though my dreams aren't enough, working with Cain does the rest: watching him command a room, discussing ideas, strategy, debating next steps and ultimately coming to an agreement that we are both happy with. I never thought it possible.

Liam and I had a working relationship that stemmed from our love of programming, of software, of building something and having it do what you need.

Cain has never shared that love. He's always been a sports fanatic, intelligent, but fun-loving. When he was younger he wanted to live a little before getting serious with his career. That had been fine by me—until that fun-loving side had cut him out of the business and sent him running.

He obviously learned some hard lessons fast, because within five years of leaving us behind his start-up hit the headlines. Its record-breaking market capitalisation made sure everyone knew the name Cain O'Connor, but his own family were forced to read about it second-hand.

I shouldn't be surprised, therefore, that he can command a room, a board, an edgy investor or two. I shouldn't be surprised at his marketing skill, his seemingly off-the-cuff competitive analysis, his strategic decision-making, his even hand.

But I am.

The Cain of old contends with the Cain of today, and I'm struggling to merge the two, to keep my wits about me and my heart intact. He's the man who crushed me seven years ago. Who left without a backward glance.

But all I see now is the man he has become—and his charisma isn't just winning over the people who matter to the business, it's winning *me* over. It's getting under my skin and messing with my head.

And that brings me to this evening: the night of the function he asked Sheila to arrange. His welcome back do.

He's using it—*we're* using it—as an opportunity to present the company's roadmap and put to bed any remaining doubts over the company's future. I'm doing most of the talking—at his insistence— and I'm a nervous bundle of energy.

I know I'm up to the task but I argued that people would rather hear it all from him. His response had been a sharp 'no' as he insisted that *I* was the face of the company, the one who'd given it their all for so long and above all, it was what Liam and Robert would want.

He made me feel alive with his words, his faith, his belief. The fact he could say it all, say it all and mean it, without the bitterness Cain-of-old would have possessed is eye opening.

Eye opening and ever more threatening to my heart and head.

So here I am, fluttering. Nervous about what's at stake—nervous about what to say, how to say it. And most of all I'm nervous about being with *him*. Standing by his side for a whole evening. Providing a united front that is starting to feel less front and far too real.

I eye my reflection in the hall mirror. Scan my outfit which has taken too long to choose. I've gone with a deep purple dress down to the knee. It fits like a second skin, the square neckline not too revealing, the stiletto heels classic black patent. Perfectly professional and one hundred percent feminine. I'm going to rub my gender in their faces whether they like it or not.

And then I spy my unadorned ears. We can't have that.

I turn to walk down the hall, back towards my bedroom, and my apartment buzzer breaks through the quiet. *Shit.* I check my watch. Seven-fifty. He's early.

My heart flutters in my chest—an uncontrollable reaction I've come to expect every time he's near.

I head back towards the door and press the intercom. 'You're early, Cain,' I say, trying to resist the urge to gaze into his face as he looks up at the camera.

It's too tempting to watch him unobserved, to indulge in the need to enjoy his appearance when I know I need to keep my distance. Our non-verbal agreement to stick to business at work and 'safe' topics when in the presence of Marie, is working too well to crush it now.

He grins—and too late I realise I'm looking, feeling, enjoying...

'So sue me...' He shrugs, his hands casual in the pockets of his dinner jacket, a move he does a lot around me...and I wonder...is it because he struggles to hold himself back, just as I do. 'I'm eager to get tonight done and dusted.'

I shake my head, but can't resist grinning back—which is ridiculous, because he can't even see me.

'You want to come up and wait? I'm almost ready.'

'Sounds great.'

I buzz him in and force my smile to dampen.

Feeling excited about seeing him is one thing.

To let him know it is another.

And to feel it in the first place is just plain dangerous.

I take the stairs to Lexi's penthouse, admiring the converted Georgian home as I go. It's full of character, impressive and bold, and definitely Lexi all over. The vibrant colour in the paintings and the contemporary sculptures that feature on every white-walled floor remind me of her fiery hair and alabaster skin.

It's a foolish comparative, born of a long-forgotten romantic streak, and I scorn it even as I think it. But, hell, that streak is getting stronger, coming back with a vengeance the more I'm around her. The more time I spend with her and try to control it.

My stomach ramps up another gear in its chaotic fluttering as I get closer to her floor. *Gut-flutters, for fuck's sake.* My hand practically trembles as I rake it through my hair and I try to breathe through it. This doesn't work for me. This constant state of nervous energy, of anticipation, of arousal.

I live for our every meeting. Even a fleeting glimpse across the office and I'm there, watching until she passes out of sight again. It's as if seven years of absence have only made this connection stronger, all the more consuming, and I'm powerless to stop it.

Something has to give.

I mean, *Christ*, I've not banged one out with my fist in years. I haven't needed to. I date. I fuck. I move on. The women I see have a similar ethos. Sex is sex. Nothing more.

Only I haven't wanted just sex since I came back here. I've only wanted *her*. And she's forbidden.

She doesn't want me.

I don't want her.

That's what our sense dictates—what our past determines. Except I'm starting to listen less to reason and more to my aching cock, which fears a case of blue balls if something doesn't change soon.

Yes, it's all about your aching manhood. Nothing to with your heart that's never quite healed.

'Shit.'

I'm on her landing, staring at her door. For all I know she's staring back at me through the peephole and wondering why I'm standing here frozen to the spot and swearing to myself. It's enough to shake me out of it and I stride forward. A quick rap of my knuckles and the door's swinging inwards and…

Oh. My. God.

I lose my tongue. It's hanging somewhere in my mouth. The only reason it's not hanging out is that my jaw is clamped so tightly there's no escaping it.

'You going to come in?'

She cocks her head at me, her words slow, her smile oh, so curious and her eyes dancing. She's wondering why I'm dumb, mute… What would she say if I told her the truth? That her beauty, her appeal, has me wanting to forgo our plans for the evening—plans that are critical to the company—and slake this thirst.

Would she say *Go to hell*?

Or would it be *Come on in*?

Would we screw until neither of us can walk straight? Until the past is a distant memory and our present is all that matters?

Hell, it would work for me. But then life isn't that simple, kind or easy.

I step forward and resist the urge to touch her, giving her a wide—*safe*—berth.

'Nice place you have here,' I say as she closes the door and proceeds to walk me through into what appears to be an open-plan arrangement: a kitchen, a diner, a living room and a study area… A study for *two*.

I swallow.

'We liked it.'

Her words merge with the sight I'm seeing. Two

desks at right angles to one another, sleek monitors, stationery, even matching charger cables. It's as if at any moment Liam could walk back in and I'm frozen to the spot, my body chilled, my throat seizing up.

'Can I get you a quick drink? I just need to find my earrings.'

She's moving off. I try to say no, but I can't speak. I can't break away from the scene building in my mind. This was *their* space, where they worked and lived together every day. Did they share a pot of coffee, a bottle of wine, between desks? Did they laugh, joke, design together just there?

I sense her pause.

'Cain? Are you okay?'

She comes up alongside me, her eyes following the direction of mine.

She takes a small breath. 'I haven't had the heart to change it. It's exactly how he left it.'

And there it is. The confirmation of how much she loved him, of how much she's lost—hell, how much *I've* lost. My only brother.

My insides feel as if they're being crushed, my lungs are incapable of drawing breath—and then I feel it: the burn behind my eyes, the need to cry. Again.

I can't stand here any longer. I need to go. I need to get air and empty my head. My heart. The lot.

'Cain?'

Her hand is on my arm, soft and warm even through my shirt and jacket, and still I can't speak. I shake my head and walk away.

'Cain…?'

I force down the lump in my throat just enough to say, 'I'll meet you outside.'

'Cain!'

She calls after me, but I can't stop… I won't.

I race down the stairs. Floor after floor. My breath comes faster and faster and I fight the urge to run back up the whole lot, to seek the burn that will take this pain away.

Idiot. You should've known you were walking into their space and yet you went in, pumped up on your dick. You absolute heartless fuckwit. You deserve the pain, the grief—

I break out onto the pavement and heave in air, heave until my pulse calms…

No, not heartless. I loved her first. She was mine first. I—

'Sir?'

I focus through the haze to see Chris, my driver, a few strides away, his frown telling me I'm far from composed. Far enough that I'm worrying him.

And I never worry my employees. I never warrant concern. I'm a man who prides himself for his control—the control I lacked when I ran away seven years ago rather than face up to my emotions.

I've been back two weeks and I'm losing it more and more with each passing day.

I nod at him. 'We'll be along shortly.'

'Very well, sir.' He moves back to the driver's door, respectfully giving me the space I haven't asked for but so obviously need, and my head starts to clear. The apartment evaporates, the desk, *his* desk...

Breathe...

It took me by surprise, I try and reason. The sudden swing from desire to grief. It would make anyone weak.

But to feel someone's presence and know they're not there and can never be again... To know Lexi passes that space day in, day out.

Her husband. My brother. Gone.

Stop it, Cain. You haven't time for this now. You have a company to save. For Liam. For Dad.

I rake my hands through my hair, stare up at the stars and swear I'll do right by them. I'll see their company back to full strength. To hell with my own hurt and the part they played in it.

And this time I will be above reproach.

Lexi will be grateful.

Mum will be grateful.

And my conscience will be clear.

CHAPTER SEVEN

THE EVENING IS going swimmingly. The food was excellent, the presentation perfect, the response better than I could've hoped for.

Yes, swimmingly—so long as I discount the bit beforehand, back at the flat.

I know I should be glad—should be happy that the investors have lapped up my words, are paying me and the company the attention it deserves. But I'm too focused on Cain.

I can't get his expression out of my head. His pain. His anguish. I wanted to press. I wanted him to let me in, to open up and tell me exactly what he was thinking. Christ, I *wanted* him to show me the true grief I'd glimpsed at the funeral. Instead he'd run. Again.

I should be glad of that too. I should be glad that he left before I could feel any more than I already do. Because seeing Cain in pain—it breaks me. It breaks my resolve…it breaks everything I've fought so hard to keep in place for the last seven years. Even now my hand goes to my stomach, to soothe, to take away the chilling ache.

'I'm impressed, Alexa. I can't deny it.'

I look to Ethan Tennant, our most influential board member, and smile my most dazzling smile— the one that masks it all. Because he's the biggest reason I have worries at all; he's the one whose negativity has spread through the ranks and brought Cain back to my door.

'I'm pleased to hear it.'

I've only told the room the exact same things I've been saying for months—but in a presentation with Cain by my side. And it's not the presentation that's made the difference.

We're now in wrap mode…sipping the finest champagne before going our separate ways for the evening…and I'm ready to do just that. I'm tired. I'm sick of delivering platitudes when really I want to rant and rave at what they've put me through these last few months.

'Excuse me a moment while I pop to the restroom, Ethan.'

While I pop to the rest room and scream blue murder, releasing the words I so desperately want to lay at your feet, Ethan.

'Am I intruding?'

I feel a heated palm through the fabric of my dress, hear his voice trickle like honey down my spine, and just like that I am no longer chilled.

'Not at all.' I look up at Cain with a smile, and it's genuine. I don't need to force anything. And it's strange, the warning siren—the one that says there's no future here, the past will always stand between us—is quiet.

'I was just telling Alexa how impressed I am with the roadmap.' Ethan gestures to the presentation slides cycling through on the big screen—a mini-promo video of what we're proposing.

'It is. You seem surprised, though, Ethan?'

I send Cain a warning glare. I can't believe he'd say such a thing—especially in front of me.

'What can I say?' Ethan clears his throat, his awkwardness clear and making my skin flush. 'It's all down to the exceptional delivery.'

Exceptional delivery. I can't stand here for this. 'Excuse me gentlemen.'

They both nod in my direction and I feel their eyes on me as I leave. I force my stride to remain steady, measured, my ears burn though. *Please drop it, Cain.* If I can drop it for the sake of the company then he sure as hell can.

But will he?

'I can honestly say I'm impressed, Cain.'

I study Ethan Tennant's weathered face. He's aged over the years since I saw him last, filled out too. He was my father's best friend. His biggest backer. He's also the man to blame for the loss of faith in the company, the man who sparked the spread of scepticism about Lexi's ability to lead.

And it boils my blood.

I take a sip of champagne, keep my cool on the

surface. 'She's an exceptional CEO; the company's lucky to have her.'

He eagerly nods his agreement.

'So, tell me, Ethan, why the surprise? Why the negativity? Why the unease spreading through the board that she's not up to the job?'

He frowns at me, a cough rumbling at his double chin. 'Why, I don't… I'm not sure what you mean…'

'Come on, Ethan.' Both my smile and tone are purposely conspiratorial. 'You know exactly what I mean.'

'Well, I…' He clears his throat, his cheeks taking on a ruddy glow. 'Look, you can't blame us.'

'I don't blame "us". I blame you.'

I can't keep the menacing tone out of my voice now. I'm too angry, too disappointed in him—a man I've always respected, believed to be wise, honest, loyal. Hell, he's known Lexi almost as long as me.

'Now, hang on, Ethan.' He waves a hand at me, but he doesn't meet my eye. 'I don't know what you've heard, but I can assure—'

'It's not just what I've heard—it's who you are. You keep these board members in check. What you say goes. It's been like that since I was a boy and I'm sure it'll be like that for a long time yet…'

My tone is back to being level now. I want him to know I'm serious, and that means taking the emotion out of it. Making it about the business.

'Unless, of course, I have something to say about it. Maybe it's time the board had a shake-up.'

I know the power I wield. My money and my influence buy me the ability to deal with things as I see fit—and even someone of Ethan's reach and influence can't fight that.

I can't deny that using my power to address his treatment of Lexi feels exhilarating. Far too satisfying to be purely business-driven.

'Seriously, Cain, you can hardly blame me.' To my surprise he visibly relaxes. 'You'd have done exactly the same in my position.'

I can't believe he has the audacity to say it, let alone believe it. And I know he does believe it. It's written all over his face.

'Look, Alexa and Liam were a team,' he continues. 'United, they were a force to be reckoned with. Apart…'

I grit my teeth as I bear the weight of his words, wait for the familiar stab of jealousy, the grief that I can't afford to succumb to…

'She's a force on her own,' I say.

'I agree. But you can't blame us for having doubts.'

Christ. I'm not jealous—I'm angry. Angry at their lack of faith in her.

'She has given the company everything to ensure its success, to ensure Dad and Liam's legacy lives on. You should have trusted her.'

He faces me head-on now, his forehead crinkling as he raises his brows. 'Okay, I'm going to level with you—but you may want to be careful what you report back to Alexa.'

It's my turn to frown. I'm completely thrown, flummoxed. 'What the hell are you talking about?'

'Yes, she's an intelligent, talented programmer; yes, the employees and the clients love her; yes, she leads and people will follow,' he says. 'But you're forgetting that she's lost the only father figure she has ever known *and* her husband, her best friend, her business partner in one fell swoop. Losing just one is hard enough. Christ, I took a month off when my wife passed—'

He breaks off, his eyes flicking away, and when they come back to me they glisten with such sorrow, such heartache, that I'm lost for words, guilt crushing me. It isn't that I've forgotten, but it isn't like I was here either. I haven't even paid my respects.

'I was so sorry to hear about Louisa,' I say, when I can manage it.

He shakes his head at me. 'Two years and still it hurts like hell. But what I'm saying is, even that month wasn't enough. I couldn't think straight. I had to pull in extra support. Alexa...' He shrugs. 'She was like a woman possessed—back in the office within a week, like nothing had happened, issuing directives, taking control... I know she was proving she could do it, proving that your father's faith in her, your brother's too, hadn't been misplaced. I tried to tell her to let it go, to be with Marie, to take some time, that we would organise interim support.'

'But she was too stubborn?'

His lips thin into a tight smile as he avoids giving me the answer I know he's thinking. But I'm not letting him get out of it so easily—not when it hurts Lexi.

'So—what? You worked behind her back to see her pushed out?'

'It wasn't like that.'

'It's how it seems.'

'Why do you think Marie came to you?'

I'm taken aback, thrown once more, and my brain reels, trying to process where this is going and what it means.

'She came to me because she was worried about Alexa's health,' I say. 'The fact that she was working so hard. She knew things in the company were unsettled and...' Suddenly it all clicks into place. '*You* spoke to her?'

He takes a second to respond, and then he acknowledges it with a nod of his head. 'I did. I had to. She had her own grief to come to terms with. She couldn't see what was happening to Alexa under her nose. How exhausted she was. How overworked, under-rested... Not to mention she wasn't grieving. Not properly, at any rate. She was too busy protecting your mother from seeing anything bad.'

Now I truly am lost for words. It makes sense now—so much sense I can't believe I didn't see it for what it was. How did I not guess Ethan's motivations from the off?

But it was a risky strategy. Using the company to do it, risking its reputation—not to mention he played *me*.

'I'm sorry if you thought it backhanded,' he says, as I quietly process it all, my conflicted emotions likely playing out in my face. 'But Alexa needed someone to break through that exterior of hers, make her realise that it's not a weakness to accept help, and that someone was you.' He shrugs again, and this time his eyes sparkle, a true smile playing about his lips. 'Judging by the two of you this evening, I think I called it quite well.'

His suggestive comment has those gut-flutters taking off again and I cover them with a stern statement of fact. 'You risked the company to do it.'

'No, Cain.' It's his turn to be severe. 'Alexa needed help, and Alexa is the company. You both are.'

I don't want to dwell on whether he's right or not—whether I *want* him to be right or not, I'm still reeling from the fact he set us up and I was blind to it.

'So you played us?'

'Don't sound so defeated about it. I was playing these games when the pair of you were still in nappies.'

A surprising laugh erupts from within me. Shock, I guess. Shock and a sea of other emotions I can't begin to identify.

I take a swig of champagne, my eyes sweeping the room, looking at the people who have welcomed me back with open arms. But the only person I want to greet me in that way is currently in the ladies', and all I want to do is go to her and tell her I'm sorry. Which is madness when I think about the past and all she's done to me. It doesn't stop the urge, though.

'And it wasn't just for the good of the company...'

Ethan's voice is thick with emotion once more and I look back to him, my eyes narrowed. 'No?'

'It was for your father too.'

The drink catches somewhere between my stomach and my throat, burning like acid. 'What do you mean?'

'It was always his dream to have you come back, to have both his boys at the helm. He never realised his first step in that direction would send you running...'

He has the good grace to look apologetic about raising what my father did, cutting me out, but he carries on anyway.

'And then, when you got so big all on your own, he knew he could hardly go asking you to return. He never gave up hope that you would to do it of your own accord, though... One day.'

My stomach churns and my ears whirr as blood races too fast through my system. I need to breathe, but I can't pull in air. Dad was right. I always intended to come back. I even had a house built—a home not far from theirs, made ready for when that day came.

Only I waited far too long and fate stepped in. And their deaths brought an anger that I've clung to in order to avoid this crippling force inside me, this desolation, this agonising loss.

Mum has helped me to understand my father's motives—helped me forgive, even. And Ethan's words only reiterate what she's told me many a time.

The regret I feel at never being able to fix it, to make amends...it's crushing. But Liam... My head shakes. My battle with him is about so much more. It's about *her*. Lexi. My twisted heart taunts me with my age-old feelings for her—feelings that no amount of jealousy or hatred have been able to quash.

How can I forgive them?

But do I really want to hold this grudge for ever?

I can't make amends with Liam, but I can with her.

And do I truly want to? Is it even possible?

I think of our relationship now, when we put aside the past. I think of how easy it is, how right it feels—how my need to be with her is as real as my need to breathe. And then I think of *them* together, of that shared kiss on the registry office steps, and my stomach lurches just as it did then.

'She's coming back, Cain.' Ethan says it under his breath. 'Look, let's not be morbid. Let's look to the future, hey? With you and Alexa taking the company forward, no one will stand in your way.'

I'm not really hearing him. I'm already lost in the sight of her gliding through the room. My heart pulses in my chest, telling me exactly how I feel about her regardless of it all. As if she hasn't tortured me enough already…as if I'm willing to go back for more.

I'm a bloody fool. I know it even as I say to Ethan, 'You're right—we should be focusing on the future, a fresh start.'

And there's another thing I know: *this* Lexi—the one who has worked so hard to reach this point— deserves to end the night on a high, to know how exceptional she is, and she needs that truth from me just as much as the rest of the room.

They've done their bit. Now it's my turn.

'Thank you for being honest with me, Ethan.' I turn to place my drink on the side. 'Now, if you'll excuse me, I have someone I need to celebrate with.'

I feel his smile against my back as I head straight for her.

Christ, she's stunning—all elegance and sophistication, but with a hint of awkwardness that's always lured me in. A geek-like edge that tells me she wishes she were in her jeans and an oversized hoody, pinned to her computer screen, her nose wrinkling as she concentrates.

The image grips me, conjured up from the recesses of my brain.

Fuck, why didn't I stay and fight? Fight for her? For the life I wanted for us?

I have to stop my fingers reaching for her when she's close enough. I have to remember who she is, where we are, and that she's not mine. The presence of that ring on the hand now resting over her abdomen reminds me of that.

I cock my head and gesture to her tummy. She does this move a lot—it's like a nervous tic, but it's not one I ever noticed when we were younger. 'Are you feeling okay?'

'Absolutely.'

She's all breathy as she says it and my eyes lift to her face, to the flush of colour in her cheeks, the darkening in her eyes.

'You want to get something to drink?'

'I thought we already were?'

She turns and takes a champagne flute from a passing waitress, raises it to me before taking a sip. A sip that seems to be full of teasing, although I know it's just my mind that sees it that way. My twisted desire to have her want me like I want—

'I mean a real drink.'

She smiles around the rim of the glass. 'Too fancy for you?'

'You could say that. So, a drink? My place?'

'With you?'

The hint of a line appears between her brows and I have the ridiculous urge to kiss it away.

'No, with the Queen—she's staying for a few days.'

She surprises me with a playful punch. 'Funny.'

'So, what do you say?'

Her eyes waver over my face and she pinches her bottom lip with her teeth.

'Your place?'

'Or a bar, if you prefer?'

I see her hesitate, and then she kicks back a gulp of champagne.

'Your place is fine.'

I let go of a breath. 'Great, let's go.'

Her eyes widen. 'Now? But we have all these people. We have—'

'You've done enough. I promise.'

'You mean, *we* have.'

'No, *you* have. Now, come on—before Ethan insists on joining us.'

She rolls her eyes. 'Don't mention his name. I've not forgiven him yet.'

I take her gently by the arm and start to manoeuvre us towards the door, nodding respectful goodbyes as we pass people.

'You may want to go easy on him, you know,' I say between my teeth.

She glances at me sharply. 'What's that supposed to mean?'

'It means things aren't always what they seem.'

'You're going to need to do better than that.'

'I will,' I say. 'Later.'

'When, later?'

'Do you always have to question everything?'

'Do you always have to act so mysterious?'

I laugh and shake my head. 'You are a pain in my arse. You know that, right?'

'Takes one to know one.'

But she's laughing now, and the sound is so easy, so happy, so very different from how things have been between us. I know what I'm risking, I've been there and done that, but there's no putting the brakes on, not now.

'Cain?'

My name is a soft request from her lips and I pause to look down at her. She's so close I can smell her perfume, see the tiny flecks of black in the blue of her eyes.

'Thank you for tonight.'

I want to kiss her. I want to so badly my lips thrum with it.

'The night isn't over yet, Lexi.'

CHAPTER EIGHT

'YOU WERE REALLY impressive tonight.'

He's sitting on one side of the car, me on the other, and his voice is filling the space between us and drawing me in. I want to scoot over, curl up against him and rest my head on his shoulder. I want to close my eyes and empty my head.

It's what I would have done years ago. It's what I would do now if there weren't this chasm of hurt between us.

'Thank you.'

I keep my eyes on the window, my hands clenched in my lap. I can't bring myself to look at him. I'm wary of the admiration warming his voice, the admiration that's shone in his gaze all evening.

I can almost forget the fact that he ran from me hours before. That pain, that anguish, so obvious in his face.

Maybe this is a foolish idea.

What do I hope to achieve by going back to his place?

Do I think that he'll open up, tell me how he's

truly feeling, and we can go some way to repair the damage of the past? Am I hoping this will be my chance to tell him the truth? Get it all out in the open and face whatever comes my way? Whatever I deserve? Am I really ready for that?

I wet my lips and ask, 'How far is it to your place?'

'Ten minutes.'

I nod. I can still change my mind. Ask that he take me home.

I grip my fingers together tightly. *No. Get it done now, before too much time passes.*

Too much time with him back in my life. Too much time when I've had the opportunity to be honest and haven't been.

Because, let's face it, I could have told him the truth years ago. Once I knew how to reach him I could have tracked him down, made him listen and dealt with it head-on. When Liam and Robert were still alive…when there was a chance for him to make amends.

Oh, my God. The realisation hits me like a slug to the stomach, the air leaving my lungs on a rush and my eyes tearing up. It's my fault it's too late. *Mine.*

'Lexi?'

I hear the frown in his voice.

'Are you feeling okay?'

'Yes.'

My lie is obvious in the pained whisper, but he doesn't press, and I stare unseeing at the passing world outside, knowing that this is it. It's time to tell him everything. He deserves the truth. I owe it to him and I owe it to Liam. I owe it to Rose, too. Her father should know she existed—*still* exists as a part of me, of us.

He doesn't talk again and I'm grateful. My nerves are shot, my head and heart a mess. All he needs do is ask if I've changed my mind and I'll be going home instead.

But then I'd be the one running.

And I refuse to run.

I'm nervous.

It's a weird state of mind.

After everything we've achieved these past two weeks I should be used to her, to this, to the whole chaotic lot. But this is different. This is my home. The home whose existence I only recently disclosed to Mum, and she was stunned.

No surprise, really, since it took almost a year to build and was completed well before the plane crash. It's helped convince her I was serious about returning, and I guess it'll do the same for Lexi.

'So, you had this built?'

Her eyes are wide as she literally twirls on the spot to take it all in.

'Yes.'

'When?'

Here we go...

'The contractors finished last year.'

And there it is. She stops, the tip of one heel clipping the polished marble floor of the hallway as she asks, 'An investment?'

'A home.'

'But you… When we talked you suggested…made it sound like it wasn't a done deal—that you were *considering* living here, not *actually* living here.'

'I know. I guess I wasn't sure myself—not entirely.'

'But you had this built before—?'

She breaks off and I know she can't mention the crash. I'm not sure I want to either, so I say, 'Yes.'

Her smile is laced with sadness. 'It's amazing.'

'You like it, then?'

My ego is waiting for her answer. Hell, it was designed to my own specification, every last centimetre agonised over. As if I wanted to create perfection to lure me home, to make that transition easier.

She frowns at me and I can see the question in her eyes before she even asks it. 'Does it matter to you if I do?'

Does it? *Yes.* Regardless of my ego, I want her to like it for reasons I don't want to explore—just as I don't want to examine my real reasoning for bringing her back here.

'Yes.'

Her eyes glisten and she looks away, moving through the hallway under the pretence of exploring. But I know she's trying to hide from me. I follow her, captivated by every brush of her fingers over the surfaces, the sweep of her eyes. She looks through doorways, takes in the vaulted ceiling high above, the occasional piece of art. There isn't much of 'me' here in terms of possessions—not yet—but the shell, the fixtures and fittings…that's all me, thanks to my design team.

'It really is incredible,' she says softly.

My heart soars more than I'd like. 'I'm glad you approve.'

She walks into the open-plan kitchen, with its sleek black work surfaces, the white units that show no handles, the range cooker that I wouldn't know how to use…much to Mum's chagrin.

Lexi would, though. The thought is impulsive, and now it's there I can't let it go. I imagine her…fluffy jumper, silly socks, all casual and baking, earphones in, singing…the idea warms me from the inside out.

'Is that a swim spa?'

'Hmm?'

I pull my eyes from the stove, back to her. The real her, not the imaginary version. And it's just as appealing, just as damaged, and just as perfect with it.

She's in front of the glass that runs the full length of the room. Outside, the hard-landscaped garden is illuminated with subtle lights that enhance rather than glare and, as she so rightly surmised, there's my steaming swim spa, just waiting for its lid to be rolled back and enjoyed.

Beyond that is the open sea.

It's private, secluded—a real oasis.

An oasis in which I could lie her back in the bubbling water, her flushed skin bare to my gaze, my hands, my tongue… The image plays out, my body overheating with it.

She turns to look at me and I realise I haven't answered her.

'Yes,' I say.

The simple word is gruff, and I wonder if she can spy the cause. I can sure feel it. The tension building, the anticipation of where this night could be heading...

'A bit James Bond, don't you think?'

She cocks a mocking brow, but I know she's teasing—and, hell, she's right. What boy didn't want to grow up to have a Bond house? I sure did.

'Built into the craggy cliff face...dark and sleek... fully pimped-up.'

'Does that make me double-oh-seven or a villain?'

'Why don't you tell me?'

She runs her teeth over her bottom lip and I swear she's flipped from sad to flirtatious. I want it to be the latter. I want her to flirt with me.

Her eyes flick back to the spa and there's a definite longing in her gaze that I can't miss.

'You're welcome to come here any time you like,' I say thickly, without thinking, and now that the offer is out there, I can't take it back. 'There's an indoor pool downstairs too, protected from the onslaught of the Irish coastal weather.'

'A pool?' She lets out a hushed laugh and it feels wistful, distant.

'What is it, Lexi?'

She doesn't speak. I don't even feel like she's heard me. I walk up to her, about to ask again, when she takes a breath and turns to me.

'So, about that *real* drink…?' she says.

There's a sudden strength to her voice, to her smile, but I know it's all front.

'A Jameson's?'

Her lashes flutter and I know she's remembering. It was *our* drink, *our* whiskey. On a night after all was said and done, when I'd pulled her away from work—*from Liam*—we would lie back on the sofa, switch on the TV and crack open a bottle.

'Perfect.'

It rasps out of her. There's so much we aren't saying, so much that needs to be said, and I feel like we're dancing around it, neither willing to go first.

I turn and head back into the kitchen. The clip of her footsteps follows me, beating in tune to the pulse in my ears. I take out two crystal-cut glasses and place them on the side, the sound of them hitting marble loud in our silence.

I lift up the whiskey that's already there, waiting, as if it's always been waiting for this moment, and I pour a healthy measure in each, the slosh of the liquid echoing around us.

As I lift both glasses I turn to face her and she's even closer than I expect, her proximity stunning me still. Then she offers a small smile, her hand reaching out for one, and I smile with her.

'Cheers.'

She clinks her glass against mine and takes a sip, her eyes closing, her hum of appreciation almost provoking the same from me.

'Cheers…' I murmur, my eyes locked on her as I raise the glass to my lips.

She gives a small sigh of pleasure, her eyes opening and glowing against the pink creeping into her cheeks.

'Still like a real drink, then?' I ask.

'It has its place.'

We stay like that, our eyes hooked on one another, our drinks halfway to our lips, and say nothing. The silence is heavy, weighted.

'I wish you'd never left.'

Her admission has me sucking in a breath—not just because of what she's said, but because of the raw emotion in her voice, in her eyes. I throw back a gulp of whiskey, feel it burn as the words resonate within me, hammering home how much I feel the same. I know I do.

'You and me both.'

Her eyes waver and then they look up at me, searching my gaze, looking for answers.

'Then *why* did you? *How* could you?'

Her eyes glisten, and the desperation in her words rips through the heart of me.

'You know why I left, Lexi.'

She takes a shuddery breath, the hand holding the glass before her lips trembling. 'No—no, I don't.'

'You were there when Dad announced his intentions,' I say slowly, my voice low with warning. I don't want to relive that night, but she's forcing me to do so now. 'You were there when I told you how much it had hurt, how much I needed you to side with me, how much I loved you and needed your support.'

'*No.*'

She's shaking her head at me vehemently, anger sparking in her glistening blue eyes.

'Don't you *dare* throw love into this. That night had nothing to do with your love for me and everything to do with your own selfish expectations.'

I stagger back a step, shocked that she would throw the same words at me now as she did then, when she knows the damage they caused. 'How can you say that?'

'Because it's the *truth*. You left us sitting at the dinner table…your mum in tears, your father mad, Liam… Christ, Liam didn't know *what* to do. He'd earned that position with your father—he'd worked hard for it and he deserved it. And you—you just expected to be *given* the same because you were blood.'

She's shaking from top to toe now, and I can't even speak. Her argument is something that's gone around and around in my head for so long.

'You expected me to walk out on them—on your *entire* family, *my* family too—because you felt hard done by.'

'You were my partner,' I say coolly, trying to keep my anger at bay. 'They were only your family because of me.'

She gives a harsh laugh, 'You said the same that night, if you remember?'

I remember, all right. I remember accusing her of playing brother off against brother, hedging her bets until she settled on the one who would give her the most.

Wasn't that why I turned up at the registry office? To see for myself that I'd been right to leave? That she was just as scheming as I'd accused her of being?

'I said a lot of things that night, Lexi, and all of them still hold true.'

She pales, her lips parted in shock. 'How can you *say* that?'

'How?' I shake my head and walk away. I need air that's not tainted with her perfume…space without her body's warmth in it. 'Because you did exactly what I accused you of. You went and *married* him, for fuck's sake! For years I watched the two of you getting closer and closer, huddled together in the lab, working on project after project. I used to come in, try and coax you out for dinner, drinks—anything but work. And you'd spare me the merest of smiles and tell me, *"Later, Cain, later."'*

She drags in a breath and then she laughs, the sound high and grating.

'Spare me the *woe-is-me* tale, Cain. I *loved* you. Loved you so much your accusations crushed me. You made me feel like a dirty whore who would sleep her way to getting what she wanted.'

I flinch. My entire body trying to deflect the harsh vulgarity of it. A whore—no, never. But… 'You got to keep my family. Hell, you even got to be CEO of the family firm when all was said and done.'

She clutches her stomach with her free hand, her

skin ashen now. But *she* brought the past into this and I can't stop the words from coming now.

'You see, the thing is, Lexi, I can forgive my father. Yes, I'm still hurt that he didn't even consult me, didn't even offer me a chance to prove my worth before doing what he did. That he didn't seem to care how it would affect me, how pushed out I would feel. But I can understand his motives—sympathise with them, even. I've had years of building up my business, understanding the graft that goes into it, understanding how hard Liam must have worked and why he was worthy—why *he* deserved it and I did not. But you and Liam…together…'

I shake my head, nausea swelling at the sight of them in my mind's eye.

'How can I *ever* forgive that?'

'*Jesus*, Cain!' She shakes her head fiercely. 'Your brother and I were geeks. We understood each other…shared the same love for programming. He was *my best friend*. We didn't care that we weren't popular, or cool, or part of the "in" crowd… We weren't like you. We—'

'You think the fact I was popular with a bunch of idiots at school made me invincible? Stopped me feeling insecure within my own family? With you?'

She slams her glass down on the side, the liquid sloshing over the side, over her hand. 'I never once gave you reason to doubt me. Your own jealousy did that for you.'

'And after?' I say, ignoring the seed of doubt she's sowed. 'When you walked up the aisle with him?'

I place my own glass on the side, feel a toxic mix of jealousy, anger and desire raging like a storm within me. I stalk towards her, half expecting her to back away, but she doesn't.

'Or are you saying you married my brother in some reckless move of your own just to get back at me?'

It's a ridiculous notion. She would never…

But her eyes flare as I pause before her. Her lips are silent. No, she wouldn't have done that. She loved Liam; I know that. She even told me so that fateful night. She loved him as a friend, as a brother, she claimed.

But that doesn't stop my eyes burning down into hers, seeking an answer. I see how she looks at my mouth, how her pupils swell with the need I so easily trigger in her, but she's not getting out of this.

I raise her chin with my fingers, brush her lips with my thumb and feel the air she sucks in pass over it. 'Tell me Lexi, did he make you feel like this?'

Her eyes snap to mine. She gives an infinitesimal shake of her head and my heart soars even as my chest tightens with the twisted question.

'No…?'

'That's not… I mean… Don't do this, Cain.'

I press her back against the kitchen counter, her breasts crushed against my chest, and the carnal sensation is bittersweet in its intensity. I look at her mouth, parted beneath me, and I lower my head. My tongue teases inside, sampling the hot whiskey taste of her. She whimpers, the sound small and clamped inside her throat.

'I want to know, Lexi...' I brush the words against her lips, my fingers lifting to caress her neck, just like she used to ask me to. 'Did he kiss you like this...?'

My fingers start to trail down as I slant my mouth over hers, feel the softness of her lips. And the ease with which she lets me tells me I have her. She's mine.

I circle my fingers over her breasts, feel their hardened nubs press against the fabric of her dress as she rocks into me.

'Did he make your breath catch and your body ache like I do?'

I rotate my hand over one nipple and raise my head to look down at her. She's all wanton, swaying into every touch, every sweep of my lips, and I'm losing control. I can feel it shuddering out of me.

Did he make her feel like this? Did he make her wanton, lustful, desperate?

The twisted questions sear my brain, my body, push me, goad me. I want them gone. I want her begging me. I want her demanding that I fuck her. Demanding that all trace of any man, be it my brother or another, be gone from her mind.

'Are you wet for me, Lexi?'

Her lashes flutter open.

'*Are* you?'

'Yes.'

The admission is small, a whisper, and the colour rushing back to her cheeks is an added confirmation.

I stroke my fingers down her belly. 'Show me.'

She wets her lips. My brother would never have done this. He would have had her on a pedestal, all perfect and pristine. But I want the Lexi I know that's inside her—the one who would perform for me, drive herself crazy while I watched.

'Show me.'

She lowers her hands from where they grip the counter-top and strokes them down her thighs. I step back—just enough to give her room, to give myself a better view. *Fuck*, she's exquisite. Desire thrums through me, tightening up my muscles; my cock straining against my zipper, painful, ready.

Slowly she ruches up the fabric of her dress, taking it higher and higher, until the black lace of her knickers comes into view.

'Show me.' The repeated command scrapes out of me, hoarse with need and the worry that at any moment she will stop. I don't want her to. I don't want this crazy state of need ever to ebb.

She hooks her fingers into the waistband of her knickers and eases them down her thighs.

'That's enough.'

She pauses mid-thigh, her eyes lifting to mine, the burn of her need blazing in their depths.

'Step wider.'

She straightens, and the sight of her spreading her legs is almost my undoing. I groan as my cock bucks painfully inside my trousers.

'Now show me.'

She lowers her fingers to part herself for me, those fingers delving in deep and coming out coated in her wetness. I drag in a breath and watch as she pulls her fingers back over her clit, her hips rolling into the move. She moans softly, her eyes fluttering closed.

'*No*, Lexi, no… *Look* at me.'

I want no other man to be in her head. I want it to be me. Always me.

Her breathing is erratic, hitched like my own, but she does exactly as I command, her eyes locking with mine as her climax builds with the tempo of her fingers. The lace band of her knickers bites into her thighs as her legs widen and lock, her other hand flying out to grip the marble top.

'*Cain… Cain…*'

My name pants from her lips. She's close, so close, and I realise I want to taste her. I want to capture her release with my tongue, my mouth.

I'm already stepping forward and dropping to my knees. I urge away her fingers so that I can surround her with my mouth. *Fuck*, she tastes so damn good. So perfect. So right.

Seven years fall away. There's no pain, no hurt… only this. Our bond.

She cries out above me, the pleasure-filled sound ringing through the room, her hands forking through my hair, harried, desperate.

'Yes, Cain, *yes*.'

I look up, see her eyes on me, the flush to her skin, the waves as they roll through her body. And I know this is all for me. That no matter our past, no matter what *they* shared together, we have this. We *still* have this.

And now I want so much more.

CHAPTER NINE

'TELL ME, LEXI, did he make you feel like this...?'

I rock back against the counter, my body and mind shaken by what's just happened—what I *let* happen and what I *did*, driven by his perverse questioning, his need to compare and contrast.

I should have stopped him.

I should have come clean there and then, in the midst of our argument.

Instead I became lost in his lascivious game, his words, his command.

And where does it leave us now? Where does it leave me and what I need to tell him?

Slowly, he slips my underwear back into place, his stubble grazing against the inside of my thighs as he traces sweet kisses over the sensitive skin. My legs tremble, my body quakes. I daren't snap my legs together, or moan at his continued touch. Because, no matter the torment inside me, I still want him. So much it hurts.

He smooths my dress back down over my thighs and rises up, but he's as close as ever. His chest brushes against mine, teasing over my nipples which are sensitised in the aftermath and willing him to do more.

I look up into his eyes, scared of what I'll see, and I wet my lips—as a result of nerves rather than desire.

'I'm sorry I used my brother like that.'

His apology surprises me, as does his guilt, his remorse, but the passion is still there. The fire in his gaze… He cups my jaw softly and lowers his lips to mine. His breath is all whiskey and me as he brushes his mouth over my parted lips.

'I just…it's tortured me for years…' He squeezes his eyes closed. 'The idea of you and him…what you did together…him replacing me, surpassing me.'

I silence him with my lips. I can't bear him talking of those years—not when he doesn't have the full story. I want to tell him. I do. But now is not the time.

When will it be? I ask myself.

I kiss him harder, forcing out the questions, the doubt, the worry. But he breaks away, lifts his head to rake his eyes over my face.

'I hate it that he gave you everything I could not, that he took the most important thing in my life…'

His eyes soften into mine, his love of old as obvious as his desire, and I'm caught in it, unable to breathe.

'I know I left you, that I have a part to play, but you went to him. He asked you and you went. And all it took was three months.'

His voice is raw, his pain as real as if it were yesterday, and my heart squeezes inside my chest.

I reach for his face, cupping it in my hands as I stare up into his tortured gaze and tell him what matters in that second. 'We *never* had an affair. I *loved* you. I promise that I loved you with every part of me.'

And then I kiss him. I seal my vow with it. I can't rewind history and write a better path. I can't change the fact that I still haven't told him the full truth.

And when I do, will he hate me all the more? Will he see it as the greatest betrayal of all?

My stomach rolls with the thought of it even as he lifts his hands to my face, mimics my hold on him, his eyes searching mine as his thumbs stroke against my cheeks.

'I loved you,' I say again, desperate for him to see the truth of it.

His groan is half-anguish, half-desire, and he kisses me. Slow, savouring this time. It's not like the kiss in my office, or his seduction born of anger just now. It's something far more intense, far more powerful. And it's this *something* that binds us, that's stood the test of time.

I'm so tired of fighting it—tired of being alone, tired of feeling nothing but emptiness and grief. Grief for Robert, for Liam, for Rose—

Rose.

I kiss him back. Kiss him until there's a combating force strong enough to smother the pain. My tongue slides against his, rough, probing, sinking deeper. I lower my hands to his chest and feel the heat, feel the muscles flexing through his shirt, the race of his heart beneath.

'Cain…' I whimper against his mouth.

And he answers with a groan that's all desire, his hands urgent as they tug me against his hardness. The feel of his need, the evidence of his desire, has me burning up inside. That throbbing ache returns ten-fold as my hips writhe and my hands rake over him.

I need this. *We* need this.

But he's tearing away again, his head shifting to one side, his body totally still. I open my eyes and he's looking away, his shoulders heaving for breath, for control. But I don't want control. Not any more. I'm sick of it.

I reach for his face and pull him back to me. 'Kiss me,' I urge.

Kiss me before I say something that we can't come back from. Kiss me before the truth brings this to an end.

I nudge his mouth open, dipping my tongue inside to gently coax his own, and a shiver runs through his body. I feel it beneath my palms, hear it in his shaky breath.

'I need to know you want this,' he rasps out, his eyes dark and glittering into mine. 'I need to know that you want *me*.'

I go to kiss him again, to show him how much I do, but he presses me away.

'Walking away from you in your office…'

He closes his eyes and shakes his head. When

he opens them again, they're blazing with hurt and need, pain and desire.

'It all but killed me. But I can't play second fiddle in your bed, Lexi. I won't.'

My heart aches inside my chest. His vulnerability is raw, honest, and all the more powerful as it breaks through the controlled, commanding exterior I've been accustomed to these last two weeks, knowing it's all because of me…

But my heart has no place in this. This is sex. Primal. Safe.

Don't confuse it. I recall our conversation in Marie's living room, but so much has happened, so much has changed…

'I want *you*,' I stress, 'like I've never wanted anyone in my whole life.'

It's the truth, and it's more than he's asked for. I'm making myself vulnerable by admitting that he's always been the one, but it's impulsive and it's driven by his honesty.

It's also the perfect time to tell him everything… not to shy away from it for fear of the damage it will cause.

'Tell me, again.' He presses his forehead to mine, his eyes staring down at me.

'I want you, Cain.'

Now. Tell him now. Tell him it wasn't a real marriage. Tell him why Liam married you. Tell him about Rose.

But his lips are already crushing mine as he turns me away from the counter and propels me back against the glass doors to the terrace. I can't think any more. It's dizzying, disorientating, discombobu-lating. His body covers mine from head to toe, hot, urgent, and I'm on fire, the delicious throb of plea-sure whipping up inside me all the stronger for my recent release.

I take the onslaught of his kiss and return it just as fiercely, just as desperately.

Seven years without anything coming close to this. Seven years of feeling empty, of being alone. And now this—mere minutes after I lost it under his mouth.

I fork my fingers through his hair, down his neck, inside his jacket as I shove it from his shoulders.

A seven-year wait—for this. I can't trust him with my heart. I won't. I can't survive that pain again. But this—*oh, yes, this*—I can trust him enough for this.

It isn't about love—it's about need.

And I need him more than I need my next breath.

His jacket hits the floor as his hands force my dress up my thighs. His fingers against my skin are rough—shaking, even. Or is it me who trembles?

'Lexi.'

My name vibrates out of him and I realise we're both trembling, both unsteady as we try and slake this hunger.

I yank at his tie and nip at his bottom lip, deliv-ering a sharp hit that has the breath hissing out of him. He growls and kisses me harder, almost pun-ishing me in return, and I'm losing it. Desperate to have him naked and not able to summon the skill, the wit, to do it.

Buttons are too fiddly, zips catch. I moan in frustration as I claw at his shoulders instead, one leg lifting to curve around him. I draw him close, shamelessly riding his hardness as his tongue plunders deeper and deeper still.

Our kiss is suffocating, neither wanting to break it to draw breath, neither wanting to create any space between us at all, and the friction is so goddamn perfect. My clit is getting the continual grind of his cock as he strains against the confines of his trousers.

'Oh, my God, Cain…'

I start to pant, my ability to kiss him back breaking as my mouth turns slack, my movements stilted. I'm going to come. I can feel it curling up from my toes, pulling at my core. My body tenses as the delicious heat swells rapidly around me, through me. I try and stave it off, talk it down—*not yet, not yet*. And then Cain takes the driving seat. He knows and he grinds against me, pressing me back into the glass. His mouth returns to my neck and then his hands are on my breasts, rough, groping…

I want more…so much more… I want his hands on my bare skin…his mouth on my nipples.

'Damn this dress.'

It's Cain who says it, as though he's in my mind, seeing what I want. He finds the zipper at the back and yanks it down. I think I hear it tear but I don't care.

He parts it over my shoulders and I wriggle to help.

My exposed back meets the cool glass and I buck away. But his hand is there, curving me against him. I lower my leg to let my dress fall to the floor and my bra swiftly follows. My bare nipples brush against his shirt, the accidental caress as erotic, as charged as anything, and then his palms are there, weighing, caressing, thumb and forefinger rolling, plucking.

'Fuck.' I'm going out of my mind. I clutch him tighter, whimper more.

'Lexi.'

He says my name as if he can scarcely believe this is happening. Hell, *I* can't. It's too intense, too dreamlike, too heady.

He twists my hair around his fist, pulls my head back against the glass as his hot mouth trails across the exposed skin of my neck, sucking, devouring. He cups the back of my knee to lift my leg around him once more, delivering that perfect hit of friction again, each grind taking me higher and higher.

My nails bite into his shoulders. I'm unable to move, rigid with the spiralling heat, the knowledge that I'm close…so close. He pinches my nipple, squeezes it tight, almost painfully, and my clit pulses. He does it again. And again.

And then his hand is between us, slipping inside the elastic of my knickers. I bite into my bottom lip, hold my breath, and then he's there, slipping down into my wetness, the brush of his fingers circling over me.

'Cain!' It bursts out of me—a warning? A plea? I don't know.

'You're so wet,' he says against my collarbone, his kiss feverish upon my skin.

And then he drops lower, sucks in one pert nipple, the hot cavern of his mouth surrounding it, his tongue rolling over it, and I tremble in my rigid state, my body not knowing which sensation to focus on more: his fingers over my clit, his mouth, or his hand over my breast.

'I need to taste you again, Lexi.'

The heat pulses between my legs, my belly contracts and I drop my head forward, look down into eyes that gaze up at me imploringly. His tongue flicks out to tease at the nipple jutting at him, begging for more. He keeps my eyes trapped in his gaze as he tongues the sensitive flesh, his fingers picking up their pace inside my knickers...the same dizzying pace of his tongue.

'Yes, Cain...*yes*.'

His hand slips out of my underwear and he drops to his knees. My legs lock tight as I fear I'm going to collapse, but then he's cupping one of my ankles, coaxing me into bending my leg to step out of the dress, which is pooled at my feet. He returns my foot to the floor and does the same with the other, purposely widening my stance as he does so.

Cool air sweeps over the dampness of my knickers, arousing and shocking in one, and then his hands are easing softly upwards, stroking up the skin at the backs of my calves, my thighs, my bum... He leans forward, his nose nudging against my clothed seam and—God help me—I jerk into the simple touch.

He smiles up at me and does it again…slowly…
very slowly…

He breathes over me. 'Tell me again.'

I don't even have to ask to know what he wants
to hear. And then I realise he *needs* to hear it—he
needs to be the one and only. Not because he's staking his claim, or possessing me. It's because of the
same vulnerability that drove him away seven years
ago. The fear of being the outsider.

For all his confident, outwardly arrogant persona
back then, he was vulnerable. And for all the man he
is now, he still has that fear deep down. It crushes
me. I should have realised back then. I should have
seen it for what it was and talked him round. But instead I pushed him away. I made it worse.

My throat closes over. Tears prick. The heat of
desire and the burn of my failure, intensifies everything as I bury my fingers in his hair.

'I want you.'

It's a whisper, but it's there, and then his hands
are easing the fabric aside, his tongue is flicking
out and he's pressing it against me, parting me. The
merest hint of friction sends me rigid, straining for
more. My knees quake, my thighs tremble and, as if
he senses my weakness, he palms my arse, holding
me fast against him.

'I want you…' I moan again, grateful for the sensation that's overtaking the pain of all that lies between us.

He groans over me, the rumble working its way
through my body. *Oh, yes.* His fingers curl into the

waistband at my hips and slowly he drags it down, over my thighs, my knees. I step out for the time it takes to strip it away, and then he's on me again, wasting no time. His fingers part me for the arrival of his mouth and he sucks me…

Oh, God, yes.

'You taste so good,' he says over my clit, his lips brushing, his breath caressing, and then he dips his fingers inside me and runs the flat of his tongue upwards.

'Cain…'

'I love hearing my name from your lips…your Irish lilt…' His fingers delve in deeper, pressing on my G-spot, his words separated by the sweet circle of his tongue 'It's so fucking hot… It's like coming home.'

And I haven't got time to process his words because he's driving me to the precipice of release, with fingers and mouth and tongue. It's a dizzying dance that he knows of old and I'm lost to it, ecstasy rolling through me as I let go.

I rock against the glass, against him, as the waves ricochet through me. I cling to the pleasurable heat, wanting to make it last, to feed it, to have it go on for ever, and I stave off reality because I'm content to stay like this always.

'Cain…'

Another breathy whisper, and slowly he releases me, his mouth trailing kisses from the tip of my pubic bone to my belly button to my clavicle. And then he's there, face to face, and I'm gazing into those eyes which are so familiar, and yet not, and I want to cry. Both pain and happiness are merging into one.

'Yes?'

I shake my head. How can I speak when I don't even know what I'm asking? I don't know how to make sense of what I feel, how to tell him what I must. What I *do* know is that I need him. I need him inside me, filling me so completely that it wipes out this age-old pain, even for a short spell.

And maybe that's all I need to ask of him.

'Make love to me.'

His smile is slow, seductive, and it triggers another sweep of ecstasy through my overactive body that hasn't had its fill.

'Your wish is my command.'

He scoops me up in his arms as if I weigh nothing, and I hear the soft whirr of the glass door sliding open behind us. I have no idea how—a secret panel on the wall? Some psychic connection to its owner?—but I'm impressed… Until I register the cold night air over my bare skin.

'Don't worry,' he says, holding me tighter as I tense. 'No one can see us here… There's not even a boat close to shore.'

I look out into the darkness. He's right. There's nothing but the sound of the rolling sea, the sight of the waves breaking and the salty sea breeze that rushes over my skin. I curve into his body, seeking his heat, and then I feel steam at my back. Warm, alluring steam. And, just as the door slid open, the cover of the swim spa rolls back.

'Is there anything this house doesn't have?'

I laugh as I say it, and look up into his gaze, but my laugh freezes with my breath. The intense sincerity in his face, his eyes, pulls me up short.

'You, Lexi. It doesn't have you.'

He didn't… He can't… He can't possibly mean it, but my heart throbs longingly all the same. Do I dare to believe, dare to hope…?

No, you were fool enough to hope once. You can't do it again—you can't risk it again. No matter the role you played in his departure. How can you trust him not to run again?

'Well, I'm here now.' I make it jovial, as light-hearted as I can.

'True.' He grins as he lowers me to my feet. 'Step in.'

I do as he asks, my hand in his as I feel for the steps with my toes. The heat of the water seeps into my skin, warm, tantalising, soothing my goose-pimpled flesh.

'I'll get our drinks.'

He walks away and I tie my hair high on my head before settling back. It's heavenly, almost other-worldly, being cocooned in this delicious bubbling warmth while looking out on blackness, on the never-ending sea. I can feel my mind threatening to wander into risky territory, into fanciful what-ifs, and I claw it back, focus on the immediate present and indulge in the fantasy for what it is—*temporary.*

I hear his step behind me and turn my head. It immediately empties. He's naked, with two glasses of whiskey in his hand. I raise my brow—it's about the only outward response I can muster, even though my tongue wants to flick out and wet my lips like some sex-starved vixen. Because all I can think about is how I want to devour the thick, hard length of him that's protruding, proud and unashamed.

I'm like a woman possessed. A woman seeking her younger self and clinging to it desperately. A woman who never went through pain, who has never suffered between then and now.

'Nice to see you appreciate the finer things in life.'

My eyes snap to his, which are glittering with laughter and a far more carnal, overriding urge.

I almost say, *It's been a while*, but it's too close to the truth—the truth he has yet to learn—so I laugh softly instead.

He slips into the water beside me, his bare leg brushing against mine and setting off a frisson of excitement in its wake. He leans back and passes me one of the glasses, offering up his own in toast.

'To us.'

My throat tightens. Hope and fear collide.

I want there to be an 'us'—my heart pulses with the very thought—but can there really be an us when all is said and done?

His eyes narrow as he lifts his glass higher. 'And to the O'Connor firm.'

I want to breathe a sigh of relief, but I mask it in a smile. It's a toast I can agree to.

'Yes,' I say, raising my glass. 'To the O'Connors.'

We drink, and I force myself to hold his eye, even

though the fear of what's to come hangs over me, endangering it all.

Now we have this moment, this closeness, I don't want to break it. It's selfish—but, hell, I've lived my life for others for so long. Just for one night…a few hours, even… I want to let it go.

And I *will* tell him.

Very, very soon.

I can't take my eyes off her.

She's glowing, the light from the water reflecting off her skin, glittering in her eyes. She has droplets of water clinging to her cheeks, her neck, her collarbone. I reach out and trail a path along her skin, sweeping some away, and I love how her lips part and she leans into my caress.

'You are beautiful, Lexi.'

She looks at me, her smile small, thoughtful, and I wonder what she's thinking. She's been quiet since I joined her in the water and made that impulsive toast. The toast that had her eyes flaring in what I can only interpret as alarm.

I thought I'd recovered the situation well enough, but the last few minutes have passed by in silence, only the bubbling water and the sound of the ocean breaking up the quiet.

Is it my toast that has her so contemplative? My suggestion of an 'us'? Or is it more than that?

I find her hand in the water and pull her towards me. To my relief her smile slinks higher and her body comes willingly, gliding through the water.

'Lonely over there?' she teases.

'Positively isolated.'

I bring her across my lap, feel her body brush over my eager cock as it bucks to meet her. I'm still hard from making her come, from the taste of her, the feel of her coming apart for me. Twice over. If I recall it in enough detail I could come on the memory alone, and it's that which has me clamping my jaw shut and trying to think of something off-putting—anything to stave off the heat.

My old science teacher—she's perfect. She hated me. She wore insipid green, wrinkled-up tights around her ankles, and had the most fascinating wart on the tip of her nose. Yes, perfect.

'Why so tense?'

She strokes my jawline as she says it, one finger brushing over my stubble, teasing, provoking, and I dip my head to surround it with my mouth. The move is impulsive, necessary—payback. I circle it with my tongue and watch her eyes glitter, dark and needy, before I release it.

'I'm not sure… Could it be that all I want right now is to sink myself inside you and never let you go again?'

It's raw. It's honest. And it makes her eyes flare—but not with alarm this time, thank fuck.

She wriggles her arse, and I don't know whether it's intentional or not, but my cock isn't fussy.

'You feel so big,' she rasps, her cheeks blushing with her observation, so bashful.

I want to choke. What man wouldn't love to hear

those words? But when she says it like that she isn't saying it to boost me. She says it because she's genuinely thinking it.

'Carry on like that and I'll be taking you here and now.'

'Here?' Her eyes narrow, as though the thought hadn't occurred to her. It's been seven years—has she really not *lived* in seven years?

'You've never done that?'

She shakes her head and bites into her bottom lip, excitement sparking in her gaze.

I want to focus on the thrill of being another first for her, want to get caught up in those pools of blue, but instead I'm caught up in those missing years. In Liam and Alexa and what they must have done. What new experiences they must have shared. Hell, they must have done plenty, and the idea chills me.

I used him as a game earlier—a game driven by anger, by jealousy, by the need to be the one in control—but I want none of that now.

'Never,' she says in verbal confirmation, trapping her lip once more as her eyes fall to my mouth.

I force my focus on that look, on the hunger in her eyes and the feel of my cock pulsing between us. *Better.*

I raise my fingers to her chin and drag her bottom lip from between her teeth. It's plump, swollen from our kisses, from her teeth, and I'm about to kiss her when she dips to take my thumb inside her mouth. She sucks over it, her tongue rotating, doing exactly what I did with her finger, and Holy Mother of—

I feel like it's my cock she's sucking.

Her cheeks are hollow with the move, her eyes alive with suggestion.

'*Lexi...*' I croak.

I'm not about to come like a horny teen—but, *Jesus*, if she keeps doing that, with her arse massaging my cock, I might. Shame or no.

She does it again, and I drag my eyes lower, to where her breasts bob on the surface of the water, the bubbles teasing nipples which are taut and ready. *Oh, fuck.* A thrilling shiver runs through me, my hips buck, and I snap my eyes to hers just as she slides my thumb from her mouth.

'It's my turn to taste you...' she purrs.

'*Lexi...*' I'm shaking my head and I don't know why.

'It's only fair.'

She gives me a pout and it's so goddamn sexy that my body bucks again.

'Just the idea of you...' I rub her lips with the pad of my thumb, my head already imagining it, and lustful heat rips through me. My words are tight as I admit, 'I'll lose it.'

She gives a soft laugh. 'Isn't that the point?'

Yes.

So why am I hesitating?

Because you want her, you want to be inside her. As much as you want her mouth, you want her.

So why not have both?

'Stay the night with me?' I say, before I can over-think it.

Her frown is instant.

'If you stay the night, I get to have you in all the ways I want.'

She searches my gaze. 'I…'

I drop my hand beneath the water, curve it over her thigh, smooth it higher and higher. 'You…?'

She whimpers low in her throat as I slip one finger between her legs and then pull it back to find her taut little nub.

'You…?' I ask again as she gives a breathy moan. 'Hmm?'

'Cain.'

She rocks into my touch, her cheeks flushing pink, and the sign of her so turned on washes through me like an aphrodisiac.

'That's a dirty trick,' she pants, but she doesn't stop rocking and I don't stop circling.

'I like to play dirty.'

I lean forward to nip the delicate skin of her throat, feeling the tension slip from her body, feeling her clit swell beneath my touch. I know I have her.

'Will you stay?' I ask.

'Yes, Cain…*yes*.'

She hangs her arms around my shoulders, rides my fingers like I'm her everything—and, my God, how I want to be. It's a terrifying realisation but I can't shift it. The need for her to be mine, for us to be together again—it's all I can care about, all I can think about in this second.

'You'll stay?'

She grinds down on my cock and stares at me in determination. *'Yes.'*

'Good.'

I claim her mouth with mine, sup from her as she rocks and explodes against me. Her abandon pushes me ever closer to my own release. And then she's turning into me, her body still quaking, and I think she's about to settle down, rest her head into the curve of my neck. But instead her teeth scrape at my earlobe, her lips lift to my ear.

'My turn.'

I shiver as the words send her breath rippling down my ear canal. Never have two words sounded more sexual, more filled with promise.

'Up,' she commands, coming to her feet with a certainty that has me surprised as much as turned on.

I rise up with a lopsided grin.

'Now, sit.'

Sit? I raise my brow at her bossy demeanour— but, hell, I'm loving it, and my cock is standing proud and waiting.

'Happy?' I say as I sit back on the cushioned edge of the spa.

'Like I said,' she practically purrs, 'it's most definitely my turn.'

And then she's sinking to her knees in the water, the steam rising around her. The cold night air wraps around me from the knees up, but I don't feel it. I'm only concerned with her hands wrapping around my cock, her grip tight, her eyes locking with mine.

'Do you taste the same?' she murmurs around my tip, her lips brushing against the head.

I grip the edge either side of me as I drag in a breath. 'You'll have to tell me.'

I'm rewarded with a smile, and then she's sinking me inside her mouth, her blushing pink lips wrapping around me and taking me so far in I'm shaking with the effort to restrain. But I need to hold out.

I'm not fighting it to be a man, to delay my own satisfaction. I'm fighting it to *show* her. I don't want to be that weak. I don't want her to control me so easily. But, hell, I wish to God someone would tell my body that. Because she's sucking me back so hard, her tongue caressing me, her lips playing with my tip as she stares up at me.

Oh, God.

'Nice?'

Did she really just ask me that?

Then she licks at the slit, at the pre-cum forming there, and I grasp at her hair, my words choked. 'You have no idea…'

She laughs, her tongue flicking out to repeat the move. Jesus, she has me so easily.

And then she takes me in deep, her mouth wrapped around me, her suck so powerful I see stars. My fingers in her hair claw more than I want them to but, hell, she's making me tremble, and my release is so close…

'*Christ*, Lexi…' I groan the words and I'm transported back over a decade, to when she perfected the same move, and the old merges with the new. 'Like that…just like that.'

She smiles around my tip. 'I know—I remember.'

She's with me in my bedroom at my family home, having sneaked in during the hour before dinner. We're learning what makes each other tick, what tips each other over the edge. Christ, so many firsts, so many mind-obliterating experiences—is it any wonder I never moved on from her? Any wonder that she is my life, my soul, my everything?

And then my mind quits as my balls contract, tingling with my imminent release. I'm trying to warn her with the tightening of my fingers in her hair, my body clenching as I struggle to speak, but she doesn't let me go. She does what she always did. She drinks me down, every euphoric pulse disappearing into her, and it's like no other pleasure I have known.

I haven't been a saint. She knows that, I'm sure, and I know it. But no one has ever come close to her, and as I caress her hair and gaze down into her triumphant gaze I believe she knows that too.

'You are a minx,' I whisper.

'Better the minx you know, right?'

Oh, my God, yes.

I shake my head and stand, pulling her up against me, breast to breast, cheek to cheek. 'You will stay?'

She nods. 'For now.'

I don't know what 'for now' means, but it's enough for me. In this second, it has to be. I comb my fingers deep into her hair and clutch her closer as I kiss her shoulder and inhale.

It has to be enough.

CHAPTER TEN

JUST AS HE carried me to his hot tub, Cain carries me to his bed, and despite every warning in my brain telling me to leave, that it's gone far enough, I'm too loved up. And I use 'loved up' in the loosest sense of the term—because I can't be *in love* with him again.

I'm just emotional because of all that he's said, raking up the past, the role I unwittingly played in it. Not to mention the crazy rush of desire and endorphins that have lain dormant all these years.

He lowers me to his bed and I'm surrounded by luxury: soft sheets that welcome me in, envelop me; low, deep music that plays a strumming rhythm in tune to my heart, and him—oh, God, *him*.

He's naked and striding towards me, a filled champagne flute in hand.

'Cain…' I shake my head at the glass. I don't need any more alcohol. I only need him. His mouth, his fingers, his—

'Drunk too much already?'

I laugh. 'No, but I only need *you*.'

He smiles, and it's so full of feeling my breath catches.

'Indulge me.'

Oh, God, how can I not? He's my past, my present…*my future?*

It doesn't matter how locked-down my heart is— he still has the power to crack it open and break it if I let him.

He leans over me on the bed, the glass hovering between us. 'Drink.'

It's a command, not a question, and I raise my mouth and angle my head to take a sip. It's cold… ice-cold. The tiny bubbles fizz over my tongue in a sensation far more powerful than it was at the presentation meal, and I wonder if it's because this is the real deal—the best money can buy—or if it's just that my senses are heightened, desperate to cling to any sensation he delivers?

'My turn…'

He takes a swig, but I don't see him swallow. Instead he lowers his head—not to my lips, but to my breast. He surrounds the peak with his mouth, ice-cold bubbles fizzing over the sensitised flesh, and I cry out, my hands flying to his hair.

Oh, yes.

How can it feel so good? So intense? So soon?

But I'm still tender from his earlier attentions, so the delicate fizz, his flicking tongue, his grazing teeth are all enough to send erotic shudders running through me.

He moves to the other breast, does the same, and

I cling to him, watching his every move, my mouth slack with unrestrained need.

What you should be asking is how you walk away from this? How, Lexi? How?

I whimper. Sex. Fear. Need. A mix that I can't get a handle on. I just know I want this crazy, almost delirious heat to continue, to overpower all the rest, to stop the past from breaking in.

But it's there—haunting me, taunting me.

I cry out, frustrated that my brain won't quit, and he gazes up at me, his teeth sharp over one taut peak, his fingers sinking low. There's a question in the depths of his eyes, a question I can't answer, and I throw my head back onto the pillow, beckon with my hand in his hair for him to continue.

And he does, but I feel the question still hanging, burning into his every caress: *What aren't you telling me?*

I grind against his fingers as they slip between my legs. I won't let the pain back in. I have lived with it for so long and right now I feel alive, born again. Let me lose it…let us lose it together.

He parts my legs with his body and rises onto his knees, the glass still in his hand as his eyes trail over me, coming back to mine. No question now, only desire.

'You are stunning.'

His voice is rough, setting my skin alight as he watches me. He tips the glass and dribbles a path of champagne from my breasts to my belly button… I suck in a breath as the liquid pools and trickles either side of me. Then he moves lower still. His fingers part me to the flow of liquid and I arch my back, whimpering as it seeps between my legs, a cold caress.

'Lexi and champagne...the perfect cocktail.'

He bends forward to cover me with his mouth. The heat after the cold liquid is a striking contrast that has my hands clawing into his bedsheets, my body arching further.

'Yes—God, yes.'

He groans over my clit, the vibrations firing spasms through my body.

'I want... I want...'

I'm trying to articulate my thoughts, but I can't keep my breath long enough to finish. I'm panting, gasping for air as my climax builds, and Cain is unrelenting, the tip of his tongue stroking me in a fierce dance that has my toes curling, my legs tensing. I can't believe I'm going to...again...already, but I'm going, I'm going—I'm gone, roll after roll of pleasure shaking me to the core.

He dips down to tongue my wetness, to take all that he has milked from me, until my body twinges in its hyper-sensitivity and I'm pulling his body up to me. He lets the glass of champagne, now empty, roll off the bed onto the plush grey rug beside it, and covers me from head to toe.

'I don't think I can ever tire of making you come,' he says.

'You and me both.' And oh, how I wish that could

be the case, that we could stay like this always. Close, connected, happy.

I rake my hands down his back and pull him closer.

'I'll crush you,' he warns, but I can't speak.

I don't trust my voice not to betray my inner turmoil. Instead I continue to tighten my arms around him, feeling the reassuring weight of his body on mine before he plants his elbows either side of me and eases up onto them.

He looks down at me and I feel his hardness pressing urgently into my thigh, telling me that although his hands are soft as they sweep over my cheeks, his face calm, satisfied, he still wants me.

I haven't let anyone make love to me since Cain—since the night we made Rose. Not even Liam and I could ever get that far. I want to tell myself it's okay, that this is what I want, but the pain has me clamping my eyes shut, my teeth biting into my lip.

'Hey, I told you I'd crush you.'

He tries to move off me but I pull him back, my eyes flying open and pleading with his.

'Don't go.'

I want Cain. I want him to replace that memory with a new one. And I want it now.

'Make love to me?'

The request chokes out of me—a thousand memories, a thousand spasms of pain and want—and as he searches my gaze I'm convinced he's read them all.

'I want nothing more.'

I curve my legs around him, urging him closer,

telling him with my actions that I feel the same. The tip of his cock nudges inside my opening and I hold my breath, ready…so ready.

And then he freezes. His entire body is rigid.

I open my eyes and see his are squeezed shut now, his breathing ragged.

'Don't move.'

His command is gruff.

'But—'

'I need to get a condom,' he explains.

I'm relieved and stunned in one. How could I be so stupid, so wrapped up in the moment, not to think…?

He drags in another breath and withdraws, and the effort it takes for him to do so is etched in every hard line of his face, his corded neck, his straining cock.

My body pines for the loss of his, but he doesn't leave the bed.

He stretches across to the sleek white bedside table and pulls out a small foil packet. He tears it open with his teeth and sheaths himself in a way that tells me he's done this a thousand times before. Not only that, but the presence of condoms in his bedside drawer tells me he's always prepared— even here. And surely that means I'm not the first woman he's brought back to this amazing house and I won't be the last?

I close my eyes, wanting to block out the unwelcome truth, wanting only to care about the here and now.

'It has only ever been you, Lexi.'

I open my eyes and he's there, lying on his side, gazing down at me. He lifts a strand of hair from my face, twisting it around his finger.

'You don't need to say that,' I whisper. 'I don't need you to say things to make me feel better.'

'I'm not saying it to make you feel better...'

I cock an eyebrow at him.

'Okay, I am...but it doesn't mean it's not the truth.'

I raise a hand to his hair and pull his mouth towards mine. 'Less talk, more action.'

He shakes his head, but then he's kissing me back with all the passion, all the need, I know he feels. I wrap my arms around him and pull him on top of me. He nudges my legs apart with his knees, his tip pressing into me once more. I curve my legs around his hips, encasing him, welcoming him, and he drives into me, forcing my unaccustomed body to adjust to his size.

I cry out as the intense sensation rips through me.

He stills and I stare up at him. 'Don't stop.'

His eyes penetrate me. 'Are you okay?'

I nod fiercely but he frowns, his eyes locked to mine. 'Are you sure?'

I can hardly announce that seven years of celibacy is to blame. It feels foolish. Inadequate. And, yes, it hurts to be made love to again, but more than that is the overwhelming pleasure of being filled so completely, so perfectly, by him.

'Did I hurt you?'

His cock pulses inside me, buried so deep, but he's refusing to move, refusing to do anything without my assurance. And his concern is killing me, exposing me, breaking me.

'No, Cain, no…please, I want you.'

Still he frowns, and his sincerity is reaching inside me and chipping away at every defensive wall I've put in place. I squeeze my thighs around him and wriggle my body to get comfortable.

'Please.'

His eyes flicker and slowly, so slowly, he eases out of me, tension pulsing in his jaw. 'Stop me if it hurts.'

He looks so serious, torn between taking his own pleasure and looking out for mine. I love him for it. *No, not love—desire.* I desire him all the more for it.

'It's only ever been you,' he repeats softly, and my wetness is slick along his length as he re-enters me, my body taking more and more of him with each gentle thrust until he's striking at the very heart of me and I can feel the tension vibrating through his body.

'Only *you*,' he stresses emphatically.

The spasm of pleasure as he enters me is all the more powerful for his words and I don't know how to respond. My messed-up thoughts merge into each other and I keep quiet, losing myself in sensation, in every heartfelt thrust of his body. I match his tempo and as it turns jagged, I grip around him, keep him where I want him, where I need him and I don't think any more. I say what's in my heart and let go. 'It's only ever been you, Cain.'

* * *

'It's only ever been you...only ever been you...only you...'

I'm between sleeping and waking, her words replaying through my mind, and I grin as warmth spreads through me. I roll over, blindly seeking her out, and wake with a start. I'm alone. Very much alone.

I launch bolt upright up in bed, my palms pressing into the mattress either side of me as I scan the room.

Where the hell is she?

I blink through a sleep-induced haze to see the sun is only just creeping through the blinds, and as I sweep my palm over the space next to me I can feel her residual body heat still there.

Is she in the kitchen making coffee? Making breakfast?

My heart soars and then immediately plummets, my fingers clawing at the bedsheets where she lay. There is no distant sound of movement, no smell of coffee in the air, and I know in my heart that she has gone.

I fall onto my back and stare up at the ceiling, replaying the night in all its glory—everything we did, everything that was said. We were desperate to sate our thirst, eager to fill the gap of seven years apart. Hell, we were eager to show one another how much we'd cared, how much we still cared for one another... Or so I thought.

Why didn't she at least wake me? Say goodbye?

I throw off the quilt, push off the bed and pull on my gym gear, keen to sweat every answer out of me.

Because there's only one reason. No, two…

Either she's still in love with Liam or she can't move on from the past… And that means she can't love me back…

Love me back?

My throat convulses. I am in love with her. I never stopped being in love with her. Despite the betrayal, the years apart, I love her more now than ever.

And she's gone.

CHAPTER ELEVEN

I'M RUNNING SO FAST that my lungs are burning and my heart is thumping like crazy in my ears, but I press my earphones in tighter and up my pace. I can't let the guilt in, the pain, the pleasure…the incredible, intoxicating pleasure of being back in his bed. I can't be that weak again. I won't be.

But you love him—you know you do—that's why it hurts all the more.

I pound the trail harder, my tear-streaked face looking out to sea, grateful that Howth Head is quiet at this time of the morning. Dawn is only just breaking over the horizon and it's virtually just me and my four-legged Ed against the world. It's a liberating time of day. Where nothing can encroach and there are no time pressures—just us and the track, the sea and the birds.

But today my gut is weighted, my legs threatening to slow against the burden of it all.

Even now I can hardly bear to think of Rose, to face the pain head-on and cry—because it terrifies me how much it hurts, how I can't feel whole again without her, how I feel as if something is always missing.

And now with Liam gone, and Robert too, it's just too much.

The very idea of passing that grief on to Cain, of it haunting him like it does me…

But I have to. I know I do. He deserves to know it all.

It was hard enough thinking about telling him before. Now that we've slept together—now that he's shared so much with me and opened up…now I know how much I've failed him—how do I break it to him?

I fell asleep in his arms so readily—only to wake up in the early hours with my hand clutched to my abdomen and a cold sweat across my skin. I could hardly wake him to tell him something of that magnitude. I could hardly lie back and go to sleep either. Not with the reason for my guilt so very present.

And so I left, like the broken, nasty piece of work I feel I am, and now he'll be waking up with me gone.

I didn't even leave a note—something to thank him for the night, something to make him realise I wasn't running from him. Not for the reason he would think, anyway.

I left because we had a child—a child he knows nothing about—and she died.

How do I even begin to tell him that?

I'm so sorry I didn't tell you, but you weren't around. And when you were back on the scene too much time had passed, too much stuff had happened.

'Christ!' I shake my head against the chilling wind and Ed looks at me over his shoulder, his tongue hanging out. 'Don't look at me like that... you have it simple.'

He gives me a bark that I take to be agreement and I smile at my own madness. Talking to animals? What will I be doing next?

I run harder, for longer than my body or Ed can take, and it's him that has me reining myself back in, forcing myself to return before I'm ready. But then, I don't think I'll ever be ready to face up to the reality I've created for myself.

I take Ed back to his house, fill up his water bowl and then head back to mine. It feels quieter than usual, but then I'm earlier than usual. My neighbours in the building are still making the most of their Saturday lie-in.

I set the coffee machine going and take a shower, hoping that when I come back to the kitchen the soothing aroma of caffeine will help to ease the cloud that's hanging over me.

But it doesn't work.

I stand before the window, my mug cupped in my hands, my nose hovering just above the rim as I breathe it in.

And nothing.

Outside the sun is shining, streaming down on me in all its warming glory, but I don't feel it. I only have to close my eyes for a second and Cain is there, looking down at me as he fills me so completely.

'Only ever you.'

It's so strong I can sense him in the room with me and my eyes shoot open.

Of course he isn't here.

The street is quiet below. Save for the odd car moving, the city is still quiet. And that's when I see it, glinting at me in my reflection. The ring on my left hand.

I hold it out, admiring the simple band, and a bittersweet smile lifts my face. Liam. Dear, sweet, intelligent, Liam. We had a pact, after Rose, that should either of us ever meet someone, fall in love, we would divorce and give each other our blessing. It just never happened. Our arrangement was so easy, so comfortable, with work filling our days, and our nights quite often too. It filled the void…helped to keep the pain of loss at bay.

I lower my mug to the desk, where our monitors still face one another, and I know it's time. I know that in order to move on I have to accept that he's gone—my best friend, my husband in all the ways that mattered to us at the time. No matter what happens with Cain going forward, I can't hang on to the past any longer.

And, as per the pact I had with Liam, I can't wear his ring when I love another.

I twist the band on my finger, ease it over my knuckle and with a tug it's off. I stare at it in my palm and a single tear drops to meet it.

'I'm sorry, Liam.'

I don't know why I'm saying sorry. We were never in love in that sense—never boyfriend and girlfriend before we became husband and wife. It was always about being a mum and dad to Rose...being a family.

I clutch the ring in my palm and raise it to my lips as the sobs rack through my body.

'I miss you.'

I don't know whether I'm saying that to Rose, to Liam, or to both, but I do know I need to move on. To take control of my life again and start afresh. To look forward rather than back and hope that in some way I can take Cain with me, make him a part of it...

It's eight in the evening and I know I shouldn't be here. I know that chasing her down when she so obviously wants space is wrong. But after everything we've shared she owes me something. *Anything.*

I've had no call, no text, nothing. I'd say it was wounded pride, but I'd be lying. I know it's my heart that's breaking.

I press her buzzer and step back, gaze up at the ancient building to the sash windows that I know belong to her and the soft glow of a lamp or two that tells me she's home. Not that she's answering.

I press it again, looking for movement even though I know that unless she steps right up to the window I'll see nothing. It's not like I can yell up at her. She has no windows open and I'm likely to disturb all the other residents before she even hears.

But I want to. I want to yell until my lungs hurt—until I can't feel my panic-ridden heart any more and she speaks to me, tells me what the hell is going on.

'Lex—'

My outburst is cut off by the door release. I stare at it for a second, disbelieving, and then rush forward before it clicks shut.

I take the stairs two at a time and ignore the weird angst inside me because I have to face Liam again by coming back here. I have to accept their past together to be able to move on. And I will.

I'll do anything to be given another chance at happiness and I need her to see that. There's nothing we can't get through together, I'm sure of it, and whatever made her run, it can't be bigger than my love for her.

'Lexi—' Her name rushes out of me as I exit the final flight of stairs and see her standing in her doorway.

Her skin is pale, her blue eyes glittering in the overhead lights. I slow down, not wanting to spook her. She looks like a frightened bird, about to take flight, and as she cradles her belly I see her hands are shaking. I reach out as I near, wanting to offer comfort for whatever this is, and as I close my hands around hers, I squeeze them softly.

'Can I come in?'

She looks up at me with a nod, wets her lips as if she's going to speak, but drags in a breath instead. She pulls her hands away as she turns, and that's when I feel it—the obvious difference on her finger...

'You've taken off your ring.'

She pauses, nods. 'It was time.'

Oh, God, is that why she ran? Was it guilt? Guilt that she'd slept with me when her heart…?

I can't even finish the thought.

'I'm sorry.'

She shakes her head. I follow her through into the kitchen area and watch as she pours water into the kettle and switches it on.

'Can I get you a drink?' she asks. 'Tea, coffee, wine?'

Her voice is expressionless and the panic inside me swells.

'I really am sorry, Lexi. I don't want to cause you more pain… Hell, I don't want to hurt you at—'

I stop. She's looking at me as if she's seen a ghost and I know I've called this so wrong.

'There's something I need to tell you,' she says, and she takes a shaky breath that has a chill sweeping over me. 'Something I should have told you a long time ago, but…but it was never the right moment.'

She trembles on the last words, her hands falling to her stomach in that gesture I've become so familiar with over the last few weeks.

Weeks? Christ. Has it really only been weeks?

I quickly count. Not even three full weeks since I came back. Since I acknowledged my love for her has never really waned. Since I accepted that she's what I've been missing for the last seven years.

I take my jacket off and place it on the side. I want to comfort her, reassure her, and I step forward.

'Whatever it is, baby, you can tell me.'

She raises one trembling hand between us, her

finger wagging, her eyes widen and spill over, a steady stream of tears that has the panic building within me.

'We had a child.'

It's quiet, so quiet. I can't have heard her right.

'A child?' I say, wary, disbelieving.

But she nods, rapidly, her pallor, her tears all the more severe. 'She died.'

No— No, no, no. My stomach lurches. I feel goosebumps pricking all over my skin as my body chills. I could never have imagined…never have guessed…even for a second…

'You and Liam had a…' I take a choked breath '…a child?' She says nothing and desperately I push. 'When? How? No one said…no one called…'

My ears ring as I strain to hear her answer, and yet I don't want her to all the same. I had a nephew? A niece? And no one told me? Not even when they died?

'No, Cain. Not Liam and I. *You* and I.'

Her trembling hand goes to her mouth. Her other hand clutches at her stomach, at the fabric of the simple navy sweater that she wears, and I can't blink, I can't process, I can't…

'What are you saying?'

She lowers her hand to her throat, the skin around her fingernails turning white as she claws into her skin.

'I'm saying…' She swallows and winces in one. 'I'm saying…'

But my mind is racing ahead now. I know what

she's saying and I can't believe it—I won't. Is this how she thinks she'll get rid of me? Does she loathe me that much?

'Spit it out, Lexi.' It's low, menacing, my fury lacing every word as I say it between my teeth.

'When you left, I was pregnant…'

She whispers, but in my head the words are loud and getting louder, reverberating through my skull.

'I didn't know for a few weeks, and when I found out…when I found out I was almost three months gone.'

'Three months…?' I don't want to believe her. 'What makes you think it was mine? You were so quick to hop into Liam's arms, it could have—'

'I never slept with Liam.'

'Come on, Lexi, drop the act,' I say desperately. 'You married him within three months of my departure—how can you expect me to believe that?'

'Because Liam and I never slept together. *Ever.*'

I stare at her, dumbfounded. None of this is making any sense. Lexi, pregnant? A child, dead?

My child.

No, just no…

My head is shaking but I'm barely aware of it.

'Liam married me because I was pregnant and you—' she sucks in a breath '—you were gone… He knew I'd never want to bring a child into this world alone, how much it pained me to think of a child growing up without a family, without a mother and a father, like I did.'

My head is shaking and spinning all at once, and

the griping sensation in my gut is making it roll until I'm sure I'm going to be sick.

'He married you…' it's barely audible '…to be my baby's father?'

'I know how it sounds,' she rushes out. 'Believe me, I know! But I was so confused, so emotional, so heartbroken and abandoned. And the idea of doing it alone…' She shakes her head. 'He was my best friend. He understood. He had no interest in relationships at the time. He was married to his job and that suited me. It suited us both.'

I say nothing. I can't.

'I loved him, Cain, but not in the way I love you.'

'Love?' I repeat on autopilot, catching the present tense and not knowing how to feel.

I'm too many things in that second. Confused. Devastated. Bereaved… Fucking betrayed. Lied to.

'Sit down, Cain.'

I stare at her, my eyes widening. 'Sit down?'

'You look like you might fall down.'

She takes a hesitant step towards me and I spin away. And that's when I see it. The empty desk. Liam's desk. His equipment is in a box on the floor next to it, ready to be packed up. I grip the kitchen counter, heave in a breath, and another, my eyes seeing, my heart disbelieving.

'I wanted to tell you I was pregnant. Of course I did. But you were gone. We had no way of reaching you. Not even Marie had any way of contacting you, not for that first year, and by then…'

Her hand is gentle on my shoulder, the warmth of her touch at odds with the chill beneath.

'By then there was nothing to tell.'

'What happened?'

Silence. I look at her, ignoring the devastation in her haunted gaze.

'What happened, Alexa?'

Her lashes flutter and I know she's reliving it, but I can't care. I *won't* care. I need to know. Christ, I *should* know. I should have been there.

'I was eight months pregnant when Rose stopped moving...'

Rose? My child was called Rose?

I drag in a breath, but I can't seem to fill my lungs. I feel like my vision is tunnelling, the world closing in, my chest suffocating.

'I tried to tell myself it was okay, that she was just getting too big, too snug to kick out. Liam was so supportive. He told me not to worry—that the midwife would check and all would be okay...'

Her hand falls away from me to clutch at her stomach and then I understand it—the gesture I've become so used to. I understand it and it crushes me.

'But it wasn't okay. There was no heartbeat, no sound other than my own body. She was lifeless, gone... My body killed her.'

Her cry of anguish is like a slap to the face and I spin to pull her against me, burying her head beneath my chin and holding her against my rigid body. I ignore the swelling sickness in my throat.

'I should have *known*,' she stresses. 'I should have

known something was wrong and told them sooner, so they could get her out, make her better... I had to give birth to her. I had to go through labour knowing I was bringing her into the world just to say goodbye.'

She's shaking in my arms, her whole body racked with sobs, her tears soaking through my T-shirt. But I feel dead. Frozen solid. Unmoving.

'Do they know what happened?'

She shakes her head. 'Not with any certainty. A problem with the placenta that stopped her...stopped her getting what she needed.'

I clear my throat and ask the question that burns through me. 'What did you...? What did you do with the body?'

'We scattered her ashes.'

'At Howth Head?'

She nods against me. Of course they did. It's where Dad is now. Liam too.

'You should have told me.'

I can't keep the anger, the hurt, from vibrating through my voice, but I can't release her either.

'I know. But reliving the pain of her death, reliving it and having to tell you, having you suffer too... To what end? It doesn't change the fact she's gone.'

'You stayed married, though. You and Liam. Even after...'

'I needed his strength more than ever. I couldn't have you, so I had the next best thing.'

'He was second fiddle.' *Not me.*

'Don't say that.'

I see red. I thrust her away from me and stare down into her anguished face, wet with tears. I see her hair clinging to her cheeks and my heart shatters inside me.

'I thought *I* was second fiddle, Lexi. For years I hated my brother for taking everything that was mine, for taking you… I *hated* him, Lexi, and it was all a lie. It was *your* lie.'

She grips her stomach and that breaks me even more. She drops to her knees on the floor, her body rocking back and forth. 'I know. I know. *I know.*'

'How could you do that to me?' I force it out, making myself ignore her harrowed state. 'How could you let me believe you loved him? How could you give birth to my child without me there? How could you rob me of the chance to say goodbye?'

I retch and cover my mouth in horror. I need to leave. I need air. Space. I need to be anywhere but here.

She says nothing, only rocks, and I'm done. I can't stay here and witness this. I can't stay here and come to terms with it all.

I run. Just like I did after watching them on the registry office steps all those years ago.

Only this time I have the facts, and the reality is far more crushing than the fabricated world I've spent the last seven years believing in.

Half an hour ago I'd believed there was nothing to come between us and the future I so desperately wanted.

But nothing had prepared me for this. *Nothing.*

I think of my mother, think of her easy acceptance of their marriage, and I know that she must have known the truth. They all did. All except me.

The outsider.

And now I have nowhere to go. I can't go to Mum. I can't go back to Lexi.

I walk and walk, until I can't walk any more, and then the lights of a bar lure me in.

A drink. Something to numb the pain…

Then maybe I can start to make sense of this mess…of my whole goddamned life.

CHAPTER TWELVE

I DON'T KNOW how long I stay on the floor after Cain leaves. I only know that the water in the kettle is stone-cold when I go to pour it and the sounds of the people on the street, in the flats below me and next to me, have tapered off. It's just me and the flat, which feels far too big and empty now that Cain has gone.

Oh, God, what have I done?

I grip the kettle tighter as I place it back on its rest and switch it on.

You've told the truth. No more secrets. No more omissions.

Whatever the future holds, at least it's all out there now. That has to count for something. But his face, his departure, his...

I don't realise I'm crying again until my knees give way and I'm on the floor once more.

It hurts. It *really* hurts.

Cain, Rose, Liam, Robert. The O'Connors. The whole heart-wrenching lot of them...

I wake to the sound of buzzing in my ear, my body

stiff and uncomfortable. I'm curled into a tight ball, the floor beneath me hard and cold.

What the...?

My eyes protest as I try to open them, crusted with dried on tears, and I wince as I rub at them. I see my kitchen sideways on and I realise where I am and why. *Oh, God.* My stomach starts to churn and I wrap my arms around my knees, squeezing tight.

The buzzing starts up again and I remember why I woke. I look towards the hallway. Someone is eager to see me.

The clock on the oven tells me it's past midnight and I feel a flutter of hope rise up in my chest. *Cain.* It can only be him.

I push myself to stand, ignore my protesting muscles and head to the intercom. The second I see him on the screen the tears are back, and I cover my hand with my mouth to trap the sob that wants to come out.

His lips are moving, as if he's saying something on repeat, but there's no sound forthcoming.

I don't know whether to buzz him straight in or speak to him first, but I'm conscious of disturbing the whole building.

'Cain?'

It's so quiet I'm surprised he hears me, but he does. His whole body tenses, and his eyes are wide as he leans into the camera.

'Lexi, thank God. Please...let me in.'

I press the button and swiftly he disappears through the door. I head into my bathroom and splash my face with water, towelling it dry. I glance at the mirror. I look like hell. My eyes are puffy, my face blotchy and my hair... I pull it out of the ponytail it's in and shake it out as I go back into the hall.

I take a breath and open the front door. My stomach is an anxious knot, my heartbeat wild as hope upon hope builds.

He appears on my landing and then freezes. 'Lexi.'

His voice is raw, thick, and I can't say anything. I can't even swallow to shift the wedge in my throat as the tears are threatening to make a return.

He steps towards me and I back away to let him enter the apartment. His fingers tremble as he rakes them through his hair, and as he passes me by I get the scent of cold night air mixed with the strong scent of beer. He's been drinking.

My senses sharpen. Cain sober and hurt was crushing. Cain drunk and hurt...

I close the front door and press my palms against it, my head bowed as I take a breath.

It'll be okay. Whatever he's here to say, it'll be okay.

I lock the door and keep my head bowed as I walk past him into the kitchen and put the kettle on again. I can hear him follow in a silence that's strained and stretching to the point where my nerves can't take it any more.

I snap. 'Why are you...?'

I turn around and the question dies on my lips. He's staring at the box by the desk. Liam's desk...

Liam's things. His eyes are so filled with anguish that I'm chilled to the bone.

'Marry me, Lexi.'

My heart skips a beat; my eyes narrow. I can't have heard him right. I can't have.

I raise unsteady fingers to my face. 'What did you say?'

He turns to me now, his eyes ablaze. 'You heard me. I want you to marry me.'

I shake my head. 'You don't mean that.'

'Don't I?'

My heart is screaming at me to shut the hell up. To say yes and live the life I always dreamed of with him. But, no—not like this.

'You don't know what you're saying…'

'I'm not a child, Lexi. Credit me with knowing my own mind.'

'You've been drinking,' I say quietly, my arms falling to wrap around my middle.

'And?' He laughs, but it's deranged. His eyes are dark and glittering as he pins me with their glare. 'After the news I've just received, I think I deserve a drink, don't you?'

I don't say anything. I can't.

One second passes. Two.

The bubbling kettle fills the void.

He looks away and takes a ragged breath, rubbing his hand over his face as if that will somehow sober him up.

'I'm sorry, Cain.'

It's all I can think to say, and the words come from the very heart of me, quiet but no less earnest.

'I'm sorry I didn't do more to reassure you, to understand you, to convince you of my love for you all those years ago, and I'm sorry I didn't tell you the truth—that I didn't tell you about…about Rose sooner. I'm sorry. I truly am.'

'I don't want your apologies,' he says, his eyes coming back to me. 'I want you to be my wife.'

'Why?'

'Because you should have been my wife seven years ago. You should have married me. We should have had our child together. We should have…'

His eyes fall to my stomach and I see him quiver. Tears well in his eyes and I can't bear it any more. I close the distance between us, wrap my arms around him and hug him to me. He doesn't move, doesn't react. He's like a statue in my hold.

'We should have said goodbye together.'

I squeeze my eyes shut over his whispered words, hear his heartbeat under my ear and the air that shudders through his lungs.

'I'm so sorry.'

He grips my arms and sets me away from him so that he can look into my eyes.

'Then marry me. Help me fix this.'

Fix this? I shake my head, my voice cracking. 'It can't be fixed. Not this kind of pain.'

'Let me try.'

I remove myself from his hold, knowing I need to be strong, knowing that no matter how much it hurts, this isn't right; it isn't the answer. Not when the reason is guilt, an act of desperation.

'I married for the wrong reasons once. I won't make that mistake again.'

'We belong together, Lexi. We always have. I should have made you mine seven years ago. I never should have left.'

'Made you mine.'

It's all I can hear—and his words from my office all those weeks ago come back to me.

'I'm back to take all that I'm owed.'

I shiver. Have I got this wrong again? Does it really boil down to possession rather than love?

'I'm not some possession you can lay claim to, Cain.'

'No? My brother got to do that, though, didn't he? He got you *and* my child.'

His tormented words stab through the very heart of me and I straighten against them. I put my hurt into strength. I know he's speaking through his pain, through the drink. If I can sober him up maybe we can have a real conversation, a real future.

'Let me make you a coffee and then we can talk properly.'

'Save it, Lexi. I came to ask you to marry me.'

I want you to tell me you love me, my heart screams. *That you want to marry me because you love me.*

'And what about love, Cain?'

He goes very still, very quiet, his eyes fixed on me for the longest time.

'What about it?'

'Don't you want to marry for love?'

His skin pales, his eyes flash. 'You didn't love my brother in that way, yet you still married *him*.'

My world plummets. He doesn't love me.

'And, like I said,' I say quietly, 'I won't marry without love again.'

He hesitates, the pulse in his jaw working to a rhythmic beat, and the kettle chooses that moment to click off. The room is so silent, so cold.

'Then there's nothing left to say. Goodnight, Lexi.'

He turns and walks away, taking my hope, my heart, my world with him.

There's a banging in my skull—incessant, painful. I try and cover my ears, but the movement makes my stomach lurch.

I groan as I roll onto my side and my body suddenly falls. I swing backwards to regain the ground beneath me and realise I'm not in bed. I'm not even at home. The air smells different. It smells of…

Mum.

I'm on Mum's sofa.

'Oh, hell.'

The night comes back to me in broken snippets. Lexi's confession, the pub, my—*my proposal.*

'Fuck.'

I press my fingers into my throbbing temples as the nausea swims inside me.

'Oh, you're awake, then?'

I squint through the haze to see Mum leaning over me, a steaming mug in her hand.

'Mum…' It's a croak. My throat feels like sandpaper, my tongue too thick for my mouth.

She harrumphs and places the mug on the coffee table. 'There's a fresh coffee. Black, two sugars. Drink it and then maybe you'll talk some sense.'

Every noisy syllable sends a shooting pain through my head and my gut lurches again. I fight against it, pushing myself to sit up and placing my head in my hands as I lean forward.

'I'll be amazed if she ever talks to you again. In truth, *I'm* only speaking to you because you're my son and I have to.'

I grimace. In my hunched position, all I can see are her slipper-clad feet, tapping as she looms over me, and I can tell she's pissed off with me. Really pissed off.

'I told you what happened…?' I manage to say eventually.

'I think you gave me the edited highlights; Alexa supplied the rest when I called her this morning to apologise on your behalf.'

I groan. 'It was really that bad?'

'Worse.'

'She shouldn't have let me in. Why did she let me in?'

I shake my head. It's a bad move because it sends my stomach on another roll.

'Oh, I don't know… The fact that you were buzzing her apartment at midnight and she has neighbours to consider? Or maybe, just maybe, she did it because she loves you?'

'She doesn't love me.' I say it quietly, and the pain of it hurts me all the more now that I no longer have the numbing effects of alcohol in me. In fact I have the exact opposite—the morning-bloody-after effect to accompany her crushing rejection.

'Is that so?' Mum chirrups. 'For a clever man, you really are stupid at times.'

'Mum!'

'Don't "Mum" me. That girl has loved you for as long as she's known you.'

I fling my head back to stare up at her, my emotional pain obliterating the physical effect of the move. 'If that was the case then she would have said yes.'

'To your marriage proposal?'

'What else?'

'That was no marriage proposal, Cain. That was you staking your claim—competing with Liam.'

I shake my head, not wanting to hear her, not wanting to think about it. 'You don't know what you're talking about…'

'I know *exactly* what I'm talking about. You were so angry when you came here. Do you remember what you said?'

I rack my brain, trying to fill in the blanks. I rub my temples and stare at her painfully bright slippers so hard I could burn a hole through them.

'I was angry to learn that you were complicit in keeping my daughter—'

Oh, God, my daughter.

I swallow and try to breathe. It doesn't feel real. It can't be…only it is.

'We made a mistake, love, your father and I,' she says, quietly now. 'But it wasn't our place to tell you.'

'You let them get married…'

'I know we did. We stood by them because it was what they wanted and because they loved each other in their own way. They were best friends. They stood as good a chance as any to make it work and provide a stable home for…for Rose.'

Rose. My heart squeezes tight.

'But what about me?'

'What *about* you? You were gone, Cain—who knew how long for? Life didn't just go on hold when you walked out. And when they lost her…when they had to go through all that…they had each other. And I was glad of it because you were still gone. No word, nothing. We lost you and then we lost Rose too. And now your father and Liam.'

Her voice trembles and guilt swamps me. I abandoned them all for my own selfish reasons. It was unforgivable.

'I came back, months later, but I came back.'

Mum sighs and drops down onto the sofa beside me. 'I know you did. Alexa told me. She explained that you saw us…'

I look up to the mantelpiece on autopilot, but the picture isn't there.

'I've put it away,' she says softly, guessing at my focus. 'We've all made mistakes, Cain, but the truth is that Alexa loves you—and I think you love her too.'

She places her hand on my back and I realise I'm crying. I wipe my hand over my face as I turn to look at her.

'But she said she wouldn't marry without love again?'

She stares at me until realisation dawns—Lexi wasn't talking about her lack of love for me, she was questioning my love for her.

'Oh, God. I didn't tell her. I didn't say.'

Mum gives me a gentle nod; her smile one of understanding, of love and sympathy.

'But how could she even doubt it,' I say, 'when I love her so much it hurts?'

'After everything you've been through? You need to hear it from her lips as much as she needs to hear it from yours.'

Her words sink in and I replay my actual proposal, and Lexi's reaction, again and again. I can't believe how stupid I've been.

'How the hell do I fix this?'

'I don't know, son.' She leans into me, her head coning to rest on my shoulder. 'But you two belong together. You'll think of something.'

CHAPTER THIRTEEN

MONDAY MORNING COMES around all too soon, and the idea of walking into the office and knowing Cain will be there has me dragging my feet.

I've heard nothing from him since Saturday night—unless you count the apology Marie gave me on his behalf—and I have no idea how this is going to play out. But we have a job to do, a company to run, and that's what gets me across the threshold.

He's nowhere to be seen, though, and I'm hardly early. I figured arriving at nine would mean the office would be abuzz with people—an audience, a reason for me to act normal.

I dump my bag on my desk and then hesitate. Do I ask where he is? Or will that look like I'm checking up on him and arouse suspicion among the staff?

I turn on my computer and open up my email, my eyes flitting to the door in my continuing debate. I could ask Janice in passing if she's seen him... Ask Sheila, perhaps...

My emails roll in and then I see it. His name. Sent at six-thirty this morning.

I stare at it, my cursor hovering, and then I open it, heart in mouth.

Alexa,
I have some business to take care of in the States. I'll be gone a couple of weeks.
    It will do us good to have some space.
    I have left John with you. Please use him. He is excellent at what he does, and you can trust him to share the load. Please let him help.
    I am sorry.
Yours,
Cain

I stare and stare until my eyes sting and water. He's run away. Just like he did seven years ago. My gut sinks and I don't want to believe it.

He says he's sorry, though. He says he's coming back.

A couple of weeks...

He will come back, won't he?

I want to believe him. I want to believe he'll return. But the past taints everything.

He might not love me back, but the idea of never seeing him again...

No, just no.

I click to reply and my fingers hover over the keyboard, the blank email glaring back at me. What do I say?

A rap on the door makes me jump.

'Yes?'

My voice cracks a little and I clear my throat as the door opens. It's John.

I force a smile. 'Hi.'

'Morning.'

He returns my smile, although his shows none of the strain I'm sure to be showing.

'I thought we could schedule some time to work out a plan of attack for the next few weeks?'

I nod. He's clearly up to speed on Cain's disappearance but his polite expression gives nothing away.

'Sounds great.' I'm relieved it comes out normal. 'Just give me ten minutes.'

'Sure. Coffee?'

'Please.'

He heads off and I look back to the screen and type my reply.

Safe trip. Thank you for John. And the apology. I'm sorry too. More than you can know.

See you in two weeks.

Lexi

I stop myself adding Don't run, although I type it and delete it several times over before I hit 'send' and pull myself away to focus on the only part of this I can control: the business.

Two weeks since Cain left and not a word. I know he's talking to John, though, and that he's keeping abreast of company matters. Maybe even me too.

I wonder if he asks about me. I wonder if he asks Marie too. But I don't dare ask either of them, refusing to acknowledge my weakness so openly.

Work is busy, as always, even with John's assistance, and I'm grateful for it. It gives me less time to dwell, less time to drive myself crazy wondering if I made a huge mistake in saying no.

So many times, I've wanted to go back on my refusal…and if it hadn't been for him leaving the country, I likely would have.

Three weeks since he left and still no word. It's also a week past his promised return date.

I don't want to feel the sadness that accompanies that thought, the crushing disappointment, the realisation that he likely won't return.

That he has run.

What will happen to his beautiful house? Will he sell it? Rent it out?

Will he ask John to stay on permanently? Wash his hands of everything but the shares? Wash his hands of me?

'Alexa, what do you think?'

'Hmm?'

John is looking at me expectantly and I realise I've not listened to a damn thing he's said for at least the last ten minutes.

'Sorry.' I shake my head. 'My mind was elsewhere.'

'No problem.' He gives me a smile that smacks

of sympathy and I wonder just how much he knows; how much he's learned in these last few weeks.

'Do you think we can take this up later? I have a migraine coming on.'

I feel bad for feeding him a lie, but it's not entirely untrue. I do feel under the weather. It just has more to do with my heart than my head.

'Sure.'

He picks up his papers, but doesn't move to leave. Instead he looks at me, and I swear his cheeks colour.

'There's just one more thing.'

I look at him expectantly and wonder what could have got such an unflappable man turning pink.

'Cain has asked that you fly to New York this week. He has a meeting lined up with some investors and thinks your presence is essential.'

Even his name has my pulse skittering. 'And he didn't think to ask me himself?'

John gives a shrug. 'He's pretty busy out there, and I said I didn't mind passing on the message.'

It's been weeks—*weeks!* And he uses John as a go between. He can't even give me the time of day. I'm mad. I'm hurt. I'm… I don't know what I am, but I'm not taking this lying down.

'Well, when you speak to him next, can you tell him I'm too busy *here* to jump to his beck and call and make arrangements on such short notice.'

How *dare* he do this? How *dare* he not ask me himself?

'He's made all the arrangements,' says John, his voice steady in spite of what he must perceive as an overreaction on my part. 'He cleared it with Janice, so your diary is being updated as we speak. Your flights and accommodation are all—'

'Janice!'

He shuts up at my shouted call and within seconds Janice is rushing into my office.

'Yes?'

'Have you and Cain rearranged my dairy for this week?'

Now she's turning pink, and this time John definitely colours. The pair of them are looking at me as if I've just caught them snogging behind the bleeding bike sheds.

'Yes,' she blurts, her lips returning to a zipped-up line almost immediately.

'And didn't you think to check it with me first?'

'Well, I… It's… I… It's important…'

'Very important,' John adds for her.

I'm a simmering pot of rage, but I know it's not them I should be angry at. No, it's Cain. And when I get my hands on him I'll make sure he knows *never* to pull such a stunt again.

But at least he's not running...

No, he's not—he's asking me to come to him. For business. But still…

And if I'm honest, it's not *all* rage that has my body overheating.

CHAPTER FOURTEEN

I AM NERVOUS. More nervous than I can ever remember. I wasn't even this nervous when I played in the big football matches at school, when I took my driving test—hell, at my first corporate job interview without the family name to help me.

In fact what I felt then was excitement—overwhelming excitement. Because I knew I was going to succeed. I was going to get what it was I had my heart set on.

Now I have no clue.

The biggest gamble of my life and I have no idea which way it's going to go.

Lexi is either going to kill me, and go to great lengths to make me suffer while she's at it, or she'll make me the happiest man alive.

I cast my eye over the room one last time. The penthouse suite is the finest New York has to offer, both inside and out. The towering view over Central Park beyond the expanse of glass—beautiful by day, atmospheric by night—will soon be cast in the soft glow of the setting sun. Perfect. I hope.

The scene is set and this time I won't get it wrong.

I can't.

* * *

By the time I'm Stateside I'm not just a simmering pot of rage. I'm bubbling over and steaming.

I'm angry that I've had no chance to prepare for this meeting, that I don't even know who the investor is—least of all why they're so important.

John and Janice would give nothing else away. They just insisted on me coming, showing the kind of fear that would make you think their jobs were at stake. And Cain didn't respond to a single email or phone call.

I'm angry that he's wasted good company money on first-class plane tickets—an expense too far, in my book—and then topped it off with a private chauffeur-driven car to get me from the airport to *this* place. Which brings me to another reason why I'm fuming. The hotel is ridiculously OTT. Every stretch of glass, gold and perfectly polished wood floor tells me that those plane tickets were a mere drop in the ocean when compared to my accommodation fees.

But more than all that I'm angry that he hasn't even shown his face yet. Not even another email to explain the purpose of this visit in detail, or a *Hey, no hard feelings, right? Work is work...* message.

I would have taken that. I would have taken any personal contact over the last three weeks in preference to this.

'Here you go, Ms O'Connor,' the receptionist says to me, her smile perfectly polite. 'Andrew will take you to your room.'

'I can take my—'

'Ma'am.' Andrew is beside me, one hand already on my suitcase, the other gesturing towards the grand lifts.

I feel my cheeks colour, as if my mental tantrum has been outed, and I force a smile through my teeth as I fall into step.

Hopefully I'll see Cain soon and I can wring his bloody neck.

The lift is as smooth as the hotel staff, arriving within seconds of being called and taking us to the relevant floor without giving me too much time to think. I don't even register the room number, simply follow Andrew blindly until he comes to the end of the corridor and we're presented with double doors into what I know is going to be a suite.

A bloody suite? Really, Cain?

And…

Oh, my God.

The doors slide open and I'm gazing at glass walls far ahead, with a view that has me walking towards it, mesmerised. Forgetting Andrew. Forgetting Cain. Forgetting everything as Central Park stretches out before me, bigger than I could ever have imagined.

'I hope you enjoy your stay, ma'am.'

'Oh, yes—sorry, thank you.'

It's beautiful, truly beautiful, and it's not until I hear the door click shut that I turn away and remind myself that I'm here for work. Not to stand around all day, gazing at the amazing view which must have cost the company a fortune.

Another reason to have a go at Cain.

Determined, I head for my suitcase and freeze midstride. I'm in the living area; to my right is a curved sofa, designed to make the most of the floor-to-ceiling view, and on the table, in its centre, is the most beautiful arrangement of burnt orange roses.

I can't ignore it.

I step closer and their fragrance reaches me. Closer still and I realise it isn't an arrangement of cut flowers. It's an actual rose bush.

This really is taking luxury a step too far, but I'm still lured by their beauty, my fingers reaching out to cup one bud as I lean in, close my eyes and take a deeper breath. Their scent is delicate, as beautiful as they look.

My eyes open and I spy an envelope among the buds with a solitary handwritten name: *Lexi*.

Flowers—*no, an actual rose bush*—to welcome me on a business trip?

No.

I find my hand is shaking as I bend to pluck the stark white rectangle from the vivid burst of colour and open it, anticipation coursing through me even though I know it's foolhardy.

I step back towards the window and let the sunlight warm me as I read:

I wanted to do something special to remember our Rose. I know I can't turn back the clock and be there for you when you needed me most, but I can be there from this day forth.

Love always,
Cain x

I'm stunned. Hot and cold at once. This isn't about business. This is about us. About us and Rose.

Our Rose.

I look back at the flowers, find my legs moving towards them, and then I see the label protruding from a stick at its base and its name.

Little Rose O'Connor

I choke back a sob, my eyes overflowing, disbelieving. I pull out the label, stare at it some more, and then realise it's official. He's had a variety of rose named after our daughter. And I know the colour is no accident.

'Mum told me she had hair like yours.'

Cain.

I spin towards his voice and almost feel as if he's a figment of my imagination. He's there beside my suitcase, wearing a navy sweater and jeans, the epitome of casual. But the intensity of his eyes takes my breath away. He steps forward, just a few strides before he pauses. He's hesitant.

'Do you like them?'

'Do I…?' I say dumbly, the card and the label clutched to my chest, my eyes flickering towards the rose bush and back to him. I don't think I've blinked. They're watering that much. I feel starved of oxygen and have to heave in a breath.

'But I… I don't understand…' I wave my hands at the roses, my suitcase, the whole room. 'I thought… I thought I was here…we were here…for business… for…'

I can't speak any more. I'm shaking. I clutch my arms around me and look back at him.

'I'm sorry. I didn't like having to lie. I didn't like making John and Janice do it either. But…'

He pockets his hands, his uncertainty so obvious and only adding to his appeal.

'I was scared if you knew the truth you might not come, and I wanted to get it right this time. I wanted to be honest with you regardless of how scared it makes me feel. I needed to see you face to face and tell you.'

Anticipation has my heart beating out of control, and my words are hard to form. 'Tell me what?'

'That I love you, Lexi.' His eyes glisten as he says it. 'I've loved you ever since I came across you in that school corridor, lost and alone. I've loved you every single day of those seven years apart, even when I thought I hated you… I wish to God I'd never left, and I'm sorry for the time we lost, the time I lost with my family. I regret it so much. But I don't think I'd be the same man now if I hadn't gone. In truth, I don't think I deserved you then, but I hope I'm the man to deserve you now…if you'll have me.'

I'm listening to him, and I can see the sincerity in his face, feel his love filling the air between us.

'But when I told you I would only marry for love, you said nothing.'

'I said nothing because I was a fool. I thought you didn't love me—that it was your way of telling me it could never be.'

I'm shaking my head now. 'You wanted to own me?'

'No, I wanted to marry you and spend the rest of my life loving you.'

He steps forward, his arms reaching out, but I instinctively step back.

'How can I trust that this is real? That you won't run away again when life gets hard? When...when things outside of our control crush us?'

I look to the flowers and I know he knows what I mean. I don't need to spell it out.

'Because I know we're stronger together. Because I've learned from the mistakes of our past. I should have been there for you then, Lexi. I should have been there for both of you.'

Slowly I bend to place the card and the label back on the table. 'So, what...?' It's not accusatory, it's soft, inquisitive. I'm trying to understand. 'You had a rose named in our daughter's honour?'

He gives a soft laugh that's shaky with sadness. 'Don't say it like that if you ever meet Peter—which I hope you will. He's certainly eager to meet you.'

'Peter?'

'He's the rose breeder who created her. She's been years in the making—almost a decade, in fact.'

'And he just happened to let *you* name her?'

His smile is slow. 'For a price. But when I told

him the reason I wanted to name it…when I told him about you and our Rose—'

His voice breaks a little, his smile falters, and I want to run to him. But I feel rooted, my heels stuck in the luxurious rug beneath me.

'I think he let me haggle him down.' He looks to the flowers. 'She's worth every penny, though.'

I don't know whether he means the rose or our daughter, and I can't trap the tiny sob that erupts.

'Oh, God, Lexi, please don't cry.'

He rushes towards me, pulls me into his arms and his warmth envelops me, his scent, his comfort, his love.

'Shh, baby, shh…'

'It's just so beautiful.'

I sniff, and it's so unladylike, but I'm incapable of caring. I can't believe this is happening. That I'm standing in the most beautiful suite, with the most beautiful man, and the most beautiful rose named after our beautiful daughter.

'I can't even begin to understand what's going on.'

'It's simple,' he says, his hand soft on my hair. 'I love you, Lexi.'

I push up off his chest and he looks down into my eyes, his hands stroking my face as his eyes rake over me. 'And if you love me too you only have to say it. You don't have to marry me. You—'

'I don't *have* to marry you?'

He looks at me quietly for a moment, so serious. 'No, not if you don't want to. It's enough to know you love me.'

'And if I do want to marry you?' I say.

He lets out a soft laugh, his expression lifting. 'I'll be taking you to Tiffany's in a few hours.'

'Tiffany's…?' Realisation dawns and brings tiny flutters of excitement rising in my chest. 'You mean, you haven't bought a ring yet?'

'I thought that would be too presumptuous.'

'And bringing me to New York *isn't*?'

'No, that was about making my proposal perfect… this time.'

My lips curve into a grin I can't contain.

'What?' He frowns and goes from sexy to nervous to cute—and so utterly mine. 'Too clichéd?'

'No—no, it's perfect,' I say, looking towards the window and the glorious view of Central Park. The sky is pink and peachy in the setting sun and the room glows with it, setting off the roses in all their colourful glory. 'But what if I'd said no? All this effort and…?'

'You would have had a few days' holiday—something you haven't done in a long time.'

'How do you know?'

'Janice.'

'Janice.'

We say it in unison, our smiles matching.

'Why a few hours, then?' I tease, my smile becoming a mock pout.

'A few hours…?'

'Before we go to Tiffany's?'

The happiness inside me is bubbling up so much I fear I'm going to burst if I don't tell him I love him soon. But I'm holding out. I've waited so long to say it without fear hanging over me.

'Won't it be closed then?' I ask.

'Not for us, my love. They've been forewarned that they may have some late-night shoppers.'

'You're kidding?'

'Not at all.'

He hooks his hands low down my back, his blazing eyes falling to my lips. I know exactly where this is going.

'But I have three weeks of absence to make up for—not to mention seven years—and I plan to start immediately.'

He lowers his head, and his lips are almost on mine when I press my index finger against them. 'You're insatiable.'

'Sue me,' he murmurs against my finger, and I laugh, shaking my head at him even as I know the time has come.

I curve one hand around to cup his cheek and raise the other to do the same. I gaze up into his eyes, holding him just where I want him.

'I do love you Cain.' I brush my lips against his. 'I've always loved you.'

And then I kiss him with everything I have. No more holding back, no more fear. No secrets, no lies. Just us and our love for one another and our dear sweet Rose.

EPILOGUE

Five years later

THERE'S ONLY ONE THING you need to know about me.

I love my family.

Even when they're driving me to absolute distraction.

'Liam Robert O'Connor—if you don't put those wellies back on this instant…'

I'm using my 'boardroom voice', as Lexi calls it, but it's having zero effect, and I look to her imploringly as our three-year-old monkey swings his footwear around like two propellers and heads for the biggest puddle on the trail.

'Please can you sort him out?'

Lexi merely laughs as she squeezes Bella, who's on her hip, and presses a kiss to our daughter's rosy cheek. 'Mummy needs to go and take care of your brother before Daddy has a tantrum.'

Bella giggles and Lexi bends to put her down, straightening out her bright red jacket as she does so, her auburn curls escaping its hood and blowing in the wind.

'At least you have the sense to keep your wellies on, Bella.' I take hold of her chubby little hand and smile down at her. 'It's a mud pit out here.'

'Their favourite kind,' Lexi murmurs, placing a kiss on my cheek before heading off after Liam.

I watch her go, feeling the warmth, the love inside me, swell. It's not raining now. The clouds have cleared, the sky is blue and the seagulls are circling. It's picture-postcard-perfect—even with my rogue little man front and centre.

How anyone copes with twins is beyond me. Even with three adults to their two I feel outnumbered. Not that I'd change it—not in the slightest.

I smile as I watch Lexi tackle Liam, watch Mum trying to help, but she has Ed pulling her in circles.

And in the distance I see the waves crashing around the Bailey Lighthouse and feel the presence of Dad, Liam and Rose.

This is our Sunday routine now—a walk around Howth Head with all of us together. Sometimes we talk about them, sometimes we don't, but they're there in our thoughts and that's enough.

I feel a tug on my hand and Bella pulls out of my grasp. I lower my gaze just in time to see her drop promptly to her bottom, her hands going to the muddy heel of one welly…

'*Bella Rose*, don't even think about it…'

* * * * *

OUR LITTLE SECRET

For you, Mum.
I think Raf would've been right up your street.
Shine bright, crazy lady!
xxx

CHAPTER ONE

Castello d'Amore, Tuscany

'YES, TYLER. YES!'

I trap a groan as Dani's lustful cry breaks through the stone walls. *Again.*

I mean, it's her wedding week. The rustic and seriously lavish Tuscan castle in which I lie is her chosen venue, her dream escape, and I'm lucky enough to have come along for the ride, all expenses paid. And, as I'm maid of honour, my room is just as fabulous as the leading lady's, my bed is just as huge and as luxurious and my veranda, with the views over the glorious Tuscan hillside, is heaven.

So the least I can do on day minus one of seven is cope with the all-night romping next door. Only...

I roll over and look to the open balcony doors, the light drapes that blow in the breeze and the soothing view beyond. All cast in moonlight, it's just as beautiful as it was this morning when we arrived, high on in-flight bubbles and Dani's excitement.

No, I shouldn't be blue. I should be happy, buoyed

up on her excitement and the seven days of fun ahead.

But then I zone in on the untouched pillow beside me and the deep ache inside resonates. I finger its softness, press my palm into it where Bobby's head would have been and feel torn between longing and loss.

I long to have the good back—the sex, the passion, the companionship. Hell, I want to be the person I was before our marriage became stale, before I started sleepwalking my way through life on some kind of autopilot.

'Yes, Tyler! Yes, just there, *just*… Oh, yes!'

I want *that*.

Not even Bobby and I quite reached those heights.

It's been a year since our divorce, two since our separation, and nothing, not even a sexy encounter in a club, has resulted in anything more.

Truth is, I don't want a drunken fumble with nobody special, an awkward date that leads to an even more awkward goodbye, and I sure as hell don't want to deliver a fake orgasm in order to protect a guy's ego. I left all that nonsense behind in my teens. But I really don't want to be here either: twenty-eight, divorced and very much single.

Not to mention horny.

Such a great combo when you're situated next door to at-it-like-rabbits.

'*Fuck*, Dani, you're the best, just like…argh!'

It's as if they're doing it on cue now… I fist my

hand in the vacant pillow and drag it over my head, wrap it around my ears and scream into it.

There. Can't hear them now.

Only, my mind is replaying Tyler's gruff exclamation, Dani's reciprocal moan, and my skin is prickling up, my nipples tightening against the delicate fabric of my silk cami. Their unashamed lovemaking, a tease to my neglected body. And I know there's no faking it for Dani; she's told me far too often and in far too much detail.

They're great in and out of the bedroom and have known each other since she was in nappies. Tyler would have been… I do the maths, my trail of thought proving a good distraction from the squeaking bed springs next door…*seventeen*. He would have been seventeen-*ish*. And, yeah, put like that, it's a bit ick. But he's best friends with her seriously older brother and it took a full-on seduction by Dani to get him to succumb.

Now I smile, my head shaking as I ease the pillow off my face and remember the lengths Dani went to. Gotta give my bestie credit; she knows how to get what she wants. They've been inseparable ever since.

They would have married two years ago if not for her big brother's misgivings. 'Misgivings' being an understatement. Tyler sported a black eye for weeks following *that* revelation.

If not for the black eye, I'd have thought the big brother was a myth. A legend. More fictional than real. No photos, no appearances, nothing. He's not attended any of the parties or family gatherings over

the years, not even their engagement. The engagement of his only sibling and his best friend! I mean,
what kind of weirdo doesn't turn up to such an event?
Especially when he's been the man of the family
since they lost their father when Dani was a child.

He cited work as the excuse, but really, is it too
much to expect that the guy sack off such commitments for his little sister...?

At least he's had the good sense to commit to
the wedding. Verbally, at least. Dani still has me on
standby to give her away. Unorthodox, yes, but after
her family's no-show today I'm plugging as many
holes as I can.

We were supposed to have had dinner together.
Me, the bride, the groom, the mother of the bride
and her brother. Both mother and brother were missing. So hell, yeah, maid-of-honour-cum-father-of-
the-bride? I can totally rock that. I can even do the
mother malarkey if need be. And if Tyler wants to
distract Dani from her elusive family by delivering
a night of...

'Oh, baby, yeah, just like that, suck it, yeah...'

My sex-starved body pulses, tuned in, turned on,
and I toss the pillow aside. I can't stay for this. It's
weird. Too weird. 'Time to get some air.'

I thrust myself out of bed and pull on my robe.
It's sheer but it beats walking through the castle at
night in my silk cami and shorts. The entire ensem-
ble is brand-new and an indulgence too far, but one
I couldn't resist when I saw this place in the online
brochure and fell in love. The stifled romantic in

me clawing its way out and taking over for a rampant few hours of online shopping fuelled by wine.

And now is the best time to enjoy the castle and its grounds. Tomorrow the place will be teeming with the other guests. Right now, it's just me, Tyler and Dani, plus the odd very obliging member of staff. I can stroll through the grounds in the subdued evening heat and really take it in: the sounds of nature, the glistening pool, the row upon row of vines and the tall Tuscan Cypress trees, so slender and majestic as they map out the pathways and the curving driveway.

Yes, perfect and soothing to my over-active body that is too willing to respond to the activity next door!

From its ice bucket, I lift the half-drunk bottle of bubbly Dani gifted me as she bade me goodnight and hook my sandals in my fingers so as not to make a sound on the polished marble floor.

I pull open the door and make my way past their room to the winding staircase that leads down to the triple-height entrance hall. It's grand in both size and antiquity, and the portraits on the stone walls flaunt stories of people and years gone by.

Suddenly I feel as if I'm trespassing. My breath feels too loud in the vast space and my heart pounds in my ears as I clutch the bottle and sandals to my chest. It probably has more to do with the fact that I'm wandering around in the dead of night, wearing nothing more than fancy lingerie, than it does with the foreign surroundings. And I know I'm being silly.

It is, after all, exclusively ours for the week and to-night I'm free to do what I want.

Tomorrow I can throw my focus onto making these seven days all about my best friend and her happiness. The perfect week. The perfect wedding. The perfect maid of honour.

Perfect. Perfect. Perfect.

And in a venue such as this…

The heavy wooden door creaks as I open it and the breeze carries with it the scent of the rambling rose that decorates the stone archway, adding to the romantic ambience and making me smile.

Yes, perfect. Nothing can ruin this week.

Nothing at all.

'Basta! Enough, Marianna! You get in my car, *alone*, or so help me—'

'So help you what, Rafael? I'm your mother, not some employee that you can order about.' She gives a flustered laugh, her face pinking up as she tries to smile at her latest toy boy and, *Diavolo*, I'm over age differences—Tyler and Dani have put that one to bed. But this one… I look to the man-child she has hooked on her arm and he has the common sense to back up a step.

'Hey, no sweat,' he says, more to me than to her. His smile is one-sided and so cocky it makes my blood boil. 'You get yourself off and we can hook up when the wedding is over.'

'No!' my mother protests, her attempt to downplay my rule forgotten now. 'This is my daughter's wedding and I get to bring *whomever I want.*'

She stares at me, just enough of a crease in her otherwise Botoxed brow to tell me she's displeased. Seriously displeased.

That makes two of us.

I step forward, and in spite of her statuesque height I still dwarf her. 'Do you honestly think that turning up with a boy younger than your daughter is acceptable?'

Her laugh is wry now, pitched and grating. 'Like you would refuse a twenty-year-old on your arm.'

I glare back at her and she wavers on the spot, her eyes flitting between her toy boy and me, before she straightens her spine and flicks her false golden waves over her shoulder.

'I have a right to have a partner with me, Rafael.'

I don't even blink. 'You have a right to a partner who is presentable to a room full of your daughter's nearest and dearest...' Which will include Nonna, her mother, and Aunt Netta, her sister... I'm quick to shake off the image of that particular showdown before it takes hold. 'Not some...*ragazzo.*'

I flick him a look. It's not even his fault. My mother still has her looks and, thanks to the knife and her injection regime, looks half her age. But this is Dani's wedding and I won't let her ruin it. Not via embarrassment, drunken debauchery or any other such nonsense my mother is prone to.

She's ruined enough of my sister's life already.

'I am not going without—'

'It's my car, my rules and you *will*, if you want to see Dani married.'

The familiar shudder returns. *Married*. But it's what Dani wants, and I trust Tyler to look after her, to do right by her. But married…the holy state of matrimony… No. Just no.

I stop my teeth from grinding and stare Marianna down. Watch as she blusters anew, assessing me for weakness and finding none. I'm cold, I'm ruthless and people do as I say. My mother included.

I see the second it registers, the high colour deepening beneath the thick layer of make-up as her shoulders sag and she blows out a breath.

Acceptance. Finally. *Grazie a Dio*.

My own shoulders ease, the throbbing ache in my skull ramping up now the tension has eased.

Painkillers, a nightcap and sleep. That's what I need.

I just need to keep it all ticking along nicely for seven days. No drama, no mishaps, no mess.

I should have been at the castle hours ago. I should have been there to greet Dani and Tyler. Instead, I'm here, collecting my mother from the arms of her latest lover before she can bring this humiliation to my sister's wedding.

Not a great start.

I scowl at her back as she fawns over him now and says goodbye.

What I wouldn't give to have a normal mother. Not some ex-model with a non-existent heart and delusions of grandeur that well surpass her own income. Not to mention her string of lovers…

Seven days. She just needs to go without for *seven days*.

I certainly am. No plus-one. No distraction.

This week is all about Dani.

Keep one woman under control and the other happy.

Simple.

Or so it should be…but the emerging headache and our family history tell me it will be anything but.

I'm not sure how long I've been outside, but I have no wish to go back in. Not even the distant rumble of a car on the private driveway some time ago could pull me away from this little oasis, with the buzzing cicadas and crickets in the air, and the pool lapping over its infinity edge just beyond my feet.

I could lie here all night on the linen-draped cabana, a mattress as big and as soft as the one inside beneath me, the starry sky peeking through the latticed, vine-covered roof above. There's just something so peaceful about the music of nature and the gentle ripple of the water, all softly lit and glowing aquamarine. The temptation to dive right in and cause ripples in the calm water, swim until my muscles ache, until I'm fatigued enough for sleep, calls to me.

I trail a lazy hand over my front. I really should have worn my bathers. I doubt the chlorine would be kind to my silk lingerie…but there's always skinny-dipping. It's what Dani would do for sure. Me…?

It's what I would have done. Pre-Bobby. Pre-marriage. Pre-grief.

I roll onto my front and force away the melancholy. I want to keep hold of this magical moment. This feeling of freedom, of just living and enjoying the world. I look at the water still calling to me and my lips curve up. I could so do this…

You haven't got the nerve.

My smile dies. It's Bobby's voice in my head now.

When did you get so boring?

Hell, I don't know, Bobby, maybe when my mother died and I realised life wasn't made of roses. Maybe when you told me to wear the high-cut dress and the opaque tights, to downplay the make-up and the attempts at seduction, effectively killing off everything that was sexual about me. Maybe then!

I suck in a breath full of the Tuscan air: wildflowers, herbs and the distant sea.

Am I boring, though? Would the old me really have stripped off and dived right in? The one that existed before Mum died, before I got the promotion that set me above Bobby, before our hasty marriage took a turn for the worse…?

Yes! Bloody hell, Faye, yes! You were that woman. You were fun, you were adventurous!

And, Christ, it's Dani in my head now. Telling me to forget Bobby, to be me again…and I'm going to start right now.

I push up off the bed and pad to the water's edge,

letting my robe hang loose. The breeze coaxes it off my skin to the floor. I toe the water. It's balmy. Inviting.

I glance up towards the castle and see only darkness, save for the subtle lights that weave through the many paths that feed down the hillside. Spikes of blackness reaching up into the moonlit sky as the cypress trees separate the pool area from the rest of the grounds and help to create a secluded little oasis. A sheltered, private oasis.

And, right now, it's all mine.

The castle is quiet now that Marianna has enjoyed a nightcap—the best she could find in the bar, having turned her nose up at my *grappa*—and hastened to her room.

I'm finally alone with my thoughts and the place I call home surrounding me: Tuscany. I don't get to come here as much as I should, and I miss it. I miss the sense of belonging that comes when I'm standing amongst the vines, breathing in the Tuscan earth that I spent my childhood exploring. It gave me what I needed—a place to run to, a safe place to avoid the chaos at home.

I stroke my hand over the rough stone wall that surrounds the veranda on which I stand. It grazes my fingers—rough, solid, safe. I look out at the castle's grounds and the rolling hillside beyond; yes, this is home. And this castle is now mine. A purchase I wouldn't have made so soon if not for Dani's wedding and her dream to marry in a venue such as this.

Am I mad to buy it and then live in it for seven days with a family as messed up as ours? Who even does that?

I sip at my *grappa*. Seems the answer is me, thanks to Dani's disillusioned view. She would have been better off eloping than insisting on even this small, intimate affair. But then Dani never did suffer the same reality as me. She didn't have to grow up with our parents at each other's throats. Their failed attempts at living together in harmony followed by bouts apart. But they never could stay away. They loved each other regardless and, if that's what love does to you, then frankly they could keep it. It's a fate worse than death.

Not in my little sister's eyes, though. To her marriage is all roses and happiness, love and laughter, and maybe I envy her just a little for having that outlook.

I throw back the remainder of my drink and push away from the wall. A restless energy floods my veins that even a day of travel can't rid me of, and I know it stems from unease about the whole affair and keeping a lid on my family.

I place my empty glass on the long mosaic table fit to host a *real* Italian family. Large, boisterous, happy. And even that taunts me as I pick up my stride, aiming for the path that weaves down to the tennis courts, the pool and the small private villa that I'll use to escape to.

I'm already unbuttoning my shirt and easing it from my body. A swim. That's what I need. An all-out lung-burning swim and then I'll collapse into bed, grateful for the rest.

But as I near I hear the water sloshing and the definite sound of someone swimming.

I check my watch. One in the morning. Who on...?

I break free of the trees and the question no longer exists. My entire head is empty.

There's a woman. In the water. Naked.

Make that a siren, graceful and serene as she glides with ease through the water, and I'm held hostage. I can't move, I can't speak. I blink, though. Blink to make sure what I'm seeing is real. Blink to try to clear my mind and tell myself that this is wrong, that I should turn away, announce my presence, anything but watch. Hooked. Mute. Hard.

I swallow.

Cazzo.

CHAPTER TWO

WHAT A GREAT DECISION! I feel so free and relaxed—liberated, even—as I move through the water. The persistent fog in my brain lifts enough to make me realise just how busy I've been for so long, how I've distracted myself with work to avoid the bad—to avoid dwelling on Mum's death, my break-up and the things I can't control.

I used to love swimming. It was a daily ritual—a few lengths of the leisure centre when I was younger and at the gym when I was older. But in recent years running has taken over. It's quick, effective and suits my heavy work schedule. For the next seven days, work is parked, though, and I get to do this.

And it's all the more thrilling for being naked.

The rush against my skin, my nipples, between my legs… Skinny-dipping isn't something I've done before and now I'm wondering why.

Er…maybe because you don't frequent nudist camps?

I laugh inside, not wanting to stop. But I know I have to. Yes, the house is asleep. Yes, the grounds are empty. But the longer I'm here the more risk I run. And I need to be up bright and early for day one of wedding fun.

I slow my stroke, preparing to get out at the end of this length, but something snags my attention, some movement off in the darkness. My kick falters as my heart lurches into my throat. What the...?

I squint in the direction of the sound, but I can see nothing. It's all blackness and shadow beyond the pool lights.

I must have imagined it. But...

Adrenaline pulses through my system, the hairs at my nape prickling against the water. I don't feel like I've imagined it.

Time to leave. I hurry to the edge and push myself up. The water rushes over my sensitised skin as the goose bumps spread and I clamber up.

'Holy mother of crap!' The words rush out of me as I both straighten and fold in on myself at once.

There's a man emerging from the shadowed path.

A half-naked man staring straight at me.

And, I mean, *straight* at me. His dark eyes glint as the light from the pool dances over his chest...his very toned and very rigid six—no, make that eight-pack. *Oh my.* I lift my gaze higher, to his face, to his shadowed jaw, chiselled cheekbones, straight nose. And those eyes... Those *eyes*...

I swallow. I have an arm over my breasts and one over my very naked nether region. What the actual crap do I do?

Heat flushes my cheeks, the burn offsetting any

hint of the cold air as it teases the water droplets forming over my entire length. For one delirious second, I think I've conjured him up like some sex-starved fantasy because, fuck me, is he hot!

Like, Italian god, golden-skinned, dark-haired hot.

'I'm sorry.' The god suddenly comes alive, his English heavily accented and definitely dream-worthy. His eyes dart around the pool edge as his pec muscles ripple and he clutches what looks to be his shirt to his own nether region that is very much clothed. 'Don't you have a towel?'

'No,' I squeak. I hadn't thought that far ahead. I start sidestepping to the right, to where my robe and cami set await on the cabana bed, and he mirrors my movement in just as awkward a fashion. I'm torn between laughing and dying of shame.

No one has seen me naked since Bobby, and even then I don't remember a fire in his gaze as scorching as that of Mr Italian Stranger.

Even if he does look as alarmed as I do.

'I'm sorry, this is so awkward,' I mumble. 'Do you mind?'

'Mind?' He frowns at me and then his brows swiftly lift, eyes widening with understanding, and I swear that even in the low light I see his cheeks flush before he spins to look the other way. His rear is almost as appealing as his front: broad shoulders, tapered waist, a great, pert behind encased in beige chinos. *Yum*.

'Apologies.'

His gruff voice has me snapping my eyes back up

and remembering what I'm supposed to be doing. But the warmth in his tone, the rasp in the blurted apology, has me smiling and totally at ease.

I take up my robe and pull it on, struggling as the fabric clings to my wet skin, but eventually I have it tied around me. I know it doesn't cover half as much as the additional cami and shorts would, but I'd struggle even more to get them over my wet skin, and there's no way I can pull them on quickly enough to get this encounter over and done with.

'You can look.'

He turns, his fingers raking through his thick, dark hair, his eyes on the floor, and then they lift and trail upwards…from my feet to my calves to my semi-concealed thighs and further still. Boy, do my nipples prickle as his eyes graze over them before finally connecting with mine. I sweep a shaky hand over my hair to hide the way my breath catches, my lungs struggling to take in air as I'm presented with the sexiest man I've ever seen outside of a glossy magazine.

'It's not often I'm lost for words,' he says, his mouth quirking to one side.

'You and me both.' I step forward and smile, offering out my free hand and praying that my other, which clutches the rest of my clothing to my chest, is covering enough of my body beneath the sheer fabric. 'I'm Faye. I'm here for the wedding.'

He eyes my hand, then my face, before slipping his fingers around mine and giving me a grin that steals my breath anew. His jawline really is bold, chiselled and, oh, so masculine. His facial hair is angled in such a way as to draw attention to his lips, all sensual, full and… Oh, my God, I just licked mine. I flick my eyes up. Did he notice?

Yes. Yes, he did!

There's amusement in his depths now, amusement and fire, and his continued grasp around my hand is all warm and firm and I'm tingling everywhere. I lower my gaze and take in our handshake, that shows no sign of ending, and his torso just beyond which is as naked as I feel and dappled with hair. Manly hair. Hair that thickens as it disappears into the waistband of his trousers… I want to wet my lips again. He's utterly delicious, and I'm practically eating him with my eyes, and—

He's not some bloody piece of meat, Faye!

'And you are?' I say over my mental admonishment, forcing my eyes back to his.

'The owner.'

'The what, now?' I blurt, expecting a name, not a… Oh God, he's the owner, and I've just been caught swimming naked in *his* pool. This can't be happening.

'The owner…' he repeats, releasing my hand to wave it about us, his eyes not once leaving mine '…of this pool, the land, the castle.'

I nod. It's all I can manage as the embarrassment swells. But then…he doesn't seem to mind. If anything, he's still looking at me as though he wants to wet *his* lips. And *I* want to wet them. Their luscious curve makes me want to taste, to probe, to do all manner of X-rated things that I haven't been inspired to think of, let alone act on, in so long.

I surprise myself by smiling, surprise myself even more when I step a little closer, a fire I've missed so much coming alive deep inside. 'You have a lovely place here.'

I watch his throat bob, watch as his eyes do their little trail over my body again, and I know by the raw hunger I see flaring back at me that the damp, sheer robe has me as good as naked. And it's not embarrassment that runs hot through my veins now, not even close…

Boring I am not, Bobby darling.

Starting right this second, I'm throwing off reserved, stuck-in-a-rut Faye. No more feeling blanketed and oppressed by Bobby, by life's cruel twists and turns. I'm giving my instincts free rein and it feels so good.

'Seems you can't sleep either?' My voice is all throaty, my inner seductress making the most of being given airtime at last.

'I've not long since arrived.'

'Been out of town?'

'Si.'

'Needing a swim to wash the day off?' He'd been on his way here, after all, half-naked.

'You could say that.'

'Well…don't let me stop you.'

'I…' He stalls, his grin slow to return, and when it does warm little flutters take off in my lower belly. 'Okay, *grazie.*'

He turns away. He's going to swim and I... I lower my arms and toss my cami set back on the cabana bed. 'You mind if I stay a while?'

He's midway to stripping off his trousers as he flicks me a look, his eyes burning into the robe that now clings to every damp stretch of skin. 'No.'

He gives that grin again and nods to the bottle of fizz I've been nursing, and which I've left at the foot of the bed. 'Make yourself at home.'

He goes back to stripping off his clothes. It's only when his hands hook into the waistband of his boxers that I realise he's about to be as naked as I was.

I swallow and turn away. It seems Bobby's wife is still too close to suppress entirely, and I hear him give a soft chuckle seconds before the break of water echoes around us.

His chuckle works its way through me, teasing the old me, coaxing out the new. Hell, why did I turn away? I'm not Bobby's wife any more. I am *me*. I am the person who skinny-dipped, the person who walked up to him wearing no more than this robe, and wet her lips like some needy vixen... *Oh, yes*.

I round my shoulders and take a breath, then turn, my eyes seeking him out. My mouth is agape and it doesn't quite close again. I'm too caught up in the delight of a man as fit as the god Poseidon himself, slicing through the water, and he's bronzed *all over*. No shame in bathing naked for this man. But then, if you owned a place such as this, why wouldn't you swim naked when it feels as good as it does?

I smile as I make myself at home, just as he suggested, and watch him as avidly as I would any movie.

Swimming shouldn't be a turn-on. Dancing in a club, the gyrating of hips, the roll of a very sexy body—yes. But right now…with the music of nature, the scent of the Tuscan vines, the herbs, the sea… swimming is as sexy as a striptease from the man of your dreams.

And I'm settling in for the show. My very private, one-on-one show. And wherever it will take me.

The old me, the new, they are one and the same. Bobby's Faye is long gone.

Faye!

As in Faye Davenport, my little sister's best friend Faye!

I speed up my stroke, swimming harder and faster as I let it sink in.

My sister and I don't see each other often, but we talk enough for me to know who she is.

And she's off-limits.

She's not just a wedding guest but the maid of honour, the one I'm depending on to make this week go without a hitch.

Too young. Too messy. Too complicated.

But, instead of telling her who I am and putting a stop to our not so subtle flirting, I've been evasive. Instead of digging out a towel from the pool house and waiting for her to leave, I let her stand there with that see-through thing clinging to her body and told her to settle back and enjoy the show.

And why?

Because I lost all good sense the second I saw her.

Because she is captivating, intriguing, different... and I want to carry on enjoying the thrill of it. Of this. The attraction, the heated push and pull, the flirtation.

Because, let's face it, I've not experienced anything as remotely stimulating outside of work in a long time.

And now what?

Now she's lying on her front, her elbows planted in the bed, her head resting on her palms as she watches me as though I'm the most interesting thing she's ever seen. And it feels good. Too good to tell her to leave.

Her eyes are too far away for me to make out their colour but, having seen them up close, I won't be forgetting them any time soon. They're the palest blue and so piercingly clear. As for how they made me feel when my hand held hers... My skin prickles beneath the water. They struck through the very heart of me, exposed me... Me and every debauched thought that had raced through my brain.

But she's Dani's best friend...

And she's lying there all at ease, her legs bent in the air and hooked by her slender ankles, the little chain she wears around one glinting in the pool lights. She could be a nun and I'd still want her.

I execute a turn under water, my back to her now, but her presence is no less teasing. I'm aware of her eyes on me, aware of her enjoyment too, and it thrums a reciprocal beat through my body that's suddenly decided I've gone too long without sex.

I try to remember all that Dani has told me about her. I know they met at uni and lived together. Aside from that, nothing. I feel a stab of guilt. We don't talk enough, my sister and I.

Another turn and I'm facing her again, quashing the guilt with rising curiosity about the brunette who's still giving me the come-to-bed eye. I know she's here alone this week, and that likely makes her single and very much available... *All thoughts you shouldn't even be entertaining.*

This week is about Dani and her happiness. It certainly doesn't involve me getting lucky with her hot—and likely just as young—best friend.

Tyler wouldn't let me live it down. Not after the hell I put him and Dani through over their age gap.

And Dani. She'd crucify me.

But Faye... I look to her before I turn in the water again and our eyes meet, a brief clash, but long enough to see the reciprocated desire firing back at me. She swings her legs, the anklet flashes and I imagine hooking my finger beneath it, tracing its line around the curve of her ankle, smoothing my palm up her calf, her thigh...

My blood rushes south with the very vivid thought even as my mind plays judge, jury and executioner in one: *She wouldn't look at you like that if she knew who you were.*

Or maybe she would.

Maybe she'd push this as far as I'm willing to go.

Not helping...

But I do need to tell her, and I do need to put a firm end to anything more. Because this week is about Dani and not the complicated mess I could get myself ensnared in if I pursue this attraction further. A mess that would detract from what is important: Dani and her wedding day.

Si, I'll tell her...once I have a towel wrapped around my waist and my nagging erection under control.

Cazzo.

I swim harder, losing track of the number of lengths as I focus on taming my uncooperative body so I can stand before her and not succumb to the offer so brazen in her gaze. Part of me hopes she will tire and leave. Another part hopes it's enough to exhaust my overactive organs into neutral. And another part, so determined to rear its head, wants me to say to hell with the consequences and dive right in.

But she's not leaving, and eventually I'm forced to cave. I swim to the pool edge closest to her, sink beneath the water and rise up, flicking my hair out of my eyes as I look to her.

'Could you do me a favour?'

She cocks a grin and I sense her mind racing with the many, many favours she could do...each of them as tantalising as the ones my mind is too eager to offer up.

'Sure.'

She rises onto her knees, that sheer robe clinging like a second skin and dragging my eyes south.

I swallow the swell of desire and force them back to hers. 'Could you get me a towel from the pool house, *per favore*?'

Her smile lifts to the side. 'You mean to say *you* had access to towels all this time?'

I can't help the grin that forms. 'I did.'

'And you didn't think to get me one.'

'And spoil my view?'

Cazzo, Rafael. That's hardly playing it cool and giving her the brush off.

'Well, in that case, I think it only fair you do it yourself...'

She lies back down and rolls onto her back, her eyes on the heavens now as she trails a hand down her front. From this angle all I can see is the tip of her head, the peak of her breasts and her nipples taut against the fabric as her fingers trail between them.

'You can get me one while you're at it...*per favore*.' She teases with the Italian and I know she's smiling even though I can't see her face.

A chuckle erupts; I can't help it. I like her confidence, her easy tease. Not many people dare tease me. I'm too cold, too controlled, too severe—labels I've been given plenty of times in the past—but not now, not with her, not with someone who doesn't know me from Adam.

And it's liberating. I don't have to be Rafael Perez. *Only, you do...*

She runs a hand beneath her neck and flicks her hair up, sending water droplets my way. 'I'm still quite *wet*.'

My body tightens over her double entendre and her fingers cease their exploration of her front as she shifts her head to eye me. One second, two… she rolls back onto her front, her smile wicked, her eyes sparkling. 'Problem?'

'No. No problem.'

Unless you count an unhindered erection.

'Sooo…' she drawls, her eyebrows gesturing towards the pool house.

I give a tight smile and launch myself up and out. I watch the play of emotions flicker across her face, the way her eyes brazenly fall to my hardened length, and my ego takes a good, long stroke. I turn and walk away, unhurried, practically strutting as I enjoy her eyes on me and, hell, if my smile doesn't relax and grow…

'I take it you swim naked a lot?' she calls after me.

I pause and turn my head just enough to see her. 'What makes you say that?'

'Your behind is as tanned as the rest of you.'

She runs her teeth over her bottom lip, her eyes locked on my arse, and my cock bucks. I shake my head and carry on my way. She's right; I do bathe naked. But this, between us, this is wrong and it has to stop. Only, it's fun, so much fun and, *Gesù*, when did I last find fun in anything?

Why does she have to be Faye? Why couldn't she be some random person with no connections to my family? To the wedding that has to go off without a hitch, and certainly without me crossing a line with my sister's best friend and the maid of honour.

Because, no matter how much I'm enjoying the anonymity and the desire, I know I need to fess up and be me.

I damn my own good conscience as I enter the pool house and take a fresh towel off the rack. If I were my cousin Dante I wouldn't hesitate. In fact, I'd put money on him going all-in tomorrow when he sees her. She's just his type: brunette, big blue eyes, a broad grin that rounds her cheeks and lights up her entire face.

Diavolo, she's *my* type. Not that I ever considered having a type before.

I wrap the towel around my waist; it's safer to have at least one proper layer between us. That robe of hers counts for nothing. It's worse than her being naked, teasing over her curves and making me wish it were my hands upon her, tracing the same path, the same wet trails…

I grab a second towel for her more roughly than I need to and stride back out. *Confess. Leave. Confess. Leave. Confess…*

She's standing before the bed, the said robe shifting in the light breeze, pulling taut against her tummy, her breasts. She twists her hair over one shoulder as though wringing it out, but I sense it has a more seductive purpose as it dips her chin and forces her to eye me from beneath her lashes, her smile all sultry.

'Thank you,' she says as I mutely offer her the towel.

My confession is on the tip of my tongue. I haven't

lied, as such. I *am* the owner, as of six months ago, when I bought the place to ensure Dani could get married here. Only, my sister doesn't know that. No one does.

'You're welcome.'

She opens the towel up and starts scrunching at her hair. The move is hypnotic and sends wafts of her shampoo my way, mixed up with chlorine and the scents of Tuscany. It shouldn't affect me like it does.

'I'm sorry you found me like you did,' she says softly. 'It's been a long day of travelling and I hadn't planned on going for a swim. The urge just…'

She gives a cute little shrug and drops the towel on the bed, turning away from me, and before I realise what she's doing the robe slips off her shoulders.

'Think I'll need to hang this out to dry,' she says, letting it fall from her fingers to the bed. She's an arm's reach away, entirely naked, and as she eyes me over her shoulder I swallow, open my mouth to say something and close it again. Because all I want to say, all I want to do, has nothing to do with confessing that I'm Dani's brother.

She bends forward, every movement drawn out, maximising what I get to see: the delicate frame of her shoulders, the line of her spine, the way her hips splay outwards and the valley of her arse, the gentle curves as they jut out to me…

Oh, Dio. I grip the knot in my towel tight.

She scoops up her own towel and straightens, turning to face me once more as she dabs her cheeks, her neck, her breasts, her stomach, her…

Cazzo.

I wet my lips and rake a hand through my hair.

'It's late,' I rasp out. 'We should…we should call it a night.'

Her lips quirk, her eyes flicking down and back up just as quickly. 'You don't *look* ready for bed yet.'

'You'd be surprised.' I'm so ready for bed…if I get to take her with me.

She pouts as she cocks her head to one side and runs the towel across her back, forcing her chest to thrust forward and her breasts to lift. I grip my towel tighter.

'Look, as much as I want to…'

I can't stop my eyes from lowering, from drinking her in, and she chooses that moment to step forward, her eyes on my obvious erection beneath the towel. 'I can see how much you want to…'

'But we really can't.'

'Are you spoken for?'

I frown. 'Am I…*what*?'

'A wife, a girlfriend?'

I laugh. It's a bark, thanks to the top-to-toe tension holding me in place.

'No, nothing like that.'

'Then…what?'

I swallow. I don't want to tell her. The moment I do, I know this is over. Which is as it should be, but…

'Because I'm kind of a lady in need—a damsel in distress, if you like—and you're…' She drops her towel to the floor. 'You're my perfect fantasy.'

She steps closer and I'm too caught up in her spell to make her stop. I'm used to confident women, sexy women, women who go after what they want, when they want. But there's something about how she says it, about what she says… A damsel in distress, a lady in need. Hardly strong, confident words, or maybe they're more confident for the honesty they touch upon. I'm too intrigued not to probe. 'What makes you a lady in need?'

She smiles, her fingers soft as they meet with my chest, and my gut contracts, my lungs scraping in air to fend off the frisson of excitement.

'You see, I've not had…*fun*…' Her lips part and I get a glimpse of a glistening pink tongue. 'I've not had *fun* in far too long, and for seven days I am my best friend's maid of honour. I aim to be perfectly behaved, doting, selfless.'

As do you, Rafael, remember…?

'But tonight is my chance to let my hair down, and I can't think of a better way to do it than…' She steps closer, so close the air is filled with her scent. My chest is warmed by hers and her nipples brush ever so lightly against me. 'Having some *wicked* fun with you.'

She closes the remaining gap, treating my erection to the unyielding pressure of her body. Her eyes lift to mine and I'm gone. Gone and pulling her against me, my mouth crushing hers. But she's just as fierce, just as wanton. Her tongue plunders, twists and tastes. She's all champagne, and something else, something that's all her. I can't stop this. I can't.

She whimpers and it's as though she's repeating my state of mind back to me. Not that she could know how close I am to ending it. How close I am to losing it.

But you're losing it with Faye Davenport. Your little sister's best friend.

'*Cazzo.*' I grab her by the arms and wrench her away from me but as I do my towel hits the deck.

She gives a soft laugh. 'You look better without it.'

I shake my head, fighting for clarity, anything to lift the lustful haze that is so determined to descend.

I press my forehead to hers and drag in a breath. 'We can't do this.'

'So you keep saying…'

She brushes her lower body against me and I close my eyes, trying to concentrate on what I need to say.

'I'm Rafael.'

'Okay, Rafael, it's nice to meet you. Now, can…?' She frowns, and then her eyes widen just as swiftly, and her body stills. 'Wait. The owner, Rafael. Not… not Dani's older brother Rafael?'

'Owner. Brother. One and the same.'

Her cheeks flush crimson and her eyes widen further. 'No, no, no, no…'

She spins away, grabs her towel, her clothes, her sandals and clutches them all to her chest before spinning back to me, her head shaking. 'And you didn't think to say anything?'

What looks like a pair of silk shorts fall from her grasp and I fight the urge to bend for them, especially when it would only bring me closer to the delightfully pink nipples still so ripe and needy for me. I pin my eyes on her face and away from temptation, but she heaves in a breath, one that has them lifting, begging… She blows it out in a gust and ducks down, blindly reaching for the garment as her eyes stay fixed on mine, and she pats at the floor.

'Hell, I knew you had issues.' She grabs at the shorts and bolts upright again. 'But I didn't think a lack of manners would be one.'

Issues? What's that supposed to mean?

'Look, I'm sorry…' I don't get to finish. She's already legging it away, her naked behind rippling and teasing me even as the panic rises. I wrap my towel around my waist and race after her.

'Faye, wait.'

She spins on the spot, struggling to pull her own towel around her with all the other items in her grasp.

'Let's save it for tomorrow, hey?' she blurts. 'When we can be introduced properly…*in clothes*?' She waves a hand between us, her eyes lingering slightly too long on my torso and her cheeks flushing more deeply when she realises it. 'Goodnight, Rafael.'

And then she's gone, and instead of cursing, instead of being relieved or feeling guilty, I have the most idiotic smile. I know it's idiotic as I don't recognise the feel of it. Much like the churning underway in my gut and the intense, unsated desire.

Is this what the next seven days have in store then? My testing family and a constant tease at every turn?

And, now that I've seen what's underneath the

clothes, now that I've witnessed her in full-on seductress mode, how do I rewind?

Cold showers. Cold showers at every opportunity,
if that's what it takes to keep this week focused on
Faye... *Dani, maledizione! Dani and Tyler!*

No one else. Because, for once in my life, I won't
be the cold, heartless bastard my family think I am.
I'll be the proud and doting big brother.

*You can still be that and have a bit of discreet
fun on the side...*

The smile makes a comeback.

CHAPTER THREE

'HAVE YOU SEEN my mother, Faye?'

Dani comes racing into the breakfast room, straight for me, and I do a double-take. It's only seven in the morning and I'd expected to be alone this early. Alone to get over my burning humiliation of last night and to bolster my confidence before the inevitable introduction to a certain god-like Italian.

Of all the people to choose to let loose with, it had to be the elusive brother. The elusive, seriously sexy, older brother.

The one who's string of conquests Dani has often bemoaned to me. And last night it was my lips he'd been exercising that well-practised skill over... A sigh works its way up my throat, my head leaning off to the side as my lips softly curl.

'Faye!'

Oh, God.

'Sorry.' I straighten sharply, blinking away the image of him naked, and clear my throat. 'Your mother?'

I frown as I take in the sight of Dani up close.

She's frazzled. Her glossy black hair is tied back but sticking out at all angles and her face is devoid of make-up—very un-Dani. 'What's wrong?'

She shakes her head and scans the deserted room. There's only one discreet staff member on hand at the breakfast bar; the room is ours.

'I had a ranting text message from her, something about her bedroom being too tucked away, and then some comment about the size of her bed and having no man to fill it.'

She steals my coffee cup and takes a big gulp. 'Sorry, babe, hope you don't mind. I need the caffeine, or a mimosa might be more apt. I mean, this is my wedding week, right? I can drink this early if I want to!'

It all comes out in a frantic rush and I stand, taking the cup from her and placing it on the table, before holding her arms and forcing her to face me. 'Breathe, honey. I will sort you out a mimosa.'

She gives me a weak smile. 'You will?'

'Yes. And I'll go and find out what's troubling your mother. You need to go back the way you came and cosy up with that gorgeous hubby-to-be. Leave the niggly things to me.'

'Niggly? She's more a giant pain in the—'

'Dani.'

She gives me a cute little pout. 'You sure?'

'It's what I'm here for. Now, go. I'll see you get some drinks sent up to your room, pastries and all.'

Her eyes widen. 'No, no pastries, not until *after*

the wedding day; there isn't a millimetre to spare in that dress.'

I roll my eyes. 'You're crazy! Excitement alone will burn through all that excess.'

Not to mention the super-loud extra-curricular activity too...

'Rafael will help you.'

I start at her mention of his name, hot off the back of my extra-curricular thoughts.

'He's the fixer,' she adds. 'He sorts everything.'

Rafael, the fixer. Oh, yes, I imagine there are lots of things he could fix, my sex drought included. My insides spin as my cheeks flood with so much heat I swear I look sunburned.

'You okay, Faye?' She squints up at me. 'You look like you're having a hot flush.'

A hot flush…and then some. Thanks to the afore-mentioned fixer, my body is in overdrive, seeking out gratification for the heat he's sparked. To feel that thrill again after so many years… Hell, who am I kidding? I've never felt a thrill *that* intense. I could blame it on my extended celibacy, only… I conjure up the fire in his eyes, the cut to his jaw, those lips… *God, those lips.*

'Faye?' She waves a hand in front of my face.

'It is warm, isn't it?' I rush out, faking a smile. 'So, you were saying, your brother…?'

She's still squinting at me and I pretend not to notice.

'Yeah…he's around here somewhere, not that I can find him. Maybe he's wandering the grounds…'

And then her eyes narrow even more. 'Speaking of wandering, where did you disappear to in the middle of the night?'

My brows twitch up, my pulse too. 'What do you mean?'

'I heard you come back in the early hours. At least, I think it was your room. Yours is the closest.'

And it's too close, much too close.

'I couldn't sleep. I went for a stroll to get some air and wind down…'

'Sounds perfect.'

It was. Too perfect. And so wrong.

'Well, if you see him, get him to lend a hand, won't you? You really shouldn't face one of my mother's moods alone and, though he looks scary, he's actually a doll.'

I laugh now, wholeheartedly. 'A *doll*?'

'Oh, yeah, totally. A heart of gold but a front that would send you running.'

'Right, okay.' I nod, letting this new version of the Italian god sink in. 'Serious. Severe. Doll-like. I won't be able to miss him.'

'You won't.' She gives a little grimace. 'But don't fall for his charm either.'

I nod slowly, my smile too amused to hide. 'Right, so he's now serious, severe, doll-like but a total charmer. He's quite the enigma.'

Dani gives me a wry smile. 'Don't tease. You know exactly what I mean, and consider yourself fully warned on that front.'

'On what front?' Maybe I shouldn't play dumb,

but right now I'm remembering just how susceptible I am to his particular brand of charm. And that was before he said much at all.

'The whole charming the pants off any female he takes a fleeting fancy to.'

'Oh, yes, that little trick.' Only, last night I wasn't wearing any pants to charm off...and neither was he. I swallow. 'Consider me warned.'

'Good, and anyway, Dante arrives today...' Her smile is full of mischief now. 'I have high hopes that my cousin will come to your aid no problem.'

'Oh, God, Dani!' I lower my voice as the eyes of the solitary staff member flick our way. 'My sex drought isn't your problem.'

'No, but I would like to see it taken care of, and Dante is perfect hot fling material.' She gives me a wink and a little nudge in the ribs. 'It's about time you put that hot bod to good use again.'

'*Dani.*'

She laughs properly now, her eyes alive, her stress of seconds before momentarily gone. 'Hey, I'm just looking out for my bestie. You have a week off work, a week to remember just how fun life can be if you relax a little, enjoy yourself... And, if my cousin can help with that, I'm all for it.'

'I'm so glad you feel your wedding is a chance for me to get laid again.'

'Well, what can I say?' She plants her palm against her chest and bats her lashes at me innocently. 'I'm nothing if not generous.'

I roll my eyes and shake my head at her, my laugh

bubbling up and suppressing the nagging guilt for keeping last night's encounter to myself. 'So let me get this straight—Cousin Dante is permitted but older brother Rafael is…'

I can't quite finish. I don't even know what possessed me to ask. *Liar*.

'Definitely not.'

'Because?'

'Because my darling brother leaves a trail of broken hearts in his wake and I don't want yours to be next.'

'Fair enough.' Though my frown tells her just how odd I find it all. 'And that's not the case with Dante?'

'Not at all. He's…he's just different.' She waves a hand at me in dismissal. 'You'll see what I mean when you meet him.'

I shake my head even more. Dani is Dani. You'd think I'd be used to her by now, but she still manages to surprise me.

'Yes, well, never mind me getting some action…' I physically turn her away from me and point her towards the door. 'You need to get yourself back upstairs to Tyler and leave the niggly things to us, yeah?'

I give her a gentle shove and she blows me a kiss over her shoulder. 'Just make sure you wear the black cozzie for the pool later…or the red one…you choose! Either's sure to be effective.'

I laugh at her tenacity. 'I'm so glad I let you talk me into buying them.'

'You can thank me properly later…once you've had a proper seeing to!'

She prances from the room, much lighter than when she came in. At least the poor state of my sex life has the power to do her some good. But let's face it, she wouldn't be quite so light on her feet if she knew I'd already met Rafael and just how close I'd come to…*not helping*.

I walk up to the discreet staff member hovering by the breakfast bar and arrange for a breakfast tray complete with His and Her mimosas to be sent up to Dani's room. Next, I head outside because I know where Rafael is. He's out running. Just as I would've been if I hadn't come out of my room at five-thirty this morning and caught him doing the exact same thing ahead of me.

I smooth back my ponytail, brush down my maxi dress and scan the grounds. Really, I should wait for him to be showered and fully clothed before I bring this to his attention, but I get the sense that Marianna's going to have the whole castle turned on its head if she isn't dealt with soon. I've only met her a handful of times and that was enough.

My stomach flutters as I wait. Nerves, excitement, anticipation. I tell myself it isn't my fault he found me naked in his pool last night, or that I was so sexually frustrated that I propositioned him. My cheeks flush even now at the way I behaved, the brazen way I ogled him, the words I used…

I clear my throat.

But then I remember how he looked at me. The reciprocation in his eyes, in his kiss, in his... *Oh, yes.*

And of course he chooses that moment to appear, emerging from the path in a burst of power while I'm recalling his impressive manhood. *Jesus.* I snap my gaping mouth shut, straighten to fend off the heat determined to melt my insides and smile. Yes, smile. Be polite. Put everything in neutral and start over.

At least I'm clothed this time and he's... No, he's not... He's...pulling off his tee and my mouth is open again and dry, so dry. He's a few strides away when he spies me. His eyes sharpen, his mouth lifts to the side and...

Close your bloody mouth!

'*Buongiorno*, Faye.'

I'd forgotten how thick and sexy his accent is, and the way he says my name has me wanting it on repeat, again and again and again.

'Good morn...'

It comes out high and I don't quite get the 'ing' out as I watch him tuck his shirt into the side of his shorts. Oh, how I want to run my hands all over every slick inch, explore, discover, tease...

I flick my eyes up to his and flex my fists that itch with the urge to touch. 'Nice run?'

He combs a hand through his hair, and I physically fight to keep my mouth shut. I cross my arms in front of me.

His eyes flicker in the direction of the move, his throat bobs and I latch onto the gesture, hoping I'm not the only one suffering with this dogged attraction. It makes me feel better. Not a lot, but a little.

'It was decent.' His eyes come back to mine. 'I'm going to get a drink. Want one?'

'I'm fine, thanks.'

He smiles and gives me a polite nod, averting his gaze as he goes to move past me. 'No problem.'

'Wait!' I reach out on impulse, finally remembering why I'm here…and it's not to ogle, touch or do any manner of the things raging through my brain. 'Before you go in, can I have a quick word?'

He pauses, his brows drawing together, and now he's close, really close. His slicked-up body glows deep bronze in the sun, brilliant, blinding, and I can feel the heat pulsing off him in my outstretched palm. It's not sweat I smell, it's a heady mix of male cologne, all musky, sensual and… *Jesus*, Dani's right, I just need to get laid, already.

'Sure.' He hesitates, his eyes darting to the castle interior and back out to the path before coming back to me. He steps closer, taking me with him so we're out of sight of the open entrance. The flutters reignite inside my belly, clambering all the way up through my throat as I blink up at him.

'Look,' he says 'if it's about last night, I—'

'No!' I blurt, wetting my lips quickly and backing up a step. 'I mean, it's not about that. Though we probably should talk about that too. But maybe not… Well, I mean, it's not… It wasn't…'

And fuck me, I'm rambling! I can work a conference centre of hundreds without getting flustered but a one-on-one with Rafael Perez has me floored.

Great maid of honour I'm going to make if I can't remain close to the bride's brother without losing my cool. And, to make it worse, he's laughing. His rich brown eyes positively dance in the morning sun now, flecks of honey-gold shining through, all warm and amused.

'This isn't funny.'

'I didn't say it was.'

'You're laughing at me.'

'I'm not.'

'You are.' I resist the urge to poke him in the chest as I know one single press of my finger against that hot, naked skin and I won't be able to stop my palm moving in next. 'I can see it in your face.'

He crosses his arms and his biceps bulge—*eyes up, Faye!*

'I'm sorry.' He purses his lips, swallows. 'I confess to finding your bluster…endearing.'

Endearing. I scan his face. As in sexy-endearing, cute-endearing, silly-endearing? I want to ask. My ego begs me to ask. But that's not what I need to talk to him about.

'Stop distracting me.'

'Distracting you?' His lips twitch at the corners; his body quivers.

'You're laughing again.'

'I didn't make a sound.'

'Your insides are laughing.'

Now he bellows with it, an almighty chuckle that

has him looking ten years younger, no sign of the serious, severe Raf-like behaviour I've been fore-warned of and… *And he's bloody well laughing at you, Faye.*

'Okay, I surrender, I am laughing.'

'It's not acceptable.'

'Which bit?'

'All of it. The laughing, the distracting, the not telling me who you were last night.'

'In my defence, last night I was a little distracted.'

I drag in a flustered breath. '*You* were distracted?'

'You were naked.'

'*You* were naked.'

'You were naked first.'

'Oh, my God.' I shake my head, waving a frantic hand around me. 'I can't even believe we're argu-ing about this.'

'I prefer to call it a debate.'

'A what?' I stare up at him, wide-eyed and I know I truly must be flushing scarlet, but inside I'm torn between wanting to jump his bones, put him in his place over not fessing up over his iden-tity sooner and running the other way before I do anything that has the power to detract from Dani's special week.

'A debate. I don't argue.'

He's so resolute, I frown. 'You *never* argue?'

'Never.'

My frown deepens. 'Never ever?'

He chuckles. 'Never ever. It's a waste of breath. And as for the debates, I always win in the end.'

His smile is so cocksure that it bolsters me, giving me the mental slap I need. 'Is that so?'

It's a rhetorical question. I know he means it; I can read it in his stance. Even half-naked he has an air of authority, a don't-mess-with-me attitude that speaks of many years at the top, of being the boss of his domain.

And I'm not about to feed that mammoth ego.

I fist my hands on my hips and focus on what I'm really here for.

'Well, Mr I'm-Always-Right, we have an issue that needs fixing—so if you're done with your morning exercise, and our *debate*, we have your mother to sort.'

'My mother?'

He curses under his breath and I know I have his attention now. The right attention. The kind of attention that keeps us clear of the teasing and the flirting so that Dani can enjoy herself without worrying about her mother.

'I'm going to need a shower for this.'

I swallow, or gulp, rather. Why does my mind have to project the image of him under the jets, all soaped up?

'Yes, you shower, and I'll… I'll…'

'Come to my room. Top of the stairs, turn left, last door on your right. Ten minutes.'

'Your room?' He's already moving off and I stare after him. He can't be serious.

'Ten minutes.' He looks back at me just long enough to add, 'Don't worry. I promise I'll be dressed appropriately by then.'

I don't need to see his face to know he's grinning as he walks away now. And I shouldn't be smiling too. But I am. I press a hand over the excited thrum in my lower belly and curse my body for misbehaving.

Ten minutes. I have ten minutes to get this under control.

And then, to his room. Just him and me.

To discuss his mother, Faye.

Yes, just a discussion, nothing more. Nothing more at all…

CHAPTER FOUR

Si, I INVITED her to my room.

Si, I'm asking for trouble.

Si, it's hardly discreet, but I did it anyway.

And do I regret it?

Diavolo, no.

Never mind the elevated heart rate from pounding the trail for a good ninety minutes, just seeing her again has it falling over itself.

It seems that coming face to face with a blushing Faye in a top-to-toe dress, an insipid yellow of all colours, is just as powerful as seeing her naked. Or maybe it's that I've *seen* her naked, that I know what the dress hides, that has me overheating again and losing all good sense.

Maybe if we'd actually gone through with *something*, gained some release, this would be under control now. I curse my noble streak, the one that had me confessing my relationship to Dani and putting an end to anything happening last night. I can't forget how she looked while propositioning me, her voice all sultry and soft.

I'm kind of a lady in need—a damsel in distress, if you like—and you're my perfect fantasy.

Screw fantasy, I want to make it a reality. And I will. Just as soon as she gets my mother off her chest.

We'd be perfect together in bed. I know because I've tasted her, felt her responsive body pressed against mine, felt it tremble with a need as powerful as my own. All from a kiss. A kiss that was far too short and far too teasing with it.

One solitary kiss.

I hit the shower, turn it to cold and grit my teeth as the icy shards pummel me. I need to moderate this. Get it under control. But it seems even the chill can't dampen my desire. And it's madness. She's just another woman. A woman I should be able to shut out until time and circumstance permit. Instead, she's haunting my every waking thought and, as I tug on my nagging erection with the intention to clean myself, I know how foolish I am, how hooked I am. And I blame it entirely on how we met.

Her body gliding through the water, naked, lithe, captivating. Watching her push up out of the pool, her hair a dark, sleek mass down her back, the water streaming down her front, her outthrust chest, and those nipples, taut and pleading. *Cazzo.* That's at the heart of this. That vision. And it was no illusion; it was real.

I'm barely aware of my fist pumping faster, harder, my mind filled with her. I drag in a breath and plant both palms onto the wall, leaning into it as the water pounds the back of my head and my neck. There's one solution that offers the greatest satisfaction for both of us, because I'm not imagining the way she looked at me outside, the way the colour flooded her cheeks, the way her eyes feasted over me. She still wants me.

She wants me like she did last night, *before* she learned who I was. And I want her. Want her so much that a hurried hand job isn't going to cut it.

I push away from the wall and lather soap over my body while my mind focuses on my proposition. I can pitch in my sleep. I've just never pitched something of a sexual nature before. My grin lifts to one side. I've never met a woman for the first time when she was naked and look where that's left me. Like this. Hard and dissatisfied.

I'm dressed and at the door with a minute to spare, my cock stiff and throbbing against the zip of my chinos. *Idiota.* I'm like a loaded gun. I adjust my crotch and unbutton my shirt another notch, not that it's the cause of the tight feeling in my throat, or the dryness either. That's all nerves and anticipation, both of which are alien to me and just as frustrating with it.

Diavolo, I don't let people get under my skin; I don't obsess over them. Work, *si*. Working out, *si*. But people…those outside of my family and close friends…no. Getting emotionally invested leads to dependency, an addiction you can't live without, a bond that can break you…and the sooner I can get Faye out of my head, the better. And sex will do that. It's worked in the past and it will now.

Ultimately, people are too self-serving, too mercurial to warrant any more.

Not that Dani and Tyler believe that. I've done that conversation to death over the last year, trying to convince them marriage isn't necessary.

On the plus side, thinking about marriage has the desired effect in the trouser department, just in time for her rap on the door. I breathe over the kick in my pulse, the excited rush that floods my body, and I pull open the door.

'*Ciao.*' My smile lifts as quickly as the ripple of awareness straight to my groin. Have I mentioned I hate mustard? Mustard in any form, but the colour in particular; it's so unappealing. But on her…that dress…

'Are you going to let me in?' She scans the hallway either side, her hands wringing in front of her as she bobs on her heels. She's worried about being caught. *And you should be too!*

'Sure.' I step back, pulling the door further open and bow my head to her ear as she passes, allowing myself a second's appreciation of her heavenly scent before I add, 'Don't worry, you're here on official wedding business. Knowing my family, this will become quite the regular occurrence this week.'

And if I have my way…

Her lashes flutter as her lips part, her cheeks flush that delicate shade of pink and she gives me a small smile. 'They can't be all that bad.'

I laugh, the sound deep and throaty thanks to her proximity. 'You better believe it.'

I swing the door closed and watch her carry on into the room.

'Wow,' she says, breathless, her eyes lost in the room. She tilts her head back to look at the vaulted ceiling and turns on the spot, taking in the fresco above. 'Is this original?'

I follow her line of sight to the garden scene above and see it with fresh eyes. It is ethereal, captivating, romantic even. Not that I go in for the latter.

'It was restored by the previous owner, I believe; this was his private domain.'

'While the rest of the castle was rented out to guests for holidays, events…weddings?'

'*Si.*'

She flicks me a look. 'Care to tell me why Dani doesn't know you own it now?'

I shrug. 'I haven't told her yet.'

'Why?'

'Because she'll think it a step too far.'

Her smile sparkles with curiosity. 'A step too far in what, the doting big brother stakes?'

'Something like that.'

'So you did buy it for the wedding?'

'I bought it because I knew how much she wanted to get married within the year and venues like this are booked years in advance.'

She laughs. 'And what about the people that likely had this one booked before you swept in and took over?'

'They were well compensated.'

She laughs more, her head shaking. 'You're quite something.'

My eyes narrow, the question itching to get out. *In a good way or a bad way?*

'Don't worry.' She must spy the apprehension in my gaze. 'Your secret's safe with me.'

'That's not what I was worried about.'

'No?'

'I was working out if *you* thought it was a step too far.'

She looks to the floor as she considers it, her smile soft, and when her eyes come back to me, they're warm and full of...*appreciation?*

'I think if you can afford to take such measures to make a loved one happy, then why not?' She wets her lips. 'Though buying an entire castle and its estate does seem...' she squeezes her thumb and forefinger together '...a teensy bit overboard.'

I pocket my hands and shrug.

'I was going to buy something in this location anyway, eventually.' Another shrug but it's awkward, stilted with the alien need to defend myself. It's as though someone up there is having a laugh at my expense, putting Faye in my path to see how much she can push me out of my comfort zone.

'You were?'

'*Si,*' I say firmly, trying to calm my reaction. 'The wedding just forced my hand.'

She eyes me with continued curiosity and I find myself elaborating. 'Tuscany is the only place I've ever truly felt at home.'

I can't believe I've admitted it, let alone said it out loud. What is wrong with me?

I clear my throat and move deeper into the room as I head for the breakfast that was sent up while I was in the shower. Not that I'm hungry. At least, not for food.

And it is the truth, Tuscany is the only place I've ever felt happy. But those days were so long ago, they almost feel like a dream. A dream that quickly morphed into a nightmare.

I sense her frown following me and I know she wants to probe further. Even I can feel the words rising up within me.

'Dani never mentioned that you lived here.'

'Can I get you something to eat, drink? I ordered plenty in case you hadn't eaten.'

'I'm okay, thank you.'

I pour the coffee and hear the click-clack of her sandals as she approaches, closer and closer. I keep my attention fixed on the coffee.

'I wonder why she never said anything. It feels like a big—'

'We left when I was seventeen.'

I flick her a look and see her eyes widen at my abrupt interruption. I wince into my coffee as I take it up, breathing in the familiar aroma and forcing my shoulders to ease and my voice to soften before I look back to her.

'Dani was just a baby; it was never home for her.'

'But the UK was?'

'In the beginning, then the States.' I sip my coffee

and tell myself it's okay to reveal this much, though I can feel my heart race and my discomfort rise. 'We flitted between the two until she finally settled in the UK with our mother and completed her education.'

'But you, where do you live? From what Dani tells me you spend your time hopping from country to country. Or are you saying this is it now, you live here? A secret hideout from your family once we all leave?'

Her smile blooms on the last question. She's teasing me, trying to lighten the heaviness in the air, in me.

'I hope so,' I answer truthfully. 'It will be nice to have more of a base. Much of my work can be done via technology these days; location isn't so important.'

So long as Marianna steers clear. I travelled the globe distancing myself from my mother. I don't plan to welcome her here once this is all said and done. She and her series of lovers and her ridiculous theatrics can stay well away.

'I think it makes for a very beautiful home, all the more so with the memories of this week. Dani will love visiting you here…when you finally tell her.'

'I will…*after* the wedding, when it's too late for her to have a meltdown.'

'She'll only berate you out of love.'

Warmth floods my chest from nowhere and I smile. '*Si*, that much is true.'

The atmosphere changes, eases and she opens her mouth to say something and closes it again. I sense more probing. I don't know what it is about her, or why I feel like the past is rising to the surface, but it has me needing to busy myself with something. Anything.

'You sure I can't offer you a coffee while we talk? A pastry, even?' I swap my coffee for a *cornetti* and offer it to her. 'These really are to die for, especially the cream-filled variety.'

'No, I'm fine. And we really should talk about your mother.'

'It's still early.' I hate the way my hackles rise with the mere mention of her. 'Even my mother can't have caused that much mischief by now that we need to get straight on it; she hasn't been here a day yet.'

She gives a weak grimace.

Oh, Dio, here we go...

I drop the pastry back on its plate. 'I take that back. What's happened?'

I fold my arms and perch on the table edge, my eyes glued to Faye's anxious frown and the way she chews the corner of her lip. Does she even know she's doing it? Running that full, swollen bottom lip underneath her teeth and making it blush scarlet...

'Dani was in a bit of a tizz this morning.'

'A what?' I'm trying to focus on her words but all I can see is her luscious lips. It's almost an offence that she should gnaw on them as she does. I would more than willingly gnaw on them for her.

'A tizz, you know...?' She flaps her hands about, pulling my attention away from her lip's reddened state and making me focus on her dramatic physical display as if it explains it all. I shouldn't be finding this entertaining, I really shouldn't, not when it all leads back to Marianna. But my lips still twitch, and I get the feeling I could listen to Faye all day. Mother at the heart of it or not. 'You know, a flap. A bit of a state. Are you laughing at me again?'

'No.' I straighten up some more and gesture with one hand. 'Continue.'

Her eyes narrow; she doesn't believe me. Her soft humph confirms it.

'I'm listening,' I add for good measure.

'Like I was saying…' Her eyes are still narrowed. I'm forgiven enough for her to speak but not so much that she's at ease. 'Apparently your mother texted her this morning to complain about her room, something to do with it being tucked too far away, and that her bed…her bed was…was…'

Her cheeks pink up, contrasting with the colour of her dress in the most intriguing way, and, *Diavolo*, I'll never criticise mustard-yellow again. Not when it works such magic with her complexion.

And focus, Rafael.

'Her bed?' I prompt.

She chews the corner of her lip again, her eyes working hard to steer clear of me now. 'Well, I don't think it's the size of her bed as such, more the fact that she seems quite put out at having to sleep there alone…you know…' She gives me a quick look. 'No plus one?'

'Her and me both.' I smile slightly. 'I'm sure she can survive.'

'Well, yes… I don't feel the need to parade a man around with me this week either, but she's the mother of the bride. Maybe she feels like she *ought* to have someone.'

'She'll have her mother and her sister, our cousins, the family.'

'Yes, the family.' She pulls the slightest face. 'Only, I thought…'

'You thought?'

She lifts her chin a little. 'I get the impression that she doesn't get along with them…not all that well, anyway.'

'And *that* is her own fault,' I say. She'll hear no sympathy from me. 'If she made an effort once in a while, actually cared about someone other than herself, then maybe things would be different.'

Faye's eyebrows almost touch the ceiling. I know how I sound: hard, unyielding.

And, again, I've revealed far too much.

'What I mean is…' I try again. 'She will be surrounded by family, and isn't that what weddings are supposed to be about?'

'Family and loved ones aren't necessarily the same thing.' Her eyes are hooked on mine, probing deep, exposing. 'I just think that maybe it would help her relax if she was able to have a friend, perhaps. Dani just wants her guests to be happy. She's no bridezilla, but she does have an ideal in her head, which surely includes her mother being happy. And I know she wouldn't mind if your mother were to have someone; in fact, she expected her to bring—'

'I rejected him.'

Her brows are up at the ceiling again. 'You rejected him?'

'He's younger than Dani, Faye, so yes, I refused to let him join us.'

'He…what?' Her eyes almost pop out of their sockets but then she shakes her head and swiftly recovers. 'Right, well, perhaps if she was to invite someone less…contentious…surely that—?'

'No,' I snap, my anger quick to fire in the face of Marianna. 'My mother doesn't get to bring someone. She doesn't get to have everyone running around making her happy. This week isn't about her and her petty antics. This is Dani's week and, as much as I think the whole wedding a foolish stunt, I—'

'Foolish?' she interjects, her frown severe in the face of my sudden anger. 'You mean to say you *still* don't approve?'

Her crystal-blue eyes narrow further and I can see her concern, see her love for my sister and her desperate desire for this week to go well, all in that one look. I can also see her concern that I'm not the wedding's greatest fan. *I* put that look there.

I press away from the table and close the distance between us. I don't think about my intention until my fingers are beneath her chin, tilting her face up.

Her eyes widen onto mine, the move surprising her just as much as it does me.

'Scusi, bella.' It comes out so much softer than I intended, but this close I can't draw a full breath. Everything seems to catch and ignite—the air around

us, between us, inside me. 'My family brings out the worst in me.'

Her lashes flutter as she inhales softly. 'But it also brings out the best.'

Her reassurance is a whisper and I know she's speaking of my grand gesture, my purchase of the venue itself. I fight the urge to run my thumb over her lower lip, to feel her appreciation in the warmth of a kiss, to caress her cheek, to comb my fingers back through her hair that flows so freely around her. And then I realise that she's freed it from the ponytail it was in outside. Is it a sign? Is it a physical move for what she wants deep down? To let go and give this desire between us free rein...?

'I think Dani's hoping this week will go some way to healing your fractured family, Rafael.'

Rafael. I love my name on her English tongue. It's enough to ease the burden of her words.

'And if I can help to smooth the way a little, please use me, please tell me what I can do.'

I want her to do so much, but none of it revolves around making the wedding a success, healing my family or the greater good. None at all.

'Our priorities are the same, Faye.' I feel the connection pulse in the air between us, holding us captive, but I need the first move to be hers. She has to drive this. We're in my room, my domain, because I asked her to come here. The rest has to be driven by her.

'Are they?' She doesn't look as though she believes me, and it goads me, regardless of how close to the truth she is.

'*Si.*' I nod. She has to understand that I love my sister, regardless of my mother and the anger that exists. Regardless of how much I loathe marriage. I want Dani and Tyler to be happy. 'We both want this week to be about Dani and Tyler; we want it to be perfect for them. How I feel towards my mother and weddings in general doesn't come into it. I want them to be happy.'

She gives a relieved sigh—or is it more wistful, dream-like? 'Yes, that's exactly what I want too.'

'No blunders, no disruption, no family fallouts.'

'Yes.'

'You clearly know my family well enough to realise it won't be easy, that they'll need constant watching over…taming, even.'

She gives a sympathetic smile, her shrug small. 'Families are never easy; even the strongest ones have their moments.'

'Be that as it may, it will take effort on our part. We can't afford to be…distracted.'

She frowns. 'Distracted?'

'*Si*, by this…' I gesture between us, my eyes resting a beat too long on the nervous pulse ticking in her throat that I want so much to kiss, to tease with my tongue, to nip with my teeth. 'It is distracting, no?'

'I'm not sure—' She breaks off, all flustered, and I laugh softly.

She raises her hand to her throat and brushes her fingers over that pulse point as she avoids my eye.

'You want me.' I wait for her eyes to meet mine. One beat, two… 'As I want you.'

Her lips softly part, the colour returning to her cheeks. I stay silent, daring her to deny it, and she rewards me with a look that roams all over my clothed state before she nods. The action is so contained and I wonder at her restraint. The power of it. I compare it to the Faye I met last night, the one who's now caged inside her, and I want to release it. I want the seductress back.

'You remember what you said to me beside the pool? That you were a damsel in distress, a lady in need?'

Another nod.

'That you've not had fun in far too long?'

She nods again as her lashes flutter. Her cheeks heat further, but not with shame. No, I see the need flaring in her eyes, the thirst I want so desperately to quench.

'That you have a week ahead of being the perfect maid of honour?'

'Yes.'

'And so one night of fun would be almost like a reward upfront?'

She laughs now, the sound low and breathy. 'Yes, but that was before I knew who you were.'

'Is who I am a problem?'

She steps back, the shake of her head weak. 'You know it is. It complicates things.'

'Not if we keep it discreet.'

'You make it sound so simple.'

'It is that simple.'

She wets her lips, the sheen that now covers them luring me closer.

'If you're as affected by this as I am, we can't go on…what is the word you English favour…pussyfooting?'

'Pussyfooting?' I love how her lips quirk at the corners, her eyes sparkle.

'*Si.*' I carry on walking towards her as she continues back, the wall only a few steps away. She's running out of space, but I don't need much more. 'I say we satisfy this need here and now.'

'Now? But your mother—'

'Can wait a few more minutes.'

Her brows lift and her eyes sparkle more. 'Minutes?'

'I'll sort her room issues before she has to sleep another night in her current one. As for her…loneliness, if she wants to choose someone respectable to join her, I have no issue with it.'

'And that's what you'll tell her?' She's pressed up against the wall now, her palms flat against it, her chest rising and falling with each elevated breath.

'I will.' I plant a hand onto the wall above her head and look down into eyes that are so blue, so hot, so fiery. 'Happy?'

She gives a soft scoff. 'It's not me you need to ask.'

'Marianna will be happy with whatever I tell her.'

'Do you always call her by her name?' Her sudden frown takes me aback. 'Never Mum or Mamma?'

'*Mum? Mamma?*' I almost choke at the suggestion, thrown by the very idea, let alone the oddity, of her question. And then I realise she's still probing, still trying to understand the Perez family better, to understand me better. 'It bothers you?'

Her stare is bold as she works hard to read me and I fight the urge to look away. I refuse to be scared of what she might see: the truth.

'I just can't imagine calling my mother by her first name.'

'Then you clearly have a very different relationship.'

'Had.' It blurts out of her and her cheeks lose some of their colour.

Cazzo. 'Had?'

'She died a couple of years back.'

'I am so sorry.' Her crystal blues swim with pain but she doesn't look away; she doesn't hide it from me. 'I'm sorry. I didn't mean to cause you any upset.'

She shakes her head, her breath vibrating through her body. 'It's not your fault.'

'Still…' I hold her eye. The silence beats with growing awareness, our bodies edging closer. I cup her cheek and her lips part ever so softly. 'You were both lucky to have what you so clearly did, *cara mia.*'

Her lashes flutter. 'What does that mean?'

I stroke her cheek with my thumb. 'What?'

'*Cara mia.* You called me *cara mia.* Doesn't it mean…?'

My thumb stills as her voice trails off. She's trying to deduce the meaning while I reel with it.

I did call her *cara mia*. And I meant it. It has many connotations and can mean many different things, but all of them are deeper than what we have here.

And who are you trying to convince?

Dio. I barely know the woman. And yet, I know how much Dani loves her and how much she loves Dani in return. I could blame it on that. A mutual love for my sister.

But that has nothing to do with the heat pounding my veins or the pain I felt in the face of hers.

'It can mean many things—"my dear", "my beloved". It's a term of affection.'

'I thought so.' Her smile is small. 'A little early for that, though, don't you think?'

'I can't pretend to know what you went through losing your mother, but I do know just by looking at you how much it hurt, and I am sorry for that pain.'

She shakes her head, her eyes wide, as if she's heard something monumental, unbelievable even, so the last thing I expect is to have her hands suddenly clawing through my hair. Then her lips are on mine and they are just as hungry, just as forceful. I lose it all in a groan and press my body up against hers, my fingers deep in her hair as I do what I've hungered for all night and all morning.

Only, this is so much better than fantasy.

'Rafael.' She tears her mouth away and her eyes blaze up into mine. 'Promise me, this will go no further.'

'I won't speak a word of it.'

She searches my gaze. 'Dani, Tyler…they can't know.'

'*Lo prometto.* I promise.'

'*Perfecto,*' she rhymes, pulling my mouth back to hers, her clear blue eyes sparking into mine and drawing me in mind, body and soul…

I only hope I can move on as easily as my promise suggests, because right now I feel as if I'm drowning in her with no hope of rescue.

CHAPTER FIVE

HE TASTES DELICIOUS. Seriously delicious.

He's not taken a bite out of the glazed goodness on the arrangement beside us and I'd warrant he tastes better. And no matter how deeply we kiss, how much my tongue twists with his, I can't get enough. I can't.

But an annoying little voice full of apprehension reminds me that there's been no one since Bobby, and no one other than Bobby, for too many years to count.

What if I've forgotten how this works? What if I'm being too desperate, too eager? Am I really ready for him to see me naked?

What? He saw you naked last night and it didn't bother you then.

But then I had the confidence of alcohol and he was just a sexy stranger.

I break away. Words flutter past my lips, rambling, disorientated, as he traces kisses along my jaw, his fingers buried in my hair. 'It's been a long time, Rafael.' *Breathe.* 'I'm not… I don't know…'

'What is it?' he murmurs against my skin, his

tongue flicking beneath my earlobe before taking it between his teeth. *Oh, yes!*

'I don't want to disappoint.'

He chuckles low in his throat, the sound rumbling through me and provoking my throbbing, orgasm-starved clit. 'Never.'

I bite into my lower lip and clutch his head to me as his hands rake down my sides and beneath my breasts, the light fabric of my dress doing nothing to hinder the heat of his touch.

'Your skin is so soft, your scent…intoxicating.'

The compliments run off his tongue and merge with the sweetness of his sympathy and his compassion. I'm not boring in my grief, not to him—a man who doesn't even enjoy a healthy relationship with his own mother.

Strict, severe, controlling, hard… All words I've heard to describe him, words I'd have used myself based on what I knew of him. Hell, Dani wasn't entirely convinced he'd even show up this week. *She* doubted him. Meanwhile, he's been off buying a whole castle and vineyard to match, all to make his little sister happy.

'You're making me dizzy…' Dizzy on the rush, dizzy on the confusion. How can Dani have doubted him?

'I'm about to make you more so.'

His head lifts, his eyes burning into mine as he slips his hands beneath the straps of my dress and bra. My skin thrums beneath his delicate touch as he traces the line of my shoulders. Heat floods my belly, my breasts, my blood, and my nipples prickle, ready for the first sweep of air as he coaxes my clothing away.

'Ever since I saw you last night, I have fantasised about you.'

Fantasised? About me? I can't breathe as the excited rush of his confession consumes me. It sounds too good to be true, feels too good to be true. Yet looking into the fire in his eyes I know he means it.

'Your eyes...' he murmurs, reaching round my back and unhooking my bra clasp. I lower my arms and let it fall to the floor, my eyes lost in the sincerity, the passion, of his.

'Your lips...'

He eases my dress down and it pools at my feet, the coolness of the air-conditioned room caressing my naked skin. He leans in, his shirt a delicate tease against my breasts, and it's enough to make me whimper. His mouth lifts at the corners and his eyes flare. He raises his fingers to my chin and runs the pad of his thumb over my bottom lip, dragging it down as he slips his tongue inside, deep, unyielding, slow. I've never felt anything more erotic, never been more aware of every touch, of every sound.

'Your mouth is made for sin, *cara mia.*'

Sin... It sounds even sexier on his tongue, with his lips brushing against mine, his breath merging with my own.

'It's enough to drive a man insane. The way you wet your lips, the way you bite down just here... The things it makes a man think of...'

My clit pulses. The things he's making me think of right now…

'The things it makes me think of…' It's as if he's in my head. The raw edge to his voice projects every one of those thoughts into my mind and the liquid heat spreads between my thighs, upping the throbbing ache down low.

I want to take him in my mouth. I want to wrap my lips around him and tease him.

I want it all.

'But your body…'

He steps back and the cool air sweeps between us, making my skin prickle up, making me feel exposed and self-conscious. Sunlight streams in from the large glass doors, illuminating my naked skin, my thong and sandals all that I am left in.

'No, *cara*.' He reaches for my hands as I attempt to cover myself, his fingers gentle around my wrists as he moves them back to my side. 'It's a crime to have your body so unloved, so neglected. Let me fix that.'

Dani's words come back to me. He is the fixer; he'll make everything right. I almost laugh.

'Then come back here.' I lift my chin, injecting the confidence I want to feel, reminding myself that this is the new me. A better me. With the lust for life I used to possess. I've been through the wringer and come out stronger for it. 'Do as you say.'

'Patience.' His eyes dance and burn in the sunlight as he steps close again. 'Sex cannot be rushed.'

Now I laugh, soft and breathy. 'I beg to differ.'

'Okay, sometimes it can be rushed.' His grin makes my pulse skip. 'But not when you've been without for so long.'

He combs his hands through the hair at the base of my neck and my skin zings beneath his touch. How is it possible that a simple caress can make me feel this alive head to toe?

'I intend to make sure that this one time...' his fingers massage into my scalp, stroking, soothing, hypnotising, as his eyes fixed on mine work the same magic '...is something you remember long after we part.'

I shiver with his promise, with the knowledge that I know he can deliver on it, but there's the persistent voice at the back of my mind, the responsible one. 'We don't have long; we need to get out there and deal with your mother.'

'My mother...' his eyes flash '...will be in her room, having ordered a breakfast she will hardly eat, making up for it with champagne and taking several hours to put on her face. She will not bother Dani any further for now.'

'How do you know?'

'Because I *know* her.' He kisses me deep. 'And now I want no more talk of her. Agreed?'

'Agreed.'

'Eyes closed, *cara*, just feel...concentrate on my touch.'

I dutifully do as he asks.

'Bene,' he whispers, close, so close I can feel his

breath sweep against my cheek, his fingers light and soft as they trail tantalisingly down my sides.

I suck in my stomach, try to contain the wild flutters taking off inside. Everything is so much more like this. Blind. Unexpected.

His fingers splay out, his palms smoothing down, beneath the waistband of my thong as he takes it with him, leaving it caught around my ankles.

'I want to taste you.' His breath sweeps over the wet curls between my legs and I shiver with the delicious little ripple that runs through me. He's there. Right, *there*! And I claw the wall, wait for that first touch, his mouth, his tongue…but he rises, his fierce kiss cutting off the frustrated whimper I can't contain.

'Your mouth tastes of heaven, but your pussy…' he murmurs, his hands cupping my jaw. 'That will be the true feast.'

I bite into my lip, arch back as he takes his time to travel down once more, licking and nipping at my flesh. He rolls his thumb and forefinger over one nipple and I tremble. His mouth surrounds the other and he sucks it in deep. The combined onslaught making me moan, my body writhe.

'Part your legs for me, *cara*.'

I do as he says, pulling my thong taut against my ankles.

'*Bene.*'

I know I'm spread open to him, that he can see it all, and I can hear the passion in his voice, the way my surrender makes him feel. His tongue scoops inside my seam and parts me, flicking over my hammering clit, and I buck, my cry loud, desperate.

He does it again and again, surrounding me with his mouth, and he sucks back hard.

'*Molto bene.*'

Tasty. He thinks I'm tasty. I fling my hands out, bury them in his hair. He has me going out of my mind. Never have I been so devoured, so thoroughly tongued and ravished. Never have I felt so desired.

He separates my folds with his fingers and I feel his eyes burning into my clit. I want to see; I *need* to see. I drop my head forward and open my eyes to watch him dip to my exposed clit, and softly—oh, so softly—his tongue circles over me. The colour streaking his cheeks tells me how much he's into this too, how much he wants me in return.

'*Rafael...*'

It's a groan, a plea. His eyes flick to mine and the fire, the hunger, sucks away my ability to breathe. He leans back in, surrounding me anew, his appreciative growl rumbling over the clustered nerve-endings and my entire body quivers. I'm going to come. I'm really going to come. But I don't want to. Not yet.

I want to draw this out. I want to prolong the pleasure, the illicit heat that's whipping through me. I just need to hold onto it. Keep it there...

I run my hands through his hair and watch as his long, lithe fingers part me to the fierce work of his mouth, his tongue. I feel suffocated by the fight to contain it, the pleasure-filled explosion that I'm on the cusp of experiencing.

I try to drag him up, to tell him with my actions that I want him inside me, and he shakes his head.

'No, *cara*, you will come for me like this.'

His mouth descends, his tongue flicking over my clit in a rhythm that has my eyes wanting to roll back in my head. I arch back, my hands locked in his hair, my body rigid as every sense hones in on his attention. There's the pressure of his fingers as he holds me in place, the air-conditioned breeze that sweeps over my sensitised skin, and the heat of the sunlight that streaks across me.

I know how wanton I must look, I know how desperate, but never have I felt more alive, more in control of my own pleasure, of taking what my body needs. *Argh!*

I explode from within, my entire body pulsing with such acute pleasure that my cry erupts from deep inside, animalistic and foreign to my own ears. I'm shaking and bucking. Ripple after ripple runs through me as his mouth stays fixed upon me, his tongue softening over the sensitised nub. I claw at his hair and clutch him to me as my head falls forward, my eyes latching on to his as the aftershocks work their way through me, and so much passes in that one look. Gratitude rises up. Gratitude and so much more.

'Thank you,' I whisper.

He presses a kiss to my curls, to the inside of my thigh, and looks up at me, his grin carnal, his mouth all wet with my need. 'You wish to thank me, *cara*?'

'Hell, yeah.'

He gives a throaty chuckle, a sound I'm quickly getting hooked on, and rises slowly up my body, taking his time over my skin, nuzzling every curve, kissing every sensitised spot he has uncovered.

'I don't need thanking...'

He reaches my lips and teases them apart, his tongue grazing softly against mine.

'I believe I enjoyed it just as—'

A rap on the door cuts him off and we look to it, wide-eyed. Panic rises up inside me, my entire body flushing with heat that has nothing to do with my orgasm and everything to do with being caught.

Another rap. 'Rafael, you in there?'

Our eyes lock together.

'Tyler,' we say in unison.

'I'll deal with it.' He presses a kiss to my gaping mouth and heads to the door while I wriggle back into my thong and scramble to collect up my clothing.

He pauses with a hand on the door handle to give me time to race across the room to the bathroom that I can see through a stone archway. I hear the door open as I disappear around the corner and pin myself to the wall. Hastily, I pull on my bra, shoving my breasts inside. It's not as though Tyler can see me, but the idea of standing just a few strides away unclothed...

As for Rafael, he's currently sporting an erection in his beige chinos that no one could miss. Tyler included. *Oh, God.*

'Tyler, what's up?'

I'm impressed at how normal Rafael sounds. As if he hasn't just been tongue-deep in my pussy. And even the thought alone reignites my clit. I bite into my lip and step into my dress.

'Hey. It's your cousin, Dante.' I hear Tyler walk into the room and press myself back against the cool Venetian plaster, eyes on the ceiling as I focus on the pattern in the plaster work and silently plead for him to be quick. 'He's been trying to get hold of you.'

'He has?'

'Yeah. Hey, you all right? You look a little… flushed.'

Flushed. I squeeze my eyes shut. Okay, so Rafael sounds fine, but he clearly doesn't look it. I just hope Tyler doesn't look below waist height!

'I'm fine. Not long been back from my run and I went at it hard.'

My eyes open and I press my lips together. He went at it seriously hard. My mind wanders to what else is *still* hard, and the pining throb in my clit deepens.

'I should have joined you.' He blows out a breath and I trap the laugh that's desperate to erupt. It emerges as a squeak and I clamp a hand over my mouth. 'What…? Did you hear that?'

Silence. I hold my breath.

'No. Didn't hear a thing. Anyway, you were saying Dante's been trying to reach me?'

Tyler lets out a heavy sigh. 'Yeah, he has. Seriously, man, I swear we should've just eloped.'

'Like my sister would have let you.'

'True. But it's only day one and I already feel like a storm is approaching.'

Rafael gives a laugh. 'Welcome to the Perez family!'

'Thanks for the encouragement.' I can hear Tyler's grimace.

'You'll get used to it soon enough. Just tell me what's going on. You and Dani are supposed to pass all the stress my way this week. I know Marianna's kicking up a storm, but I'll deal with that shortly. What's up with Dante?'

'I'm not sure, just that it's urgent and he's been trying to call you, but you're not picking up.'

Rafael curses under his breath. 'I must have been in the shower. I'll give him a call now. In the meantime, why don't you take Dani out to enjoy the grounds before everyone else arrives and chaos truly descends?'

'I think I'd rather hit the bar. Remind me why your family is so complicated?'

I wince. I can just imagine the shutter falling over Rafael's expression.

'You were the one who decided Dani was worth dealing with the rest of us.'

Tyler laughs. 'It's true. That woman is worth putting up with every one of you eccentric Perezes.'

I hear them make for the door and the gentle creak of the antique hinges as it swings open.

'On a serious note, though,' Rafael says, and I can hear the sincerity in his voice. I feel it warm me to my toes. 'Leave the stressing to me, *si*?'

'Will do, Raf. And thanks.'

'Prego.'

The door clicks shut and I let out a breath. *Thank goodness that's over.* I push away from the wall and head back into the room.

Rafael has his palm pressed against the door, his head down and shoulders hunched.

'That was close,' I say quietly.

He spins to face me, his smile not quite reaching his eyes. 'What's life without a little danger, eh?'

He walks to the bedside table, picks up the phone that's there and grimaces at the screen. 'I need to call my cousin back.'

'Of course.' I chew the corner of my mouth. This isn't awkward. Not at all. I'm kind of in limbo. My body is still reeling from an orgasm so intense I feel like jelly inside and out, but there's a pressing urge to express something, anything. 'I'll… I'll leave you to it.'

'Faye?' His fingers are soft as they close around my wrist and he waits for me to meet his eye. 'I'm sorry I need to deal with this.'

I shake my head. 'I'm the one who's sorry. Hardly seems fair that I get to have fun and leave while you…' I shrug.

His smile lights up his eyes now and it makes everything better in an instant. 'I had fun, believe me.'

I laugh softly. 'You know what I mean.'

'I do.'

One second passes, two, and I force myself to

pull away. He has to call his cousin; he doesn't have time for this.

'Wait,' he says, and my heart lurches. 'Let me check the way is clear.'

I don't know what I hoped he would say, but my heart sinks just as quickly. He walks ahead of me, scooping up a pastry on the way, and opens the door. He does a quick sweep, turning back a second later.

'Clear.'

I laugh again. 'I feel like a naughty schoolgirl sneaking about after hours.'

His eyes flare. 'Are you *trying* to tease me?'

My lower belly comes alive. 'I wouldn't dare.'

I smile as I pass him, feeling lighter than air, happy that the connection between us is just as strong as it was before I got my rocks off.

'Take this with you.'

I cock one eyebrow at the pastry he offers to me. It looks very much like a croissant. A very sweet and carb-loaded croissant. 'Doesn't it defeat the point of going for a run this morning, eating all this naughtiness?'

'*These* are the reason I run.'

I take it from him with a grin. 'You have a sweet tooth?'

'And that surprises you?'

'Yes.' My grin widens. 'You're really not what I expected, Rafael Perez.'

He frowns as his eyes sparkle. 'What did you expect?'

'I don't dare say. You'll have to ask Dani.'

He laughs, low and husky. 'Fair enough. Now go, and when you bite into it, and your taste buds dance, know that it tastes only a fraction as good as you do.'

I'm on cloud nine as I walk away, nibbling at the delicious pastry, his soft, *'Ciao, bella,'* following behind.

CHAPTER SIX

Danielle and Tyler's Wedding Week
Monday: Dive and Dine. Poolside, two p.m.

'Si, DANTE, CIAO.'

I end the second call with my cousin that day and place my phone on the antique *escritoire* that sits alongside the opening to my balcony. It's positioned to make the most of the view, and as I take up my drink, I do just that. I try to lose myself in the rolling hills as I massage the knot at the base of my skull.

It's no use, though. Neither my fingers nor the view can work the same magic as Faye and take away the pressure that's been building since my showdown with Marianna. As for her 'issues', I've had the staff move her to a room at the front of the house, which makes the most of the stunning landscape but brings her far too close to my wing. And I had the 'talk' about suitable male companions—more to pay lip service to the idea than actually to acquiesce and, for now, she is quiet.

And quiet means temporarily out of trouble.

I left her changing for the pool, where all the guests are gathering for an afternoon of fun and food, and escaped to my room to call Dante back. He should have been here by now but his call this morning was to let me know that Nonna had had a fall and it had delayed their trip to the airport. Cue missed flights and the rigmarole of having to source new ones, as well as making sure Nonna was still fit to fly. Turns out her own stubborn refusal to accept aid down the stairs resulted in her little accident and Dante getting a flustered apology from Nonna and an ear-bashing from his own mother, my Aunt Netta.

As for Aunt Netta herself, no sooner had I cut the call than the phone had rung again, with Netta herself informing me that, regardless of what her sister Marianna had told her, she was bringing her plus-one, and if her sister didn't like it she could shove her phone where the sun don't shine. And, me being me, I said yes. Yes, to get her off the phone, and yes, to rile my mother more—which is damn stupid but, the way my head is throbbing, I'm passed caring about my mother's petty issues.

And, truth is, I have a PA who could deal with all this chaos, even the kind caused by my mother. Hell, even the wedding planner would have stepped in. But it's my family, my mess, my responsibility. No one else deserves the aggro of it, or the embarrassment.

So here I am, at two o'clock in the afternoon, sinking a *grappa* and contemplating hiding for the rest of the day, even though I can't. The wedding itinerary says 'dive and dine poolside'—yes, in those exact words—and that's what I'll do. I've yet to greet the latest arrivals—Tyler's parents and his best man, Harry, who I've met many a time before, but not his wedding date.

Plus… Faye will be there.

My blood fires of its own accord and I head for the third cold shower of the day. One pre-Faye, one post-Faye and now pre-Faye-in-a-swimsuit.

I blame it entirely on the impromptu end to our fun. To the memory of her coming hard against my mouth and having to let her leave without sinking myself deep inside her and achieving my release.

She certainly got hers.

Me…

I'm left in this state of semi-arousal that makes donning a pair of swim trunks wholly unadvisable. And yet necessary.

I take a deep breath and hit the cold jets, all with a sense of déjà vu and the acceptance that it won't be the last time I try to freeze my head out of my pants this week.

Faye is different. My reaction to her is different. And that makes her a problem.

A problem I don't know how to fix…other than to try to get my fill of her.

I squint into the full-length mirror in my room. It's okay if I do that. The sheer mesh panels in the front of my swimsuit merge into a more opaque, solid co-lour and my skin's not so on show. Damn Dani and her outrageous tastes.

Or maybe I should curse the fizz we consumed during our trip to the exclusive swimwear boutique she took us to. We had the entire place to ourselves, three sales assistants and more attention than I knew what to do with.

But the result…

I peak through one eye. It's not *that* bad. I turn in the mirror and eye my rear; that's perfectly sedate. Yes, just focus on the rear, not the front, not the barely concealed curve to each breast, the nipple just about hidden. One wrong move and—

My phone pings on the bedside table and I lunge for it, eyeing the swimsuit positioning after the boldness of the move and finding my nipples still have their dignity. That's something at least…

I look to the phone. It's a text from Dani:

Come on, slow coach, I'm waiting. Dante's just arrived, and I can't wait to see his eyes pop out of his sockets at your…

I shut the screen down without reading the rest, my cheeks flushing crimson. This is wild. Too wild. And she's incorrigible.

But I love her. And she's right to nag. I shouldn't be wasting time standing in front of the mirror, fretting about the revealing swimsuit. This is all part of the new me and, if I've learned anything, it's that being daring pays off big time. I recall Rafael between my legs, tonguing me deep, his eyes wild, my climax wilder still. Hell, yeah, I totally need to embrace the new me.

And if I can get more of that then, yes—yes, please.

Just keep it discreet, Faye.

The warning is very real. I don't want to upset Dani and I certainly don't want to steal her thunder this week of all weeks, but when am I going to have another opportunity like this, with a man such as Rafael?

As for the erection he'd been sporting, that very *impressive* erection he never got to satisfy, well, I owe him...and I can't wait to pay up.

My thighs clench, my clit pulses and my nipples perk up, their pebble-shaped mounds obvious through the thin fabric of the bathing suit. *Oh, God.* I can hardly go to the Dive and Dine with a full-on booby boner! I go to rub them and stop; that isn't going to help. I pull my top away and blow down at the blushing pink tips, as though that will somehow douse their heat. Nope. They are pert and alert. All ready for their next Rafael encounter...

I scan the room and spy my vibrant red kimono tossed over the back of a chair. I slip it on; it's light and sheer but it'll help detract from the twin peaks situation below. I grab my straw bag from the bed which contains my latest romance read, my phone and my oversized shades. I pull out the latter and slip them on; next comes my wide-brimmed hat and I'm ready for anything.

Even the hot and sizzling Rafael Perez.

My smile nudges my cheeks into the rim of my shades. I wonder how he's feeling right now? I mean, I'm needy and my nipples are more than willing to demonstrate just how much. But Rafael… That erection…

My body gives an excited little shiver.

It's Dante who Dani wants you to be all hot on, my conscience reminds me.

But it's hardly my fault I saw Rafael first…

She's not here yet. It's the first thought to enter my head as I arrive at the pool and the pang of disappointment is as surprising as it is strong. I rake a hand through my hair and shake my head at my crazy behaviour.

'Hey, don't you be shaking your head at me, *polpetto*.' Nonna wags a finger up at me from her temporary wheelchair as Dante pushes her towards me. They've just arrived too.

'I wouldn't dare.' I grin down at her enough to make her blush. It's good to know my smile hasn't lost its charm after all these years. 'It's good to see you, Nonna.'

I lean down and press a kiss to her cheeks.

'And you.' She slaps the arms of her chair and gives it a good shake. 'Maybe you can tell Dante I don't need this blasted thing.'

'If you'd listened to Dante in the first place, you wouldn't be in it now.'

'Don't start that argument again, cousin.' Dante gives me a neck-slicing gesture above her head. I'm guessing he's had this the entire journey and is more than ready to call it quits.

'I take it back.' I give his back a welcome pounding. 'It's good to see you too. But, Nonna, you should be making the most of it. Your entire family at your beck and call for a week? What more could you want?'

'More of a family, *raggazzo mio*.' I walked right into that one. 'It's wrong that there are so few of us. Call us Italians.' She shakes her head vigorously, tsking away. 'Not a single great-grandchild between you…or a wife, for that matter. What's wrong with the pair of you?'

I meet Dante's eye and know he's suppressing an eye-roll. It's the same at every family gathering and it's getting old. Dante is still enjoying his freedom too much and I never intend to go down that road. Ever.

'In that case, this wedding must make you very happy indeed.' I take the focus off us and put it squarely on Dani, who is currently making out with Tyler on the same cabana Faye used last night. Try as I might not to think of it, my brain projects the teasing image anyway and makes me glad of Nonna's presence. There's nothing like your grandmother to keep your hormones in check.

Dante grins wide, his eyes finding them too. 'I have a feeling your dreams for more great-grandchildren will soon be satisfied.'

I send him a look.

But Nonna laughs, all wistful and happy. 'Yes,

they look happy. Very happy, just like me and Nonno once were…' And then she frowns, her eyes sweeping the area. Tyler's parents are sitting at the bar under the shade of a vine-covered pergola. Harry, the best man, is swimming laps, while a blonde who I assume is his date is stretched out on a sun lounger with a glass in one hand and a magazine in the other. Nonna's eyes narrow as she looks back to my cousin. 'Where's your sister and her family?'

'They're arriving tomorrow. Less time for the kids to cause chaos, if I'm to interpret my sister's reasoning correctly.'

'Wise.' She nods. 'And Antonietta… Marianna… where are they? Surely they can be trusted to be here by now?'

I grimace. I'm not sure I trust them any more than the kids.

'Mamma will be joining us for dinner this evening,' Dante supplies, eyeing me warily. I know he's thinking the same.

'And Marianna is just getting changed. She'll be down soon enough.'

I don't need to look to know Nonna's scowling. It's not just Dante and me sensing the war about to rage. The last time they were both under the same roof, all hell broke loose.

But this will be different, I mentally reason. This week they have Dani's happiness to put first. And, as if she senses my thoughts, my sister turns in our direction.

'Ah, Nonnina!' Her smile lights up her face as

she rises up from the bed and tugs at Tyler's hand to bring him with her. 'At last! What did you do with her, Dante? You were supposed to be here hours ago…and what's this?'

She places her hand on the arm of the wheelchair and leans in to kiss Nonna, squeezing her tight.

'Never you mind what this is, I'm perfectly fine without it!' She tries to stand and winces. 'Okay, maybe I get up later.'

She plonks herself back down and Dani turns to Dante, embracing him with a beaming smile. 'So glad you're here, cousin!'

But her eyes gesture back to Nonna and the chair. Dante gives her a warning look and she gets the message quicker than me.

'Nonnina, you remember Tyler?'

'Of course I do.'

Tyler leans down and plants a kiss on my grandmother's cheek. 'It's lovely to see you again, Greta.'

'Ah, nonsense…' Her cheeks flush. 'It's Nonna to you now.'

I'm already tuning out, my eyes back on the path behind us. Where is she? She doesn't strike me as the fashionably late type, looking to make an entrance. Unlike my mother.

'You okay, Raf?'

It's Dani who asks, her frown curious as I look back to her. How long had I zoned out for?

'Of course.'

'We're just taking Nonna over to the shade.'

I nod and watch them go, save for Dante, who lets out a huge sigh.

'That bad, eh?' I say.

He shakes his head. 'Would you object if I go and swim in a vat of *grappa*?'

I laugh. 'Only if you don't leave me to deal with this alone.'

'Families, eh? Who'd have one?'

'Not me, that's for certain.'

He eyes me and I feel the question burning, the one that comes out at every family function from young relations and old alike. I head for the bar before he has a chance to ask it. I am, after all, forty-two, and showing no sign of settling down any time soon.

'Now, about that *grappa*...'

He chuckles after me and we join Tyler's parents at the bar. I do the introductions and, as they talk, my eyes go back to the path, searching, anticipating... And then I see it: a flash of red on the sloped path that runs from the house to the pool. I catch glimpses between the trees: a red kimono blowing in the breeze, long, tanned legs, a straw bag under one arm, fashionably large shades and a wide-brimmed sun hat. My pulse picks up; my eyes are transfixed.

I follow her progress until finally she's at the other end of the pool, surveying her surroundings. Her eyes behind her shades meet mine. I know they do, as her head dips just a little and her lips curve up. Is she wearing red lipstick too, or is it a trick of the light, the sun reflecting her bright kimono?

I get a nudge from behind and a murmured, 'Who's Red?'

I flick Dante a look and see his eyes fixed on her, as well as the intent behind them. Just as I predicted. And my blood fires with it.

It? *What's* it?

It's not jealousy. I don't get jealous.

'She's the maid of honour.'

'Really?' He gives a low whistle close to my shoulder, discreet enough for only me to hear. 'This wedding just got a whole lot more interesting.'

I have the overwhelming urge to call dibs.

To call dibs. Gesù!

I reach past Dante to take up the freshly poured *grappa* he's just been served and throw it back.

'Hey…' He's not watching her now; he's frowning at me. 'Get your own.'

'Don't worry, there's plenty more where that came from.' I'm already crossing the poolside…

Getting there first isn't quite as obvious as calling dibs.

It's merely polite behaviour befitting the host— even if no one knows I own this place. No one except the woman in red inspiring all manner of illicit thoughts.

I'm staring intently at Dani as I arrive, but every fibre of my being is aware of Rafael. He's moving in the same direction, his eyes pinned on me, burning into me, and even if the sun were behind a cloud I'd feel just as on fire.

He's changed out of his clothes from earlier and into a light shirt, unbuttoned, and a pair of—I swallow—swimming briefs. *Holy fuck.* He's like a swimwear model and he's coming straight for me. I struggle to draw breath, struggle even more when a breeze threatens to take my hat with it, and I pin it back in place, which frees my kimono to open up around me, instantly calling attention to every exposed inch. Mesh panel, or not.

I pretend not to notice the slight falter in his stride, the flare in his eyes, or the fact that I feel more eyes drawn to me from the bar, and from the blonde that I know to be Harry's date for the week.

Why, oh why, did I buy this thing?

'Faye!' Dani straightens up from where she's been bent over a lady in a wheelchair who is dressed top-to-toe in black. *Dani.* She's the reason I bought it. And her white swimsuit—which, to be fair, is even more revealing than mine—screams 'the lady of the moment' and I can hardly kill her now. On *her* wedding week.

'It's about time you got down here,' she admonishes, walking towards me, her grin wide as she gives me a quick once-over. Her eyebrows do the same little waggle she pulled off in the swimwear boutique as she declared an impending end to my sex drought.

If only she knew the truth. I hadn't required swimwear to sort it… I swallow. It hadn't been the man she'd had in mind either.

'Sorry!' It's a bit high-pitched and I smile more brightly and force my shoulders to relax as I embrace her and give her a peck to both cheeks. My eyes are drawn to Rafael, who is still heading in the same direction, before I snap them back to her. 'Just plucking up the courage to come out in this thing.'

She gives a flighty laugh. 'You're kidding, right? You look hot as…'

She hooks her arm through mine. 'You must come and meet my grandmother. She's heard so much about you.'

Yes, the grandmother—not the suave, sophisticated, too-hot-for-words older brother who's about to join us.

'Ah, and my brother too. Did you find him earlier?'

'Yes.' My voice hitches and I pray she doesn't notice. 'We…we talked about your mother. Everything's sorted on that front.'

At least I hope it is…

'Ah, thank you.' She leans in conspiratorially. 'Well, now I can introduce him properly. Just remember, he's not the ogre he first appears to be.'

'Ogre, right.' My giggle is loaded with nerves, guilt and a sudden desire to defend him. 'He seemed perfectly pleasant to me.'

'*Really?* Maybe he's on his best behaviour. Miracles do happen!'

If that's his best behaviour, my body is already wishing it could see his worst. I suck the inside of my cheek to kick back the heat and curse my body that's too keen to travel down that road. I also wrap my kimono around me as I feel the swift return of twin peaks.

'Maybe you just need to see him through fresh eyes.'

She murmurs something I don't quite catch, and I don't have time to probe without being overheard by an audience.

'Great to see you, Faye.' Tyler gives me a warm embrace. 'Sorry I missed you at breakfast.'

His eyes sparkle as he releases me and I get the distinct impression he's also thanking me for sending his wife-to-be back to bed. Not that he need thank me. My little errand saw me rewarded in a very similar manner. I smile over the heat that's made it into my cheeks, grateful that my sunglasses conceal so much.

'No problem. It was nice to get a quiet one in before all the guests arrived.'

Though, Raf never quite made it in, did he? Jesus!

'Nonna…' Dani places a hand on her grandmother's shoulder and gestures to me '…meet my fabulous friend, Faye. Faye, meet my fabulous grandmother, Nonna… Greta to her friends.'

'It's such a pleasure to finally meet you, *signora*. Your reputation precedes you.' I grin down at the lady who is every bit the Italian grandmother. Her brown eyes sparkle and crinkle at the corners with her smile and the wisps of grey that have escaped the knot at her nape soften the bronzed lines of her face. 'All good, I promise,' I add in my best Italian. I'm not fluent, not by a long stretch, but I've picked up enough to impress over the years.

'Greta, *per favore*.' She beams up at me. *'Ciao, bella.'*

She reaches out and I place my hands in hers, lean down, and she kisses each cheek as is the custom for friends, and I immediately feel welcomed in... welcomed in and...sad.

It's a sudden pang of loss as I acknowledge how different our situations are, Dani's and mine. I have no elder to look up to within my own family, to be loved by and to love in return. No one, save for Dad. And the lack of a female, of that maternal connection, suddenly feels huge. It makes tears spike out of nowhere. I close my eyes and breathe through it. It's such a silly thing to get caught up on, right now of all times. But then, grief doesn't abide by any rules.

I straighten back up and frown as I take in Greta's chair. I don't remember anyone mentioning her being wheelchair-bound and I make a note to mention it to the wedding planner, if Dani hasn't already.

'Nonna had a fall this morning,' Dani chips in, spying my focus. 'She's sprained her ankle.'

'Ouch.' I look to her feet which are hidden beneath the skirt of her dress. *'Ti fa ancora male?'*

'Adesso, va bene. No fuss.' She waves a hand at me and goes to raise her foot with a wiggle but winces almost immediately.

'I think we should get some ice on it, just to be sure, and get it raised,' I say. I was a first-aider back in my swimming days. Lifeguard duty at weekends was a great way to bring in extra pennies and, looking at her swollen foot, ice is definitely a good idea. But I sense nothing happens without Nonna's buy-in. 'What do you think, Greta?'

'*Si, buon'idea.*'

Or Rafael's buy-in, it seems, as his deep baritone fills the space and he comes up alongside us, so close I can breathe in his scent, and it makes me remember everything we did this morning. Me, naked. His mouth between my...

'Ah, Raf...' Dani beams. 'I hear you've already met Faye.'

Our eyes meet and his mouth twitches.

'I have. Though I didn't realise you speak Italian.'

I give a sheepish smile. I know he's remembering how I questioned the meaning of *cara mia*. But the query was genuine. It's hardly the kind of vocab I'm accustomed to hearing when touring the globe conducting pharmaceutical sales.

'I speak a little. I travel a lot with work.'

Or I used to...

'Work?'

'Pharmaceutical sales. Though I'm more UK-based these days.'

His brows lift marginally and I feel not only Nonna's eyes, but Dani's and Tyler's flitting between us. No one speaks. Not even Dani, who speaks enough for the entire population of Italy. And I feel the heat creeping ever more into my cheeks, along with the carnal recollections that seem desperate to clamber up into my sex-starved mind.

'About that ice...' I say, needing to break the silence and the burn of being caught out, even though we haven't been. Not even close.

'*Si*, why don't you give me a hand?' Rafael suggests. Is it my imagination or has his voice dropped an octave or two? And is he seriously suggesting we go off together? He must sense the series of questions searing my brain as he smiles encouragingly, his eyes too suggestive. And again, is that my mind putting that suggestion there? And do I even care when it means we can be alone again?

'You sound like you know what you're talking about,' he continues.

'I was a first-aider—lifeguard duty in my teens.'

'Is that so?' I feel the appreciative burn of his gaze all the way to my toes. Surely everyone else can read it too? 'Well, in that case, I'll point you in the direction of the first-aid kit. I'm sure we can fashion together some sort of compress.'

I swallow. 'Great.'

'It's just in the pool house. This way...'

Us. In the pool house. Alone. Won't Dani suspect?

But Raf is already heading that way.

Dani nudges me in the side. 'That's my brother all over, issuing a command and not waiting for a response.'

I look to her, my own eyes wide behind my glasses, but hers are laughing. She looks happy, not suspicious. Not suspicious at all. My own conscience is doing the guilt thing for me.

'Right.' I clear my throat. 'Okay. One cold compress coming up.'

I follow his luscious rear and don't look back. I sense Dani's eyes following us, and I'm not entirely sure we've escaped undetected after all, but I'm already being sucked into the impending heat, high on what's to come...

The pool house is a stone building with a terracotta roof and a stunning pink rose rambling over its walls. It's pretty and unassuming, the little cobbled path that leads up to it dainty and cute. But, as he opens the door and stands back to let me enter, my heart rate soars, my blood zinging with the look in his eyes. It's no innocent structure now.

I enter and remove my sunglasses, slipping them into my bag as I scan the walls, the racks of towels and what look like laundry bins, a fridge, a freezer...

I hear the door click shut behind me and start to turn. 'The first aid—'

I don't finish. He's upon me. My hat and bag hit the deck, our lips mash together and I'm pressed up against the wall, my entire body covered in the hot, hard heat of his.

He growls low in his throat. Hungry, fierce. '*Cazzo*, Faye! This outfit. This swimsuit.' He drags in a breath, his forehead pressing into mine. 'Are you trying to kill me?'

My laugh is high, giddy, my hands clawing into his shoulders beneath his shirt; his hot skin sears my fingertips. I feel his cock pulse against my belly, his unrestrictive shorts doing nothing to conceal his need for me, and the throbbing ache in my core wants nothing more than to satisfy him whole.

'I could say the same to you.'

He kisses me harder, his tongue delving inside, his

hands raking beneath my kimono, shoving it aside as I hook one leg around him and press him tighter against me. His hardness pulses against my clit and I cry out, muffling it in our kiss as I ride him with shameless abandon.

'I want you.' His demand is gruff and I'm nodding into his kiss, telling him I want him too.

'Now.' He grazes over my lips. 'Here.'

'Here?' I break away and stare up at him, biting my lip.

'*Si.*'

His eyes blaze into mine and I look to the door.

'They won't come in.'

'How can you…?' He spins me into the door and presses us up against it.

'They won't have much luck.'

It's daring, it's risky, but it feels too damn good and I can't stop this. I'll surely die if I don't come soon, but…

'Do you have a condom?'

He's already releasing me and unzipping a pouch on the side of his shorts.

'You haven't?' He has… He's pulling out a small foil packet. 'I don't know whether to be offended or relieved.'

'What can I say?' He tongue-fucks my mouth. 'I'm always prepared.'

'Like a proper boy scout.' I tangle my fingers in his hair, marvelling at his seriously sexy good looks, and try to imagine him as a child. Vulnerable. Young. Studious.

His grin cocks to the side. 'That's me.' He rips the packet open. 'In the interest of speed, you want to get yourself out of that cock-teasing number?'

A ripple of excitement runs through me. I love his dirty mouth. Bobby was never like this. Never direct, masterful, so hot for me… I toss my kimono to the side and shove the straps down on my swimsuit, eager to be free of it as quickly as possible, but the sight of him shoving down his briefs makes me still.

I wet my lips and swallow. He's big. Big, long and so fucking hard.

'Hurry, *cara*, I need you.' He's already rolling the condom down, fisting his length, gripping the base tight. The tension is thrumming off him, his entire body pulsing tight, all muscular and bronze. 'Now.'

I shove my swimsuit to the floor and step out. I'm not even out of my nude wedges before he has me lifted against him, my legs wrapped around his waist, his cock jutting between us as he presses me back against the door, his lips claiming mine once more.

He reaches back to lock my ankles together, his fingers pausing to toy with my anklet.

'I love this. *Molto* sexy.'

My heart flutters. I could listen to him spill over with the compliments all day.

'You know what I find sexy…?' I shove a hand down between us and grip him hard, lowering him to my wet and ready pussy. With one thrust he is deep inside, so deep, so big, and my poor neglected womanhood stings with pain and pleasure, my cry swallowed by his low growl. He breaks away. Stills.

'Are you ok?' His eyes are desperately searching. 'Did I hurt you?'

'No, *fuck* no.' I lift a hand to his hair and drag him back to my mouth, my other hand clawing into his shoulder, gaining purchase, grinding down. 'Don't stop.'

He hesitates a split-second more and then he starts to move, starts to thrust, his movements long and drawn out and so tight against me, his entire length working against my clit and filling me deep. It's incredible, intense, and my belly pulsates with the erotic thrill of it. Of where we are. Of the talk and the laughter on the other side of the door. Of what we are doing here, now.

Pleasure pulsates out from my core, coiling through my limbs, making movement impossible as I surrender to his every thrust. I keep my mouth pinned to his, my wanton moans merging with his unhinged grunts, trapping them inside.

And I can feel his climax building, feel his thrusts turning jagged, and I tear my mouth away. I want to watch him come. I want to see this beautiful man, so powerful, so controlled and so secretly loving, spill his load inside me. I want to be the woman capable of doing that.

Our eyes lock as he grips me tighter. His neck cords up, his jaw pulses and my mouth falls open. My pants are enough to tell him I'm tipping over and he's there with me. His body jerks, a sharp thrust that sends me up the door, and I drop my head forward and bite into his shoulder to stop the cry that's desperate to emerge with my orgasm. But his growl doesn't have the same point of rescue, and I cover his mouth with my hand and feel it vibrate against my palm as he lets go.

He rides it out inside me, against me. It's quick, it's intense and it's mind-altering. I feel reawakened, as if I'm stepping out of the dark and seeing life for what it is—full of possibility, of potential, of so much more if I just take a leap.

'Wow.' It comes out of me softly, full of wonder, and as I raise my head to smile at him I feel his lips lift beneath my palm and see the same smile in his eyes. Their golden hue, intense, alive.

'That was fun,' I say, lowering my hand from his lips, and he chases it with his mouth, kissing the palm.

'Very much so.'

I feel like warm, mouldable putty, incapable of standing, let alone walking out of here. But we have to and soon. There's only so long we can disappear for under the pretence of fashioning a compress.

'So…' I say. 'The first-aid kit?'

He chuckles low in his throat and pulls out of me, careful to wait for my feet to be planted before he releases me completely, and my body immediately pines for the loss of his.

'That's what we came in here for,' I remind him, meeting the mischief in his face.

'Absolutely. What else could we have possibly needed?'

I watch him move away, his laugh teasing my blissfully satiated body, and bite into my lip. How is it possible to want him again? Already?

I don't know, but I do know that this week is turning out better than I ever could have imagined...

We make ourselves presentable, and focus on constructing the compress for Nonna, but I feel the awareness still thrumming in the air, the desire that we can't seem to burn out. As we go to leave, he grabs my hand and pulls me back in for a kiss that promises more, so much more. Soon, very soon.

I should feel guilty. I know I should. Dani made her thoughts clear as far as Rafael and I are concerned. But that was when she was worried about potential heartbreak. And I'm not foolish enough to fall in love with Rafael. He isn't a man wanting a future. He's a man wanting super-hot sex. And I'm all for that.

The new me is one hundred percent all over it.

CHAPTER SEVEN

Danielle and Tyler's Wedding Week
Monday: Bridal Party Dinner. Terrace,
eight-thirty p.m.

AKA TORTURE ON the terrace. And it was always going
to be torture…even before Dani made it clear she had
high hopes for Faye and Dante getting it on. Her not-
so-subtle matchmaking has been full-on since we
emerged from the pool house and, no matter how
much I remind myself that it was me cock-deep in
Faye, bringing her to climax twice in one day, I can't
stop the way it riles me.

She made sure they sat together at the poolside
and encouraged them into a game of water volleyball
with Harry and his wedding date, Lisa. It quickly
morphed into what Dani declared as a chicken fight,
and there was no way the designer of Faye's swimsuit
envisaged it being worn during that. No way at all.

Not when her legs were hooked on Dante's shoulders, his hands grasping at her thighs as the couples
sought to up-end the females into the water. I mean,

one wrong move and that mesh would surely tear, or a breast would pop free or, heaven forbid, come away all together. It seemed far too delicate, the mix of mesh and opaque fabric curving around her body in just the right way to conceal the crucial points, but one tug, one mistimed move, and…

It didn't happen, but it could have, and the idea had my entire body rigid for the duration.

As did the fact that it was Dante's hands on her.

I shouldn't have been so hooked on their easy fun together. I should have made myself busy talking with the other guests and catching up with Nonna. And I tried. I really tried. But when Nonna looked at me with that far too astute gaze of hers, and asked if I felt I was missing out, the smile tugging at her lips telling me she saw far too much, I knew I'd all but failed.

It was the cue I needed to make a hasty exit, citing work as the excuse. I'd been there long enough, surely? But in reality I wasn't ready to admit that I was jealous. Jealous and envious of their easy camaraderie. The fun so readily available to them while I sat on the sidelines.

And I know I'm the older brother…the serious, responsible one. I know fun doesn't come easily to me, not when my family is near. But not once did they seek to include me. I'd been lumped in with the older generation and forgotten about, save for Faye. She would send the occasional look, one that was more curious than anything else.

She's doing it now. As we all sit round the table

for dinner, the chatter incessant, her eyes keep finding mine...or is it that I keep pulling her my way because I can't stop seeking her out? It's as though I'm magnetically drawn to her and no amount of mental talk will stop me from doing it.

'Isn't that so, Rafael? *Rafael?*'

I turn to see my mother staring pointedly at me from further along the table. Tyler's parents across from me are also looking rather expectant, but I have no idea what I'm supposed to be responding to.

'*Scusi*, what was that?'

My mother rolls her eyes and shakes her head. 'You've hardly been with us all afternoon. What's wrong with you?'

I take a sip of wine and lean back in my chair. 'Work.'

The lie is easy. Far easier than the truth. That the woman two seats down from me, with Dante between us, is causing my mind to wander. Hell, maybe it bothers me more because I know Dante is a better match for her. Dani certainly thinks it's the case.

'Of course.' My mother looks to Tyler's parents. 'No change there. He's all work and no play, my son.'

Tyler's father murmurs a respectful, 'He has the success to show for it too.' While his mother beams at me.

Marianna, on the other hand, looks as if she's sucking on a lemon. 'That may be, but it would be nice to have your son's attention once in a while.'

The wine turns bitter on my tongue and I'm about to respond when Faye's voice reaches me. 'It's such a beautiful part of the world here. Rafael told me you used to live here when he was a child, Marianna?'

My mother's eyes leave me to find Faye and her face softens, a wistful smile touching her lips. 'We did. It feels like a whole other lifetime ago now.'

'Do you miss it?'

Now my mother really does smile, and an unexpected sheen fills her eyes. I'm frozen as I take it in, witnessing an emotion that's not anger, either acrid or cold. There's no petulance, no arrogance. And yet the strength of it, its sincerity, guts me.

'I do. I often wonder if I should come back, but in my heart I know it wouldn't be the same as it once was. It's the people that make a home. It was…it was Eduardo who made it home.'

I watch Nonna reach out for my mother's hand and give it a squeeze, a rare sign of affection between the two, and I feel the mood around the table turn sombre with reflection. I can't breathe. It's the first time I've heard my mother say my father's name in too many years to count and it resonates through me. A grief I haven't allowed for so long assaults me without warning and it's suffocating. The pressure of it pushes down on my chest and I need to get out of there.

I push back from the table, the iron chair legs screeching against the travertine floor and through my skull, but I don't even wince. My apology, when I utter one, is practically mute as I head for the steps that lead towards the gardens.

A hand grasps mine, making me pause. It's Dani, smiling softly, mouthing *It's okay*. But it's not.

I don't want to make a scene. I've already made enough of one and I need the air. I need the space.

So much space.

I watch him go. I watch Dani watch him go. And the need to go after him burns through me. Why hasn't she gone after him?

Even with his well-tailored jacket enhancing the line of his shoulders, they look drawn in, tense, and nothing can take my focus away from his retreating form.

He doesn't look back, just keeps going until he's lost amongst the darkness and the foliage. But still I can't focus on the conversation that picks up around the table. Everyone tries to fill the awkward lull save for me. I'm too annoyed that no one else is going. I look to Dani, my eyes urging her to go and check on him without actually coming right out and saying it.

She leans into me, her hand coming to rest on my own. 'It's okay. He'll be okay,' she says in a hushed tone for my ears only. 'Mum's forever winding him up when we're together and he'll take himself off for a time-out to calm down and—'

'A time-out?' My whisper is rushed, breathless with disbelief. 'He's not some naughty toddler being sent away, Dani.'

Her eyes widen with a laugh. 'I didn't say he was, but now you—'

She breaks off abruptly at the continued concern

in my face. 'Okay, okay, if it'll make you feel better, I'll go and check on him.'

'No, it's fine, I'll go.'

I'm already rising, but her hand reaches out for me again. 'Hey, are *you* okay?'

I frown down at her. 'I'm not the one you should be asking.'

My voice is still too low to be overheard above the general hubbub around us, but I'm aware I stand out. I'm standing at the table with Dani's hand clasped around mine, her concerned gaze on me, *for* me, when I should be concerned with making sure *she* stays happy, not the other way around. I immediately regret my snappy retort.

Hell, who am I to get between them? What do I know about sibling relationships? I just know that he didn't look okay when he left and I'd like to think that, if he was my brother, I'd go after him.

Dani's eyes quietly search mine and I plaster on a smile.

'Sorry. That didn't come out right. What I mean is, I'm fine and I'm going to make sure your brother is.' I lean down and press my cheek to hers, giving her shoulders a gentle squeeze. 'It's my job as maid of honour to smooth over any troubles this week, and I'd feel happier knowing he's okay rather than assuming it.'

I feel a small stab of guilt that it's not quite the full truth. That in actual fact my few encounters with her brother have shown me another side to him, one that Dani doesn't seem to know exists, and it's that knowledge of him that has me wanting to go to him now.

He's done so much to ensure this wedding comes off without a hitch that to get up and walk out during dinner isn't something he would do lightly.

But I can't let her know any of that. Not right this second, at any rate. Instead, I give her one more squeeze. 'Save some Eton Mess for me, won't you?'

She taps my hand, her smile one of gratitude now. 'Will do. And don't let him keep you too long. We thought we'd play cards after dinner. If you can coax Raf away from his work, it'd be nice if he could join us too.'

'I'll see what I can do.'

One last smile and I'm walking in his direction, hoping he has stuck to the softly lit path, because if he hasn't I'm never going to find him. It's hard to hear anything over the chatter back at the table and the ripple of the insects in the undergrowth. The further I walk, the more the insects take over, and I realise I have no idea where he is. I'm almost at the pool when I sense movement off to my right and see a shadow in amongst the vines. *Rafael?*

I squint into the darkness but it's no use. I start blindly in that direction, hoping there's nothing in the undergrowth about to attack me. I feel oddly vulnerable leaving the path behind, the vines running either side of me, the trill of the insects even louder now; I breathe in deeply and let the scent of Tuscany soothe my elevated pulse.

'Rafael?' I call out softly and the shadow becomes

a definite figure as he turns to face me. His eyes glitter in the darkness, the moonlight cast through the vines streaking across his face, and I can make out his hands shoved deep into his pockets. 'Is everything…is everything okay?'

'What are you doing here?' His tone is hard, so hard I wonder if I've misjudged the situation. Maybe I'm the last person he wants coming after him.

'Sorry, I just wanted to make sure you're okay. I can… I can go.' I start to turn away and he steps forward, his hand closing softly around my wrist and sending a zip of warmth right through my arm.

'No, *I'm* sorry.' He stops to stand before me, so close I can feel his breath brush against my hair. 'Like I said before, my family—or, rather, my mother—brings out the worst in me.'

I look up into his eyes and search their harrowed depths for the answers I so desperately want, even though I hardly know him. It's been less than twenty-four hours, yet it feels like a lifetime, and I can't stop the question from surfacing. 'Why did you leave?'

He shakes his head and rakes a hand through his hair as he looks to the darkened vineyard rather than me. 'You won't understand.'

'Try me. *Please.*'

He flicks me a look and I can see the hesitation in the line forming between his brows.

'I *want* to understand.'

He wets his lips and I sense his nervousness. The severe, strong, confident Rafael is nervous and my heart flutters with the realisation.

'My mother never speaks of my father. She never speaks of Tuscany or our time here. It…it was a shock.'

'It hurt you.'

He scoffs. 'It made me uncomfortable.'

'Why? Because it makes you realise that perhaps you and your mother have more in common than you think?'

'We are *nothing* alike.'

I place a palm on his arm. 'She seemed very genuine.'

Another scoff.

'You don't think she was?'

His mouth is a grim line and I don't press. I wait patiently, hoping he will open up.

'No, I think she meant it, that's why…why it got to me.'

Why it hurt so much, my brain supplies for him, because it does hurt him; I can see it in his face as I turn him to look at me.

'You should talk to her about it, let her open up to you, and you can do the same in return. Life's too short not to try to salvage a relationship with her, Rafael.'

I feel the pain of my own loss, my own mother, who I'd give anything to have back in my life once more.

'Perhaps.'

His eyes are so dark in the low light, dark and pained; the lines bracketing his mouth, severe. I want to reach up and smooth them away. I want to kiss his lips and make them soften, make them smile or slacken with desire. Anything but this.

And it's something I have the power to do. He's opened me up to new possibilities, to pleasure, wild and abandoned... My lips feel parched with the memory of it all and I wet them, watching his eyes flare as they trace the move, and I know I'm not alone in riding this fresh wave of heat.

The air seems to thicken and wrap around us, the sound of the insects falling away as our elevated breaths blend into the same rhythm.

'You should go back to the table before you are missed.'

He says the words, but his hand doesn't release me. Instead, his other hand lifts to cup my cheek. His fingers are gentle and his eyes roam over my face, intense, searching.

'I want you to come back with me.' I remember that's why I'm here. To make sure he's okay and bring him back for dessert, for cards with his family. But my feet are as rooted as the vines around us.

'I will...' His gaze rests on my lips and his head lowers slowly, so slowly. 'Soon.'

And then his mouth sweeps over mine and the tiny little tremors that have been building ever since he grabbed my wrist take off inside. The whimper I utter, their outlet. My mouth moves in time with his and I angle my head to let him in deeper, to let his tongue graze mine. *Oh, yes.*

He releases my wrist to wrap his arm around me, drawing my body up against his, tearing his mouth away to find the sensitive skin of my throat. His stubble is rough as it scrapes against my skin, making me shiver and shake. The lust so powerful it consumes me from within as I fork my hands through his hair and cling to him for support as my knees weaken.

His hand leaves my cheek to stroke down my front, over the light fabric of my dress, my bra… He palms my breast, his thumb sweeping over one taut peak and making my hips roll.

He comes back up to claim my mouth, to swallow my moan that is quick to follow, and his arm around me tightens. I palm his chest and kiss him deeply, feeling his heat permeate my fingers, feeling his heart beating as wildly as my own.

'I think it's my turn to give you a happy ending…' I look at him from beneath my lashes, waiting for my meaning to register as I lower my fingers to his belt and start to unfasten it. His body stills. His fingers are quick to close around mine as he struggles to drag in air. His jaw pulses and his throat bobs. But I don't look away. I don't stop, either, and his fingers slacken over mine, letting me continue.

He's staring so hard into my eyes, their glittering depths hypnotic, and I'm high on it. The power, the control, the risk, even… I unbutton his trousers and ease his zipper down. The sound of it cuts through the air as illicit as any erotic touch. His cock strains to greet me and I trace a fingernail down his clothed length, savouring the way his jaw pulses and his nostrils flare with his sharp inhalation. I wonder if lust has stolen his voice as I slip my hand inside his briefs and feel him pulse within my grasp.

I pump his cock and his hands fly to my hips. '*Dio*, Faye.'

My smile is small and teasing, my eyes drinking in the tension rippling through his body. 'Do you want me to stop?'

He shudders, the breath hissing between his teeth as I move over him again, my hand twisting and undulating.

'*No, no.*' The words are as tight as his body. His eyes squeeze shut, his fingers flexing against my hips. 'But you will be my undoing.'

'Good,' I whisper. 'And, when you're sated, we can return to play cards with the guests as though nothing is amiss.'

'And you?'

He opens his eyes and stares down at me as if he can scarcely believe we're doing this, in the vineyard, with the chatter of the guests blowing on the breeze, the vines cocooning us.

That makes two of us. But…

'This is about you.' *And my sexual awakening*, if I want to be even more honest about it. I lift up on tiptoes and brush my lips with his, parting them with a flick of my tongue, and it has his eyes flaring into mine. 'No one knows what we're doing. No one can know but us. It's our little secret and I want to take advantage of that.'

He bucks into my grasp, his groan reverberating through me. I clench my legs together tight, nursing the ache that's building with his pleasure. I feel his pre-cum slip through my fist and I bite into my lip.

He shakes his head. 'Faye…'

'I want this. I want to make you lose control like you made me today. Let me have this.'

I stroke him harder, let him grind into my grasp as I set the tempo. His hands lift to my shoulders and he throws his head. *'Si… Si, cara mia.'*

His Italian endearment merges with his heightened need and I am so lost to the moment, so lost that I forget I want more, that I want to taste him, like he tasted me.

'You need to stop before…*before*…' I look up into his flushed face and see what he means staring back at me. But it's my turn to shake my head as I lift my dress to my knees and bend to the ground.

'It's my turn,' I repeat, and his hands lift to my hair, his eyes burning into my lips as I bring them to the tip of his erection and flick my tongue out to tease at his slit.

His cock bucks in my hold, his, 'Are you sure?' a growl.

Jesus. I'm on my knees before him, his cock at my lips, and he's asking me if *I'm sure.*

How can Dani not know her brother as I do?

He loves.

He cares.

And right now he cares too much to let his wicked desires take over and drive this. My answer is to surround his head and sink him in deep, so deep he reaches the back of my throat, and I know he's holding back. I know the reason his body is so rigid is that he doesn't dare fuck my mouth as deeply as he desires. That *I* have to take him there.

I cover his hand in my hair and I hold him there as my other hand grips him, sinking him in deeper and sucking hard, telling him with my actions what I want, what I need. Slowly he succumbs, his fingers tightening in my hair as his body rocks faster, harder. I moan around him, telling him, *yes, yes, yes, come for me.* My eyes burn into his, urging him on. The moon enshrouds him in white. He is a dark shadow with eyes that glitter, his panted breaths overtaking the trill of the insects around us, flooding my ears and my clit with heat. I drop the hand over his to the skirt of my dress and hook it under to find my swollen, wet heat and I rock into my palm.

I won't orgasm. I won't. This is for him. But I can't ignore the acute beat that demands something, anything.

'Faye… Faye… Faye…' My name erupts with every rock of his body and then he bucks sharply, his head thrown back, growling to the heavens, and I cry with him as he fills my hungry mouth, my body grinding hard on my fingers. *Yes, oh, yes, Rafael.*

It's incredible. Other-worldly. Never have I… Outdoors like this…

'Faye! Rafael!'

Shit, it's Dani!

I scramble to my feet, cup him and pull up his zipper in one, my 'Jesus!' and his *'Dio!'* coming in unison. I'm trying to feed his belt back through the loop when I hear steps on the path behind us and he takes over so I can wipe the back of my hand across my mouth.

'There you are. I thought the vines had swallowed you both up for a second,' she calls out as I spin to face her and conceal Rafael as best I can behind me. 'You ready to play cards, the two of you?'

'Yes, absolutely. Raf?' I turn to look up at him, grateful that the darkness will conceal his flushed cheeks.

'Si, un minuto.'

Okay, so he's just saying 'in one minute', but still my insides quiver over it as if it's the sexiest utterance I've ever heard.

I smile at him, my pleasure at what we've done shining in my face.

His eyes fall to mine. His lips are soft—no grim line now, no hardness, sadness or regret—and my heart squeezes in my chest. I did that. I did that to him, for him, and it feels so good, so dangerously good.

He's not yours to worry about. He's not your lover, not your brother, not your concern.

Only, I do care, and there's nothing I can do to stop it.

We might not have a future, but my heart isn't fussed. I know this is bad, really bad, but if I can enjoy my week like this, if I can go some way towards healing Rafael and his relationship with his family, it can't be *all* bad.

Can it?

'Well, are you coming? They're getting restless up there.'

Dani fractures the moment completely and I've never been more grateful.

'Coming!'

I feel his palm press softly into my back, sending far too thrilling a shiver up my spine as he encourages me on. 'I'm ready.'

And then it hits me, really hits me: I'm falling for Dani's commitment-phobic brother and there's not a damn thing I can do about it. Nothing at all.

I practically run up the path ahead of him, my smile all about masking my panic, but I'm hoping she'll take it as reassurance that her brother is okay... not that she was the one worrying in the first place.

'So, what are we playing?'

'How about strip poker?'

I'm so off the beat that I merely stare at her in stunned silence.

'*Dio*, Faye. I'm just kidding!' She rolls her eyes theatrically. 'Do you really think I'd play strip poker with my brother, let alone my mother *and* Tyler's mother?'

My laugh is high-pitched and as ridiculous as I feel. 'I forgot myself for a second.'

She sends a curious look past me to Rafael and I don't want to second-guess what it means. She hooks her arm through mine and starts marching us back to the castle. 'Yeah, you sure did.'

In more ways than you can ever possibly imagine, Dani, my brain unhelpfully adds.

I raise my chin and focus, matching her stride for stride.

You're having fun. For the first time in a long while, you're having real, honest-to-God fun. Don't ruin it by getting all serious now.

I start to question whether it's the afternoon drinking at the 'dive and dine' on top of the wine consumed at the bridal party dinner that has me acting like some over-concerned, smitten hussy. Yes, all of those things. But one look back at Rafael and the way our eyes meet, the way the fire in his eyes connects with the very heart of me, tells me I'd feel this way regardless.

I go back to looking straight ahead, to the softly lit castle, beautiful even at night, and try to ignore the panicked little flutter deep inside.

CHAPTER EIGHT

Danielle and Tyler's Wedding Week
Tuesday: Wine Making and Tasting.
Two p.m. NB Dress to get your feet wet!

I CHECK THE TIME and fight back a grimace. Aunt Netta is due any minute, along with my cousin Sienna, her husband Lorenzo and their kids, Isabella and Leo. It's not their presence that worries me; it's the effect it will have on my mother. I've avoided being alone with her since her surprisingly sentimental outburst at dinner last night.

I feel a conversation brewing and it's not one I'm ready for, not this side of the wedding, in spite of Faye's encouragement to think otherwise. It's waited all these years; it can at least wait another week or two, or more.

It was hard enough being cracked open for all to see at the dinner table. Losing my composure, this week of all weeks, and in such spectacular fashion…

No. I will deal with it later.

Much later.

As for Faye…she's the perfect distraction from it all and one that I'm more than willing to entertain if it will keep my mind from veering into the past and whatever pain I glimpsed in Marianna.

I understand why Faye is encouraging me to talk to her. Her relationship with her own mother had been a good one, a healthy one, and one that she still so clearly mourns. The pain I glimpsed in her, the anguish still swimming in those pale blues, chips away at something buried deep inside. I rake my fingers through my hair, take a breath and force the image out.

Dio. Since when have I cared so much for the personal baggage of a woman I sleep with?

Sleep with?

Hardly.

It's been a sensual trip up against a wall, a risky encounter in the pool house and again in the vineyard. All bring the hint of a smile to my lips even now, pushing out the stress of the new arrivals.

My veins instantly fire up, lust heating a path straight to my groin. Its intensity is at odds with the fact that she took me to the edge last night. And all through the game of cards I watched those fingers, those lips, those eyes and remembered what we'd shared. I was so badly distracted that I lost the game. And I never lose.

It was something which Dani commented on as she pulled me aside before bed and advised me to talk to our mother. I almost laughed. How would she feel to know the truth—that it wasn't Marianna on my mind during the card game. It was her far too appealing maid of honour who also wanted to push the same advice?

Talk. I've done enough talking with Faye already, telling a woman I barely know things that I can hardly get a handle on myself. All this by day two of seven. What am I going to share in the next five?

The sound of raised voices invades the sanctity of my bedroom and I snap to attention, my eyes on the closed door as though I can see through it. Not that I need to.

Aunt Netta and Marianna.

At war already.

I pocket my phone and give the mirror a second's glance. Black linen shirt, chinos, and I've forked some product through my hair. My eyes are remarkably clear, no sign in them of the restless night I endured. All perfectly presentable for an afternoon and evening of entertaining…or refereeing.

As I open the door, the voices hit me harder, louder, and I pick up my pace. What is wrong with my family? What did I do in a previous life to deserve this?

I hit the stairs when the noise tapers off and I slow my stride. My eyes lift to the entrance, to the two women who not one minute ago had been making enough noise to shake the rafters. But they are quietly listening to someone else. Someone I can't see. And then they are talking. Actually talking. With smiles. Real, genuine smiles.

I leave the stairs and make my way across the entrance hall.

'She's a miracle worker, whoever she is.'

I turn to see Sienna walking up to me, her grin wide and welcoming.

'Cousin! It's good to see you.' We embrace, kiss cheeks and she adds an extra-tight squeeze before giving me a slap to the chest.

'It's been far too long, Rafael. I'm almost surprised to see you.'

'Don't you start.'

She laughs. 'You're right, I'll save it for *after* we've sampled the vineyard's finest.'

She elbows me in the side and nods to the entrance. 'So, who's the stunning brunette currently wooing Mamma and Aunt Marianna into silence?'

We start to walk to the entrance and, though I can't see her, instinct tells me that Faye is involved. Even without my cousin's apt description.

'Let's go take a look. Where are the kids? Lorenzo?'

'Leo had an incident with an ice-cream so Lorenzo's getting him changed, and Isabella decided to change before the tour. Seems she's ten going on twenty.'

I laugh at her eye-roll. 'Takes after her mother, then.'

'More like her grandmother and great-aunt. Do you think the two of them realise how alike they are? Though your mother is a tad less…flamboyant. If I'm honest, I'd also be changing, if not for the slanging match.'

'You and me both.'

'And it seems we needn't have bothered.' As

we round the corner, all three ladies are laughing. *Laughing!*

'*Si, si*…and then I said, you know what else looks like a monkey's bottom?' Aunt Netta is positively rumbling as she says it and then she spies us approaching. 'Shh…shh…we have an intruder in our midst! Rafael, *regazzo mio*, it's so wonderful to finally see you again.'

She bustles through the middle of the women, heading straight for me, her cheeks aglow, her dress almost an exact copy of my mother's, only hers is neon pink to Marianna's pastel shade. 'Let me look at you.'

Her hands are already launching into the air and I have the awful feeling she's about to… Too late. She's already pinching my cheeks and I'm cursing my own stupidity for leaning down.

I hear a stifled giggle and look over the curly mass piled high on her head to see Faye biting her lip. I'm not going red. I'm not. I'm a forty-two-year-old man; I don't blush. It's the sun, the heat…it's Faye, all Faye. My dawning frown quits as Aunt Netta pulls me in for a hug and then thrusts me back so she can stare up at me.

My red-faced smile is tight. 'Aunt Netta, it's so good to see you.'

'You know, I half thought you wouldn't turn up!' She wags a finger at me. 'We had money on it, didn't we, Sienna? And look, here you are, handsome as ever! Please tell me lovely Faye is the person we have to thank for putting this colour in your cheeks and getting you all the way here. It's about time, *regazzo mio*, about time!'

My frown returns. It's all noise flying at me, a flurry of words, but some are sticking. Does anyone else want to accuse me of being so heartless as to not attend my little sister's wedding? Is that really the impression I've built over the years—the workaholic bachelor with no time for anything or anyone else? As for the assumptions regarding Faye…

I sense movement behind Netta and it's Faye, her skin calmer, her eyes…sincere. Why does it feel as if she can read me? Every intense, uncomfortable second?

She's wearing a simple summer dress that ends just above the knee, nothing elaborate or sexy, but still my body warms, my heart beating that little bit faster the closer she gets.

She reaches out for Aunt Netta, her hand soft on my aunt's shoulder as she laughs softly. 'No, I'm afraid you have Dani to thank for me being here. I'm the maid of honour.'

'Of course you are!' Aunt Netta announces so loudly I want to cover my ears. She turns her attention to Faye and, before she can duck away, she's getting the cheek-pinch too, though just the one side, not my double helping. 'Dani always had excellent taste!'

'And I don't?' I tease.

She rounds on me with a harrumph. 'You, my boy, have yet to bring anyone home, *maschio o femmina*, for me to establish such credit. At least Dani comes to Tuscany often enough.'

'Well, he's here now.' Faye positively beams.

'*Si, si*, you're right, he is,' my mother chimes in, coming up alongside Aunt Netta and giving me a look I don't recognise. 'Faye, this is Sienna—Rafael and Danielle's cousin.'

Sienna smiles at Faye. 'It's a pleasure, a real pleasure.'

Her eyes flit between the pair of us and I have the distinct impression she's putting two and two together and coming up with a very accurate four.

'Let's not stand here all day,' I say, keen to shift the focus off us. 'The tour is due to begin shortly. The rest of the guests should be in the gardens waiting.'

'Speaking of which, Mamma,' Sienna says, 'what have you done with Giovanni?'

'He's making himself look pretty. He'll join us shortly.'

I frown. 'Giovanni?'

'*Si,*' my mother's smile turns forced. 'Antonietta's plus-one. You know—the plus-one you wouldn't let *me* have? You may even recognise him; he and your father were good friends.'

'The best.' Aunt Netta nods furiously. 'God rest his soul. Eduardo was a good man, such a good man, it was a cruel—'

'Sienna,' I turn to my cousin. I can't do this right now. 'Do you need to go and fetch Lorenzo and the children…? Ah, no need, here they come now.'

Leo and Isabella are running through the entrance hall towards us, a rather flustered Lorenzo on their tail.

Whatever he has to be flustered about, it can't be anything close to my discomfort, and I'm already walking away from the source of mine, eager for some grounded male companionship in place of the emotional rollercoaster of being around these four women, especially Faye. No matter how much I try, I can't push her out of my mind or get my body under control whenever she's near.

Clothed, unclothed, blushing, stoic… It doesn't matter. Faye just gets to me.

She also *gets* me. More than my own family have ever been able to.

And I have no idea how to feel about it.

I'm so glad I opted for a light summer dress. The tour of the vineyards is scorching, and I'm already a hot, sweaty mess having to be in Rafael's company again. I do my best to keep people between us, to act as a buffer, anything to try to lessen the effect of his presence.

But it's no use.

My every sense is attuned to him. He moves and my eyes follow. He speaks and little tremors work their way through my body, relishing the sound. He passes by and the slightest touch, the slightest hint of his cologne, has my knees turning weak.

It's driving me crazy and I'm more than a little relieved when we enter the wine cellar and the temperature drops dramatically.

'So, you see…' Diego, the winemaker, turns to us all, bringing us to a quick stop that has someone walking straight into my back. I know who it is before I hear his hurried, *'Scusi.'*

Rafael. He's pressed up against me, only for a split second, and then his hands are on my hips as he takes a step back. My legs want to move with him, to keep him close, and the effort it's taking not to do so, especially when he releases my hips, has all of my attention.

Dante, to my right, flicks us both a look, a smile twitching at his lips, and I wonder what he's thinking. Up front, Diego is still talking, something about the Valentini family who built the castle, and I try to focus but my mind keeps wandering back to the man behind me. The man whose grief seems far too raw after twenty-five years have passed. The man who has the reputation of a workaholic, caring more for his job than his own family. But I know different and I wish everyone else did too.

I can already feel myself falling…but that's the sex talking, I try to tell myself. The explosive, mind-blowing sex. Nothing more.

I cross my arms in front of me and feel the goose bumps that run over my skin. I shiver. It really is cold down here.

Cold, right? It has nothing to do with realising how emotionally invested you are. That it isn't just sex at all. That you enjoy his company and can see it becoming more. That you care.

'Are you cold?'

His voice teases so close to my ear and his body warmth radiates down my back. I risk a glance up at him and the low light of the cellar makes the atmosphere feel far more intimate than any guided tour. His brown eyes soften into mine, his concern creasing at his brow, and my heart gives a tiny squeeze, punctuating my realisation from seconds before.

'I'm okay,' I whisper. At least, I think I'm okay. I don't even know how to feel. I didn't come to Dani's wedding to get caught up in some fling with her brother.

He starts to say something more but Diego encourages us to move on and I hurry forward, through the tunnel of stone that's lined with casks, into another tunnelled room. This one has several upturned barrels laid out like tables, with wine glasses at the ready and wooden stools for the guests to use.

Dani giggles softly and it echoes off the stone wall. I look across to see Tyler whispering something into her neck; their love and passion, so clearly on display.

A smile touches my lips. Perhaps it is possible for me to have both too: love and passion.

Perhaps Rafael could be that man. In spite of all I know of him, perhaps this is different for him too. As different as it is for me when compared to my relationship with Bobby.

'You look cold, Faye.' It's Dante who says it, his frown mirroring Rafael's. 'Here, take my jacket.'

'No, no, it's fine.' I wave a hand at him. It feels far too intimate when I know Dani has been determined to set us up together, and I have the man I do want standing right behind me.

'I insist.' He's already shrugging it off and wrapping it around my shoulders, his clean, masculine scent taking over Rafael's. It's pleasant, stronger than Raf's, but it does absolutely nothing for me.

I give him a smile and feel his residual warmth take the edge off the chill. 'Thanks.'

'No problem.'

His attention goes back to Diego, who is describing the Chianti we are about to sample, and I sense Rafael's eyes on me. I want to turn and look at him. I want to tell him with my eyes that he's the one I want. But when I risk a look his attention is firmly on Diego.

Maybe he doesn't care either way. Maybe all this is very one-sided. And maybe, just maybe, the lust really is getting in the way and blinding me to what this really is between us. Just great sex.

I shiver in spite of Dante's jacket and throw my focus into the wine, into the tour, into the history of the castle. And I succeed, to a point. I sip the wine. I laugh over my silly attempt at swilling, tasting and spitting, and Dante is the perfect companion. He laughs with me. He's easy. Fun.

Rafael isn't. He's aloof. He's more detached than I've seen him before and I'm getting a glimpse of what his family are used to. I know because Dante doesn't bat an eyelid at his behaviour. His quietness, his apathy, his lack of involvement…

Don't get me wrong. He tastes the wine along with the rest of us. But he's robotic with it. There's no curve to his lips, no spark in his eyes, and the habitual grim line has made a return. He watches Diego as he talks about the next wine we are to sample and his eyes flit in my direction—a second's pause, and my heart flutters as I hope for something, a small smile, anything.

Nothing.

He takes up his wine glass that looks far too big for the small amount of wine we are sampling and swirls it in his hand, his eyes falling to the drink, intense, pensive, and then he raises it to his lips. Those lips that I can scarce believe have laughed, let alone been buried between my legs. I tense as my clit pulses over the vivid recollection and his eyes flick to mine. They lock on and, hell, I know he reads me now.

Colour streaks my cheeks and I go to look away, but then I see that hint of something more in his eyes at last, a twitch to his lips before he draws a little air in over the wine and begins to taste it like an expert. I normally want to giggle at this—I wanted to when I watched Diego instruct us on how to do it properly; I've wanted to at every other wine demonstration I've attended—but with Rafael, as I watch him move the drink around his mouth, I am captivated. I wish I could be part of that tasting, my tongue twisting with his, enjoying the depth of body, the hit of grapes.

And then his throat bobs, and I'm so wrapped up in the move it takes me a second to realise he hasn't spit. Or, to use Diego's polite term, expectorated. And, as my eyes lift once more to his, I understand why. I'm not the only one who feels as if their throat has closed over with the rush of heat inside.

'Are you not tasting this one?' He raises a brow at me and I see the laughter rising in the heat of his gaze, the twitch to his lips.

'I was enjoying you tasting it.'

It's out before I can stop it and it's quickly followed by a sharp cough from Dante as his own wine catches the back of his throat.

Really, Faye? Really?

Thank God no one else seems to have overheard. I focus on taking up the wine. I throw it back and get far too big a sampling; I swirl it with far too much gusto and attempt a spit. *Bollocks.*

You'd think with the force of my response I'd have nailed getting it in the dump bucket. Instead, I end up with an unattractive river running off my chin. I hurry to grab a napkin, but Rafael beats me to it, and as our eyes lock together once more, his finger and thumb are on my chin, angling my head back as he dabs away the mess I've made. *Oh, God.*

'Nice?' he murmurs, his eyes falling to my lips.

Oh, yes. Too nice.

And I don't mean the wine. I actually can't speak. My throat is wedged shut again and the whole room is falling away. It's just me and him and this connection that is determined to exist against all the odds. And the truth is, I have no idea about the wine, because everything tastes and feels good with him this close.

His eyes flick away and he releases me so quickly,

I almost slip from my stool, but as I follow his eye line I realise why. Dani's watching us, the speculation in her gaze enough to tell me exactly what she's thinking.

I give her a big grin, gesture to the glass in my hand and throw a thumbs up. She's slow to return my smile, but when she does it seems genuine enough.

Diego calls for our attention and we all look to him as he starts to go through the next wine. I fixate on him. I don't let my eyes stray. I don't look at Dante unless he speaks to me and I don't look at Rafael even when he *does* speak.

It doesn't stop us accidentally brushing against one another, be it our fingers reaching for our glasses, a movement on our stool or a graze of the knee. Every slight contact sets my body alight, making me want, making me need, making me wish we were anywhere but here.

And alone. Very much alone.

CHAPTER NINE

'SIGNOR PEREZ, ARE YOU joining us?'

I turn from the view to see Diego looking at me, his eyes narrowed. And I can't blame him. It seems I've zoned out long enough for the rest of the party to be halfway across the courtyard on their way to the rear of the castle where there is to be a hands-on, or rather feet-on, demonstration of the traditional grape-stomping. Something Dani insisted she wanted to experience, and the team were more than happy to oblige in their desire to please me, their new employer.

I know I look less than pleased now and, though my scowl is directed wholly at myself, poor Diego won't know that.

'*Si.*' I force a grin as I gesture for him to lead the way.

I should be happy. Dani is happy. My mother and aunt are getting along well—a miracle in itself—and Giovanni, technically Aunt Netta's plus-one, seems to be more than happy entertaining the two of them. Everyone's smiling and laughing and I want to be too. I want to feel at ease but, every time I've felt at ease this week, I've let Faye in or exposed a part of me I've long kept buried…

Up ahead, Dante trails behind the rest of the group, and as I near he turns to me, his grin alive with teasing.

'So, come on, tell me all…' he urges, his swift Italian for my ears only.

I look back to the wedding party, to my niece and nephew chattering excitedly as they race through the vineyard, their faces aglow with the bronze of the sun bouncing off the vines and the earth.

'I don't know what you mean.'

'No?' He tosses his jacket over his shoulder, the same jacket that warmed Faye's shoulders in the wine cellar, and I feel the same weirdly possessive surge. It's ridiculous, but my body doesn't seem to care. *I* wanted to be the one to warm her, to caress her goose-flesh until it returned to silk, to murmur all the things I wanted to do when that wine trailed down her chin.

'Anyone ever tell you you're a rubbish liar, cousin?'

My laugh is tight. '*Si*. You. Just now.'

'If you're trying to keep it subtle you need to re-think all this…'

He waves a hand up and down my length and I frown. 'What on earth are you talking about?'

He cocks his head to the side and bats his lashes. 'This.'

Heat courses through me. Another damn blush! 'Don't be ridiculous, Dante.'

'Hey, don't get worked up about it. It's obvious she feels the same way.'

'You don't…'

His raised brows cut me off.

'Be careful, though.' He turns all serious on me. 'Dani is all for encouraging me to show her friend a good time off the back of her failed marriage, but I'm not so sure she'd take too kindly to it being you Faye has her rebound fun with.'

Wait, what? Rebound? Marriage?

'You didn't know,' he says, spying my confusion. 'She hasn't mentioned it?'

I think over our conversations, but I know she hasn't. I'd remember something as big as that.

'No.'

'Yeah, well, it seems Dani feels she needs a bit of fun before she finds "The One".' He rolls his eyes at the label. 'Why does there have to be a "One"? Why can't there just be many and many?'

My laugh is more of a grunt. 'I think you're missing the point if you have to ask.'

'Not at all.' He shudders. 'I don't ever plan on being all *pazzo d'amore*.'

Crazy in love… *Diavolo, no.*

'You and me both.'

We join the guests just as the folk accordionist I hired as a surprise appears, his traditional music piping through the air, and Dani gives out an excited whoop, her beaming face finding me across the cobbled ground.

'Thank you,' she mouths, and I acknowledge it with a nod.

Tyler scoops her up into a jig on the spot and they laugh, carefree and happy.

'I have to say, though,' Dante murmurs around the wine glass he's managed to bring with him, 'being all *pazzo d'amore* sure suits them.'

Another nod. I can't deny it. We watch as Tyler swings Dani in the air and places her down in the giant wooden container which houses the pressing floor, covered in grapes. She gives a squeal as her feet sink into the fruit and Tyler's grin widens. His eyes are fixed on his wife-to-be, alive with his love for her. I feel a strange pang deep inside, a confused mass that I don't understand or want to examine.

'They're happy enough,' I murmur, 'for now.'

I pick up my stride as the memories threaten, memories from before my father died and after. When my parents couldn't live together, and couldn't live without each other, and then the choice was taken away. His death changed everything. My mother…

I remember how she looked last night at dinner, talking of him for the first time in so long, and the chill sets in.

It's not to say it will happen to Dani and Tyler, I try to reason. God willing, they'll live a long and happy life together.

God willing? Now I sound like Nonna.

I watch the pleasure building through the group,

watch Dani and Tyler and feel their happiness permeating the air, and it eases some of the chill.

Yes, I can be happy for my sister, for them both.

But I can never go there.

'Come on, Dante, come and join in!' Dani beckons as Tyler climbs in, his parents too.

Harry and Lisa scoot off to the sidelines as she pulls a face at the very idea of crushing grapes with her feet. Lorenzo and Sienna help their kids in and back away to join Nonna, who is happy watching with Marianna and Antonietta at her side, each with a glass of a wine in hand, content to drink and spectate. Giovanni too.

Dante shakes his head. 'You're all right! I prefer grapes in my glass, not between my toes.'

'Spoil sport.' Dani looks to Faye. 'You're going to come in, aren't you?'

My eyes follow Dani's to Faye. Her smile lights up her face and takes my breath away. *Beautiful. Così bella.*

'Absolutely!'

'Just make sure you tuck your… Yes, you've got it.'

I watch as Faye raises the skirt of her dress, hooking it into the line of her underwear, and I feel the heat of the sun inside and out.

Then her eyes lift to mine, her face flushed with colour. 'Would you mind giving me a hand?'

And in that moment I know, if I *were* that way inclined, if I were to be all *pazzo d'amore*, she would be 'The One'.

'*Si.*' My reply is gruff and my stride rigid as I approach her. I sense Dani watching. I also sense Dani wondering at her friend's choice of aid. Me rather than Dante. But it's too late to stop myself, and I don't want to.

Faye climbs onto the bottom rung of the ladder that leads into the wooden vat, but my hands are already on her hips, and I feel her little gasp through my fingers. She turns in my hold to look down at me, her eyes glowing, her fingers soft as her hands fall to my wrists. A moment passes between us, a moment that feels far more intimate because the audience around us has no idea what we've shared. It's our little secret. Our little bit of fun...

'Ready?' I ignore the way my head is travelling, my heart with it, and she gives a breathless nod.

I swing her round, her scent washing over me, invading me and making me crave. Crave more than I ever have before.

And crave what, exactly? More fun, more sex?

I lift her over the edge, letting my hands ease up her sides as she lowers herself into the grapes.

'Dante, come on, this is a blast!' Dani comes stomping up behind her, her presence forcing me to release Faye before I'm ready...before she's ready too, judging by the look in her eye. 'Tell him, Faye!'

'Dani won't be happy until you do, Dante.' Her smile is one-sided as she looks to my cousin and I sense her attention is still very much on me.

'I'm quite all right spectating, *grazie*.'

She looks at me, her smile turning soft. 'Are you not coming in?'

Dani laughs. 'As if...'

Her light-hearted tease cuts deeper than it should. She's right, this isn't me. I don't get involved in silly pursuits that serve no purpose. Just as I didn't get involved at the pool...

'It is kinda fun,' Faye says, not ready to give up. She looks down at her feet and I imagine her toes curling into the grapes as she tests out the sensation. Her nose wrinkles. 'A bit icky, but fun.'

'A bit icky?'

Amusement bubbles up inside my chest. Amusement and something else. The same flicker that came to life when I cleaned the trail of wine on her skin, when I held her seconds ago. It's there beneath the desire, the lust that I know of old...

'You sell it so well.'

Her laugh is enough to see off my hesitation and I'm already bending forward to strip off my footwear and roll back my chinos.

'He's not...' I hear Dani say.

'He is.'

I shake my head at their little interchange and straighten up. Ignoring the inner voice telling me I won't be wearing these chinos again, I vault over the edge of the vat, and my feet slide as they hit the mix at its base, launching me towards Faye.

She palms my chest to steady me, her eyes dancing into mine. 'Too macho to use the ladder?'

I straighten. 'Of course.'

She only laughs harder and shakes her head at me.

Dani whoops. 'Let's dance!'

The accordionist starts to play a fresh tune that has the spectators clapping along. Dani directs Leo and Isabella to hook arms in the middle of the vat and dance as the adults hold hands in a circle around them.

'We're going to can-can!' Dani declares, taking up Tyler's hand and turning to offer me the other. She grins up at me and I know she's as surprised as I am that I'm doing this. I take her hand and give my other to Faye. The circle is complete and we're off, our feet squelching through the grapes, the sensation between my toes the strangest I've ever experienced.

Not as strange as the lightness in my chest, though...

The tempo picks up, the noise, the laughter, the fun, and it's not just in the air now. It's rising up inside me, taking over, and I feel almost drunk with it.

'Brother!'

'Si?' I call down to my sister.

'Grazie mille!'

I give her a nod, my grin too big for my face, and lose myself in the music. The more we dance, the faster the tempo, the further the grapes fly, until we are all covered, head to toe. Even the spectators take a showering...including my mother. There's a second's displeasure on her face and then Giovanni is there, wiping it from her dress and from her cheek, and even with the chaos going on around me I see the expression in his eyes, the softness. I see the exact same look in my mother's face too.

What the…?

I look to Aunt Netta and she too is watching. Not with surprise, but with pleasure, as if it was meant to be. And then Giovanni takes my mother's hand and draws her towards the vat… She won't… She wouldn't…

She is.

They're climbing in and Dani is breaking away from me to make space for them. My mother laughs as her feet hit the grapes, her eyes lifting to find mine. Tentatively, she offers out her hand and I take it. Take it and feel my head shake.

'Couldn't leave all the fun to you,' she says, but I hear the emotion that catches in her voice, that shows in her over-bright eyes, and then we're moving again. Giovanni is in between her and Dani, the circle once more complete and alive with laughter.

I feel Faye squeeze my hand encouragingly and I look at her. Her eyes are so blue, so bright, and I see all the happiness and joy reflecting back at me, pushing out the questions, the overthinking…

I'm living for the moment, lost in it, happy. It's where I want to stay for as long as I can.

'Hey, Faye, you coming?'

I look up to see Dani beckoning me from the middle of the wedding party as they make their way back inside the castle to get cleaned up. I'm the only one left by the well-crushed vat of grapes and I can't find my sandals.

'Of course. Just finding my shoes!'

She laughs. 'Only you could lose your shoes so quickly.'

She's right. Only me. I resume my hunt as the sounds of the party disappear into the castle.

'Looking for these?'

I spin on my heel, and there he is. Rafael. Leaning on the stone archway that leads off into the kitchen garden. Grape-stained, hair ruffled, shirt unbuttoned and sexier than I've ever seen him. I wet my lips and look at the pair of sandals hooked in his out-stretched hand.

'So that's where you snuck off to?'

'I may have had an ulterior motive.'

'What motive is that?'

'To ensure you were the last guest standing.'

My laugh flutters up. Excitement, desire, nerves. I turn to see the last of the guests disappear.

'They're gone,' he says.

But I'm rooted to the spot, breathing in the sight of him, his eyes dancing with the happiness of the afternoon, his smile teasing and seductive. Gone is the quiet, aloof Rafael from the tour. This is the man who danced in grapes with his family.

This is the man I've come to know, and now his family have witnessed it too. There's a shift under-way in him, in his relationship with his family, his mother especially. It is a shift I know everyone can sense and it warms my heart. It reminds me of just how much I care. Of just how deeply I am falling, and I'm helpless to prevent it. My stomach twists with a spark of fear, knowing there can be no future and hoping for it all the same.

But if he can change with his family…is there a chance for us?

'Do you want your shoes, or am I keeping them?' His grin sees off my fear and I'm already closing the distance between us.

'I don't think they'll suit you.'

And then my hands are in his hair, our lips melding in perfect time as he lifts me, sandals and all, and swings me back into the garden, tucking us away, just him and me. It's heated and crazed after a day of abstinence and it's all coming out in the desperation of our kiss.

'I've wanted to do this all day,' he rasps against my lips, his breath as ragged as my own. 'Wishing my family away so I can have you to myself.'

I whimper over his fierce declaration, wishing it meant more, wishing things were different. 'And now you can.'

He lifts his head, his eyes burning into mine. 'Not for long enough.'

I still, my fingers frozen in his hair, my lungs unable to draw breath. Time passes. Long enough for…what? For sex? For here and now? Or for a future?

And then he shakes his head, his groan trapped in his throat as his lips crush mine.

'I need you, Faye.'

My sandals hit the deck and his palms smooth up my thighs, beneath my dress, and the heat in my lower belly swells. The carnal ache, acute, incessant.

'I need you too.'

And I do. More than I need my next breath.

I fumble over his belt, his trousers, and I shove them down his thighs to free him for my eager grasp as he palms my heat, seeking out my wetness, my clit. I clamp down on my bottom lip as I try to keep my cries contained. I stare up unto his hooded eyes that burn and glaze with the thrill of the climax building between us.

'You're so beautiful, so fucking beautiful, Faye.'

It's the first time I've heard him swear in English and it shouldn't tip me over the edge like it is. But it's so raw, so impassioned, and I... I can't... I can't think any more.

'Raf, Raf, I'm going to, I'm going to...'

His pre-cum slips inside my fist, his cock swelling thick and fast, and I realise I'm not alone; I'm tipping him over the edge too, and it's so fucking sexy.

'Faye...*fuck*, Faye.' He grinds inside my grasp, pulses, and I feel the hot spurts of his release in my hands, on my dress, on him. And I'm gone, crying out into the fresh air, unable to trap it inside as I fall against him, shuddering with it all. The truth of what I feel. The truth that just sex, no matter how great, will never be enough, that I'll still want more.

He clutches me to him, his heartbeat wild against

my ear, his breathing unsteady as he presses a kiss to my hair.

A kiss that is so tender, I could believe it meant more.

I want it to mean more…

CHAPTER TEN

Danielle and Tyler's Wedding Week
Tuesday: Dine to Offset the Wine.
Terrace, eight-thirty p.m.

I DON'T JUST need the food to offset the wine, I need
it to distract from the chaos within. I can't get a handle on anything. The afternoon with my family, the
dancing, the laughter, the fun. The joy with Faye. The
insane passion. The heat that never ebbs.

I can't remember the last time I let a woman take
control like that, made me climax in her hands, so out
of control that I didn't want to stop myself from coming in her grip. And to witness the pleasure she took
from it too… Even now the heat pulses through my
body, and I drag in a breath. I release it slowly and
force my body to calm as my knee brushes against
hers under the table.

I only have to lean to the left and I can smell her
perfume and feel her body warmth penetrate mine.
I'm hooked on her. As hooked on her as I was on day

one and I can't imagine it ever dying out. Which of course it will. But right now...

I slip my hand beneath the table and stroke her thigh above her dress. I hear the slightest catch in her breath, her eyes flickering in my direction before they go back to Dante on the other side of her and she continues their conversation. But then her hand is there, slipping over mine, and the simple connection makes me content and alive in one.

The whole table is buzzing with chatter, but I'm attuned only to her, and as she forks up a piece of Nonna's famous tiramisu and slips it into her mouth I can almost feel her pleasure.

'This is so good,' she murmurs, her hum of appreciation teasing me to the core.

'Nothing beats Nonna's tiramisu,' Dante says, raising a glass to the woman herself sitting at the head of the table.

'There's more, if I can tempt you?' Nonna says.

Faye shakes her head, her hand leaving mine to press against her stomach. 'I'd love to but I'm afraid I can't. I don't think I'll sleep if I eat any more. I'm not quite sure how you all manage to eat so late.'

'Ah, yes,' my mother chimes in. 'It is the Italian way, I'm afraid. It does take some getting used to.'

'Well, *you*, *sorella*, wouldn't need to get used to it if you came back more,' says Aunt Netta.

'Hey, Mamma, let it go.' Dante's severe frown is for his mother alone, but she doesn't need it; she's already smiling softly, her eyes damp at the corners as she looks at my mother.

'What I mean is, I've missed you, Marianna. If I'd known a wedding would bring you back here sooner, I would have been breathing down Dante's neck a lot more.'

'Well, it's not Dante's fault Sienna decided on a small, intimate arrangement for her wedding,' my mother returns swiftly.

Here we go... I lift my wine glass and take a sip, preparing to intervene as Sienna looks up from her conversation with Lorenzo. 'We're not doing this again, are we?'

'No.' Giovanni tries to intercede but Aunt Netta's already talking over him.

'It's hardly Sienna's fault, or Dante's, that Rafael hasn't seen fit to find himself a wife. Lord knows it's about time he did.'

The wine catches in my throat and I almost choke on it. 'What—?'

'Now look what you've done,' Dante says, though I can hear the laughter in his voice. 'You've almost killed the man by putting him in the same sentence as marriage.'

'There's nothing wrong with marriage,' Aunt Netta blusters. 'And the sooner you two realise it the better. If my Roberto were still alive, we'd show you a thing or two about what makes life worth living!'

She has both Dante and me in her sights now and I shake my head. *Do we really have to do this, right, now?*

'Marriage isn't for everyone.' It's my diplomatic answer, one that I hope will bring the conversation to a close, but I feel all eyes on me…on me and on Faye—or am I just being paranoid? My hand eases discreetly back to my lap. 'But it's certainly right for Dani and Tyler… In fact, let's have a toast. It's not the big day yet but there's nothing to stop us raising a glass to the beautiful bride and groom. May their love last, and may life be kind. To Dani and Tyler.'

'Dani and Tyler.' Glasses are raised, cheers are made, but I get the impression my words aren't positive enough, and Nonna's eyeing me with far too much speculation.

Still, at least no one is badgering me openly any more.

I reach for Faye beneath the table again, but she edges away.

'I'm just going to take a short walk.' She lifts up her wine glass and, though her voice is pleasant enough, she won't meet my eye as she smiles to the table. 'See if it helps all the fabulous food go down.'

I watch her go. Her pace is steady, yet I feel she's running. The question is, from what?

'I'll just go and…keep her company.' I'm already pushing back from the table. I don't care if it looks strange or if Dani suspects there's something going on. I need to know she's okay, because all my senses tell me she isn't.

I catch her up as she reaches the opening to the pool.

'Running away?' I try to make it sound breezy.

She sips her wine before turning to me, her smile small. 'Are you?'

Her eyes seem to swim in the lights of the pool, and I feel a tightness in my chest I can't comprehend.

'I asked you first...'

She laughs but it's awkward, panicked, even. I close the distance between us and she straightens and turns away to look at the view beyond the pool.

'My family are pretty full-on,' I say softly.

Yes, blame the family, it's so much easier than blaming yourself.

'Si?'

She flicks me a look. Her smile is weak, her shrug too, and I can't bear it. But what can I do, what can I say?

'I like it,' she says. 'It's nice to be part of something big, something whole. I have no one except for my father now. My parents were only children—no siblings, no cousins, no grandparents left. I sometimes wonder what it would be like to be part of something more...'

'You really don't; it's a pain in the—' I stop. It's not the time to tease or joke or to make light of her situation. 'I'm sorry.'

I reach for her before I can stop myself, my palm soft on her lower back as I wait for her to look at me. And when she does, my throat closes over at the sadness in her eyes. It's all the more painful for the smile she still tries to give.

I cup her jaw, stroke her cheek and stare down into her eyes. 'I guess it's too easy to take family for granted when you have one.'

She turns her head into my palm, closes her eyes

and breathes in softly. I don't speak. I can't. I'm lost in that look, the way she appears to take comfort from the touch, even when I've played the fool.

'They're a good bunch,' she says eventually, her lashes lifting, her eyes meeting mine.

'And you—you have a good heart and deserve more.'

'I…' She lets out a small sigh. 'That's nice of you to say.'

I replay the words and my intention. I mean she deserves to have a big family to love and be loved in return. Instead, I'm thinking of me and her; I'm thinking of Dante, of all the other men out there that she could spend her time with, better men than me. And then I remember Dante's revelation about her marriage. She had a man who promised to love her and then…what?

'Faye.' I wet my lips, my frown impossible to prevent. 'Why didn't you tell me you were married?'

She starts. And I can't blame her when my question seems to come from nowhere.

'I'm not.'

'I mean, before…'

She steps out of my hold, her eyes going back to the view, her arms hugging her middle as she cradles her wine glass in one hand. 'It didn't seem important. It wasn't… It's not like this is serious between us.'

Her eyes flit in my direction, assessing my response, and I know I'm impassive and doing everything I can not to show the confused state of my feelings. Because I don't want to confuse her. I don't want her to think that this is something more. Something serious. Something with any longevity. I'm not that man. And one whirlwind fling isn't going to change that, no matter how impassioned, how intense…

'It's hardly like we're dating.' She's trying to tease now, the jovial tone to her voice at odds with her rigid posture and her sad smile.

'No.' She's right. We're not, and I need to acknowledge it, but in the same breath… 'I don't know, though. It feels like something I should have known.'

'There's nothing for you to know. Not really. Bobby and I met at uni and married soon after. It didn't work out.'

'What went wrong?' *And why are you even asking when it only brings you closer together?*

But it seems I can't let it go. I want to understand. I want to know how a man could have the desire and good sense to commit to her and then let her go.

She drags in a breath and blows it out. 'We were young and we were busy so much of the time. We had five good years, pursuing our careers. We worked in the same role for the same company and our sales sent us all over the world. We saw each other two weeks in every four and then I got promoted. It pushed me to the top of the ladder…above him.'

'And he didn't like it?'

She takes a sip of her wine and scoffs softly. 'I thought he was okay with it, and it made so much sense for me to be the one settled in the UK more; I thought it made more sense for the place we were at.'

'Place?'

A shrug. 'The promotion to director meant I wasn't racing around the world selling any more. I was in the UK. I was at home, settled, ready for...'

She breaks off and chews the corner of her lip.

But I know where this is heading, and the truth triggers a strange twisting sensation in my gut. 'For children?'

I know I'm right. I see it in her awkward smile and the way she won't meet my eye.

'Yes.'

'You must have loved him very much.' It's come out tight, constricted by my gut that continues to writhe.

'At one time. And I'm sure he loved me too...but then everything changed.'

'He was bitter?'

'I'm not sure bitter's the right word. With me being home more, we were able to spend more time together when he was in the UK, and we did, but...' She frowns. 'I don't know. It just felt like we were going through the motions, putting ticks in boxes, fulfilling a life plan at a hundred miles an hour. Then my mum died and I just shut down. We didn't connect any more, we didn't talk, we didn't...we didn't have sex. Eventually, he'd had enough of waiting for me to come round, to go back to how I was. He accused me of being a workaholic, of being boring; he said that the person he fell in love with was no more.'

'Bastardo!'

Her head whips around to face me, her eyes flaring at my outburst. But I'm angry, so angry at a man I don't even know, because he wasn't worthy of her. He promised her so much and left when she needed him the most.

'He should have looked after you, not run.'

She lowers her gaze. 'It wasn't all his fault.'

I can't believe she's defending him. How can she not see that what he did to her was wrong? I reach for her arms, caress her skin and wait for her to look at me.

'Can't you see he shouldn't have treated you like that? Made you feel that way?'

'You don't understand. I did change. Bobby was right. I... I did lose my love of life, the ability to laugh and enjoy it. I wasn't an easy person to be around.'

'You were his wife, Faye.' I'm vehement, and there are warning bells ringing between my ears, but I can't stop. 'He swore to love you in the good times *and* the bad.'

Her eyes search mine, quietly curious, and I fear what she will say next before she says, 'Is that—is that why you won't ever marry? Because you won't promise yourself to a woman for fear of failing her? If you don't promise, you can't fail.'

I swallow and shake my head. 'I won't marry because of many reasons.'

'But that is one?'

I close my eyes and open them again, knowing what I have to say but not wanting to say it. '*Si*. But with love comes the power of pain, and the ability to destroy a man…or a woman…when it's taken away. Through fate, through choice, whatever reason. It is not a given. It is not a guarantee. You can't control it.'

'And so you run away from it? You're scared of it.'

I want to refute that. I'm never scared. I don't run away. And yet…

'I guess I do.'

'Maybe you just haven't met the right woman.'

I want to laugh. My insides tremble with the shock of it, the force of it. She *is* the right woman. If ever there was someone I could fall in love with, it's her. I know it as well as I know I can't do it. I can't let myself go there.

She takes a shaky breath and steps out of my hold. I can see her physically shutting down. 'We should get back. They'll be wondering where we've got to, and we don't want Dani to suspect any more than she already does.'

I want to stop her. I want to say so much more. I want to promise her the world, to take away her sorrow, and I can do none of that. It would only make me as bad as her ex-husband. And so I nod and gesture for her to lead the way. My gut rolls, my chest aches and I understand none of it. In all my adult life, I don't remember being this confused, this…helpless.

'There you both are!'

I lift my gaze to the head of the path to see Dani standing there, one hand on her hip, a glass of wine in the other.

'We're all ready for another game of cards, and

I'm not pairing with Mamma this time, Rafael. It's your turn.'

I rake a hand through my hair and manage a smile, grateful for the normality, even if it does come via my family.

'Cards again? Why can't we just have a quiet nightcap, a civilised early night before tomorrow's fun?'

'Are you serious?' Dani blurts.

'Maybe.'

'*Dio*, Rafael! When did you get so old?'

I wince. 'Enough of the old.'

'There'll be enough of the old when you stop being a party pooper and running away with the maid of honour!'

The air catches and Faye tenses up in front of me, her laugh too high. 'Well, this maid of honour is just going to freshen up. I'll come and join you shortly.'

She hurries past Dani and we both watch her go, the tension building around us. I know there's an on-slaught coming; the air positively thrums with it but I'm not ready to go there, not when I'm still reeling from my conversation with Faye.

'You don't need to worry about playing cards with Marianna tonight.' I force her onto a topic I'm surprisingly comfortable with. 'I think Giovanni has that role well covered.'

She eyes me as she takes a sip of her drink and closes the distance between us. 'You've noticed, then?'

'It's impossible to miss.'

'Funny story there...' She waves her glass at me. 'It turns out it was Aunt Netta's plan all along.'

'What was?'

'To bring Giovanni, to try to relight an age-old spark and see her sister happy again.'

I frown. 'They were never...'

'No.' She smiles at me, her big brown eyes soft and warm. 'But Giovanni has loved her for as long as Papà. Apparently, they met the same night but Papà got in there first. It seems Giovanni has never quite forgotten her.'

'Right.' I nod as I let that sink in. 'It's a good job I stopped her bringing her own man after all, then.'

She hums her agreement and I give a small chuckle. 'I really wasn't expecting that.'

'No, I don't think Mamma was either, but she seems happy. Happier than I've ever known her to be. It's nice... It's even nicer still to see you two getting along so much better, you and Mamma.'

I exhale softly. She's right, it does feel better. We've some way to go, but...

'Maybe you really should take some time while we're out here, away from work and life's little distractions, to talk to her. Properly, I mean...'

'Now you sound like Faye.'

It's out before I think better of it. Here I am, trying to avoid talking about Faye, and I'm the one who brings her up. I glance her way and regret it even more. Her brows are raised, her eyes glinting with something. Not quite alarm, but she's not exactly at ease either.

'Is that why the two of you seem to be attached at the hip? She's talking you through your issues with our mother?'

'Yes, we've talked about it,' I say, ignoring her exaggeration that's not as much of an exaggeration as it should be. 'She's surprisingly easy to talk to.'

Dani goes quiet, too quiet.

'Whatever you're thinking...' I flick her look. 'Just say it.'

'I'm worried.' She raises her free hand, palm out. 'I don't know what's going on between the two of you, *fratellone*, but don't mess her around, okay?'

'Says the woman who wanted to throw her to the wolves.'

She laughs, her eyes dancing now. 'I *wanted* to throw her at Dante.'

'And you think he's a better man than me?'

Why am I even encouraging this conversation?

She's quiet again and her eyes turn sombre. 'It's different.'

'Why? Because he's not your brother?'

'No.' She's resolute as she pins me with a hard stare. 'Because he is Dante. He's young, he's all about the fun, he can show her a good time.'

'And I can't?'

'You, my dear brother, will chew her up and spit her out.'

'I'm so glad you have such a high opinion of me,' I say, not bothering to hide how much it stings.

'I do have a high opinion of you, and I'm scared. With Dante there can be no confusion, Raf. She knows what she's getting, there's no risk…no risk of her falling in love.'

'In love?' I shake my head and refuse to accept how her words chime with the warning bells that are ringing ever louder. '*Sorellina*, you are deluded.'

'Don't mock me, Raf. I *know* Faye, and I *know* you.'

'Is that right?'

'I see the way she looks at you, and I know this can only ever be a bit of fun for you. But for her… She wants it all. She'll fall for you and then what? You'll pass her up, like you have done every woman before, and I'll be left with the guilt of her heartbreak and all at the hands of my brother. Don't shake your head at me.'

I don't even realise I'm still doing it, but I don't want to listen to her opinion any more. Or the way it resonates with what Faye has told me. Her dreams of a future, of children and settling down, all things I could never offer her. All things that her ex promised and took away.

But I haven't promised her more. I haven't promised her anything.

'She's a grown woman, Dani, more than capable of looking out for herself. You don't need to fight her corner.'

'I do if it means protecting her from you.' She places a hand on my arm to soften the blow of her words. '*Ti voglio bene, fratellone*. But Faye…leave her alone. You are the stuff of dreams, the Italian billionaire from the romance novels she adores. Handsome, honourable, lovable, though you try hard not to be…'

I swallow down the wedge forming in my throat. The wedge of guilt, realisation and a need to refute it all.

'You will break her heart. You won't mean to, but…' She wets her lips and attempts a smile. 'There are just a few more days left. Surely you can resist her for a little longer?'

Resist.

She's right to ask it of me. *Diavolo*, I should be telling myself to resist with all that I've learned. But to never kiss Faye again, to avoid…

'Please, *fratellone*.'

I focus on Dani's imploring gaze and feel myself nod. 'You have no need to worry.'

Because ultimately, Faye knows this is temporary. Just a hot fling. That's been clear between us, hasn't it?

And though I believe it—I do—it still leaves a bitter taste on my tongue.

'Bene.' She pats my arm and pulls me into a tight embrace. *'Grazie,* Rafael. *Grazie.'*

I barely move, as her gratitude makes me feel like a fraud, a liar, a brother who cannot be trusted. And I am none of those things. I'm not.

Only, Faye… She makes me forget myself.

CHAPTER ELEVEN

Danielle and Tyler's Wedding Week
Thursday: Seafood and Sailing.

'COME ON, FAYE! It's no good having a yacht for the day if we're going to spend most of our time docked in port.'

Dani's hanging over the side rail, her bikini-clad body a bronze vision against the vivid blue sky above, her brown eyes dancing as brightly as her teasing grin.

'I'm coming! I'm coming!' I rush out over the stab of guilt that they're all waiting for me. But then, I'd hardly been thinking clearly when we set off from the castle this morning, hence why I had to go back for the swimsuit I left behind…for a day of swimming and sailing. Yeah, I'm *that* distracted.

I look to the gangway beneath my feet, careful not to lose my footing and end up in the water. Because that would really top the day off, even the last forty-eight hours.

I'm not missing him. I'm not.

How can I when we're virtually always within talking distance? Granted, there are always people between us too, something which feels very much orchestrated by him. And I should be grateful, really, really grateful, that Rafael's preventing the temptation of anything else happening between us. But my body's less inclined to agree.

Yes, it's just your body, not something more... something more real.

But opening up to him as I did only made the connection between us run deeper, stronger...and I'd foolishly started to hope, to dream, that he could change. That he could want more from this too.

Instead, he's reaffirmed his bachelor status, and it's left me reeling. And it's not even his fault. He never promised me more. I was properly warned. I wasn't supposed to fall for him.

'All okay?' Dani descends the stairs in front of me and I swear she's glowing, her happiness radiating.

'Absolutely.'

She beams at me. 'You'll be wanting to change, then?'

She eyes my maxi dress, which is neither sailing-worthy nor swim-worthy. 'Please.'

'You brought the red bikini, right?'

I roll my eyes. 'Yes. And will you let up? I think Dante and I have established a nice, *platonic* relationship. I don't need any more meddling from you.'

'Let me be the judge of that. It's been too long, Faye.' She hooks her arm through mine and leads me deeper into the yacht. 'It's time you buried Bobby under a stack of adventurous fun, and Dante is just the man.'

My cheeks flush and I pray my sunglasses help to hide my discomfort, my guilt. *If only she knew...*

'You can change in the master suite. Nothing less for my awesome maid of honour.'

I follow her up a set of stairs, taking in the impressive yacht as we go. I've been on yachts before, mainly for corporate functions, but this is on another level.

Does Rafael own this as well? I stop myself. It's none of my business. None at all.

The engine noise changes, and I hear what must be the gangway being stowed away.

'And we're off!' Dani declares, sending me a smile over her shoulder as she leads us up another floor. 'This is the owner's deck. Everyone else is downstairs. Just follow the steps back down two levels and head towards the front when you're done. In the meantime, you have this to yourself.'

She waves a hand at the hot tub, with its outer ring of cushions to lounge on, the mini-bar complete with stools, and then backs up towards the double glass doors that lead inside. She pushes one open.

'Off you go, and don't be too long!'

I laugh as I bat her away. 'Yes, Bridezilla!'

'Hey, I'm milking the bride status for all it's worth.' She winks as she says it and I give her another playful shove as I pass her by. The door clicks shut behind me and I stop in my tracks.

Wow. Just, wow.

In a high-end hotel I'd be impressed, but on water… The contemporary grey, white and chrome soothes as much as it impresses, and I'm almost scared to touch anything for fear of leaving my sweaty fingerprints behind.

I wander on, checking through the open doors as I go. There's a walk-in wardrobe bigger than my bedroom at home, a bathroom with a sunken tub for at least six, a glass shower enclosure with double heads and a floating bed that makes the most of a glass-walled one-hundred-and-eighty-degree view of the horizon.

I carefully place my bag down on the bed and open it up, scouting out the red string bikini—another of the items Dani coaxed me into buying. I pull it out and give a little wince. It's practically non-existent and very…strappy. Then I think of Rafael seeing me in it and a thrill runs through me.

It doesn't matter that he's reaffirmed his bachelor status, that he appears to have avoided me since we talked about my divorce. He hasn't faked the way he feels about me when it comes to sex. And this thing *screams* sex.

My lips are already lifting as I head for the bathroom. There are only two days left before the wedding, three before we part ways, and I want to maximise every chance I get to enjoy him. *All* of him.

But first, a quick shower wouldn't go amiss. I'm hot and sweaty after my dash in the mid-morning heat, and while I have this place to myself with all the high-end toiletries ready and waiting... Well, it would be rude not to.

The shower is heavenly, but I don't hang about. It feels a bit like trespassing on someone else's domain. Silly, when I know it's ours for the day. I shut the water off and dry myself before picking up the tiny bundle of red.

I eye it and take a deep breath. Well, here goes. The bondage-style affair is a bitch to get into, but the effect, as Dani informed me, is totally worth it.

I only hope Rafael agrees.

I can't douse the smile building now.

'What is it about weddings that has companies adding a zero to the end of everything?'

I don't mind saying it out loud to Dante. Dani and the rest of the guests are all on the lower deck enjoying the view and the plunge pool. My niece and nephew are haranguing the deckhands, begging for a go on the jet-skis, and Faye... Well, she's here somewhere, and I'm damned if my body doesn't want to find out where.

'I wouldn't know and I don't plan on finding out. You can afford it though, Raf...' he gives a carefree shrug '...so what does it matter?'

'It matters because I feel like they see you coming. Maybe I should consider setting up a company, one that offers events at reasonable prices. Reckon it would do quite well.'

Dante erupts into a belly laugh now. 'You? The

billionaire bachelor owning a wedding company? Brilliant. Truly brilliant.'

I even manage a grin myself. 'You laugh now, but just you wait...'

My phone starts up in my chest pocket and I pull it out. 'I need to take this.'

It's the call I've been expecting, to authorise payment for some last-minute tweaks to the wedding breakfast. It's also a good excuse to hide out for a few minutes and rebuild my defences before I have to face Faye again. It's getting harder and harder to resist being around her, to resist pulling her aside and doing all the wicked things my body so desperately wants to do. And it's not just the wicked things either; I *want* to talk with her. About the wedding, my family, her past... *Diavolo*, anything.

I've managed to keep people between us since I promised Dani but the closer we get to the wedding, the closer we get to parting ways altogether and it's not sitting well. Not in the slightest.

And any second now I will see her again, wearing another blasted swimsuit, and I'll have to keep myself in check.

I feel another cold shower coming on.

Call, then shower, then Faye.

All in that order.

I swipe the phone to answer. *'Ciao?'*

I run through the details with the wedding planner as I make my way to the owner's deck. It's been a while since I've been on the yacht and I really should take more time out to enjoy it. Perhaps when the wedding is over, I should stop for a bit. Spend some time at sea. Get a woman to accompany me, a woman who can get me over my incessant need for Faye.

And yet the idea leaves me cold…

'Signor Perez? Signor Perez?'

I silently curse my loss of focus. She's not even here and she has me distracted. *'Si, scusi.'*

I throw my attention into the call, go through the adjustments and authorise the payment as I enter the cabin and head for the bathroom. *'Grazie mille, ciao.'*

I re-pocket my phone, push open the bathroom door and…

Faye!

She screams. I scream. I swear my heart has just launched into my throat. And then my eyes dart down her body and back up. What the actual…?

'Turn around!'

I spin on my heel, my brain and pulse racing. 'What are you…? Why are you…?'

I can't even get the question out. All I can see in my mind's eye is her body, arms caught up in some… some red…some red…*rope?*

'I'm getting dressed,' she squeaks.

'In red string?' I can't keep the amusement out of my voice, or the heat that's surged south. My body saw too much, far too much…

'It's a…it's a bikini. Or at least, it's supposed to be.'

'I'm sorry, I'll leave you to…' I wave a hand in the air, my grin growing by the second as I head back through the doorway.

She makes a sound very akin to a grunt and there's the definite sound of tearing. *'Shit.'*

I stop. 'Everything...okay?'

'Yes. No. Yes. *Shit.*'

'You want to make up your mind?'

'I don't believe it. This can't be happening.'

'Want to explain?'

I can hear movement and her breath straining out of her but she doesn't speak. I angle my head to the side—not enough to see her, but enough for her to see me frown. 'Are you okay back there?'

'I... I think I might need your help.'

I have to stop my lips quirking up. So many ideas are racing through my mind. None of which are conducive to my brotherly vow.

'What do you need?'

I hear her blow out a breath. 'I think I've broken my bikini and now I'm stuck.'

'In your bikini?' I say it slowly. This has to be the most surreal encounter of my life. Finding her naked in my pool comes a close second. 'We really need to stop meeting like this, you know?'

It's my attempt at humour but the flustered breath that comes out next tells me she doesn't find it funny.

'When you've stopped entertaining yourself with my predicament, do you think you could back your way up here and see fit to actually help me?'

'Well, in order to do that, you know I need to turn back round, *si*?'

'Yes.' It comes out as a resigned huff and I have to chuckle as I turn.

'Don't worry, it's nothing I haven't seen before…'
Only, it kind of is. She has one arm hooked over her
head, the other wrapped around her front, and for
the life of me I can't work out how she got herself
into the position let alone how she's managed to get
her breasts pointing this way and that.

'Don't *fucking* look.'

My eyes snap to hers. 'How can I untangle you
if I can't look?'

'You know what I mean. Stop. *Staring*. Down.
There!' She gestures at her exposed bits with wild
eyes and does a little jig that has the knot of hair on
top of her head bobbing and those bits jiggling all the
more and begging to be looked at. I want to laugh.
I also want to confess that she is still the sexiest
women I've ever set eyes on, her cheeks all flushed,
her crystal-blue depths blazing, her lips parting to
puff loose strands of hair out of her eyes.

I suppress the laugh with what I hope is a sympathetic smile and walk up to her. 'Okay.'

Our eyes meet and her fresh, clean scent assails
my senses. I see the shower floor glisten behind her
and realise she's not long been out, and all I want
to do is back her up into it and soap her up afresh.

The idea takes over… Her tied up and me…

'You know… I'm not so sure I want to help.' My
eyes return to hers and I let every carnal thought
come through in my gaze as I step closer. I mean,
give me a break; there's no way I can walk away
from this now. My vow to Dani be damned…

She swallows audibly. 'What do you mean?'

'I mean…' I reach out and trail my hand down her front, and watch her breath catch and her skin colour as she pulls against her restraints. 'Do you have any idea how sexy you are?'

'Like this?' She eyes me, disbelieving, but tiny little breaths escape her parted lips and the fresh rush of colour in her cheeks has nothing to do with embarrassment now.

'You are effectively tied up, *cara mia*. If I want to touch you… I can.'

I brush my hand ever so slightly against one nipple and she inhales sharply, her bottom lip trapped in her teeth, her eyes flaring wildly.

'You can tell me to stop and I will untangle you, Faye.' My voice is gruff, my pulse elevating with my thoughts. 'Or you can accept your restraints and let me pleasure you.'

I tweak her nipple. *'Raf!'*

It comes out like a plea.

'What, *cara*?' I circle both nipples now, my touch so light it's barely there, and she arches into the caress, her nipples forming sharp, teasing points.

'Don't torment me.'

'No?' I take another step closer and she takes one back.

'No…' She drags in a breath and stares up at me in challenge 'Not unless…'

'Unless?' I cup both her breasts and feel their heat as I roll my thumbs over each pebbled nub.

It's seconds before she can speak, seconds before

she unclamps her bottom lip as she fights the pleasure that runs through her.

'Not unless you finish what you start.'

'Oh, *cara mia*, don't you worry about that. I intend to finish…and do a whole lot more.'

Her eyes blaze and I step forward, forcing her back into the shower enclosure. I raise my hand to the detachable hose and take it off its hook.

'What are you…?'

I switch it on, ignoring her question as the water pummels the base of the shower. 'Tell me, *cara mia*, have you ever got yourself off with running water?'

'But your clothes…you're going to get soaked.'

My smile is one-sided. 'Think I care?'

Her cheeks flush deeper. 'Raf… I…'

I stare down her front to the two exposed peaks that are pleading for attention. 'Tell me, does this feel nice?'

I aim the jets at her breasts and watch her writhe beneath the pressure, her arm above her head trying to lower, the other to lift. Her whimper pushes me to go further and I raise my free hand to one breast and pinch it tight. She positively bucks, her head pressing back into the shower wall.

'And this?' I toy with the other one and watch her eyes close. Her cry is desperate and, *cazzo*, my cock swells against the zipper of my chinos, desperate for release, the fabric starting to cling as the trouser legs take a soaking. And I don't care. I have others in the bedroom. Nothing will stop me from taking advantage of this gift.

'I can do anything I want to you right now, Faye.' Her eyes flare open but they are glazed, hooded. 'Does that excite you?'

I know it does. I don't need her answer but, as I trail the jets of water over her front, I wait for it anyway.

'Yes, Rafael, Yes.'

'Bene.' I dip my mouth to hers and kiss her slowly but as she leans into me, looking for more, I break away. To control my own need as much as to tease her further.

'Do you want to see how much it excites me too?'

She nods her head, her eyes lowering to the obvious bulge in my trousers. With my free hand, I unbutton them, lower the zipper and release my cock to her eager gaze.

'Commando?' she asks, gasping.

I fist my erection, give it one long stroke and watch her take in the move. 'Now I want to feel how excited you are.'

I slip my hand beneath the arm that is still trapped across her front and feel her stomach suck in, her eyes intent on mine. There is no rejection, only desire. And, as I slip inside the tiny triangle that protects her modesty, she tilts into my touch, trying to take me deeper.

'Yes, Raf, please.'

I skim over her seam, feel her curls slick with her need, and trail back up towards her breasts.

'Raf.' She writhes, her arms pulling against the tangled red binding, her eyes pleading for me to give

her what she needs, what her body needs, but I'm in no mood to hurry this.

'Do you trust me, Faye?'

She frowns up at me, her breasts lifting with her breath, each rose-pink peak straining through the bands of red, desperate, needy.

'Do you?'

Her lashes flicker and her eyes soften into mine. 'Yes.'

It's a breathy whisper, so honest and raw, and it cuts deep. *Idiota.* I wanted her to trust me. I wanted her consent to take this further. Instead, she has given me so much more. The depth of feeling that blazes in her eyes catches in her voice.

I shake off the sudden panic. I shake it off and focus on the heat, the need, the lust that I know I can provoke, the heights I know I'm capable of taking her to. This is just sex. Great sex. An opportunity I cannot waste. Nothing more.

I spin her away from me and place the shower head back in its holder. I trace the bands of red down her body, my fingers grazing over her skin. I fist my hand in the straps between her shoulder blades and yank her back towards me. Her head turns, her mouth seeking out the crushing pressure of mine, and I delve my tongue in deep, feasting on her heady whimpers, her taste, her heat.

'I'm going to fuck you so hard, Faye. Is that what you want?'

Her nod is hurried, her eyes flaring wildly, her cheeks flushed with lust.

I slide my free hand down her front beneath the small red triangle and separate her seam to feel her wetness, to feel her clit all swollen for me. I let her roll into my touch, let her take some of what she needs, some of what I need too.

'You're so wet.'

Her hum of agreement is hitched.

I sink inside her, feeling her pulse around my fingers, and I know how desperate she is for this.

And what about how desperate you are? More desperate than you've ever been before...

I step back and release her and she goes to turn.

'No. Stay facing the wall.'

She does exactly as I ask. Her gorgeous body is bound, her luscious round arse barely concealed beneath the triangle of red, her shoulders shuddering with every breath she takes. I throw my shirt aside, uncaring of the phone still tucked inside, and shuck the rest of my clothes until I'm naked and so fucking hard I fear I'll come before her. And then I remember...condom.

I take one out of the discreet container in the vanity unit and tear it open, my eyes feasting on her bound and waiting as I sheath myself, my teeth gritted against the sensation that feels more teasing than it should thanks to my heightened state.

'I want you.' I come up behind her, my mouth to her ear. 'So badly.'

I nip at her lobe and she whimpers, her arse wriggling back, seeking out my hardness.

'I want you more than I've ever wanted another soul.'

The words are out before I stop them. But they are the truth; this is true. And I don't want to suppress it. I can be honest in sex.

I hook my fingers into the band of her bottoms and roll them down her thighs, bending my knees as I lower myself down her body, my tongue following the same teasing trail.

'Step out,' I say as my fingers brush her ankles, her teasing anklet, and strip the fabric from her feet. I toss it away and take my time as I rise back up her body.

'Step wider.'

She shuffles her feet apart, so obedient, so fucking hot.

I reach for the shower head once more and bring it over her front as I lower my mouth to her ear.

'I'm going to make you come with this.'

She goes to turn and stops, remembering my command as she turns her head instead.

I raise the shower head, my grin loaded. 'Another first?'

She doesn't have to answer me. I know. I can read it in her face. I take hold of the bands between her shoulder blades again and turn, encouraging us to rotate so she's facing the glass wall of the shower and the mirror beyond.

'See how sexy you are?'

Her mouth is slack with desire, her colour high, her eyes shying away from the image she presents.

'Look, *cara*, see you as I see you...'

She focuses, her eyes sweeping over her length before connecting with mine through the mirror. 'Do you see?'

She wets her lips, nods.

'You are exquisite.'

Her lashes flutter as she takes in my words.

'You are not boring. Your ex was a fool. You deserve to be worshipped, adored...'

Loved. I want to say loved. It's there, choking up my throat, and I force it down as I trail the jets over her front, smooth my hand over her curls and slip inside her folds. I spread her open to our gaze, to the jets that I send lower, lower still, until she rocks back against me, her cry trapped in her throat, her body pulsating against mine...

'What the...? Oh, my fucking God! Raf... Raf!' I feel her pull against her bindings. Her body shudders as the water works over her clit, unrelenting, incessant, and she's stiffening up head to toe.

'That's it, *cara*, let go.'

She's whimpering, her body lifting on her toes, pressing back against me. Her breaths turn jagged, fast, and then she bucks, crying out so hard with her climax. It's all I can do to hold myself steady, to stop myself from losing my all with my cock pressed tight between our bodies, my eyes feasting on the carnal sight before me in the mirror. It's rippling through her with such force and I drink it all in, transfixed, the lustful haze fogging up my brain and making me want to drive myself deep inside her.

I ease the water away and palm her with my free hand as I hold her sated body against me and return the shower head to its holder.

'I'm so hard for you.' My voice is thick with it.

'Then take me, Raf...' She holds my gaze in the mirror. 'Now. Fuck me hard.'

Cazzo. I grit my teeth against the intense wave of pleasure that runs through my body. It's like she's had an awakening. I see the determination in her face, the lust, the carnal wants taking over and merging with mine.

I hiss in a breath and roughly grasp her bikini top, tugging her back for a tongue-sinking kiss.

'Now lean forward,' I rasp out. She edges forward, too tentative as she tries to keep her balance with her arms all bound. 'More.'

I pull on the binding to show her with the action that I've got her. 'More.'

Her arse nudges me back as she does as I ask, bending until I stop her with my grip on her bonds. I grip my cock and shift my body lower until I meet with her tight, wet heat, and in one thrust I bury myself inside her. My growl is drowned out by her cry, her pleasure ringing through the room, through me. I grip the binding tighter, riding her deeper, harder, just as she demanded.

Our eyes lock in the mirror. Her breasts strain against the binding that tightens with my grip, her entire body rocking with every thrust, her skin pink with her orgasm. It's too much, all too much. My thrusts turn jagged. The sensation, her surrender, my power over her that feels as if it's really her power over me…

And suddenly I'm coming, so fucking hard my cry is guttural, my body shaken to the core. So shaken I can't dwell on it and I override it with more. More passion, more lust. As the pleasure tries to relax my limbs, I tug her back and pull out as I turn her, forcing her back up against the wall. I drop to my knees, my mouth on her pussy, my tongue flicking at her clit, and she's moaning, her head falling forward to look me in the eye, her body trembling, her legs quaking.

'Raf… Raf… I can't, not so soon.'

Want to bet?

She's panting above me and I see what she isn't even aware of yet: her climax building. I chuckle low in my throat as I keep tasting her. I can never get enough. I can't. I blame the abstinence, the forced avoidance over the last forty-eight hours. It makes every sensation more acute now, the taste of her, the feel of her, the sound of her.

Carnal, salacious, wanton.

And then she's bucking off the wall, her cry intense as I hold her steady and let her orgasm take over. She's so perfect and she has no idea. I stay there until she calms, stay until I think I can look her in the eye and act as if all is okay.

I press a kiss to her curls, her stomach, between her breasts. I reach her lips and cup her face.

'Now I will release you.' I smile into her eyes, fighting the surge of warmth that seems to swell around my heart.

'That was…' She laughs softly. 'There are no words.'

I grin, praying it masks the strength of feeling I can't get a grip on. 'Glad I can be of service. As for this…' I eye the bikini top. 'I have no idea how to get this off, not in one piece.'

'I've already torn it somewhere.'

'True.'

'So, you could just tear it off me.'

I try to laugh with her, but inside my gut is rolling, my heart is racing and I'm losing it, my trusty control. I grip the fabric in my hands and tear it apart, feeling a similar sensation deep inside. It takes away my ability to breathe, to think. I focus on peeling the top from her body and see the red lines marring her skin the more I unwrap. My gut rolls anew.

'Did I hurt you?'

'No!' she rushes out, her hands palming my chest, her eyes earnest, so earnest. 'Are you crazy? That has to be up there with one of the best experiences of my life!'

Her compliment should make me happy. It should provoke my ego or spur a cocky response. Instead I trace the lines with my fingers. 'Are you sure?'

She laughs softly, her hands lifting to my hair. 'Do I look hurt?'

I swallow and force my eyes to hers. One second

passes, two. There's so much I want to say, so much I can't, so much I don't understand.

'No.'

Not yet, adds my inner conscience, and Dani's words are quick on their tail: *You will break her heart. You won't mean to, but...*

I swallow again and step out of her hold. 'We should get out of here before we're both missed.'

I see the disappointment in her gaze, I feel it deep inside, and I want to kill it off. I want to fork my fingers through her hair, back her up against the shower wall and kiss her until we're high on sex again.

'You're right.' She grins, but too widely. 'I'm late enough to the party as it is.'

I turn away to sort myself out and the crumpled red fabric catches my eye. 'Do you have another swimsuit? If not, I can—'

'I'm fine. I have another.'

'Not...' I remember the pool. 'Not the black number?'

'Is that a problem?' She pulls the shower head off its rest and starts to rinse between her legs. Her intention is innocent enough but it burns through me. Right along with the memory of her in that swimsuit.

Cazzo. 'No, no problem.'

She lifts her gaze to me, her eyes sparkling now. 'Good. You want to come and get clean?'

I swallow, toss the condom in the bin and walk towards her.

But as I join her and our eyes meet, Dani's words

come back ever louder: *I know this can only ever be a bit of fun for you but for her... She wants it all, Raf. She'll fall for you and then what?*

Then what? exactly...

CHAPTER TWELVE

Danielle and Tyler's Wedding Week
Saturday: The Wedding. Five-thirty p.m.

I TAKE HOLD OF Dani's hands and give them a squeeze. 'You ready?'

She gives a rapid nod and I feel her nerves through her trembling fingers.

'Just breathe,' I say.

Her emotions have been running high ever since I entered her room this morning armed with a bustling team of hair and make-up artists ready to make us look the part. I've never seen her less than a hundred percent confident, but today there's a nervous edge to her and she actually does appear more blushing bride than the usual strutting diva.

'Good.' I beam at her encouragingly. 'It's going to be fine.'

'Uh-huh! I'm so glad you're with me, Faye.'

'Where else would I be when my BFF is getting married?'

She takes a shaky breath that's interrupted by a

knock on the door. Her eyes dart to it and I give her fingers another squeeze before releasing them.

'Here we go.'

I head to the bedroom door, preparing myself now, because I know who's on the other side and I haven't seen him since the yacht, which was over thirty-six hours ago. He, Dante, Tyler and Harry took themselves off to the private villa just beyond the pool area yesterday morning, in keeping with the tradition of separating the bride and groom the night before the wedding. But the distance hasn't helped how I feel about him, it hasn't stopped my heart which seems determined to care.

The problem is, I know who he is. I know he's a sworn bachelor running from love, but I saw the way he looked at me on the yacht, I heard the words laced with so much meaning, and it didn't feel like pure lust, it felt like more. So much more. And even when we were at our best, Bobby never made me feel like that. Not once.

But, as I pause before the door, I remember that this is Dani's day. This is about *her* heart, *her* love, *her* life. Not mine. I take hold of the door handle and take a deep breath, my eyes going back to Dani, and I give her an encouraging smile. She is stunning. Her dress is sheer and formfitting, flowers trailing over the nude under layer in such a way as to blend fabric into skin. It's tasteful, elegant, and still sexy. Her hair is tied back in a loose chignon that replicates mine, with the same baby's breath, and the addition of blush-coloured roses that match the shade of my fishtail dress. She looks angelic and sinful in one.

'Okay?' I say.

She nods, takes up her bouquet and clutches it in front of her.

I pull open the door and turn to face him. I'm ready for this.

'Hi.' It comes out as heady as I feel. *Prepared? As if!*

I've missed him. Oh, how I've missed him. And that look... His eyes smoulder and burn, his throat bobs and he raises his hand to his tie, adjusting it, though he doesn't need to.

'*Buongiorno*, Faye.'

It's a deep murmur that has my insides quivering. I touch a hand to my hair again and he smiles. It's dazzling in its intensity, breath-taking in its sincerity. 'You look...you look exquisite.'

He pockets his hands and I wonder whether he wants to reach for me as much as I do him. Is he remembering the last time he said those words to me on the yacht, in the mirror...?

'As do you.'

And truly he does. His hair is swept back high off his face, his facial hair groomed, enhancing his bold cheekbones and the cut to his jaw. The deep blue shade of his suit brings out the bronze of his skin, the molten chocolate of his eyes, and makes him appear every bit the successful and intimidating billionaire, though I know him to be so much more.

'*Grazie*.'

It's gruff, raw, and for the first time I see a smudge of black beneath his eyes and lines I don't remember being so obvious before. I open my mouth to ask if he's okay before remembering that now isn't the time.

'Nothing beats your little sister, though.' I hurry out, stepping back to let him enter.

He walks in, his eyes leaving me to find Dani. His smile stills and his eyes shine. 'Wow, *sorellina.*'

'Is that a good wow?' she asks tentatively. 'Or a what were you thinking wow?'

'Sei troppo bella.' He pauses before her and shakes his head, clears his throat. 'I only wish our father were here to see you.'

'Don't, Raf.' She sniffs and stiffens her spine. 'You mustn't make me cry, not now.'

He pulls her into a hug that's awkward due to the bouquet and the dress. 'No tears.'

But his own voice is laced with them and I don't need to see his face to know he's suffering too. My own eyes spike and it's me clearing my throat now.

'Right, out of here,' I bluster, 'before we all end up a blubbering mess and draw attention for entirely the wrong reason.'

Dani blows out a shuddery breath and rolls her shoulders back. 'Right, ready.'

'Ready?' I ask, looking pointedly at Rafael and ignoring the way my heart pulses at the emotion in his truly magnificent face. A face I can never imagine being immune to.

'Born ready.' He offers his sister his arm, his

face so full of his love for her, and my eyes well up again.

'Me too,' Dani murmurs.

They make the most glorious picture and words fail me. I see the same effect on the staff as we make our way downstairs. I catch the wedding planner dabbing at the corners of her eyes as we make our way outside and pause just out of view of the guests.

I'm to go first and, as I leave them, I clutch my bouquet tighter and mouth, 'Good luck.'

My eyes flit from Dani to Rafael and my breath catches. He's not looking at Dani now; he's looking at me. He's looking at me with such emotion, adoration...*love?*

No, don't get fanciful. Don't go there again. Enjoy today. Enjoy the wedding and what time you have left.

'Okay, Faye, the musicians are ready.'

I drag my eyes from his to the wedding planner and hear the string quartet begin Pachelbel's *Canon*. 'Here goes...'

I watch Faye disappear through the trees ahead and feel a trapped breath slowly leave me.

From the second she opened the door, I've been caught up in a whirlwind of spiralling emotion. Of fear. Of gut-clenching panic. Of tomorrow being the end. Because tomorrow she leaves, and this will be over.

The hedonistic fun. The lust.

Because it is just lust. Granted, it's more powerful, more all-consuming, impossible to sate, but it's
just lust. No more.

And yet I feel as if I'm working too hard to convince myself of it.

'It's time…' The wedding planner gives us a nod,
refocusing my attention, and I look to Dani.

'Well, here goes, *sorellina*…' She gives me a
small smile, her eyes so big in her face as she looks
up at me, fearful, nervous. 'You want to do this, *si*?'

She laughs softly. 'Yes.'

'Good, because you look terrified.'

She steps forward, taking me with her. 'I'm many
things right now, *fratellone*, but the one thing I know
for sure is that I love Tyler and I want us to spend
the rest of our lives together.'

She looks back at me as I struggle to keep in
step.

'Now *you* look terrified.'

I give an uneasy laugh; there's too much racing
through my brain. Too many questions. Too many
'what ifs'. But I focus on her certainty, on what's
important in that moment. 'It's my honour to give
you away to a man worthy of you, a man I love as a
brother already.'

Now we fall into step together, the music wrapping around us, guiding the rhythm. I remember my
toast at dinner the other night—that if life is kind
it will be long and happy and worthy of such com-
mitment.

Dani pauses beside me and I look at her. Her eyes

are locked with Tyler's, their depths glistening, her lips curving up.

'Love is worth it, brother,' she whispers, her eyes not once leaving her husband-to-be. 'You just have to open up your heart and let it in.'

I look up the aisle to Tyler's beaming expression and to Faye... *Faye*.

'One day, I hope you'll find someone worthy of it too.'

I'm barely aware of her words, of my legs moving now as we approach. I am lost in the sight of her standing there, waiting for us.

She is worthy, she is more than worthy... It's me that's the problem.

I feel her eyes on me during the ceremony, I feel them because my every sense is urging me to look back at her. To listen to the mayor as he talks of love, of marriage and of the sanctity of the vows. I listen to Dani and Tyler make their promises to one another...

I run a finger through the collar of my shirt and lower my hands in front of me, gripping them together. A gentle hand covers them, and I look down to find that it's my mother offering me comfort. I lift my eyes to hers and she gives me a smile that swims with emotion. Then she looks back to Dani and Tyler and I do the same. I don't pull away; instead, I turn my hand over and take hers in mine.

I wonder if she's thinking as I am. Worrying for their future. Worrying about what life may throw at them down the road. Will they be as unlucky as her and Papà?

My thoughts return to Faye, to her encouragement where my mother is concerned, and how right she was. I look across the aisle and see her smile, her eyes looking at where our hands are entwined before returning to my face. I smile back at her. I have her to thank in some way for this and, when I can, I'll tell her so.

And then I remember that I don't have long, that the clock is ticking, that tomorrow she leaves and this, whatever this even is between us, will be over.

Emptiness consumes me. Suffocates me.

Is this how being without her will feel?

Is this what it's like before love sets in? Or have I…?

No. Impossible.

My mother squeezes my fingers and I realise I'm gripping hers tightly. I soften my hold, shift in the seat and do my best to ease the tension that's taken hold, but it's no use. It's buried so deep and it's consuming me.

I need to get out of here, but I'm trapped.

Trapped and sinking deeper.

Like a nightmare you can't wake up from, or a dream you want to lose yourself in. A dream where you can love…you can let yourself go. A dream where everything's as rose-tinted as the couple up front and love conquers all and nothing can hurt.

What a perfect day. A truly gorgeous, perfect day.

But my feet are killing me.

It's late, gone midnight, but, as I've learned this week, it's early by Italian standards.

Still, no one will sniff at me slipping off the heels now. I toe one off, then the other, and sink my feet into the cooling grass. I'm out of the way, up on an elevated position that overlooks the outdoor dance floor with its ceiling of fairy lights that swing from tree to tree, illuminating the ground below and the people dancing beneath it.

Tyler and Dani have barely left the floor. Marianna and Giovanni have become ever closer as the week has progressed and are more than happy to entertain the young duo, Leo and Isabella, with their dance moves. Their parents caved and left the dance floor over an hour ago to cuddle up at one of the intimate tables still set out from dinner, their heads close together as they sip their wine and watch the dancing still underway.

Harry and Lisa are at another table, deep in conversation. Tyler's parents are chatting to Antonietta, Nonna and Dante, off to the side, and Rafael...

I breathe in softly.

Rafael...

He's talking to the head waiter, taking control, making sure everything is still picture-perfect and every need is catered for.

It's an intimate affair, with more paid staff discreetly waiting in the wings than there are guests, and that's all down to him.

Him and his huge heart.

Not his wallet.

Yes, money paid for all this, but it's his heart that makes it so important to him. And ever since his wobble in Dani's bedroom earlier he's been back in control, commanding, taking care of everything. And I… I love him for it.

I accept the emotion for what it is and accept that it can never be.

Because he is still Rafael, the man who will never marry.

Not that I even want marriage.

I don't need another ring to bind me to him; my heart will do that for me.

He finishes with the head waiter and takes two glasses from a tray, scanning the tables and the dance floor. I hold my breath.

His eyes find me in the shadows and something flickers in his face. Something that looks like so much more than it could possibly be. And I know I'm putting that look there, that the distance is playing tricks on me and aiding me in my quest to believe that more is possible. The drink too. All those bubbles we've consumed have gone to my head, not to mention the Chianti consumed with dinner.

I watch him approach, my heart racing, my eyes unblinking. I have the sudden desire to turn and run, which is ridiculous, but it's there.

I curl my toes into the grass and plaster on a smile. He's climbing the stone steps that weave through the lavender that grows wild up here and his eyes lift to me.

'Found me, then?' I say, feigning a confidence I don't feel.

'I've known where you are every second of every moment today.'

My heart dances in my chest, his words adding to the fanciful future I'm too quick to imagine. 'Is that so?'

He offers me a glass, his body so close now I can smell his scent, his eyes near enough to see the ambient glow from the castle behind me sparkle in his darkened gaze.

'Yes.'

I take the glass without looking, my eyes refusing to leave his.

'I'll take that as a compliment.'

'And so you should.' He raises his glass to me. 'Cheers to a successful day.'

I clink my glass against his. 'Cheers.'

We drink but the bubbles stick in my throat. Nerves, want, love…all the emotions claw their way through me, making it impossible to relax. I lower my lashes and cover my mouth on a small cough.

'Are you okay?'

I force another smile. 'Of course. Have you had a good day?'

'Si.' He frowns at me and hesitates. 'It's actually gone better than I dared hope.'

'Really?' I laugh now, wanting the mood to lighten, wanting him to quit worrying. 'You say that so seriously. I know people panic that things will go wrong at weddings but to be *so* emphatic! Are we really all that bad?'

He laughs and I treasure the sound.

'Not you, exactly, but...' He turns and looks down on the dance floor, his eyes settling on his mother and Giovanni.

'They look happy,' I say after a moment.

He flicks me a look. '*Si*, they do. Turns out it was my aunt's plan all along to bring Giovanni and remind my mother of what she could have if she would only move on from the past and come home.'

I study his face, watching him as he watches her. 'Sounds...deep.'

He gives another laugh, softer this time, reflective. 'Apparently, Giovanni has always been in love with my mother, only Papà got in there first.'

'Really?' I say, my smile genuine now, my surprise too.

'Really. And now it seems they may have a future.'

I look at them on the dance floor, their hands entwined with Leo's and Isabella's as they dance in a circle. Everyone is smiling. Everyone is happy.

'How perfect.'

He makes a non-committal sound and I frown at him. 'You're not happy for them?'

He looks at me, but not for long; his eyes are too quick to go back to the dancing figures.

'I'd like to be happy for them.' He gestures out to the dance floor with his glass. 'I'd like to be happy for them all.'

'But?'

'Life has so many other ideas, doesn't it?'

I study his pensive expression and stay quiet, sensing that the question is rhetorical and there's more to come.

'Take my mother and father. They were once happy. They argued, but they loved each other underneath it all. And I didn't make life easy for them.'

'In what way?'

His smile is small and one-sided as he looks at me. 'I was something of a hellion.'

I laugh, happy that he's opening up to me, and amused to imagine him as such. 'You were that bad?'

'Dio, si.' He sips at his drink. 'I wanted to conquer everything all at once and as soon as possible: swimming, cycling, driving, schooling. If my parents could do it, so could I. Regardless of the law, of what was wise or sensible.'

I smile. 'I'm sure they were very proud of their young hellion.'

He goes quiet and I lean into him, my head resting against his shoulder offering comfort that he hasn't even asked for.

'They would have been, Rafael. Just as your mother is proud of you now, your father would have been proud too.'

'Dani would have made Papà proud. Today…this morning…' His voice cracks and, God, it kills me. I turn into him and reach for his cheek. I can't stop it; I need to touch him, to feel him, to reassure him.

'Yes, he would have been, but he would have been proud of you too. So proud that you could do what he wasn't able to in giving her away.'

His gaze glistens and I feel my own tears well.

'You *are* someone to be proud of, Rafael.'

My eyes waver into his and I want to kiss him. I want to so much it hurts...

'You are,' I insist softly, my lips parting, pleading, and then he's kissing me, his arm drawing around me, pulling me closer.

We kiss and kiss, tongues tasting, bodies melding together, but it's not enough. Tonight is my last night. Tomorrow I leave, but I want more, so much more from him, before I go. And then I remember where we are and I fall back, scanning the ground below, making sure we haven't been seen.

'Stay with me tonight, *cara mia*.' He isn't hurried or panicked. His fingers are soft in my hair as he brushes it back from my face and I look at him, his eyes imploring. 'Please, our last night.'

I'm nodding before I think better of it. He's not offering me a future; he's telling me this is it.

We return to the guests, do our duty and wait for the last to fall. I'm bone-tired, weary from a long day; even my cheeks ache from all the smiles. But the second we cross the threshold of his room I'm alert. A hive of thrumming activity, of anticipation.

Rafael comes up behind me, his fingers soft on the straps of my dress as he bows his head to my neck, sweeps kisses along the exposed skin.

'It feels weird that it's over,' I murmur, taking a

steadying breath as I try to fight off the sadness. 'I wonder how Dani will fill her time now she has no wedding to plan.'

'I think Tyler has many ways to occupy her.' He takes hold of the zip at my back and eases it down. 'None too different to what I'm wanting to do right now.'

'Is it all you men think about?'

My dress falls from my shoulders and he smooths it down my hips, my thighs… I'm wearing no bra, just a thong, and in the free-standing mirror ahead I can see his eyes taking me in. Their burn. The emotion…

He takes hold of my hands and lifts them, entwining my fingers behind his neck so that I arch into his warm, unyielding body.

'You truly are exquisite.' His hands smooth around to my front, cupping my breasts. He rolls their puckered hearts, his lips soft on my neck as he sweeps kisses to my ear. He catches my lobe in his teeth, all the while his eyes fixed on the mirror and what he's doing to me.

'You are a masterpiece.'

My laugh catches as he pinches my nipples.

'You are, *cara mia*. Don't ever doubt it.'

His eyes are on fire, their darkened depths glinting with gold in the soft light of the room. I want to ask, if I'm such a masterpiece, why doesn't he want to keep me, treasure me? I bite into my lip. I don't want to ruin tonight with that. He keeps massaging my breasts, pinching and caressing my nipples until

I'm writhing against him, until the colour of desire is as high in his own cheeks, his cock like granite as it grinds against my back.

'Please, Raf!'

'What, *cara*?' His voice is husky in my ear, his breath coming in pants, and I swear I could come from this alone.

'I need you to touch me.'

He lowers one hand to my thong, slips his fingers inside and groans. 'You are so wet.'

He coats himself in my need, rolling over my clit, his pace matching my hurried breaths, my grinding hips. I want him to take me to the bed, I want him inside me. I want it all. But I can't speak, can't demand it. My toes curl, the delicious tension spreading through my tightening limbs. I turn my head to his, seeking out his mouth, his tongue. I see his eyes still feasting on our form in the mirror, determined, carnal, and I'm gone. He swallows my cry with his groan, his hands pressing me tight against him as he absorbs shock after shock.

He spins me into him, scoops me up in his arms and carries me to the bed. There's a strange tension to him, a desperation. I see it in the lines that bracket his mouth, his eyes that blaze and strain.

I watch him undress, his eyes not once leaving mine, and I understand. I understand, because it's the same desperation I feel. The need to get enough, to get enough and walk away. Because tomorrow it will be over.

And, even though this has to end, I will always be

grateful to Rafael. He has taught me so much. Made me realise that such passion, such love is possible.

I only have to find someone capable and willing to offer it in return.

It has to be possible.

It has to be…

CHAPTER THIRTEEN

I WAKE TO an empty bed and realise that Faye has gone. We were awake until three, so I know she's not been gone long. It's seven-thirty now, the latest I've slept in a long while, but still it doesn't feel long enough. The after-effects of the alcohol and the lack of sleep are weighing me down, clouding up my brain and making my body ache.

I roll onto my back and stare up at the ceiling fresco, a romantic scene fit for a bedroom, and feel the ache run bone-deep.

It's not just the alcohol, the lack of sleep. It's her. I miss her.

And if I'm honest I can't imagine my life without her in it…yet today she leaves.

Cazzo. I throw back the covers that still smell so sweet of her and thrust up out of bed. I hit the shower and pray it will clear the fog in my head, the ache in my body and make today…easy.

Because it should be easy. The wedding was a success, the guests all depart today and I'll have my new home to myself. Time to enjoy it while getting back to business as usual.

But I'm still mentally coaching myself an hour later when I'm pacing the hallway and resisting the urge to go to Faye's room and ask… And ask what, exactly?

Don't leave?

Stay a little longer?

Let's have sex a little longer?

Let's have fun?

Because, let's face it, I'm not about to offer more. I can't.

'Morning, Rafael.'

I spin on the spot and I see my mother coming towards me. *Sans* make-up and grinning widely.

'I'm glad I caught you. Can we talk?'

'Si, Mamma.'

She stalls, her eyes glisten and I realise what I've done. I've called her Mamma for the first time in too many years to count.

She lifts her hands to my cheeks and her smile softens. *'Mio amata figliolo.'*

My beloved son.

The words resonate through me, out of me. My own eyes spike and, *Gesù*, I don't cry. I don't. But it's choking up through my chest, stinging the backs of my eyes.

'Grazie,' she says. 'For this week, for this wedding. You have been the most incredible son, the most incredible big brother to Dani and you would have made your father proud…so proud.'

I feel her fingers tremble against my cheeks and I can't answer her. My voice is trapped in the tightness of my chest.

'I want you to know that Giovanni and I...'

Her voice trails off as her eyes probe mine, looking for encouragement, perhaps. Encouragement that I'm happy to give.

'It's okay, Mamma. I understand and I want you to be happy. It's all Dani and I could want for you.'

Her eyes spill over, the tears trailing down her cheeks as her fingers tremble more. *'Grazie, figliolo. Grazie.'*

I sense movement to our left and look to see Faye turning away. 'Faye!'

She stops and turns to us, her smile apologetic.

I look back to my mother and she is smiling all the more now. 'I want you to be happy too, *Rafael*. Go. Speak to Faye.'

Her eyes are all-knowing, and I frown as it puts the fear of God in me. I'm not about to... Does she think I'm...?

It doesn't matter what she thinks. Just speak to Faye and say what you planned to say.

Which is what, exactly?

I wait for Rafael to catch me up. Yes, I left in the middle of the night—or the early hours of the morning, depending on how you want to look at it—but I didn't want this conversation. I didn't want to succumb to the inner pressure that's begging me to ask for more. Because how much more can this man truly offer?

I'm not so deluded as to think myself capable of changing him. I'm better to cut my losses and run.

'Hi,' I manage to say calmly.

'Morning. You left before…'

My eyes lift to his and I see the hesitancy in his expression. My stomach flutters, my heart too, every bit of me so attuned to him and his alien uncertainty.

'I was… I was trying to make goodbye easier.'

'By leaving before we could talk?'

I frown at him. What is there to say other than what we already know: that this is over? And I know we can't have this conversation in the middle of the entrance hall. I move into a side room that looks as though it was once a library and hear him follow.

'I wanted to leave on a high.' I try to sound cheerful as I turn to face him. 'It was a fabulous day, and a perfect night! We don't need to spoil it with…'

My nonchalant shrug fails miserably and he reaches out, his hand gentle on my arm.

'Then let's not spoil it with goodbye.'

I laugh breathlessly. 'It is goodbye, Rafael. I fly back to England today and you go back to your life, wherever that may take you.'

'You could stay longer; you could stay here with me. I'd like it if you stayed.'

My heart races in my chest, too excited, too hopeful.

'You'd like me to stay?'

He nods swiftly.

'In your Tuscan castle, just me and you?'

'*Si, cara mia.*' He is so sincere. 'I want you to stay with me, Faye.'

'And in a month or two?' I force myself to ask. 'What then?'

He frowns, pales even.

'And a year? What then, Rafael?'

His frown deepens. 'Don't push me, Faye.'

'Don't push you for more?' My eyes widen, pressing him to admit what he cannot give. Pressing him to admit what I need to hear.

'I want you to stay.'

'And I want you to commit to more.'

He shakes his head.

'Why didn't you want Dani and Tyler to marry?'

'What's that got to do—?'

'Just tell me. It's quite clear how much they love one another.'

'You know why.' He studies me intently as his shoulders sag and his hand falls away to rake through his hair. 'Why do we have to discuss it?'

'I want you to explain it to me. I want to hear it from you.'

He eyes me carefully and eventually speaks. 'I've told you before. Love isn't something you can control. It doesn't guarantee you happiness. It isn't a certainty. And, when it's taken from you, it has the power to ruin you, to destroy you and make you… make you bitter, twisted, lost…'

'Like your mother was?'

He swallows. '*Si.*'

'And now? Do you still feel the same after seeing

your mother with Giovanni? After seeing Tyler and Dani so happy? Your cousin, Sienna, with Lorenzo?'

He's silent and I smile. But it is a sad smile. Regretful. 'It's okay, Rafael, I understand. I just needed to hear you say it.'

'I don't want to be that weak, Faye.' He stresses the words. 'Never that weak.'

I place my palm on his chest, both sympathetic and distraught in one. 'I do understand.'

I kiss him because I can't help myself, because I can't walk away without feeling his lips on mine once more. As I drop back, I bite back the tears to say, 'But please understand that I can't continue this. I have to go back to my life. It's better for us both.'

'I'm not asking for a lifetime, just a week or two or...'

My sad smile grows. 'That's just the thing, Rafael. I'd gladly give you a lifetime. I'd lo—'

'What the hell?'

The exclamation comes from the open doorway. Dani.

Shit.

'I knew it! *Cazzo se lo sapevo!*'

My sister is steaming, shoving her sunglasses back from her eyes and storming into the room, slamming the door closed behind her.

'How could you, Rafael? How the fuck could you?'

'Calm down, Dani. It's okay,' Faye rushes out,

turning away from me, a panicked hand raised up to ward Dani off.

'It's not fucking okay, Faye. You promised, Raf!' She focuses her anger wholly on me, where it belongs, where I would gladly take it, if not for Faye still in the room.

'Dani, you need to calm down,' Faye says, still defending me.

'Don't tell me to calm down. You don't understand.'

'What don't I understand?' Faye steps between us. 'You were all up for me having a little fun this week.'

'With Dante, yes!' she throws at Faye, as if it explains it all. 'But you know where you stand with him, not Raf.' She flings a hand at me 'He's complicated, so deep and contradictory, so loving, so… so… Oh, God, Faye!'

She spins back to look at me and I'm motionless. My gut isn't though; it twists and rolls.

'He'll make you think he can love you,' she continues, 'because how could he not? When he plays the perfect big brother, the fixer, how can he not be capable of falling in love himself?'

'I know all this, Dani,' Faye says quietly from behind her.

'Do you?' Dani flings back at her, desperate, panicked. 'Because the look on your face tells me differently. The look on your face tells me you've fallen for him, Faye. It's as obvious as your pain.'

Slowly Faye looks from Dani to me and inside my heart tears in two.

'Tell me I'm wrong, *fratello*,' Dani pleads softly. 'Tell *her* I'm wrong. Tell me that you can love her, that you will do right by her?'

I can't breathe. I can't speak. The crushing force on my chest is crippling.

'I don't need him to say any of that, Dani.'

Faye's desperate attempt to rescue me makes it worse. So much worse.

'Don't you?' Her eyes spear Faye now and the door opens behind her. Tyler peers inside, hesitant, concerned.

'Babe?' He scans the room, his eyes settling on Dani. 'The car is here to take us to the airport.'

Dani just stands there, her eyes shifting to me, torn, angry.

'It's okay.' Faye reaches out for Dani. 'You need to go. Everything is fine here, I promise.'

She pulls her into a hug and Dani looks at me over her shoulder. 'How could you?'

'I'm sorry,' I try. 'It wasn't planned. I didn't…'

I flounder because what can I say? There's no excuse I can give her that'll make this all right.

'Go,' Faye softly urges. 'Have a fabulous honeymoon and we'll catch up when you return and all this… It'll be forgotten.'

My sister squeezes her eyes shut. 'I'm sorry.'

'Stop it.' Faye gently pushes her away and Dani hesitates before striding up to me. She pulls me into a tight hug, her whisper for my ears only.

'Do the right thing, *fratello*, please.'

I don't even know what the right thing is, not any more, but I nod and watch her leave.

'I should go too,' Faye says into the sudden silence and my eyes snap to her.

'*No!* Please…reconsider?'

She looks at me as if I'm crazy. 'You still want to ask that of me?'

'It's out there now. Dani knows; we can be honest, open. Spend some real time together.'

'Having fun?'

'Yes,' I say, quietly hopeful, desperate. 'We work well together, we have fun—more fun than I've ever had with any other woman—and I… I'm not ready to pass this up.'

She laughs softly. 'I am, though, Rafael. I'm ready. I want more, so much more than you can give. I want to find a man who can love me as I love him.'

'*Love…*' Nausea swells and I have to swallow 'Why does it have to be about love? Why can't it be about fun? About great sex?'

'Sex isn't the be all and end all.'

'Okay, a relationship, then. We can be exclusive, a couple, until…'

'Until what?'

I can't put words to it.

'Until this chemistry fizzles out, right?'

'Yes.' It's awkward. A strange confirmation when it's something I can never imagine happening. But it will do. It *must* do. 'I don't know. I just know I'm not ready to end this now.'

'And, like I said, I *am* ready.' There's a strength

to her now, a resolve that scares me. 'The longer this goes on for, the closer I come to…the closer I come to falling head over heels for you, Rafael. And I know you never promised me anything, that it was just a bit of fun, but I'm afraid my heart didn't get the memo.'

She's already walking to do the door.

'Faye!'

She turns to look at me, eyebrows raised. 'What? Are you going to tell me that you're falling for me too? Are you going to tell me that Dani's wrong about you? That *you* were wrong and that you do want more?'

Silence. Save for the rush of blood whirring in my ears, my pulse surging with my rising panic, my legs weighed down like lead.

'Goodbye, Rafael.' Her voice is so quiet. 'Thank you for the heavenly week. No regrets, *si*?'

And then she's gone and I'm alone, more alone than I've ever felt before.

I stare at the open doorway, hear her footsteps becoming ever more distant, and I know I can't run after her. Because what can I say? *I'm a changed man? I do want more? I want it all?*

I leave the castle before the temptation to do it wins out. I don't return until nightfall, until I know she's long gone, and the risk of feeding her a pack of lies to get what I want is gone.

But I'm in hell. Miserable. Lost. Grieving. Not even the *grappa* I've consumed can numb the pain.

I'm still like it a week later, when the wedding feels like a distant memory and the castle is empty save for Mamma and Giovanni, who extended their visit at my invitation. It's a selfish gesture because I hoped they would be a distraction, a way to get over the mess in my head, in my heart, and move on.

It doesn't succeed. Not them, not work, nothing.

It's Saturday night, exactly seven days since she left, and I find myself back in the library. I'm lying on the divan, staring at the spot on which she stood, when she told me she couldn't stay, that she couldn't stay and not fall for me. Fall in love. After one week.

It's not possible. She's not. I'm not.

No.

But the pain, the emptiness deep down inside...

I fall asleep staring, remembering, hurting.

'Rafael! Rafael!' I wake with a start, the hand that's shaking me sending pain ricocheting through my skull—the delayed gift of *grappa*.

'What? What?' I focus through the haze to see my mother staring down at me.

'I brought you a cappuccino. You look like you need it.'

I catch a waft of it on the air and it wakes up my sluggish senses. I grumble a thank you and push myself up to sitting, reaching for the cup. I breathe the scent in and feel my mother's eyes on me.

'What is it?'

'Dani called me,' she says softly. 'She's worried about you.'

'I think she's more worried about Faye.'

'She's worried about the two of you.'

I take a sip of the coffee, appreciating its familiar taste, the hit of caffeine.

'She also suggested we talk. About the past, not just Faye.'

I look at my mother and my conversations with Faye come back to me—her gentle encouragement to do just this, her crystal blue eyes warm with her compassion, her understanding… My throat closes over. I miss her. I miss her so goddamned much.

'Let me shower.' It's gruff, my voice unrecognisable even to me. 'Then we'll talk.'

'Bene.'

And maybe, just maybe, I can make sense of the way I feel because one thing's for sure: I can't go on like this. I can't.

CHAPTER FOURTEEN

IT'S BEEN TWO WEEKS since I returned from Tuscany. Two weeks, and I'm walking through life like a zombie. If I don't pull myself together soon, I'm going to have bigger things to worry about than a broken heart. The career I worked so hard for will be on the line.

Last week I slept through my alarm and missed the start of a crucial debrief. Yesterday I managed to present the sales and marketing strategy for the coming year wearing my blouse inside out, and today the CEO pulled me aside with a very concerned frown and asked if I was okay, suggested I should maybe take another holiday, in the hope I'd come back like me again.

I cringe even now as I sit on my sofa and stuff another spoonful of ice cream into my mouth, trying to forget. But even dreamy cookies and cream has lost its ability to make everything feel okay.

This whole situation is ridiculous. I knew him for one week. *One* week. And now my entire life has been turned on its head. Even my house is starting to look as though it's been taken over by a bunch of youths who don't know how to clean up after themselves.

This isn't me. It's not.

I stare at the half-empty pizza box and the greasy slices I couldn't bring myself to finish and realise the truth. It *is* me. And I did fall in love. I do have a broken heart.

But...

I had an incredible week. My eyes were opened wide to the passion that's possible with the right man. And Rafael was almost that man. Almost.

And if I had my time over, I'd do it all again. Even with the pain of now.

I slap the lid back on the ice-cream carton and head to the kitchen. No more feeling sorry for myself. I need to get back in control of my life, my heart, the whole damn lot.

The doorbell goes, as though rejoicing with me, and I check the time. It's nine in the evening. Who could possibly want to call by at such a late hour? Dad wouldn't. My friends would text first. Cold caller? This late?

It rings again and I'm already walking towards it, ice-cream pot still in hand as I pull the door open with the other. I blink. Blink again. It can't be... It can't...

'Rafael?'

He's as grey as the rainy backdrop of Chelsea behind him, water beading in his hair, on his lashes, but it's him—definitely him.

'Faye.' His eyes flicker as he sucks in a breath and wets his lips. 'Can I come in, please?'

I lower my gaze and step back, opening the door wider, but I can't find my voice, can't even breathe as he enters and his scent engulfs me. I count to three. There are so many thoughts racing through my brain, so many possibilities. Is he here to apologise or is it something more? I don't dare let the hope take hold, not again.

'Faye.' He sounds as if he's talked himself hoarse, the rasp in his voice making it barely recognisable. I feel his hand on my shoulder and I duck away, turning to face him, my eyes wide.

'Please, don't touch me.' I can't stand the contact after two weeks of nothing, no call, no message, no email even. Just something, anything, to tell me I wasn't alone in my suffering.

'Sorry.' He pockets his hands deep within his designer coat and his throat bobs; the lines bracketing his mouth deepen. He looks so grey beneath the deep bronze of his skin, and now he's up close I can see those dark smudges under his eyes. He looks... broken.

I walk round him to the kitchen and throw the ice cream in the bin. It's past saving now and I need something stronger. I reach for the wine I opened earlier and pour myself a glass.

'Would you like one?' I'm on autopilot now. 'It's nothing like the Chianti on your estate but it's pleasant enough.'

He's watching me. I feel his eyes burning into

my back, provoking every nerve, but he says nothing. Nothing at all.

'You need to speak, Rafael!' I crack, spinning to face him. 'You came here to talk to me, for Christ's sake, so speak! I'm many things but I'm not a mind reader!'

His eyes widen and his voice breaks. 'I'm sorry.'

'You said that already.' And now I feel guilty. It wasn't his fault I fell in love. I did that all by myself. 'Sorry. I just… I don't know why you're here.'

'You don't need to apologise. I'm just… I'm just taking you in. Taking in that I'm really here with you.' He rubs a hand down his face. 'The last two weeks have felt like for ever, and the longer I went without you the more I wondered whether I would ever see you again.'

'Well, that was the plan, wasn't it?' I turn and take up my glass, throwing back a gulp, needing it to quash the dizzying mass rising up inside. 'To have our fun and move on.'

He drags in a breath. 'It was.'

'So…?'

He's quiet and I flick him a look, about to prompt again when he gestures to the wine. 'Can I take you up on a glass…*per favore*?'

I take another glass down off the shelf and pour, not caring when it sloshes over the side. He reaches out to take it from me, but I place it on the countertop between us—anything to avoid the risk of our fingers touching, no matter how briefly.

He doesn't react to the move, but I know he notices. *'Grazie.'*

And then I wait.

'I did as you suggested,' he says eventually, so quietly I have to strain to hear him over the rain that pounds against the patio doors. I look at it now, watching as it runs rivers down the glass, obscuring the outdoors. 'I spoke to my mother about the past, about what happened to my father and the years that followed.'

My lips lift just a little at the corners because, though I may be hurting, I still care. 'That's good.'

'We had a long talk, an honest one, and you were right. She was lonely; she was trying to fill the void my father left without risking her heart again. She chose men for fun, for companionship, but never chose anyone she would risk loving again.'

I nod so he knows I'm listening.

'She avoided love for so long but then, when Giovanni came along, it changed everything. She wants to be happy again; she wants to be with him. She's decided love is worth the risk after all.'

I give him the smallest of smiles as I recall their potted history. 'They did look happy together.'

'They *are* happy. Happier than I've ever seen Mamma look.'

I frown. 'You called her Mamma?'

His mouth twitches into a smile and it shaves years off his tormented face, making my heart bloom in spite of everything. *'Si.'*

He works a hand through his damp hair and rain flicks off the ends.

'*God*, you're soaked, Rafael.' I move into action, unable to ignore it. 'Let me get you a towel.'

He reaches out to stop me, his wet hand still warm on the exposed skin of my wrist. 'I don't care that I'm soaked. I only care for you.'

Our eyes meet and my heart stutters inside my chest.

'It's not just my mother who has changed.'

'Wh-what are you saying, Rafael?'

'That I too believe love is worth the risk.'

I take a shallow breath. He can't mean… It's not possible.

'These two weeks without you, Faye, I've been grieving. Grieving as though you were dead, when in actual fact you were here, living your life without me. I've been tormented, lost. And yet it was me that pushed you away, it's me that let you leave, it's me that couldn't commit.'

'And now?'

'Now I want it all, Faye. I want to let love in, I want to give us a chance. I know I can't change overnight, but if you'll have me I can try to be that man. I can love you and do everything in my power to make you happy, to make *us* happy.'

My lashes flutter closed, pins and needles creeping over my skin. I feel faint. The rush inside is so intense, so…

'Faye…' He pulls me against him, his arms so strong, so reassuring.

I look up into his eyes. 'Am I dreaming? Is this some cruel trick and any second now Dante's going to jump out of the woodwork and shout, *"Surprise!"*?'

He laughs, the gruff sound vibrating through his chest and into mine.

'No, *cara mia*. I am in love with you. Not even my fear could stop that from happening. And it turns out, once you love someone, losing them just isn't an option, not when they still walk the earth.'

'Are you saying I left you no choice?' A smile plays about my lips as I look up into his eyes and see all that I've come to love looking back at me.

'I'm saying exactly that.'

'Doesn't sound very romantic.'

He laughs again and rakes a hand through my hair, reminding me of the hair tie that's still in it, and the crazy mass that has escaped, and my unmade, sleep-deprived face, and… Oh, my God, I really do look a mess. But he doesn't care. He loves me. I can see it all in his molten-chocolate eyes that blaze and love in one.

'I admit to needing help in that department.'

'In being romantic?'

'*Si.*'

'Lesson one.' I smile widely. 'Close your eyes so you can't see what a mess I look.'

'No, I'm not closing my eyes when they have been starved of you for two weeks. And you look incredible.'

'Still exquisite?' I ask, my eyes wide with teasing pessimism.

'*Si.*' He strokes his fingers along my jaw and cups my head in his hands as he studies me intently, the amber flecks in his gaze glinting with emotion. '*Molto bella.*'

My eyes well up, the pain of the last two weeks fading in the warmth of his love and acceptance of his love.

'Lesson two…' I whisper.

'*Si?*'

'Kiss me.'

I glimpse the joy in his smile seconds before his lips brush over mine and I tremble in his hold.

'*Ti amo*, Faye.' He whispers against my lips and kisses me again. '*Ti amo molto.*'

I fork my hands through his damp hair and hold him to me as I look up into his eyes. 'I could listen to you say that for ever.'

'Then it's a good job I plan on telling you every day for the rest of my life,' he murmurs. 'If you'll listen to it.'

'I can go one better than just listening.'

'You can?'

'*Si.*' I smile softly. '*Ti amo,* Rafael. *Ti amo molto.*'

And then I kiss him back with all the love blooming wild inside, knowing that I have all I could ever wish for in my arms right now.

I don't need marriage, I don't need a ring to bind us, I just need this…

Our love.

EPILOGUE

Five years later, Castello d'Amore, Tuscany

'EDUARDO, COME HERE this *minuto*!'

I chuckle at Faye. I can't help it. 'You know it's better for him if you say it in one language or the other, *cara mia*. If you mix it up, heaven knows what he'll learn.'

She turns to look at me, her skin flushed, her eyes as bright and beautiful as ever, especially in the silver gown that makes her eyes appear more ethereal, her skin more bronzed, her baby bump more pronounced. She radiates sunshine and happiness and I swear my chest is fit to burst with pride.

'Stop preaching to me about using our languages correctly and start helping, Raf. We're going to be late.'

'Don't be silly. How can we be late? We are the hosts.'

'It's your mother's wedding! The mayor is a busy man; we can't expect him to hang about waiting for our *papàtino* to actually put on some clothes.'

I chuckle harder and pull her in for a chaste kiss that causes a loud, 'Eww!' to erupt from waist-high. Eduardo has returned.

'See, all we had to do is kiss and he would come running.'

We both look down to find our naked boy scrunching up his eyes tightly. 'Not looking.'

'Can you not look and get dressed at the same time?' Faye murmurs down at him.

'It's hot. Too hot.'

'Yes,' I say. 'But you can't go to Nonna's special day dressed in your underpants, and you also can't do that special job I gave you, either.'

He peeks at me out of one eye. 'The special job?'

'Si.' I nod, my eyes wide as I encourage him to remember.

'You want me to do that now?'

'I think it might be nice.'

Faye frowns at me and mouths 'Job?'

I just grin as Eduardo runs off. 'You'll see.'

He's back in minutes, his trousers on, his shirt done up all wonky and only one sock on. But it's a start.

I grin down at him. His skin is flushed from exertion, his eyes so like his mother's, his skin the colour of mine. My chest swells ever more with pride. 'You got it?'

He nods his head rapidly, his hands clasped tightly behind his back. 'Si.'

'Rafael?' Faye drawls. 'What's going on?'

'Well, since Eduardo has the all-important task

of being ring-bearer for Nonna today, I thought he could have a practice run with us first.'

Her frown wavers as she looks from me to our boy, her eyes starting to well.

'That's your cue, Eduardo…' I whisper, placing my hand on his shoulder.

'But we need to kneel, Papà,' he says to me. 'I read about it on the internet.'

I chuckle and Faye laughs shakily.

'I think you're right.' I ruche up my right trouser leg and lower my left to the ground as our boy mimics me, taking the ring box from behind his back and opening it up.

'Mamma, will you make Papà and me very happy and…?' He looks at me, his frown scrunching up his entire face.

I mouth *agree* and he nods quickly, his grin as big as his face as he offers the box.

'Agree! To getting married?'

We both stare up at her imploringly and she is shaking with joy, with laughter. 'How can I say no to a proposal as romantic as that?'

'Eww, I'm not romantic!' our boy pipes up.

She ruffles his hair. 'You will be one day!'

'And your answer?' I say.

We've talked about it many, many times, but there was no rush and, having been married before, it wasn't top of her priorities. But with a wedding in the air and the wish to share the same name as our son, our unborn child too…

'I say you no longer need lessons in how to be romantic, Rafael.'

'No?'

'No. I think you've graduated with honours.'

'And?'

'And, yes! *Si*...yes.' She cups my face and lowers her lips to mine for a chaste kiss. 'It would make me the happiest woman and...' she turns her attention to our son and kisses him too '...the happiest mother alive.'

Which is lucky, since Eduardo is already trying to shove the ring on her pinkie.

'Wrong finger, Papàtino,' I say. 'Maybe I should do this bit.'

'Si, Papà.' He shoves the ring and the box into my hands and runs from the room.

'Hey! Where are you going?'

'I'm going before there's any more kissy-wissy stuff.'

We both laugh and as I slip the ring on Faye's finger I look down into her eyes and the words flow from me. *'Tu mi completi.'*

'And you complete me, Rafael.'

* * * * *

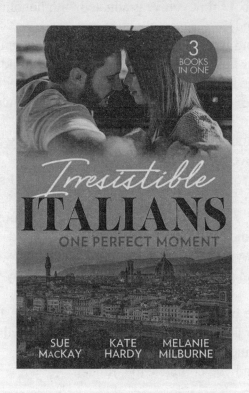

MILLS & BOON

THE HEART OF ROMANCE

A ROMANCE FOR EVERY READER

MODERN

Prepare to be swept off your feet by sophisticated, sexy and seductive heroes, in some of the world's most glamourous and romantic locations, where power and passion collide.

HISTORICAL

Escape with historical heroes from time gone by. Whether your passion is for wicked Regency Rakes, muscled Vikings or rugged Highlanders, awaken the romance of the past.

MEDICAL

Set your pulse racing with dedicated, delectable doctors in the high-pressure world of medicine, where emotions run high and passion, comfort and love are the best medicine.

True Love

Celebrate true love with tender stories of heartfelt romance, from the rush of falling in love to the joy a new baby can bring, and a focus on the emotional heart of a relationship.

Desire

Indulge in secrets and scandal, intense drama and sizzling hot action with heroes who have it all: wealth, status, good looks…everything but the right woman.

HEROES

The excitement of a gripping thriller, with intense romance at its heart. Resourceful, true-to-life women and strong, fearless men face danger and desire - a killer combination!

To see which titles are coming soon, please visit
millsandboon.co.uk/nextmonth

JOIN US ON SOCIAL MEDIA!

Stay up to date with our latest releases, author news and gossip, special offers and discounts, and all the behind-the-scenes action from Mills & Boon...

 @millsandboon

 @millsandboonuk

 facebook.com/millsandboon

 @millsandboonuk

It might just be true love...